NIGHT SCHOOL

C. J. Daugherty

GALAXY

PLUS

First published in Great Britain in 2012
by Atom
This Large Print edition published 2012
by AudioGO Ltd
by arrangement with
Little, Brown Book Group

ISBN: 978 1445 89717 2

British Library Cataloguing in Publication Data available

To Jack
Who always believed

CHAPTER ONE

'Hurry up!'

'Will you chill out? I'm almost finished.'

Her jaw set, Allie crouched in the dark, painting the last T as Mark knelt beside her holding a torch. Their voices echoed in the empty corridor. The light beam illuminating her work quivered when he laughed.

A sudden snapping sound made them both jump.

Lights flickered above them, then flooded the school hallway.

Two uniforms stood by the door.

Allie dropped the can of paint slowly without taking her finger off the trigger, causing the letter to stretch freakishly down the door of the headmaster's office to the dirty, linoleum floor.

'Run.'

As the word left her lips, she was already flying down the wide corridor, the rubber soles of her trainers squeaking hollowly in the emptiness of Brixton Hill School. She didn't look back to see if Mark was behind her.

She didn't know where the others were, but if Harry got caught again his dad would kill him. Rounding the corner at speed she turned onto a dark stretch of corridor. At the end of it she saw the green glow of a fire exit sign.

A thrill of power rushed through her as she ran towards freedom. She was going to make it out. She was going to get away with it.

Crashing into the double doors, she shoved hard

1

against the bar that should have freed her.

It didn't budge.

Unbelieving, she shoved again, but the door was locked.

Bloody hell. If I hadn't just been vandalising the place, she thought, *I'd alert the local paper.*

Feverishly she scanned the wide corridor. The police were between her and the main entrance. The only exit at this end was locked.

There had to be another way out.

She held her breath to listen. Voices and footsteps heading her way.

Resting her hands on her knees, she let her head drop low between her shoulders. It could *not* go down this way. Her parents would destroy her. A third arrest in a year? It was bad enough when they made her go to this godforsaken school. Where would they send her now?

She ran to a nearby door.

One, two, three steps.

She tried the handle.

Locked.

Across the hall to another.

One, two, three, four steps.

Locked.

She was now running towards the police. This was crazy.

But the third door opened. A supply closet.

They left the supply closet unlocked but locked empty classrooms? This school is run by idiots.

Slipping in gingerly among the shelves of paper, mop buckets and electrical equipment she couldn't identify in the gloom, she let the door close behind her and steadied her breathing.

It was black as pitch. She held her hand up in

front of her face—right in front of her face—and she couldn't see it. She knew it was there; she could feel its existence. But not being able to see it was instantly disorienting. Reaching out to steady herself, she gasped as a top-heavy pile of papers began to slip. She struggled to rebalance it without being able to see it.

Outside the door she could hear faint voices; they sounded far away. She just had to wait a few more minutes and they'd be gone. Just a few more minutes.

It was hot, airless.

Stay calm.

She counted her heavy breaths . . . *twelve, thirteen, fourteen . . .*

But it was happening. That feeling of being encased in concrete, unable to breathe. Her heart pounding, rising panic burned in her throat.

Please calm down, Allie, she begged herself. *Just five minutes and you'll be safe. The guys'll never tell.*

But it wasn't working. She felt dizzy; suffocated.

She had to get out.

As sweat streamed down her face and the floor seemed to swing beneath her, she reached for the door handle.

No no no . . . It can't be.

The inside of the door was completely smooth.

Frantic, she felt the entirety of the impassive door, then the wall around it. Nothing. There was no way to open it from the inside.

She shoved the door, scratched at its edges with her nails, but it would not give. Her breath came harder now.

It was so dark.

Curling her hands into fists, she pounded on the

smooth, unyielding door.

'Help! I can't breathe. Open the door!'

There was no response.

'Help me! Please?'

She hated the pleading tone in her own voice. Sobbing now, she put her cheek against the door and gasped for air as she slapped the wood with her hands.

'Please.'

When the door opened, it did it so suddenly that she fell forward helplessly, straight into the arms of a police officer.

He held her at arm's length, shining a torch into her eyes, taking in the wild hair and tear-streaked cheeks.

He grinned over her head at the other cop. That was when Allie saw Mark, his head down and his cap missing. His arm was firmly in the grip of another officer, who grinned back.

CHAPTER TWO

Against the constant rumble of a police station on a summer Friday night, Allie heard her father's voice as clearly as if he were standing in front of her. She stopped twirling her hair and looked anxiously at the door.

'I can't tell you how much I appreciate this. I'm very sorry for the bother,' she heard. The tone in his voice was one she knew quite well: humiliated. By her. She heard another male voice she couldn't quite make out and then her dad again, 'Yes, we're taking steps, and I appreciate your advice. We'll

4

discuss this and make a decision tomorrow.'

Decision? What kind of decision?

Then the door opened, and her grey eyes met his tired blue ones. She felt her heart twist in her chest just a little. Unshaven and rumpled, he looked older. And very tired.

He handed a few papers to the female officer who barely glanced at them before adding them to her stack of paperwork. She reached into a drawer and pulled out an envelope containing Allie's things, which she shoved across the desk to Allie's father. Without looking at either of them she said robotically, 'You've been released into your father's care. You're free to go.'

Allie rose stiffly and followed her dad down narrow brightly lit corridors to the front door.

When they were outside in the cool summer air she breathed deeply. Relief at being out of the police station mingled with anxiety about the expression on her father's face. They walked to the car in silence.

From across the street her father unlocked the door of the black Ford and it beeped its incongruously chirpy welcome. When he started the engine, she turned to him earnestly, her eyes filled with explanations.

'Dad . . .?'

He looked straight ahead, his jaw tense. 'Alyson. Don't.'

'Don't what?'

'Don't talk. Just . . . sit there.'

After that, their journey was silent. And at their house, he got out of the car without a word. Allie scrambled after him, the worried feeling in the pit of her stomach growing.

He didn't seem angry. He seemed . . . empty.

Allie walked up the stairs and down the hallway, past her brother's empty room. In the safety of her own bedroom, she studied herself in the mirror. Her shoulder-length, henna-red hair was tangled, black paint was smeared on her left temple and mascara was smudged under her eyes. She smelled of stale sweat and fear.

'Well,' she told her reflection, 'maybe it could have been worse.'

*　　*　　*

When she awoke the next day it was nearly noon. Climbing out from under the rumpled duvet, she threw on a pair of jeans and a white vest top. Then she cautiously opened her door.

Silence.

She tiptoed downstairs to the kitchen, where sunshine streamed through the big windows onto clean wooden countertops. Bread had been set out for her with butter that was melting in the heat. A teacup sat by the kettle, ready with a teabag inside.

Despite everything, she really was hungry. She sliced a piece of bread and dropped it into the toaster. She turned the radio on to fill the silence but then, after a moment, switched it off again.

She ate quickly, flipping through the pages of yesterday's newspaper without really looking at it. Only when she'd finished did she notice the note near the kitchen door.

A–
Back this afternoon. Do <u>NOT</u> leave the house.
–M

Instinctively, she reached for the phone to call Mark, but it wasn't in its usual place by the fridge.

Leaning against the wooden counter she drummed her fingers, listening to the steady ticking of the big clock above the stove.

Ninety-six ticks.

Or were they tocks?

How do you tell the diff . . .?

'Right.' She straightened and slapped her hand on the pine countertop. 'Screw this.'

She ran upstairs to her room and yanked open the top drawer of her desk to get her laptop.

The drawer was empty.

She stood still, contemplating the meaning inherent in its absence. Her shoulders slumped just a little.

*   *   *

Her parents did not return until late that afternoon. She'd been waiting anxiously—hopping up to peer through the window every time a car door slammed—but when they finally did come home she adopted an air of disinterest, staying curled up in the big leather chair watching TV with the sound off.

Her mother dropped her handbag in its usual place on the hallway table, and followed her father into the kitchen to help make tea. Through the open door Allie saw her rest a hand reassuringly on her father's shoulder for just a second before moving to the refrigerator for the milk.

This looks bad.

A few minutes later they were perched

side-by-side on the navy blue sofa across from her. Her dad's hair was neatly combed now, but he had circles under his eyes. Her mother's expression was calm but her lips were in a tight line.

'Alyson . . .' her father began, then faltered. He rubbed his eyes wearily.

Her mother took over. 'We've been talking about what we can do to help you.'

Uh-oh.

'Obviously you've not been happy at your current school.' She was speaking very precisely and slowly. Allie's eyes darted from one parent to the other. 'Now that you've broken in, set fire to your records and spray-painted "Ross is a twat" on Headmaster Ross' door, it's hardly surprising that they're not very happy with you either.'

Allie chewed on the cuticle of her little finger and fought the urge to giggle nervously. Giggling now really wouldn't help.

'This will be the second school to ask us, very politely, to send you somewhere else to study. We're tired of receiving very polite letters from schools.'

Her father leaned forward and looked Allie in the eye for the first time since he'd picked her up from the police station.

'We understand that you're acting out, Alyson,' he said. 'We understand that this is how you've chosen to deal with everything that's happened, but we've had enough. Graffiti, truancy, vandalism . . . Enough. You've made your point.'

Allie opened her mouth to defend herself but her mother shot her a warning look. She pulled her feet up and wrapped her arms around her knees.

Now it was her mother's turn again. 'Last night,

the helpful police liaison officer—who, by the way, knew all about you—suggested we send you to a different school. Out of London. Away from your *friends.*'

She said the last word with bitter contempt.

'We made a few calls this morning, and we've . . .' her mother paused, glancing across at her father almost uncertainly before continuing, 'we've found a place that specialises in teenagers like you . . .'

Allie flinched.

'. . . and today we went to visit it. We've spoken to the headmistress . . .'

'Who was absolutely lovely,' her dad interjected.

Her mother ignored him. '. . . and she's agreed to accept you starting this week.'

'Hang on . . . This week?' Allie's voice rose in disbelief. 'But the summer holiday only started two weeks ago!'

'You'll board,' her father said as if she hadn't spoken.

Allie stared at him, her mouth agape.

Board?

The word reverberated in her head.

They have got to be joking, she told herself.

'. . . which will be difficult for us to afford, but we think it's worthwhile to try and save you from yourself before you throw your whole life away. You're a juvenile now in the eyes of the law, but you won't be for long.' He slapped his hand on the arm of the sofa, and Allie stared at him. 'You're sixteen years old, Alyson. This has to stop.'

Allie listened to her heart pound.

Thirteen beats. Fourteen, fifteen . . .

She couldn't believe how bad this was. It was unbelievably bad. Record-setting levels of badness were happening right now in this room. She leaned forward in the chair.

'Look, I know I messed up. I feel really, really awful about it.' She put as much sincerity as she could into her voice. Her mother looked unmoved, so she turned to her father, imploring. 'But don't you think you're overreacting? Dad, this is crazy!'

Allie's mother glanced again at her father; this time her gaze was imposing. He looked back at Allie sadly and shook his head.

'It's too late,' he said. 'The decision has been made. You start on Wednesday. Until then no computer, no phone, no iPod. And no leaving this house.'

When her parents stood up it felt like the judge was leaving the courtroom. In the emptiness they left behind, Allie exhaled shakily.

*   *   *

The next few days went by in a blur of confusion and isolation. She was supposed to be packing and getting ready, but mostly she tried to talk her parents out of their crazy plan.

She got nowhere. They barely spoke to her at all.

On Tuesday afternoon, her mother handed her a slim ivory envelope dominated by an elaborate crest in thick black ink and the words: Cimmeria Academy. Below that, 'Information for New Students' was beautifully written in curly handwriting.

The two sheets of paper inside appeared to have been written on a typewriter. She wasn't certain— she'd never actually seen typewritten paper—but the small, square letters each made a noticeable

10

indentation in the thick creamy paper. Each page held only a few paragraphs; the first was a letter from the school's headmistress, an Isabelle le Fanult. She said she was looking forward to welcoming Allie to the school.

Oh good, Allie thought, chucking the first page of the letter aside. The second page was no more useful. It said her pencils, pens and paper would be supplied by the school. That her uniform would also be supplied. That she should write her initials using a waterproof pen or 'stitch them' on all of the clothing she chose to bring with her. That she should bring wellies and a raincoat because, 'the school campus is large and rural'.

She scanned the rest of the letter looking for the usual ominous mention of 'school rules' and sure enough there it was, highlighted in bold:

The full rules for student behaviour will be supplied to you upon your arrival. Please read them and follow them closely. Violations of any school rule will be punished severely.

And just below that, more bad news:

Students are not allowed to leave the school grounds once they arrive without permission from either their parents or the headmistress. Permission will only very rarely be given.

Allie's hands shook as she picked up the first page from the floor, folded the letter back into the envelope and set it on her desk.

What is this, a school or a prison?

Then she marched downstairs to where her

mother was making lunch in the kitchen.

'I'm calling Mark,' she announced defiantly, as she picked up the kitchen phone, which magically reappeared whenever her parents were there.

'Oh are you?' Her mother set her knife down on the counter.

'If I'm being sent to *jail* I have a right to one phone call, don't I?' Allie said in tones of righteous indignation. This had all gone too far.

Her mother studied her for a minute, then shrugged and picked the knife up and returned to thinly slicing a tomato.

'Call him then.'

Allie had to think for a second before dialling. His number was programmed into her mobile so she rarely had to actually remember it.

The phone rang several times.

'Yo.' His voice was so reassuringly familiar and normal that for a second Allie thought she might cry.

'Hey. It's Allie.'

'Allie! Bloody hell. Where have you been?' He sounded as relieved as she felt.

'In lockdown.' She glared at her mother's back. 'They took my phone away, and my computer. They won't let me leave the house. How are things with you?'

'Oh, the usual.' He laughed. 'The parentals are pissed off, the school's very pissed off, but it'll blow over.'

'Are they kicking you out?'

'What? Of school? No. Are they kicking you out?'

'Allegedly. My parents are sending me away to a prison camp they insist on calling a school.

12

Somewhere in Outer Mongolia.'

'Seriously?' He sounded genuinely upset. 'That sucks! Why are they being so lame? Nobody got hurt. Ross'll get over it. I'm going to do some community service, apologise to everybody and then it's back to normal school hell. I can't believe your parents are being so medieval.'

'Me neither. Listen, the Medieval Ones say I won't be able to talk to you once I get to this prison school, but if you want to find me, it's called Cimmer . . .'

The line went dead. Allie looked up to see her mother holding the plug, which she had pulled from the wall. Her face was expressionless.

'That's enough of that,' she said, and smoothly lifted the phone from Allie's hand.

Her mother returned to slicing the tomato as Allie stood stock still, staring at her. Over the course of thirty seconds she felt her face first pale, then redden as she fought back tears. Finally she spun on her heel and stormed out of the room.

'You. People. Are. Crazy!' The words started low, but rose to a scream as she mounted the stairs. She slammed the door to her room, and once inside stood in the middle of it, staring around her, bewildered.

She no longer recognised this place as her home.

*   *   *

When Wednesday morning arrived hot and bright, she was surprised to find that she was actually relieved. At least this phase of her punishment was over with.

She stared at her open wardrobe for half an hour

13

trying to decide what to wear. She finally opted for skinny black jeans and a long black vest with the word 'Trouble' scrawled across it in sparkly silver. She brushed her bright red hair and left it loose.

Studying herself in the mirror, she thought she looked pale. Scared.

I can do better than this.

Grabbing her liquid eyeliner, she applied a thick black swoosh to her eyelids and then coated her lashes in mascara. Next, she dived under the bed and pulled out a pair of dark red, knee-high Doc Marten boots, lacing them up over her jeans. When she walked downstairs a few minutes later she looked, she thought, like a rock star. Her expression was mutinous.

Her mother looked at her outfit and sighed dramatically but said nothing. Breakfast took place in icy silence, and afterwards her parents left her alone to finish packing. She piled her clothes up on the bed and then sat among them, her head resting on her bent knees, counting her breaths until she felt calm.

When they walked to the car that afternoon, Allie stopped and looked back at their ordinary terraced house, trying to memorise it. It wasn't much, but it had always been home, with all of the emotional beauty that word implied.

Now it just looked like every other house on the street.

CHAPTER THREE

The car journey was excruciating. Normally she would have been happy to leave the city on a sunny summer day, but as London's crowded streets gave way to rolling green fields dotted with white sheep dozing in the warmth, she felt a wave of loneliness. The mood in the car didn't help. Her parents barely acknowledged her presence. Her mother held the map, and offered occasional directions.

Huddled in the back seat, Allie stared resentfully at the backs of their heads. *Why couldn't they get a GPS like everybody else?*

She'd asked them this same question many times, but her father just said they were happy to be 'Luddites' and that 'everyone should know how to read a map'.

Whatever.

Without access to the map, Allie was left trying to figure out precisely where she was going.

She'd never been told where the school was, and the town names whizzed by (*Guildford, Camberley, Farnham* . . .). Then they left the A-roads and began to wind their way up and down hills on tiny country lanes surrounded by high hedges that blocked any view, through villages (*Crondall, Dippenhall, Frensham* . . .). Finally, after two hours, they turned down a narrow dirt track. Her father slowed the car to a crawl. The road passed into thick forest where it was cooler and quieter. After a few minutes of jostling and bumping as her father swerved to avoid deep holes in the road they arrived at a tall iron gate.

They stopped. The rumble of the car engine was the only sound.

Nothing happened for a long minute.

'Do you need to beep the horn or push a buzzer or something?' Allie whispered, taking in the forbidding black fence, which extended into the trees as far as she could see.

'No.' Her father's voice was also hushed. 'They must have CCTV or something. They know when someone's here. Last time we only waited a few . . .'

The gates shivered and then, with a clanging metallic sound, swung slowly inward. Inside, the forest continued, and the sun barely filtered through the thick branches.

Allie stared into the shadows ahead.

Welcome to your new school, Allie. Welcome to your new life.

While the gates swung open, she counted her heartbeats. *Boom-boom-boom* . . . Thirteen beats and she could see the road ahead. Now her heart sounded so loud that she checked surreptitiously to see if her parents had noticed. They were waiting patiently. Her father drummed his fingers on the steering wheel.

Twenty-five beats and the gates had locked into place with a shudder.

Her father put the car into first gear.

They were on the move.

Feeling her throat closing Allie focused on breathing. She really didn't want to have another panic attack right now. But she couldn't shake an overwhelming sense of dread.

Stop freaking out, she told herself. *This is just another school, Allie. Stay focused.*

It worked; her breathing steadied a little.

16

Her father pulled the car forward onto a smooth gravel drive that rolled through thick trees. After the rutted dirt road outside the gates, the drive was so smooth and well maintained that the car seemed to float.

Allie continued to monitor her heartbeat; for one hundred and twenty-three beats nothing but trees and shadows, then a coronary drum roll as they emerged into the light and she saw a building ahead.

She lost count.

It was worse than she'd feared. Looking out of place in the bright sunlight at the foot of a steep forested hill sprawled an enormous Gothic mansion of dark red bricks. The three-storey structure looked as if it had been ripped from another time and place to be dropped here in . . . wherever they were. Its jagged roof jutted sharply in peaks and turrets, topped with what looked like daggers of wrought iron stabbing the sky.

Holy shit.

'It is such an impressive building,' her father said.

Her mother snorted. 'Impressively ghastly.'

Terrifying. The word they are looking for is 'terrifying'.

In contrast to the intimidating structure, the gravel road ahead was transformed by the sun into a piece of ivory, curving towards a big, mahogany door in the dark brick wall. As they entered the shadow cast by the school, her father slowed the car.

The second the car stopped moving, the door swung open and a slim, smiling woman slipped out and ran lightly down the stairs. Her thick, dark blonde hair was held back loosely with a clip, and it curled up at the ends as if it were happy to be there. Allie was relieved to see how normal she looked: her glasses were pushed up on top of her head, and she wore a creamy cotton cardigan atop her pale blue dress.

Allie's parents climbed out and walked over to meet her. Lagging behind unnoticed, Allie reluctantly opened her door and left the back seat of the Ford, which suddenly seemed so friendly and familiar. She didn't close the door.

Rather than joining the group ahead, she leaned against the car and warily watched the scene in front of her. Waiting. Twenty-seven heartbeats.

Twenty-eight. Twenty-nine.

'Mr and Mrs Sheridan, it's so nice to see you again.' The woman's voice was warm and lilting; she smiled easily. 'I hope the drive wasn't too tedious for you. The traffic can be awful between here and London. But at least the weather is lovely today, isn't it?'

Allie noticed she had a faint accent, but she couldn't identify it. Was it Scottish? It added delicacy and complexity to her words, as if they were filigreed.

After more pleasantries were exchanged and the conversation lulled, the three turned towards Allie. Her parents' polite smiles disappeared, replaced with the cultivated blankness with which she'd grown uncomfortably familiar. But the headmistress smiled at her warmly.

'And you must be Allie.'

Scottish, definitely. But such an unusual accent—very subtle.

'Allie, I'm Isabelle le Fanult, the headmistress

at Cimmeria Academy. You can call me Isabelle. Welcome.'

Allie was a bit surprised to hear her nickname, rather than 'Alyson', which is what her parents always called her. To be told to call a headmistress by her first name seemed weird too.

But quite cool.

Isabelle held out a slim, pale hand. She had oddly beautiful golden brown eyes, and up close she looked younger than she'd appeared from a distance.

Allie didn't want anything to do with this place—anything to do with this woman—but she found herself reaching out. As her hand was grasped in a surprisingly strong, cool grip, shaken and then released gently, she relaxed a little.

Isabelle held her gaze a second longer, and Allie thought she saw sympathy in her expression, before she turned back to her parents with a smile and an apologetic shrug.

'I'm afraid it is our policy that parents bid farewell to their children here. When the students cross the threshold they start their new lives at Cimmeria, and we like them to do that independently.'

Turning back to Allie, 'Do you have many bags? Hopefully we can carry them between the two of us. Most of the staff are busy at the moment, so I fear we must fend for ourselves.'

For the first time, Allie spoke. 'I don't have too much.'

It was true. The school supplied most things and allowed so little that in the end she only had two medium-sized bags, mostly filled with books and notepads. Her father carried them from the boot.

19

Isabelle lifted the larger of the two with surprising ease. She exchanged a few final pleasantries with Allie's parents and then stepped back away from them.

'Work hard and drop us a line now and then,' her father said. He was still distant but he looked sad, and he gave her a quick hug.

Her mother smoothed a strand of hair out of Allie's face, avoiding her eyes. 'Please give this place a chance. And call us if you need us.' For just a second she hugged Allie tightly, and then she let go and walked to the car without looking back.

Allie stood still, her hands at her sides, watching the car turn and head back down the smooth gravel drive. She felt tears prickling the backs of her eyes, and she shook her head fiercely to ward them off. Picking up the remaining black bag, she turned towards Isabelle, who was watching her.

'It's always difficult the first time,' Isabelle said, her voice gentle. 'It gets easier.'

She headed briskly towards the steps saying over her shoulder, 'I'm afraid we have a little distance to go. You'll find this building is simply endless.'

Her voice faded as she walked inside. After a moment's hesitation, Allie followed.

'I'll give you the pocket tour as we go . . .' Isabelle was saying, but Allie hardly heard as she gaped at the vast entrance hall.

Inside it was dim and chilly, the bright sunlight filtered into colourful shade by a stained glass window far above her head. The ceiling was at least twenty feet high, held aloft by thick stone arches. The stone floor had been polished smooth by thousands of feet over hundreds of years. Candle holders five feet tall stood like sentinels in each corner. Some walls were covered with old tapestries, though Allie didn't get a good look at them as she hurried after the headmistress.

From the entrance hall they moved on into a wide hallway with dark wooden floors. Isabelle turned into the first room on the right. Inside were more than a dozen large, round, wood tables, each with eight chairs around it. Along one wall an enormous fireplace reached well above her head.

'This is the dining room. You'll have all of your meals here,' she said, pausing a moment for Allie to take it in before striding off down the hallway.

A short distance away and on the opposite side of the corridor, she walked through another arched doorway. This vast room had polished wooden floors, a ceiling nearly as high as the one in the entranceway, and was largely empty. Its fireplace dwarfed Isabelle, and huge metal candelabra hung from the ceiling on chains.

'This is the great hall. We have events here, balls, gatherings, and so forth,' Isabelle said. 'This is the oldest part of the building. Much older than the façade. Older even than it looks.'

She turned on her heel and headed back into the hallway. Allie scrambled to keep up, panting slightly from the exertion. Isabelle was surprisingly fast. Turning to the left she gestured at another door, explaining that it was the common room. Then they began climbing a wide wooden staircase with an impressive mahogany banister. Isabelle's espadrilles made a soft shushing sound as she skipped upwards, all the while reeling off facts and figures about the building. Allie was a bit dazed by it all—the staircase was Edwardian, or had she said Victorian? The dining room was Reformation . . .

or was it Tudor? Most classrooms were in the east wing, but what did she say was in the west?

At the top of two flights of stairs, Isabelle turned left and walked down a wide corridor, then climbed a narrower flight of stairs which led to a long, dim hallway lined with wooden doors painted white.

'This is the girls' dormitory. Let's see, you're in 329 . . .' she hurried down the hall until the appropriate number appeared, and swung the door open.

The room was very dark and small with a single, bare bed, a wooden dresser and desk, and a wardrobe, all painted the same clean shade of white. Isabelle walked across the room and flipped a latch Allie couldn't see, swinging open a wooden shutter covering a small arched window. Instantly the room glowed with golden afternoon light.

'All it needs is a little fresh air,' she said cheerfully as she headed for the door. 'Your uniforms are in the wardrobe, your parents gave us your sizes but let us know if anything doesn't fit. You should have everything you need. Shall I leave you to unpack? Dinner is at seven, you know where the dining hall is. Oh by the way . . .'

She turned back. 'I noticed you've been having trouble in English class lately so I've added you to my own class. It's a special seminar with a smaller class; I hope you'll find it interesting.'

Overwhelmed with information Allie nodded silently; then, realising that words were needed, she said haltingly, 'I . . . I'll be fine.'

Isabelle tilted her head to one side, studying her for a second, then nodded. 'There's lots of information about the school and your classes in the envelope on the desk,' she said. Allie hadn't

22

noticed the big envelope with her name on it at first glance, but now she wondered how she'd missed it.

'Any questions before I go?'

Allie started to shake her head then stopped. She looked down at her feet and then up again. She tugged at the edge of her T-shirt hesitantly. 'You're the headmistress, right?'

Isabelle nodded, looking slightly puzzled.

'So why are you doing all of this?' Allie made a sweeping gesture.

'I don't understand,' Isabelle said, obviously baffled. 'Why am I doing what?'

Allie tried to explain. 'Meeting me at the door, showing me to my room, giving me a tour . . .'

Isabelle hesitated, crossing her arms loosely across her chest. Her voice was gentle. 'Allie, your parents told me a lot about you. I know what happened, and I am so very sorry about your brother. I know what it's like to lose somebody close to you, and I'm aware how easy it is to get caught up in that . . . horribleness, and never get out again. But you mustn't let what happened destroy your life. You have a lot to offer, and my job is to get you to realise that. To help you get yourself back.'

Isabelle walked to the door and rested her hand against it.

Three breaths in and two out.

'I'll send a prefect around to introduce herself and answer any questions you might have,' Isabelle said. 'She'll come at six, which should give you time to get everything sorted before dinner. Mealtimes are strict—please be there on time.'

She whirled out at her usual speed, but the door shut lightly behind her and latched with a quiet

23

click.

Allie exhaled.

With the room to herself Allie had time to think. Why had her parents told Isabelle about Christopher? That had always been a private family matter. And how strange was this school? Why hadn't they passed a single student in the hallway on the way here? The place felt empty.

It was weird.

She lifted a bag up onto the bed. Unzipping it, she began pulling things out and finding places to stow them. Books went onto the narrow bookshelf beside the desk. Clothes went into the dresser, but as she opened drawers she found many were already full of T-shirts, shorts and jumpers in white or midnight blue, with the Cimmeria crest above the heart.

Curious, she opened the wardrobe to find skirts, shirts and jackets, all in the uniform's style. She rummaged through the back of the wardrobe until her fingers felt something light and filmy. Pulling out the hangers she found they held delicate frocks in various colours. Isabelle had mentioned balls, but she hadn't said that the school would supply formal gowns. She held up a dress in dark blue velvet—it looked vintage, with a full, knee-length skirt and a sophisticated, beaded V-neck.

She stared at it, baffled. What was it doing there?

She'd never been to a real dance—it was not the kind of thing her former schools offered. The idea of wearing an expensive frock and going to a proper ball sent a thrill of nervousness through her. What would she do? She didn't know how to dance.

Stroking the soft fabric, she tried to imagine

herself nibbling canapés and making small talk. She gave a bitter laugh.

Not my world.

Allie returned the clothes to the wardrobe, shut the wooden door and sat at the small wooden desk in front of the window. From the chair, her view was of blue sky and the green tops of trees. The afternoon was cooling, and the air smelled of pine and summertime. She opened the envelope and pulled out a sheaf of paper. Isabelle hadn't been joking about 'too much' information.

Inside was a map of the building, sketching out where the dormitories were in respect to classrooms, dining halls, and teachers' quarters. The second sheet held her class schedule: English, history, biology, algebra, French—all the usual suspects.

Next in the stack was a black binder on which was written:

The Rules

Inside was sheet after sheet written by hand in a lovely old-fashioned script. Before she could read it though, someone knocked on her door.

The door swung open and a pretty girl in a Cimmeria uniform—white short-sleeved crested shirt, pleated dark blue knee-length skirt—walked in. She had a serious face, Allie thought. Her straight, white-blonde hair brushed the tops of her shoulders, and she wore pink Birkenstock sandals. Allie noticed that the girl's pedicure matched her shoes perfectly and she instantly felt awkward and tomboyish.

When was the last time I painted my nails?

She got the feeling the girl was trying not to stare.

'Allie?' She had a husky voice that didn't seem to match her appearance.

Allie nodded and stood up from the desk.

'I'm Jules, the prefect for your class. Isabelle asked me to come and meet you.'

'Um, thanks.' Allie tugged anxiously at the hem of her top, wondering if she should have changed.

There was a pause. Jules raised an eyebrow enquiringly and tried again. 'She thought you might have questions that I could help you with?'

Allie struggled to think of interesting questions. And failed. 'So, are we supposed to wear a uniform every day? All the time?'

Jules nodded. 'Whenever we're anywhere on the grounds, we wear the uniform. There's a whole section on it in the papers Isabelle left for you.'

'I was just sort of reading them.' Allie wished she would quit stumbling over her words. Jules seemed so confident. 'But there's a lot to read.'

'It's a lot to take in on your first day,' Jules conceded. 'I think my first day would have been awful but my brother was here already, so he helped. Lots of kids have relatives who went here—do you?'

Allie shook her head. 'I'd never heard of the place until a few days ago.'

Jules seemed surprised by that, but said only, 'Well then I better show you around the dorm, although there's not much to it, to be honest.'

Allie took a step towards the door but Jules looked at her outfit meaningfully.

'Why don't you change into your uniform first?'

Flushing, Allie crossed her arms across her chest

but Jules didn't seem to notice.

'I'll wait outside,' Jules said. Without waiting for a response she walked out the door.

As soon as the door closed behind her, Allie yanked open the wardrobe door and pulled out a white shirt and neat blue skirt like the ones Jules wore and threw the outfit on the bed.

Had Jules been making fun of her clothes? She couldn't be certain, but she was so . . . perfect.

Of course she was making fun of me, Allie thought bitterly. *That's what girls like her do.*

Girls with perfect pedicures . . . She unlaced her boots violently and kicked them under the bed.

Girls with perfect hair . . .

She launched herself at the wardrobe to find acceptable shoes, but unearthed only practical rubber-soled black Oxfords and prim, schoolgirl white socks. She made a face as she put them on.

Stupid perfect girls.

Checking herself in the mirror on the back of the door she felt self-conscious about her heavy makeup—Jules wore only lip gloss. But there was nothing to be done right now.

Smoothing her hair with her hands, she walked out. Jules was leaning against the wall.

'Now you look like one of us,' she said approvingly as they walked down the narrow hall.

Allie didn't know what to think about that.

'This area used to be the servants' quarters,' Jules explained, oblivious to Allie's simmering resentment. 'The building was expanded over the years, though, so it's much larger than it used to be. The bathroom's here . . .' she gestured at the only door they'd passed that wasn't numbered. 'Everyone shares it so go early or late or expect to

27

wait.'

They turned back towards the stairs. The building felt busier now, with uniformed students talking and laughing everywhere.

'I take it Isabelle showed you the dining room?' Jules said. 'Did she take you to the common room?'

Allie shook her head.

'It's the most important room in the school,' Jules said, leading them down the staircase. 'Most of us are here after class whenever we're not doing our prep.'

'Prep?' Allie asked.

Jules looked at her as if she couldn't believe she had to ask.

'Homework,' she explained, opening a door at the foot of the stairs.

They stepped into a comfortable space with leather sofas, Oriental rugs scattered on the floor, a piano in one corner, and floor-to-ceiling bookshelves stacked with books and games. Several tables had chessboards painted on top. The room was empty save for one deep chair at the far side of the room where a boy sat watching them over the top of an ancient-looking book. He had straight black hair, a firm mouth and huge, dark eyes surrounded by thick lashes; his feet were propped casually on a chessboard. Their eyes met and Allie had the strangest feeling that he knew who she was. He didn't smile at her, or say a word, but he kept looking. After a moment that seemed longer than a moment, she tore her eyes away and looked back at Jules, who was watching her expectantly.

Say something.

'There's, uh . . . no television? Or . . . stereo . . .' She thought she heard a stifled chuckle from across

28

the room but she refused to look back over at the boy.

Again she saw bafflement on Jules' face, as if she'd asked her what the bright golden globe in the sky was.

'No, definitely not.' Jules' voice was stern. 'No TV, no iPod, no laptops, no mobiles . . . No twenty-first century, really. Surely your parents mentioned this to you?'

As Jules listed off the things the students couldn't have, Allie's heart sank with each forbidden device. In answer to Jules' question, she shook her head mutely.

Jules seemed astonished but gathered herself enough to explain.

'We're expected to learn how to amuse ourselves in more traditional ways. Like conversation and reading. Trust me, they'll keep you so busy with schoolwork you won't have time for TV anyway.' Jules turned to walk out of the room, 'It's all in the packet . . .'

That stupid packet. It will take me all bloody night to read it and learn more about how rubbish this place is.

Without looking back at the boy in the chair, she followed the prefect down the hall. Jules lightly touched a door as they passed it. 'This is the library—you'll get to know it very well.'

They crossed the main hall and she pushed open a heavy door, letting them into the east wing of the building.

'This is where the classrooms are. It's easiest to find your way around by number when you first start here. On your schedule, each of your classes has a room number. We all know them by teacher, but that won't be much help to you at first, since they don't put their names on the door. Rooms one to twenty are on the ground floor, one hundred to one-twenty are on the first floor, and anything higher than that is off limits to you.'

Allie shot her a surprised look but before she could ask why, Jules said, 'So, you've got about twenty minutes before dinner, and I'd suggest you read through the packet while you've got the time. That stuff is really important. Otherwise I think you'll be a bit lost tomorrow. Your teachers will give you your books in each class, by the way, so you only need to bring paper and pens; there should be plenty in your desk.'

They were climbing the stairs by that point, heading back towards the dormitory. 'I'm in room 335 if you need me, but anybody will help you if you get lost, OK?'

She waved and turned away down the hall, as Allie returned to her room.

Setting the weird-looking Rules aside for later, she flipped through the stack of papers on the desk and tried to focus on class guides ('Students must be in their seats before the instructor begins each class . . .') but her thoughts returned to the boy in the leather chair. She searched her memory for any past encounters but could find none filed there. He definitely seemed to recognise her, or, if nothing else, to know who she was. She twirled her pencil between her fingers, remembering the way his dark eyes had studied her.

As she turned over another page she glanced down at her watch.

Bollocks.

It was one minute until seven o'clock. Where

had twenty minutes gone? Dinner was starting.

She dashed out the door and barely avoided colliding with a girl with short blonde hair who was hurtling down the hall.

'Watch it!' the girl yelled without breaking her stride. Allie stepped in right behind her.

'Sorry! I didn't see you.'

The girl didn't look back, and they both ran downstairs and skidded to a stop at the dining room entrance at the same time. Without exchanging a word they walked into the room with the same air of contrived insouciance, as if they'd been chatting casually on the way down. The blonde girl glanced at her and winked before sitting at what appeared to be her regular table, judging by the way everybody greeted her.

The room looked very different now than it had appeared to her when she'd breezed through with Isabelle. Lighted candles sparkled on tables draped in white tablecloths. Plates in the school colours and crystal glasses glittered in front of each seat. Spotting an empty chair, Allie slid into it. As if somebody had hit the mute button, conversation at the table died instantly. Seven pairs of eyes gazed at her curiously.

'Is it OK if I, uh . . . sit here?' She glanced around nervously.

Before anyone could answer, the door to the kitchen opened and waiting staff appeared dressed in black and carrying platters of food. Somebody placed a clear glass jug of water at Allie's elbow. Until that moment she hadn't realised how thirsty she was, and she longed to fill her glass but she waited to see what everybody else was doing. Nobody moved.

'Please do.'

She followed the voice, with its French accent, to her left side where a boy with tawny skin, thick dark hair and exquisite blue eyes was watching her.

'Excuse me?'

'Sit here. Please do.'

She smiled at him gratefully. 'Thank you.'

He smiled back and she thought she might actually melt into a puddle on the floor. He was gorgeous.

'You're welcome. Would you be so kind as to pass the water to me?'

She handed him the jug and, to her relief, he filled her glass before his own. She drank half of the glass very quickly, and then served herself from the platter of beef and potatoes he passed to her. Silence fell again, and she glanced over at him.

She cleared her throat. 'I'm Allie,' she said.

Something told her he knew that already. 'I'm Sylvain. Welcome to Cimmeria.'

'Thanks,' she said, momentarily glad to be there.

The food was delicious. She hadn't had anything to eat since that awful, stilted breakfast, and now she ate ravenously. As she speared the last piece of potato into her mouth, though, she glanced up to find everyone watching her. The piece of potato seemed enormous and she chewed with difficulty then reached for her glass of water, which she noticed too late was empty.

Smoothly, Sylvain picked up the glass and filled it for her. His expression was sympathetic, and his light eyes glittered in the candlelight. But as Allie tried to think of something interesting to say, her thoughts were interrupted.

'You're from London.' The abrupt voice came

32

from a red-haired girl across the table.

'Yes. How did you . . . ?'

'They told us a new student was coming. You're Allie Sheridan.' The redhead stated this matter-of-factly, as if she were reporting the day's news.

Allie's reply was guarded.

'So they tell me. Who are you?'

'Katie.' Nobody else volunteered their names.

Allie squirmed a bit in their combined gaze, and felt the need to fill the awkward gaps in the conversation. But small talk had never been her strong suit.

'This school is . . . huge,' she fumbled. 'The building is kind of scary.'

'Is it?' Katie asked, sounding a bit taken aback. 'I think it's beautiful. Everyone in my family went to school here. Did your parents go here?'

Allie shook her head. Katie arched one perfect eyebrow as the girls on either side of her whispered to each other.

'How strange.'

'Why is that strange?' Allie asked.

'Most of the kids here are legacy—I am, Sylvain is, and Jo is too.'

Allie was confused. 'Who's Jo?'

Katie looked bemused. 'The girl you came in with.'

'Miss Sheridan.' The booming voice from just behind her seat cut Katie off, and Allie turned sideways to see its owner, a balding man who looked to be her father's age. He was very tall—well over six feet—and although he wore a tired-looking suit, he stood with almost military carriage. Allie sat up straighter. The room fell silent.

33

'Has anyone explained to you the rules on meals at Cimmeria?' The look he gave her felt like contempt.

'Yes.' Allie's voice quivered slightly, and she hated that.

'All students must be in this room before the start of every meal. You cut it a little too close today. As did you, Miss Arringford.' He spun on his heel and pointed at Jo, who regarded him fearlessly. He looked back at Allie. 'Don't let it happen again. New or not, the next time you're late you'll face detention.'

He strode away, his heels making a clicking sound in the hushed room. Allie stared at her empty plate, feeling the room's eyes on her. Her cheeks flushed with anger. She was *two seconds late*. He had no right to humiliate her in front of the entire school for that.

She couldn't believe it. She'd only just arrived, and already she was in trouble.

Looking over at the nearby table she saw Jo watching her. Briefly their eyes met and Jo gave a cheeky smile and another wink before she returned to talking and laughing as if nothing had happened. Allie watched as a boy rubbed Jo's arm and she rested her head on his shoulder for a moment smiling at something he'd said.

Allie felt both better and worse.

The others at her table were talking busily to one another, pointedly ignoring her. All except Sylvain, who looked concerned.

'Who was that?' she asked, folding and unfolding her linen napkin, pretending that what had happened wasn't that important.

'Mr Zelazny,' he said. 'History teacher. A bit

34

officious as you've now seen. He sees himself as the school's enforcer. I'd like to say that you shouldn't worry, but in reality you don't want to get on his bad side. He can make your life . . . unhappy. If I were you, I'd be early for meals for the next few days. He will be watching you.'

'Great,' Allie said resignedly.

Just my bloody luck.

All around them students began rising from their tables and walking out. Allie saw that they left their plates and glasses on the table.

'Don't we help clear the tables?' she asked, surprised.

The girls around Katie giggled.

Katie looked puzzled. 'Of course not. The staff do that.'

Allie turned to Sylvain, but his seat was empty. He was gone. She could hear more giggling and whispering around the table, and she'd had just about enough of that today, so without another word she joined those walking to the door.

She felt tired and defeated. What she wouldn't give to go back to her room and listen to her MP3 player while texting Mark and Harry about the weird people she'd met today. But that world seemed very far away from Cimmeria's stuffy, antiquated universe where technology didn't exist, and people were too pampered to pick up their own dinner plates and carry them to the kitchen.

Out in the hallway she saw the students were walking in several directions. Some were going outside, while others headed into the common room or library. They all seemed to be travelling in groups of friends, talking and laughing.

Alone, Allie climbed the stairs towards the girls'

rooms.

Twenty-four steps to the first floor, and twenty more to the second, then seventeen steps down the hall to her room.

Once inside she saw that somebody had been in while she was at dinner. The window was closed, although the shutter was still open. The bed was now covered in crisp white sheets and a fluffy white duvet; a dark blue blanket folded neatly across the footboard. The clothes she'd thrown on the floor had disappeared, replaced by a pair of soft white slippers. Two white towels were folded up on the chair with a bar of soap on top. The papers on the desk had been straightened into a neat pile.

Somebody around here's a neat freak.

Kicking off her shoes, Allie picked up the papers and threw herself onto the bed. She'd only made it halfway through, though, when the evening light began disappearing from the sky.

She yawned into her course schedule.

Shoving her feet into the slippers, she grabbed her toothbrush and headed towards the bathroom. She opened the door with slight trepidation, but the room was empty. As she cleaned her teeth she studied herself in the mirror. Did she look older now than she had a week ago? She felt older.

Back in her room she closed the shutter over the window and climbed into bed. But when she switched off the desk lamp the room was plunged into total darkness. It was way too dark. She groped for the lamp on the desk, knocking over her alarm clock as she hurriedly switched the light back on.

Jumping out of bed, she opened the shutter. The last light of the summer day bathed the room with a soft glow.

That was better.

Switching off the lamp, she lay watching the last glimmers of sunlight disappear and the stars appear. She'd counted one hundred and forty-seven breaths when she fell asleep.

*   *   *

'Allie, run!'

The scream came from ahead of her in the darkness. Allie didn't know why anyone felt it necessary to say that—she was already running, and running as fast as she could. Her hair flew behind her, and although she couldn't really see the trees clearly—she could just make out their shapes—she could feel the branches grabbing at her clothes; the twigs tearing her flesh. The forest floor was uneven and she knew that eventually she would lose her footing. You can't run blindly in the dark through the woods. It's impossible.

Suddenly just behind her she heard footsteps and felt the air move as if someone were right . . .

Hard fingers cut into the skin on her left shoulder and she cried out, swatting whoever it was with her hands, beating them away from her.

Then she heard a contemptuous laugh right behind her and, screaming, she was pulled off of her feet by hands she couldn't see.

*   *   *

Allie sat bolt upright. For a short moment she had no idea where she was, and she scrambled into the far corner of the bed, her back to the wall and her arms wrapped around her knees protectively.

Then she remembered. *Cimmeria. School.*

That dream again. She'd been having it regularly for weeks. Each time she woke up sweating.

The room was still dark—the clock showed that it was just after twelve-thirty. She felt wide awake and anxious, and yet somehow still groggy, as if nothing were real.

She climbed out of bed, and leaned across the desk to look outside. The moon cast the world in an unearthly blue light. She clambered up onto the desktop and opened the window, feeling the cool breeze as she rested her chin on her arms and gazed out into the darkness. She listened to the night birds and breathed the fresh air in deeply. She loved that smell—pine needles and loamy soil—it was comforting.

Suddenly she heard footsteps . . . above her? Was that possible?

She strained to see what was above her window and could have sworn she saw the faintest shadow moving on the roof.

She sat still for a moment, listening, and thought she could hear, very faintly, a susurration of voices.

She closed the window, tested the latch to make sure it was secure then climbed back into bed. She was unconscious within minutes.

CHAPTER FOUR

Allie opened her eyes to find the room filled with light. In the hazy space between sleep and wakefulness she thought that, with its pure white

38

walls and pristine white duvet, it looked like heaven.

She glanced at the alarm clock on the desk—six-thirty.

Had she ever been up this early in her life? Maybe for that trip to France with her family a few years ago, but never of her own volition. Never just for school.

She could hear voices in the hallway as she stretched and yawned. The room was cool with the fresh morning air.

She sat up straight and stared at the wide open window. Hadn't she closed it last night? She could remember doing it but now it stood as far open as it had been when she'd sat in front of it during the night.

Maybe I just dreamed that I closed it.

She climbed out of bed muttering under her breath, 'Get on with it, Allie.' Pulling on her dressing gown and sliding on her slippers, she wrapped her shampoo and toothbrush in a towel and hurried down the hall, anxious about the shared bathroom scenario ahead.

In contrast to its echoing emptiness last night, the big room was now steamy and busy, but there was one free shower. Relieved it wasn't one of those everybody-naked-in-a-brutal-concrete-cube shared showers, Allie pulled the curtain closed behind her and stepped in to find a private changing area in front of a spacious white shower cubicle. Both were spotless.

This wasn't so bad, actually. There was plenty of space, a hook on which she could hang her robe and even a polished wooden bench where she could leave her slippers high and dry. In the hot spray she felt better almost immediately. Later, with her wet hair wrapped in a towel, she found a free sink to brush her teeth and didn't really mind how busy it was. Swathed in a thick white robe like everybody else, nobody could tell she was the new girl.

Back in her room she quickly pulled on her uniform, combed her damp hair and applied a light sweep of mascara. Her hand hovered over the eyeliner . . . then she left it in the bag. This place seemed to have a different style than her school in London.

She gathered her papers and pens for the day and put them into the dark blue tote bag she'd found in the wardrobe. Swinging it over her shoulder, she headed downstairs at seven o'clock on the dot, well ahead of the seven-thirty breakfast deadline.

When she walked in the dining room door she paused for a moment—it had again transformed itself. Huge windows along one wall let in sunlight, diffused through white blinds. Gone were the twinkling candles and sparkling glasses. Most of the tables were empty and topped only with plain white tablecloths. Food was piled on buffet tables: ten kinds of cereal, a steaming cauldron of porridge and stacks of bread ready for toasting. Heated silver serving platters held eggs, bacon and sausages.

Smelling the food, she discovered she was starving again. Piling her plate with toast, cheese and scrambled eggs, she poured herself a glass of apple juice before claiming a seat at an empty table. She didn't recognise anybody in the room, which was, in its own way, nice. She smeared butter and blackcurrant jam on her toast and took a huge bite.

'Is this seat taken?'

Trying not to chew with her mouth open, Allie turned to see Sylvain standing beside her. She shook her head mutely, and struggled to swallow gracefully but failed, wincing as the food went down. For the first time she thought a smile reached his extraordinary eyes.

'No . . . I mean, you can sit here. Please. Do . . .'

Sitting down beside her without a hint of awkwardness, he took a bite of bacon. 'How did you find your first night? I looked for you in the common room but I couldn't find you.'

Her heart jumped and she looked determinedly at her cheese so that he wouldn't see how pleased she was. 'I had a lot to read last night. I thought I'd better learn as much as I could before today to, you know, get ready. Big day and all that.'

He nodded and took a reasonably sized bite of toast. 'I remember that from my first day. They seem to want you to learn everything about Cimmeria all at once. I think the information they give you is more than . . .' Adorably he seemed to struggle to think of the English words he was looking for '. . . the school in size, if that makes sense?'

Charmed, she couldn't help but smile. 'I know exactly what you mean. It's disproportionate.'

'Yes. Disproportionate.' He smiled back at her and Allie's heart jumped again.

Stop that, she told herself firmly. *He's just being polite.*

They ate in companionable silence for a while.

'So,' she said after a while, 'does everybody hang out in the common room a lot? It looks OK.'

41

Great small talk, Allie. Really smooth.

He didn't seem to notice as he sipped from a cup of milky coffee. 'The common room and the library are where people are most evenings. In the summer when it's warm many of us choose to be outside, though. I was outside last night, playing night croquet. That is why I was looking for you. I thought you might want to join us.'

Allie's fork stopped halfway to her mouth.

'You were playing croquet at night? In the dark?'

'It's more fun that way. You know, I've found that many games are more exotic if played at night.' His eyes held hers for just a second too long.

And just like that Allie lost her appetite. She tore her eyes away from his, and her gaze skittered around the room.

Chair, table, girl-with-ponytail, window, chair again . . .

She felt the warmth rise in her cheeks. When she glanced back at him a slight smile played at the edge of his lips as he crumbled a corner of toast between long fingers, watching her face.

He's flirting with me. Definitely.

'Rounders, for example,' he continued thoughtfully. 'And football without lights, although that can be a bit . . . rough.'

He balanced a piece of bacon on his fingertips while he considered the possibilities. 'Tennis with fluorescent rackets on a moonless night is incredible. I think you'd love it. I promise to find you the next time we play—wherever you are.'

She watched as if hypnotised while he took a bite.

'Allie. How nice to see you again.' Katie pulled

out a chair across the table, and sat down. Her plate was intricately decorated with slices of fruit. 'And Sylvain. What a surprise.'

Her long, curly red hair contrasted brilliantly with her milky, translucent skin. In the soft light, she seemed illuminated. She was surrounded by a small group of perfectly styled girls who watched Allie with amusement.

Sylvain looked at her icily. 'I was just leaving, actually.'

He turned back to Allie and held her gaze. 'We have English together, I believe. It's Robert Browning this week, in case you want to read before class. See you then.'

He walked away before she could ask him how he knew what classes she was taking, but he turned in the doorway for a second and when their eyes met Allie felt as if somebody had draped a warm blanket across her shoulders. When he was gone she smiled at her apple juice.

'Sylvain's lovely isn't he?' Katie's crisp west London accent cut into her reverie. Allie looked up to find her watching her knowingly. 'Those dreamy eyes and that melty accent. His girlfriend's lovely, too, isn't she?' She turned to the brunette beside her who nodded and giggled.

'She lives in Paris now I hear.' Katie delicately consumed a segment of grapefruit as Allie felt her emotional balloon burst.

Ah. Girlfriend. Right. So much for that, then.

She was not surprised to find the inevitable crushing blow of early romantic disappointment following hard on the heels of hope. Frankly, that was how things usually went for her. When she'd first met Mark there'd been something there. For

43

two weeks it had been obvious to everybody that they'd get together. Until one night he'd shown up with a perky, diminutive blonde named Charlotte who had a penchant for miniskirts and hot pink nail polish.

After that he was just her mate.

'How nice for him,' Allie said resignedly. 'Well . . . I have to go too.'

She stood up and walked away quickly, stopping herself at the last minute from looking for a place to take her plate and glass. Hearing giggles behind her, she straightened her spine and did not look back.

Outside the dining hall Allie joined other students walking down the wide hallway with oak wainscoting towards the classrooms in the east wing. The walls were lined with oil paintings—most were huge portraits of nineteenth century men and women in formal attire staring down at her haughtily. A few portrayed Cimmeria Hall from different perspectives, most from the hill outside with thick forest in the foreground. In one, the building was much smaller than it was now—before the expansion Isabelle had talked about.

Her first class was biology, in room 112, so she climbed the staircase to the first floor and found the room near the top of the stairs.

The handful of students who'd arrived early were sitting in pairs at tables arranged in long rows, as a tall, distracted-looking man with wire-framed glasses and unruly brown hair flipped through papers at the front of the room.

Allie walked over to him. 'Hi. I'm Alyson Sheridan. I'm new.'

He peered at her over the top of his glasses and

44

shuffled his papers again at length, finally emerging with one, which he waved triumphantly.

'Of course you are. A transfer student, how lovely. But I have you down as "Allie". Which do you prefer?'

'Allie,' she said, surprised. Schools always had her down as Alyson. But everybody at Cimmeria knew her as Allie before she met them.

'Then Allie it is.' He was shuffling papers again distractedly. 'I'm Jeremiah Cole. The students usually call me Jerry. Please take the second seat on the right there, next to Jo.'

She glanced in the direction he pointed to see the blonde girl from dinner last night waving vigorously.

'I'm so glad it's you. I do hope you're good at biology,' she said as soon as Allie walked up. 'I think all the sciences are diabolical—dead baby animals and parasites—what are they trying to tell us? Crikey we got into trouble last night, didn't we? Does that always happen to you?'

She had a contagious smile—white, even teeth, deep endearing dimples and little crinkles around her tiny nose—and a lead crystal accent. Allie smiled back at her before her brain realised she wanted to do it.

'It does always happen to me. If you hang around with me, it will definitely happen again,' Allie said, with a wicked smile.

Jo beamed at her. 'Brilliant! This is going to be *amazing*.'

As Allie pulled out her notebook, Jo whispered, 'Isn't Jerry snoggable for an old guy? I had a crush on him my whole first year here.'

Allie studied the teacher. He looked

like somebody's dad. A nice dad. But a dad nonetheless.

'I like that you can call teachers by their first names here,' she said noncommittally. 'My last school was so strict we practically had to call them "Officer".'

Laughing, Jo looked like she wasn't sure whether or not to believe her.

'You're going to have to tell me more about your life,' she said. 'It sounds much better than mine.'

Don't count on it, Allie thought. But she just smiled.

Jo showed her where the class had reached in the book. 'It's disgusting,' she said cheerfully. 'Today, I think we're dissecting.'

As if on cue, Jerry called for quiet.

'Today we'll be looking at the general internal construction of amphibians, thanks to the sacrifice of this little fellow.'

Reaching under his desk he pulled out a dissection tray containing a dead frog, spreadeagled and pinioned, its pale belly curving at them vulnerably.

'Oh bollocks.' Jo grimaced.

'Who can tell me why we're dissecting a frog rather than some other poor creature?' Jerry asked, looking at the class over the top of his glasses. 'Why do we torment these innocent pond-dwellers? How about you, Allie? Do you know?'

Allie felt the colour drain from her cheeks.

'I . . . I guess . . .'

'Because a frog's anatomy is much like man's.' The voice, deep and pleasing, came from behind her.

'Mr West,' Jerry said, glancing without warmth

46

towards the speaker, 'is correct as usual, although he could wait his turn. The anatomy of the frog is somewhat similar to human anatomy . . .'

Allie turned around in her seat to see who had saved her, and instantly recognised the boy from the common room yesterday. He was staring at her with those big, dark eyes, but his expression startled her—he looked almost resentful.

With a puzzled frown, Allie turned to face the front.

Science was not her best subject, and so she tried not to think about 'Mr West', and focused instead on Jerry's lesson about frogs.

She didn't look back again.

*   *   *

'You took loads of notes,' Jo said as they were walking out, 'I'm so psyched that you're really into science. I need a friend who's a science geek.'

'I'm not that into it,' Allie said honestly. 'I just think I'm going to have to work to catch up. This class is way ahead of my last school.'

'This is a really hard school,' Jo said. 'But it's fun too. Although it does have too many freaky rules.'

'Totally,' Allie said.

Pretending to straighten her bag strap, she asked casually, 'Hey, who was that guy who saved me from the frog question? Jerry called him "Mr West".'

With a knowing look, Jo lowered her voice confidentially. 'Carter West,' she whispered. 'He is totally hot. But he's a mess. So you probably shouldn't.'

Allie was so intrigued she didn't bother to deny

interest. 'How is he a mess?'

'He's constantly in detention. Thinks he knows everything and everybody else is shallow. He's infuriating. Half the teachers hate him, and the others treat him like, I don't know, he's their kid or something. And he's a notorious womaniser. He gets what he wants and then he's not interested any more. You'd be better off working that Sylvain thing you've got going.'

Allie blushed. 'I don't have anything going with Sylvain.'

'Well, I think he's got something going with you.' Jo elbowed her.

'Actually, I heard he has a girlfriend in Paris.'

'First I've heard of it.' Jo seemed genuinely surprised. 'Who told you that?'

'The red-headed girl. What's her name . . . Katie?'

'Oh, Katie.' Jo's voice dripped with contempt. 'Christ, she's such a bitch. Don't listen to a word she says. She's always had a thing for Sylvain and he's never been interested in her at all. She must really hate the way he's just fallen for you.'

Allie kept her expression blank but inside she was churning. So Katie had lied. Well that was it then.

Game on.

*   *   *

The day was a brain burner of new classes, new teachers and new classmates, and of finding out the truth about just how much schoolwork she needed to do. She had Zelazny for history, which she'd thought would be a nightmare, but to her relief, aside from a brief hard stare when she first walked into his classroom, he treated her like everybody else.

Her next class was Isabelle's English seminar, and as she walked in the first person she saw was Sylvain, leaning back on a desk, his long legs stretched out gracefully. He was talking to the boy beside him when she walked in, but she noticed that he stopped almost immediately and turned to watch her as she walked up to Isabelle.

'Hi Allie.' The headmistress smiled. 'How's your first day going?'

'So far so good,' Allie said, only lying a little.

'Good.' She handed Allie a course schedule. 'We're reading Robert Browning today. Are you at all familiar with his work?'

During her lunch break, Allie had read the Browning in her text book. 'I've read "Life in a Love",' she said.

'What do you think of it?'

Allie fidgeted. 'It was all right.'

Isabelle tilted her head to one side, looking unimpressed. 'Is that your full review?'

Allie hated poetry, but now seemed like a bad time to mention it. She leaned on the edge of a desk as she fumbled for the right words. 'To be honest . . . it seemed a bit . . . you know, stalky.'

For a second the headmistress looked as if she was going to argue, but then she stopped herself and handed Allie the class syllabus. 'Fair enough. Sit anywhere you like.'

The desks were arranged in a circle, which somehow made choosing one more difficult. After a moment's hesitation, Allie picked a seat at random. When she sat down, she saw that

Sylvain was still watching her. She raised her hand hesitantly, and he smiled at her before turning back to the boy beside him.

Isabelle stepped into the circle and leaned against an empty desk.

'I hope everybody read some Browning last night. I'm curious to hear what you all thought. He had a unique style that rebelled against many of the accepted rules of poetry of the time, so I thought some of you might relate to his approach. I presume you've all had a chance to meet our new student, Allie. Allie, I don't want to embarrass you, but would you please read the first few lines?'

Oh bugger.

Standing uncomfortably she held her book close to her face and cleared her throat.

'Escape me?
Never
Beloved!
While I am I, and you are you
So long as the world contains us both,
Me the loving and you the loth
While the one eludes must the other pursue.'

At Isabelle's nod, Allie slipped gratefully back into her desk.

'So, what is Browning saying here?' The class regarded her in silence. Allie was fairly confident that she knew, but no way was she going to say anything right now.

'It's about obsession.'

Allie hadn't seen Carter West come in, but he was sitting just a few desks away from her.

Isabelle nodded. 'Care to elaborate?'

'As long as they both exist on the same planet, he has to be with her,' Carter said. 'He's in love with her, but it's more than love. It's everything. He thinks they were meant to be together but she doesn't. So his life is spent trying to convince her.'

'Interesting theory.' Isabelle glanced at Allie. 'Anyone else?'

Allie slid down in her seat.

'Ismay,' the headmistress said, turning to a familiar-looking brunette. 'Can you read the next few lines?'

Allie chanced a sideways glance in the direction of Carter's voice, and then looked away sharply. He was looking right at her.

*   *   *

'What is it with the boys in this school?' Allie and Jo were walking to the library. Classes had ended for the day and Jo had intercepted her on the way back to her room and suggested they study together.

'What do you mean?' Jo asked.

'They stare,' Allie said. 'A lot.'

Jo smiled. 'You're pretty. And new. Boys stare at pretty, new girls.'

'I'm not *that* pretty. Boys didn't stare at me like that in London.'

'I think you're pretty,' Jo said. 'Maybe they just . . .' she shrugged, 'want you to notice them.'

They both giggled. Allie pretended to sag under the weight of her book bag. 'I can't believe how much work I need to do.'

Jo nodded. 'They really bury us in the summer, because if you're here for the summer term it's

51

because you've got, like, promise.'

'Promise?' Allie raised her eyebrows.

'You know, potential.' Jo shrugged. 'Whatever. The school is sort of, I don't know, divided up, I guess. Some come here because they've got lots of money. Some come here because their parents did. But some are here because they're super-clever. They're here most of the year, while the others get the summer off. I think we're being groomed to rule the world or something.'

Allie marvelled at how she could say things like that and not sound pretentious.

'That's why I don't mind being here in the summer.' Jo pushed open the library door and lowered her voice to a whisper. 'We have the place to ourselves, and the people who are here at this time of year are the coolest.'

The voice in Allie's head was damning: *I'm not here because I'm super-clever.*

As they walked into the library's hush, she breathed in the rich mix of leather, old books, and lemony wood polish. The room stretched further than she could see through a forest of dark wooden bookshelves that reached to the ceiling fifteen feet above their heads. Each row had its own rolling ladder giving access to the highest shelves. The floor was covered with thick oriental rugs that captured the sound of their footsteps. Ancient, wrought-iron light fixtures that surely must have once held candles hung several feet below the ceiling on thick chains, so that the books on the top shelves were lost in the shadows. Heavy wooden tables topped with green-shaded lamps were surrounded by leather chairs; many were already occupied by students, dwarfed by the stacks of books piled around them.

Intimidated by the display of studiousness and its accoutrements, Allie tried to push back a wave of insecurity. She was already so far behind: how would she ever catch up? For the first time in a long time she cared about failing.

She followed Jo, who wound her way expertly to a table neatly placed to provide a good view of the main study area while managing to be slightly out of the sightline of the librarian's desk. They stacked their books onto the table and settled into the big leather chairs. They were immersed in history when two leanly muscled arms wrapped around Jo from behind, pinning her to her seat. She gasped, and then giggled as a handsome blonde boy appeared near her shoulder, kissing her neck lightly.

'Gabe, stop it! You haven't met Allie yet. And you need to, because Allie is a goddess.' Jo's face glowed and Allie felt a twinge of envy chased by a brief surge of guilt for having felt it.

Gabe gave her a welcoming smile, his hazel eyes glittering in the lamplight. Reaching around Jo he held out a strong hand with square, neat fingernails. 'Hello Allie. I've never met a goddess before.'

She smiled back and shook his hand. 'There's a first time for everything.'

Brushing a kiss on the top of Jo's head he sat down across the table from her and pulled her notebook over so he could see it. 'What are you two working on? Ah, history. Good to see you studying so diligently.'

Jo rolled her eyes at Allie. 'Gabe's a year ahead of us. Sometimes it makes him pompous.'

He laughed and swished the end of a pen lightly

up her arm. 'Not pompous. Just experienced.'

Jo giggled again as Gabe turned to Allie. 'So you're the famous Allie Sheridan everybody's talking about.'

Allie was startled. 'Everyone's talking about me? Why would they talk about me?'

He smiled. 'Relax. It's just because you're new. Fresh meat. Those of us who are here year round can start to feel a bit cut off from the rest of the world. So a new student in the summer is about as exciting as it gets. Plus there's the whole Sylvain thing . . .'

His voice was ripe with suggestion as it trailed off, and he and Jo both smiled at her as if she'd done something wonderful.

'Oh for God's sake.' Allie had heard enough of 'the whole Sylvain thing'. 'I'm sorry to disappoint you, but there isn't a Sylvain thing.'

Jo leaned towards Gabe. 'Allie's in denial. I think they're meant to be together.'

Allie glowered. 'I'm not in denial.'

'Either way,' Gabe said smoothly, 'everybody's noticed that he's interested in you. And we're all intrigued.'

'Why is it so intriguing?'

Gabe glanced at Jo. She gave a slight nod. 'Sylvain is kind of . . . special. His parents are very important people—he's from a very old family. And he's kind of an interesting guy in his own right. Lots of girls over the years have tried to get his attention, but nobody's ever really succeeded.'

Jo chimed in. 'But then you came along and suddenly it's like he has this huge crush.'

Allie felt pressured and she always hated that feeling. 'Well, I'm sorry to disappoint everyone, but

54

I'm not sure I'm interested.'

Jo looked exasperated. 'I think she's into somebody else.'

Gabe raised his eyebrows at her, and she gave him a significant look.

'Carter,' she said, wrinkling her nose.

'Oh no.' Gabe leaned towards Allie intently. 'Seriously. You can't. Not West. He's the single worst guy you could go for here.'

'Thanks Gabe. I never knew you cared.'

Allie recognised the rich deep voice instantly, and froze in her seat, trying to figure out how to dissolve into the leather and never be seen again.

Gabe was undaunted. 'Oh, get over it Carter. You know it's the truth. You haven't exactly made a name for yourself around here as a reliable, trustworthy boyfriend.'

Giving Allie an apologetic look, Jo stacked up her books briskly. 'I was just about to dash to the common room for a break before dinner. Should we all go?'

She and Gabe stood up, but Allie was immobilised with embarrassment. Besides, leaving now would look cowardly.

She raised her chin slightly. 'No thanks. I'm going to get through a bit more before I take a break.'

Over Carter's shoulder Jo mouthed, 'I'm sorry,' at her, before walking towards the door with Gabe.

Carter sat down in the seat across from her while Allie pretended to write a note to herself in her history notebook. But her mind was spinning.

So he now thinks I've got this major crush on him. So what? Let him think it.

She counted two breaths in and out.

55

'Hey,' he said.

Looking up from her notebook she saw that he was leaning forward. His face was close—his dark eyes looking right into hers. She thought, inanely, that his lashes were really long, and his eyebrows straight and fine.

Somehow she kept her face expressionless but her burning cheeks surely betrayed her.

'I don't think we've been properly introduced,' he said. 'I'm Carter West.'

'I'm Allie Sheridan.' She willed her voice to be steady and unembarrassed and for a change it cooperated. She held his gaze fearlessly. Or at least she hoped it came across as fearless.

'I know,' he said, settling himself comfortably in the chair. He smiled cynically and she instantly didn't trust him. 'We should talk.'

'Should we?' she said coolly. 'What about?'

'You.'

'Terrific,' Allie said. 'Well, my favourite colour is blue and I love puppies. Your turn.'

'Very funny,' he said, looking like it wasn't very funny.

'Oh yes,' she said, 'and I'm very funny. Sorry, I forgot to mention it earlier.'

He was beginning to look exasperated. 'That's really useful, thanks. But what I was wondering is, what are you doing at Cimmeria? It's rather unusual for new students to join in the middle of summer term.'

Put off by his investigative tone, Allie leaned away from him and crossed her arms. He'd asked for the truth, but that was a lot of ammunition to give a stranger.

She twirled her pen between her fingers. 'I won a

contest?'

'Funny,' he said again, although his face said it wasn't. 'Seriously. Never be afraid to be honest—what brought you here really?'

So he wasn't going to let go. Fine then.

She raised her chin and met his eyes directly. 'I got arrested.'

He shrugged. 'So?'

'Three times.'

'Oh.'

'In one year.'

He gave a low whistle. 'Right. But getting arrested doesn't get you into Cimmeria. This isn't a reform school. Why are you here?'

Stung, Allie could feel her temper rising but she fought it back. 'To be honest, I have no idea. My parents told me that I was coming here, and a few days later here I was. They said it specialises in kids like me. Whatever that means.'

'Interesting.' He studied her curiously, as if she were a puzzling display in a museum cabinet.

She shot him a sharp look. 'Why is it interesting?'

'Troubled kids do come here, but not in the summer term. All the summer term students are in advanced studies.'

A flash of resentment shot through her and she glared at him.

Do I have 'too stupid to be here' tattooed on my forehead?

She stacked her books in angry piles. 'I guess it's impossible to consider the idea that I might be clever. And *troubled*.' She spat the last word out. 'Well, then I better get on with studying, right? I'll have to really work hard to keep up with all you geniuses.'

'Hey.' He looked startled. 'Don't be so sensitive. I'm just trying to figure you out.'

And that was all it took. After Katie and Jules and Zelazny, her parents and the police, she'd had it. She shoved the books into her bag and spun around to face him.

'Well don't. OK? Don't try to figure me out. Don't try to analyse me. And, while you're at it, stop insulting me. You see me in class and overhear a conversation and think you know me. But, believe me, you know *nothing* about me.'

She stormed out of the library and ran up the stairs.

. . . thirty-two, thirty-three, thirty-four steps . . .

She just made it to her room before the storm hit. The bag dropped from her nerveless fingers, and leaning back against the door she slid down to the floor. With her face buried in her hands she sobbed quietly. Why was she here? Everybody treated her like the village idiot who'd slipped in when the guard's back was turned. She could feel her breath growing shallow and she fought back a panic attack, but the edges of her vision started to go black.

She counted her breaths, the boards on the wooden floor, the books on the shelves, and the panes of glass in the window until she felt herself regain control, and her sight began to return to normal.

When she felt better, she climbed to her feet. Opening the door, she checked to see if the hall was empty before hurrying down to the bathroom to splash cold water on her face. As she smoothed her hair back, the door opened and Jules walked in. Her eyes took in Allie's tear-stained cheeks, and a worried look flashed across her face.

'Hi Allie. How are you settling in?'

Allie didn't feel like faking it. And she didn't feel like talking about it either. She just wanted to be somewhere else.

'Everything's great, Jules.' Her words dripped sarcasm but she couldn't help it. 'Everybody's being so nice. It's all just . . . great.'

Before Jules could react, she opened the door and ran down the hall.

She'd never felt more lonely in her life.

*   *   *

Allie awoke with a start, and sat up in the wooden chair. Her back was aching and the desk lamp was still on.

What time is it?

Her head foggy, she turned the alarm clock to face her. Two o'clock in the morning.

Must have fallen asleep at my desk.

She was sitting in front of the open window, a stack of papers spread out in front of her. After her meltdown she hadn't been hungry, so she'd skipped dinner and stayed in her room to catch up on her reading.

The last thing she could remember was reading The Rules.

After finishing her homework, it had occurred to her that she'd never really read them, and she'd pulled the thick stack of paper out of the desk drawer. They were so strange and prescriptive that at first she couldn't believe what she was reading.

Welcome Allie.

Cimmeria Academy is a unique place in which to learn, and we are very glad to have you here among us. The school has, for many years, operated according to rules set out long ago by its founders.

Follow these Rules closely, and your time here will be memorable and pleasant. Fail to follow these Rules, and your time at Cimmeria may be very brief indeed.

Cimmeria Academy Rules:

1. The day begins at 7 a.m. and ends no later than 11 p.m. Outside of those hours you must be in your dormitory.

2.. The woods around the school can be dangerous; students are forbidden to enter them alone or after dark.

3. No student may leave the school grounds without permission.

4. The teachers' wing is off-limits.

5. Students in certain advanced areas of study take part in Night School. Only a very few, select students are offered this opportunity; if you are not among them, you must not attempt to interfere with or observe Night School. Anyone attempting to do so will be

expelled.

6 . **The identities of those involved in Night School are secret. Anyone who attempts to find out their identities will be punished.**

7. **ALL Night School activities are secret. Any member of Night School found to be divulging the details of those activities will be punished severely.**

Suddenly she heard again the noise that must have awakened her. It was a kind of scrabbling on the roof. She switched off the lamp and moved the papers aside so that she could climb up on the desk and look out.

At first she heard nothing, and then in the distance a shout. Then a few seconds later, a faint scream. Allie leaned forward to peer into the darkness. There was no moon tonight, and clouds obscured the stars. She could see only darkness. Suddenly, very nearby, a noise—a creaking sound, like footsteps on old wood.

What the hell was that? Whatever it was, it was on the roof.

Down below, she thought she saw something dart across the grass into the woods. She held her breath to listen. Was that . . . laughter?

After a few minutes she heard a voice whisper so faintly she wasn't sure she hadn't imagined it: *'It's OK, Allie. Go to sleep.'*

She looked around the room. She was alone. She shook her head fiercely, trying to determine if she was awake or asleep.

'I'm going insane,' she muttered, and closed the window, locking it firmly, before climbing into bed.

As she fell back asleep, she could have sworn she heard the same voice chuckle very faintly.

CHAPTER FIVE

The alarm's jarring ring woke Allie from a deep sleep the next morning at seven. Groggy, she swatted it several times before finding the off switch.

Sitting up in bed, she stretched languorously. Another weird dream. What was with that voice? It had seemed so real. She blamed The Rules.

This school is just freaking me out.

After a quick breakfast, she made it to class with a few minutes to spare. Jo was already in her seat. Carter, she noticed, was not in his. Jo bubbled with questions. She barely waited until Allie was at the desk.

'What happened last night after we left? What bad luck that he walked up while we were talking about him. Gabe felt really awful about putting you in that situation.'

Allie wondered how much to tell her. She remembered Carter's maxim: 'Never be afraid to be honest'.

But then, Carter is a dick.

'We talked for a while, but all he seemed to want was to find out what I was doing at Cimmeria.' She shrugged. 'I got pissed off and walked out.'

Jo looked surprised. 'Why did you get pissed off?'

Allie tried not to sound sulky and juvenile. 'I don't know. It just seemed to me he didn't think I should be here. Like I'm not good enough to be here.'

Jo leaned forward and lowered her voice to a whisper. 'Allie, I'm no fan of Carter's as you know, but that really doesn't sound like him at all. He's sort of the last person to be snobbish about anything. He thinks everybody's too stuck on themselves here. He's always going on about it. It's one of the reasons people don't like him.'

Jerry called the class to order. Reluctantly, they both turned towards the front. Jo pulled out a piece of paper and wrote furiously. As he began drawing lungs on the white board, the door opened and Carter walked in.

Jo slid the paper across the desk to Allie. It said, 'You must have misunderstood. I promise.'

Allie lifted her eyes from the paper to find Carter watching her as he walked by. She dropped her eyes instantly and covered the paper with her hand.

She sighed and shook her head as if to physically clear it of crazy thoughts, and twirled her pen around her fingers.

One, two, three times.

And then at the bottom of the note she scrawled, 'OK. I believe you,' and passed it back to Jo, who looked pleased.

Allie tried to tune in to Jerry's lecture. She could not spend every single class distracted by Carter West.

*　　　*　　　*

63

'He just gives me the weirdest looks all the time,' Allie said. 'He's always staring at me.'

She and Jo were sitting in the dining room as the lunch crowd waned, twirling salad leaves around their plates and talking about Carter.

Jo wrinkled her pert nose. 'He probably just wants you to fancy him. He wants everyone to fancy him.'

'Well if that's the case, then he's kind of failing,' Allie said. 'God, can you believe the energy we're giving this conversation about some guy we don't even like? Tell me about Gabe. How long have you two been together?'

Jo brightened. 'Let's see. We've been together more than a year now. When I first came here I was going out with this guy Lucas, but then I met Gabe and it was just . . . like, forget it. He's the coolest guy I've ever known. The funniest. The sexiest. The . . . everything.' She laughed at her own giddiness.

'I can't believe you've been going out a whole year,' Allie said. 'I don't know anybody who's been together that long.'

Jo set her fork down. 'Cimmeria's funny that way. People who get together tend to stay together. That's why everybody talks about Carter so much. It's kind of not done, the whole one-night-stand thing. I don't know why. Maybe because we're here so much of the time. I mean, some kids here, like, never go home. They're just always here. Like this is their home. And we're their family.'

'Who does that?' Allie asked curiously.

'Well, Carter. And Gabe. And, well, me, I guess.'

Allie couldn't hide her surprise. 'You never go home?'

'Long story,' Jo said with a shrug.

She looked around the room, which was nearly empty. 'Oh bollocks! What time is it?'

They both reached for their book bags and ran out the door, down the hallway and up the stairs. As they neared the first floor landing they were both giggling hysterically.

'Late again!' Allie said as they careened down the corridor and divided to go to their separate classes.

'What are we like?' Jo giggled breathlessly.

Allie stopped at the closed door to her history class to catch her breath, then opened it quietly. In the awful sudden stillness, the students all turned to look at her.

'Miss Sheridan.' Mr Zelazny insisted on keeping an old-fashioned chalkboard in his room, and he was standing in front of it now, glaring at her. 'Class started two minutes ago. I know you're new, but I presume you know our rules on tardiness.'

Allie nodded mutely.

'Yes? Good. Well then, see me after class.'

Allie trudged to her seat, her eyes downcast.

I can't do anything right.

No matter how hard she tried to change her life it didn't work. It was as if trouble were her default setting.

*   *   *

At the end of class she waited for the others to leave, pretending to organise her books until the room was mostly empty. Then she walked up to Mr Zelazny's desk. He was writing, and did not immediately look up. She cleared her throat timidly. After a moment, he raised his head and

65

fixed her with an icy glare.

'I'm very sorry to have to speak to you a second time about tardiness in your first week. It is a very bad sign for your future at Cimmeria Academy. I know the other teachers say you have great promise, but I must say I haven't seen any sign of it.'

An angry flush rose to Allie's cheeks, but she bit her lip and said nothing. He held out a handwritten piece of paper.

'This is your detention notice. Tomorrow morning at six-thirty, meet the group outside the chapel and hand the teacher this.'

Allie couldn't believe it.

'Six-thirty in the morning? But tomorrow's Saturday!'

His expression of cool disinterest did not change. 'I've only given you one day's detention, Miss Sheridan. If it happens again I will make it a week.'

Allie walked into English class draped in an almost visible shroud of frustration. Isabelle gave her a questioning look, but Allie lowered her eyes to her book and, as the headmistress began the class, slipped, relieved, into the familiar cotton wool world of self-pity until Carter walked in five minutes later.

Isabelle stopped her lecture. 'Carter, you're usually a little late and I'm willing to overlook a little tardiness but this is ridiculous. Do you have an excuse?'

'Just running late, Isabelle,' Carter shrugged. 'It happens.'

The headmistress sighed and made a note on a piece of paper in her hand. 'You know the rules, Carter. Please stay after class to speak with me.'

When a discussion of T.S. Eliot ensued, Allie tuned out, fretting about what detention would entail and wondering (secretly hoping) if Jo had been given detention too so she wouldn't be alone. She felt a quick lash of guilt for hoping that something bad had happened to her only friend at Cimmeria.

Suddenly she tuned back in, hypnotised by the combination of words and the familiar voice reading them. She'd always hated poetry, but she'd never heard poetry like this.

'And I will show you something different from
     either
Your shadow at morning striding behind you
Or your shadow at evening rising to meet you;
I will show you fear in a handful of dust.'

She looked across the circle to see Carter sit down. He didn't look at her, but she had the feeling he was conscious of her gaze.

'So, what's he saying here? What does he mean by "fear in a handful of dust"?' Isabelle looked around the class. Impetuously, Allie started to speak and then immediately wished she hadn't.

Isabelle nodded at her.

'It sounds like . . .' she faltered, but her teacher's gaze was steady and patient. Allie thought it through and started again. 'I mean, to me, it sounds like a warning. He's saying "Be afraid of me. You will get hurt with me."?'

Isabelle nodded again. 'I think that's fair enough—there's obviously a warning or a threat in there. Does anybody else have thoughts?'

'It's about death.' Carter didn't wait to be called

upon.

Allie's heart beat faster.

'Everything he's writing about is unstoppable—unavoidable. And what's everybody most afraid of? Death.'

Allie stared at her desk but she knew without looking up that Carter was staring at her.

*   *   *

'Zelazny is such a wanker!' Jo was furious. 'You were only, like, two minutes late. I don't know how he could do that to you when you're still in your first week.'

It turned out that Jo's French teacher hadn't even noticed she was late as he'd been discussing an impending trip to Paris with some advanced students and hadn't realised that class should have begun. So Allie was going to be alone in detention. Jo had few comforting words for her.

'I've done detention so many times I've lost count. It's such a thing here because the rules are so strict and if you veer even a step outside them . . .' She made a pistol out of her fingers and fired it into the air. 'There are always at least ten students in it. But it's bloody hard work, so brace yourself.'

Allie was puzzled. 'Isn't it just reading or studying?'

Jo's tone was wry. 'Oh no. Not at Cimmeria. Here it's hard labour. You'll either be painting something or weeding, planting, clearing . . . God knows. It's always something that makes you sweat. It only lasts a couple of hours but it can be horribly dull if they give you something awful. But, you know, at least you'll get to meet the other troublemakers.'

Allie rolled her eyes. 'Oh great. Lucky me. Like I don't know enough troublemakers already.'

They were sitting at the table after dinner in the quiet dining room; most of the other students had left. Jo looked around the emptying room. 'Let's get out of here. Have you explored the grounds yet? Or have you just been imprisoned inside with dusty books and me?'

She hooked her arm through Allie's and they strolled out of the dining room. Ahead of them, the flow of students swirled in several directions; they followed the tributary rolling to the door.

They wandered out across the drive, which in the evening light had lost the ivory lustre that Allie remembered from two days ago. Now it just looked like an ordinary grey gravel path. The smooth green school lawns stretched out in all directions, and the long shadows of the trees reached out for them as Jo led the way onto the grass.

'Where's Gabe tonight?' Allie asked.

'He's working on some special project, I think it's going to keep him busy until curfew.' Jo smiled indulgently. 'OK, FYI? See that path through the trees there?' She pointed at a row of pine trees across the lawn of the east wing. Allie could just make out a path going into the woods. 'That leads to the chapel. That's where you need to go tomorrow.'

Then she pointed in the opposite direction at a pathway that wandered from the west wing of the school building down to the treeline.

'Over there,' she said, 'there's a summerhouse just beyond the edge of the woods. Sometimes we have picnics there.'

69

'So what's further out in the woods?'

Jo looked at her quizzically. 'Trees?'

Allie laughed. 'No, I mean, are there more buildings? Or things to do . . .?'

'I think there are a few houses far in the woods where staff or teachers live, but I don't know for sure. We don't actually do much in the woods, and they kind of discourage it because of, I dunno, health and safety or something. You'll like the chapel though. It's really old.'

They walked around the west side of the building and then behind it, where stone steps led up through a series of terraced lawns edged with colourful flowers. Beyond the last stretch of grass, the ground rose steeply up a lightly forested hill.

'There's a tower at the top of the hill.' Jo pointed and Allie could faintly make out a structure. 'It looks like there used to be a castle or something there but it's just ruins now. The tower's kind of cool. You can climb to the top and see everything. Some people say they can see all the way to London, but all I see are trees and fields.'

They skirted the foot of the hill and reached a long stone wall. 'What's this?' Allie asked.

'You'll see.'

After a few minutes they came to an ancient wooden door sealed with an incongruously modern combination lock. With the speed that comes of practice, Jo spun the three numbered wheels and the lock clicked open.

She opened the door and walked through, ducking to avoid the low door frame. Allie followed, and Jo carefully closed the door behind them, pocketing the lock.

'Oh wow.' Allie breathed, taking in the huge,

cultivated walled garden. Vegetables stood in rows of military precision, straight as a rifle barrel. Fruit trees crowded at the back, reaching up above the wall into the evening sun. Around the edges flowers spilled over in vivid pinks and whites and purples.

A stone path ran around the edge of the garden and Jo struck off down it. 'Welcome to my favourite place at Cimmeria.'

'It's amazing! How did you find it? And how do you know the combination?'

'Um . . . it's just this random thing. I had to work here on detention my first year. At first I really hated it—getting up at six every day to come here—but by the end of the week I realised I was going to miss it. I don't know why. I'm really good at the whole gardening thing, and this place is . . . peaceful.'

Allie wondered what she'd done to earn a week of detention, but since Jo didn't volunteer the information she decided not to ask. Besides, it seemed pretty easy to get detention around here.

Jo turned left onto a path that cut across the middle of the gardens, past a classic fountain where a pretty young girl in flowing gowns, with a slightly damaged nose, tipped an urn of water eternally onto rocks, around a blueberry thicket, and then onto the granite path on the other side.

'Now I help out after class and on weekends. I come here sometimes when I want privacy.'

Amid the lush purple wisteria enrobing the walls a wooden bench was tucked away, and Jo perched on it, gesturing for Allie to do the same. Allie pulled her feet up underneath her and wrapped her arms around her knees, breathing in the cool scent of the flowers.

'We can talk here,' Jo said. 'In fact this might be the only place in Cimmeria where nobody is going to overhear us. As you've noticed, this is a really nosy school. How are you doing anyway? It must be totally weird for you to be here. I remember my first few days here—this place completely freaked me out.'

'It's going to sound crazy. But I hate it here. And I kind of love it too.'

Jo gave her an easy smile. 'I actually completely understand.'

'It's very different from any school I've ever been to, you know? And it's a lot of work. But it's . . .' Allie thought for a minute. 'It's not my life. And that's what I like about it. It's not my life the way it's been for the last two years, and anything's better than that.'

Jo considered her. 'When I came here,' she said, her words emerging hesitantly, 'I'd been kicked out of my last school after they caught me and my ex passed out on the roof. We'd drunk some vodka and . . . Well. Anyway, my parents were unbelievably pissed off. But the thing is, it was supposed to be this great school, but it was just . . . stupid. The classes were too easy, there was nothing to do, and it was full of rich kids biding their time until Oxbridge.'

She dropped one leg and swung her foot back and forth.

'My parents sent me here next. I think they thought I'd hate it, but after I got used to how weird it is, I was totally into it. I love how hard it is, and how odd it is. How bizarre some of the teachers are. It just kind of fits. Since then, I've

72

been OK. Great, actually. It's like I'm in the place I need to be.'

Allie rested her chin on her knees and thought for a moment. 'My life has been . . . kind of crazy lately.' She stopped, and then decided to go ahead. 'I had, I think, the perfect life until a year and a half ago. I was the perfect daughter, got perfect grades, my parents loved me. Then one day . . . it all ended.'

She stopped and looked up at Jo. 'You know, I haven't told this story to anyone. Ever.'

Jo nodded and waited.

Allie took a deep breath; her next words came out in a rush. 'So I came home from school one day and the police were there. My mum was crying, and my dad was shouting at the policemen although I could tell he wanted to cry, too. It was chaos.

'My brother was missing. And they never found him.'

Jo reached for her arm. 'Allie, Jesus! That's horrible. What happened? Did he . . .?'

'Die? Who knows? We've never heard from him again.'

'I don't understand. What happened?'

Allie's voice was calmer now and steady. 'See, Christopher and I, we were super-close. He was like my best friend my whole life. Other kids fought, but we never did. We hung out together all the time. He's two years older than me, but he was always completely patient with me. He just didn't get tired of me the way some older brothers get tired of their little sisters. When I was little he used to meet me after school every day and walk me home. He'd help me with my homework, watch TV with me. My parents work a lot, but I never minded

73

because Christopher was always there. And even when I was older, he'd check up on me. Just sort of, show up after school, like it was a coincidence or something. And he'd do his homework at the same time I was doing mine, so if I got stuck on a question he could help.

'About six months before he disappeared, though, he started acting funny. He stayed out really late, got into trouble with Mum and Dad. He was never around, and he didn't have much to say when he was there. I felt like I was kind of losing him. When I tried to talk to him about how he was, and was everything OK, he would walk away. Like he would literally get up and walk out of the house and not come back for hours. His grades went from great to terrible. My parents were completely freaked out, but they couldn't do anything to help. He wouldn't let them.'

She stopped, remembering endless arguments and slamming doors. A night bird sang an elaborate melody.

When she spoke again, her tone was emotionless. 'He left a note. My parents wouldn't tell me what it said, but I overheard Mum on the phone one day talking to someone about it. She had it memorised. It was the meanest thing I've ever heard. It said, "I'm leaving. I'm not hurt, I'm not on drugs. I just don't want to be a part of this family any more. I don't love you. Any of you. Don't follow me. Don't try to find me. I don't need your help. You will never see me again".'

'Oh my God,' Jo whispered. When Allie looked up she saw that her eyes were filled with tears, which she dashed away with the back of her hand. 'Oh Allie.'

74

Allie focused on staying distant from the story she was telling, pretending, as she sometimes did, that it had all happened to somebody else. 'So then it all fell apart. I had, I guess, a nervous breakdown. I couldn't, like, talk. I sat in Christopher's room for days on end. I didn't go to school for months. They sent me to a counsellor, who I hated. My mum and dad fought with each other, and I was just this . . . nuisance to them that they had to deal with.

'It was like, whcn he left he pulled the stopper from our lives and drained everything good out. They didn't love me any more. And I felt nothing at all.'

She sighed shakily. 'Feeling something became really important to me. So I drank a lot; but actually that's kind of the opposite of feeling anything, you know?'

Jo nodded.

'I hung out with people who hurt each other. I got into a lot of trouble. Getting arrested was really scary, so I did that a few times. I . . .' she held out her left arm, exposing three neat, thin white scars between her wrist and the inside of her elbow. 'I cut myself for a while. And that hurt, which was good. But it was also totally stupid. And it felt fake. Like, if you do it to yourself like that, it's not real pain. So I don't do that any more.'

She rushed through the end of her story as if she couldn't wait to be done with it. 'Anyway, the last time I got arrested my parents had pretty much had enough of me. So here I am. They've got an empty house now. And I don't even have that.'

Spontaneously, Jo threw her arms around her and hugged her fiercely. Then she leaned back and held her shoulders looking her in the eye. 'OK.

That's fucking awful. But you're here now. And you're alive. I just met you Allie, but I can already tell you're awesome. And you might have a horrible family, but your life from now on is up to you. I want you to promise me that you'll give this place a chance. Cimmeria straightened me out. It's my home now, and these people are my family. It can be the same for you.'

Allie hugged her back, and fought back tears. 'OK,' she whispered, her voice quivering. 'I promise.'

Jo pulled Allie against her so that her head rested on Jo's shoulder, and they sat quietly on the bench for a moment, each lost in thought. Allie felt awkward; hungover. Tired.

'It's funny this place,' she mumbled. 'Time seems sort of compressed here. I can't believe I've only been here two days. This will be my third night. But I feel like I've been here for weeks.'

Jo nodded. 'It's like life concentrated. More happens here in a week than happens outside in a month.'

Curled up on the bench they talked idly as the daylight ebbed away, and the shadows filled the garden. 'I can see why you like it here,' Allie said as she stretched. 'It's kind of magical. Like that book you read when you're little—*The Secret Garden*. Did you read that?'

Jo nodded. 'I've always . . .'

Her words were interrupted by the sound of something crashing loudly at the far end of the garden. They both jumped.

'What the hell was that?' Allie asked, staring into the gloom, noticing for the first time how dark it had become.

'I don't know,' Jo whispered. She peered at her watch. 'Oh bugger! It's nearly curfew. We have to get back.'

She stood up, reaching out to Allie, and then they heard the sound again. Then footsteps.

'What the . . .' Jo whispered, then she raised her voice and shouted: 'Who's there?'

The footsteps stopped.

They stood frozen, listening to their hearts beat. 'Jo,' Allie whispered. 'Couldn't it be . . .'

They both heard the growling sound at the same moment.

Jo grabbed Allie's arm.

'Jo, what the hell is that?' Allie whispered.

'I don't know.'

'Should we . . .?'

'Run?'

'Yeah.'

'On three. One. Two . . .'

The quiet was shattered by a crash that now seemed to come from the shadows inches away from them. They screamed and hurtled down the footpath. Jo held Allie's hand tightly. 'Stick with me,' she said breathlessly and raced off the path into the orchard. In the darkness they zigzagged between the trees, and Allie could feel dropped fruit squelching sickeningly under her shoes. She tried to tell if she could hear footsteps aside from their own but they were going too fast—it was impossible to tell.

Then something touched her head and she screamed, batting at the air around her. Jo dragged her to the left, around the tangle of blueberry bushes and into a rose garden. Thorns tore at their hands and clothes. Twigs snapped under their feet.

77

Suddenly something grabbed Jo and lifted her off her feet, dragging her inside a room built into the wall. Allie could hear her trying to scream but a hand covered her mouth, muffling her.

'Shhhh.' Gabe held one finger to his lips and looked into Jo's eyes. Jo threw her arms around him and buried her face in his neck.

Gabe reached out for Allie, but now somebody was holding her arms too. She looked up wildly to see Sylvain's blue eyes watching her steadily in the darkness as he pulled her into the dark room.

He mouthed one word: 'Quiet.'

CHAPTER SIX

Allie froze and tried not to breathe.

Gabe encircled Jo in his arms protectively, and Sylvain pulled Allie behind him. They both stared through the open door, their eyes alert.

Something crashed through the garden and Allie jumped at the sound, but it sounded further away than before. And after a few seconds . . . silence.

When a few uneventful moments had passed, Gabe and Sylvain exchanged a look, and then as if they'd been given a signal they began walking quickly towards the door. Gabe scanned the area around them, then looked back and nodded, and they all ran silently out into the garden and down the path to the door, and out onto the lawn. Wordlessly, Jo handed Gabe the lock and he secured the door.

For the first time Allie became conscious of the fact that Sylvain still had his arms around her. He had a distinctive scent of pine or juniper and she inhaled deeply, relaxing into his arms. Immediately his grip tightened around her.

Faint streaks of light still glimmered in the sky as Gabe led them in through a back door that took them directly into the central hallway. In the light, Allie saw that Jo looked pale, and that she clung to Gabe tearfully. A trickle of blood ran down her cheek, and Gabe touched it lightly with his finger.

'You're hurt,' he said. 'We should take you to the nurse.'

She nodded her consent, and he wrapped his arm around her and walked her down the hall. Allie felt again the curious ache of envy. As if he'd sensed it, Sylvain stepped towards her and examined her face, smoothing her hair back.

'Are you wounded at all?' The concern in his eyes made her heart flutter. Now that he wasn't holding her any more she felt an almost irresistible urge to climb back into his arms and breathe in that scent. Everywhere he touched her tingled.

She took a shaky breath. 'Sylvain, what was out there?'

'I don't know.'

Something about his tone didn't ring true and she looked up at him sharply. She had a feeling he was holding something back—something important.

'We have to tell Isabelle what happened,' she announced. Her eyes burned with determination.

'I suppose you're right,' he said. 'Let's wait until tomorrow, though. She's probably asleep. Everyone is fine now and you do not want to appear to overreact, no?'

Even though she wanted to disagree, she could

see the logic—they had, after all, seen nothing. But after the adrenalin in the garden and the rush of the rescue, she wanted to do something. To go back outside and look for whatever that was. Or at least to sit and talk about what had happened. There was no way she'd be able to sleep.

'Maybe we should go and check on Jo?' she suggested hopefully.

'She's OK—Gabe's with her.' Sylvain paused and then continued with some reluctance as if he knew what her response would be. 'Listen, it is past curfew. You should go to bed and we will deal with all of this tomorrow.'

Allie couldn't believe what she was hearing. 'What, seriously? No, Sylvain! I want to talk about what happened. Be completely honest: what did you see out there?'

Sylvain's reply was carefully framed.

'I am afraid I saw nothing. Perhaps it was some sort of animal. Maybe you disturbed a fox or a badger.' As she opened her mouth to protest he held up his hand to stop her. 'You're tired, Allie. And I'm tired, too. You really should go to sleep.'

Allie wanted to stay, but arguing about whether or not she was tired didn't seem like the best reason to break curfew and get detention.

Reluctantly, she acquiesced. 'Fine then. Good night Sylvain.'

Her tone was brusque, but as she turned to go he caught her wrist and held it gently.

'What? No good night kiss?' he said, with a low chuckle. 'No "thank you for rescuing me, Sylvain"? Not even a "you're my hero, Sylvain"? You should never go to bed angry, *ma belle* Allie.'

His blue eyes danced with amusement and he

pulled her close, wrapping her in the hug she'd wanted a few minutes ago.

At first, out of sheer stubbornness, she resisted but when he whispered jokingly in her ear, 'It's more fun if you help,' she found herself laughing. His accent was completely irresistible anyway, and those eyes were incredible.

When he kissed her cheek his lips lingered and his breath felt warm and welcome on her skin. She leaned into him, hoping it would last.

'Now,' he whispered in her ear, 'go to bed on your own or I'll drag you up there myself.'

Allie focused on staying cool but she was melting inside.

'Whatever,' she said, turning away before he could see the effect he had on her.

But of course he knew anyway.

'Sweet dreams,' he called after her with a light laugh.

She ran up the stairs without looking back.

*　　　*　　　*

The next morning Allie was up at six and feeling oddly energetic, as if the adrenalin from last night still rushed through her veins. Standing in front of her wardrobe, she wondered what to wear for hard labour, finally deciding on a pair of tracksuit bottoms, trainers and a white T-shirt with the school's insignia on the breast. She pulled her hair back with a clip and, grabbing the detention notice, headed downstairs at a trot.

Her stomach grumbled but it was too early for breakfast. Taking a chance, she peeked into the dining room and found it empty, however one table held bacon sandwiches on a warming platter alongside a silver ice bucket filled with water bottles. She walked into the room with some hesitation.

They must be for us, otherwise why would they be there?

Picking up a sandwich and a bottle, she looked around the empty space.

'Thank you,' she whispered, holding the bottle of water aloft in a salute.

She munched on the sandwich as she made her way through the quiet entrance hall and down the front steps. The morning air was cool and the sky overcast. Leaves of grass brushed chilly dew on her ankles.

She thought it was actually quite nice being out on the grounds alone.

But I wouldn't want to do it every day.

In her head, she went over the experiences of the night before and practised describing it all to Isabelle in a way that didn't sound hysterical or emotional. It wasn't easy.

Walking past the treeline and into the shadows she shivered—it was several degrees colder out of the sun. The path was arrow-straight, shooting under pines and bypassing thorny brambles. Feathery wings of ferns delicately tickled against her calves but she barely noticed as she continued her mental vivisection of the evening before.

After about ten minutes, the path arrived at a low stone wall, which it followed for about fifty feet before reaching a gate opening into a slightly overgrown churchyard. An ancient stone chapel stood in the middle, and a small group of students clustered near the door looking bored. Allie breathed a quiet sigh of relief when she saw that they were all dressed much like her. Seeing nobody she recognised, she kept to the fringes of the group, leaning against the elaborately gnarled trunk of a yew tree.

She'd barely got comfortable when the door of the chapel opened and a woman appeared in the doorway. Casually dressed in dark linen trousers and a white button-down shirt, her long dark hair was knotted loosely on her head. She held a clipboard in one hand.

'Can I have all notices, please?'

As the students walked up she took their sheets without comment, but when Allie handed hers in, she stopped her.

'You must be Allie.' She sounded as pleased as if they'd met in the dining room over a cup of tea. 'I've heard a lot about you from Isabelle. I'm Eloise Derleth, the librarian. You must stop in and say hello. Isabelle left some books for you at my desk.'

She gave Allie a beaming smile and moved on to gather the rest of the papers together. When everything was in order, she raised her voice so the whole group could hear her.

'I know you're all eager to find out what today's chore will be. So I won't keep you waiting. Please follow me.'

Some students rolled their eyes and giggled as they trooped along behind her. Allie stuck to the edges, caution holding her back.

Eloise led them around the side of the chapel to a shed at the back of the churchyard. It was a lovely place with aged gravestones leaning higgledy-piggledy under leafy trees amid deep, soft grass. An old garden bench rotted slowly against the wall in a pool of sunshine. A man in the black work outfit worn by the staff at the school waited at the back of the building.

'Today you're going to be clearing the churchyard,' Eloise explained. 'Mr Ellison will give you everything you need and assign you tasks for the morning. Good luck!'

With a cheerful smile, she walked briskly down the path and out the gate. Allie headed over to join the group queuing to collect tools from Mr Ellison.

'I'm dividing you up into teams.' His voice was a rich, resonant baritone, and as he handed out tools, Allie marvelled at the sheer size of him. He must have been six and a half feet tall; his arms were thick and strong, probably, she theorised, from working outside all his life. His skin was the colour of espresso, and he had a wonderfully calming manner.

'These are my weed trimmers here.' He gestured at a group of boys he'd already armed with noisy devices. 'They'll trim around the graves while this group here,' he pointed at two boys and a girl pushing lawnmowers in various directions, 'do the main clearing.'

Allie was the last in the queue. As she walked up, Mr Ellison gave her a polite nod.

'You two will be my rakers.'

Two?

She spun around to find Carter standing beside her, gazing innocently at the gardener as he handed over their rakes. As she stared at him, astonished, Carter thanked him politely, then turned on his heel and strode off carrying both rakes in one hand.

She hurried after him, hopping gingerly past the

graves and stumbling on the uneven ground as the angry mosquito buzz of lawn devices filled the air.

'What are you doing here? And where are you going?' she asked sharply. And when he ignored her: 'Hey! Shouldn't we be raking instead of running?'

Carter didn't seem bothered by her attitude. 'I have detention. Why are *you* here? And can you please chill? We need to wait a few minutes for the mowers to give us something to rake. So I'm getting out of the way.'

He didn't stop until he got to the yew tree near the front of the church. He leaned the rakes against the trunk and then, stepping up on a bulging tree root, climbed onto a low branch where he sat comfortably with his legs hanging down. Holding out his hand to her, he raised his eyebrow questioningly.

After hesitating (and imagining herself standing aloof and saying, 'No thanks, I'm happy standing.') Allie reluctantly reached up. As he took her hand and lifted her up beside him, there was something in his gaze that she couldn't interpret and she felt a rush of colour to her cheeks.

She slid out along the gnarled branch away from him, then sat with one leg dangling and the other bent, with her foot propped on the branch. He turned to face her, so that his back rested against the trunk. Spinning a twig between two fingers, he studied her curiously. She watched the lawnmowers make grass disappear and pretended not to notice his gaze. From up here she could hear the sound of rushing water.

'Look,' Carter said, 'I've been wanting to get you alone so that I could apologise.'

She glanced up at him, surprised. He looked, she thought, uncharacteristically uncomfortable.

'I gave you the wrong idea the other day in the library,' he said. 'I know you thought I was saying something I wasn't. I think you have as much a right as anybody else does to be here. OK? Please believe that.'

Although she nodded, her expression was still guarded. He sighed with frustration.

'I feel terrible about this. You must think I'm a complete dick.'

She nodded again with an ironic half-smile, and he laughed. She tried to fight a smile and failed.

'I knew it. Allie, I hope you believe me. I didn't mean what you thought I did. Not at all. I hate the snobs at this school. I won't be one of them. Can we start over?'

Something in her didn't trust him. But then, she thought, something in her didn't trust anyone. And what was the point of dragging this out?

'Sure,' she said finally.

'Good. Now we're at the beginning again.' Looking out over the garden he said, 'Right. Well, that was short and sweet. Looks like they're getting somewhere. We better get started.'

He jumped down from the tree, landing smoothly, and turned to help her down. As she slid to the edge of the branch, he reached past her outstretched hand and put his hands on her waist, lifting her off the tree with ease. She was surprised at his strength.

'Off to work we go,' he said, turning away to pick up the rakes. Watching his loping stride, she followed him into the graveyard.

The gravestones gave little away ('*Emma*

Littlejohn, beloved Wife of Frederick Littlejohn and Mother of Frances Littlejohn 1803–1849 God grant ye Reste') but she found herself unable to pass one without reading it and thinking about the occupant, wondering if they'd had happy lives and what had brought them to this place.

Forty-six. Not really that old, she thought. Her own mother was probably at least that now.

The mowers had already made a pretty good start on the long grass, and Carter handed Allie a rake and began combing the grass and leaves expertly into large piles. She joined in raking as best she could, and whispering an apology to each grave.

Sorry to disturb you, Mrs Coxon (1784–1827). I'll just be a moment.

But her pile was a mess and she lost half of the grass on the way to the stack.

'You're really great at this,' Carter said sardonically.

'Shut up!' She laughed. 'Give me a break. I've never done this before.'

'Never done what? Raked?' He looked genuinely surprised.

'Yeah, I've never raked.' She shrugged.

'How have you never raked? Don't your parents make you do anything?' His tone was disapproving.

'I live in London, Carter. We don't have a garden, we've got, like, a patio with lots of pots and some flowers around the edge. I've swept it plenty of times, but I've never raked.'

He worked in silence for a few minutes then shook his head. 'London must be full of kids who've never done anything like this. That is so weird to me. I can't imagine not working outside,

87

getting my hands dirty.'

Leaning against her rake, she marvelled at how efficiently he worked.

'Where are you from?' she asked.

He made a sweeping gesture at the land around them. 'You're looking at it.'

'What, you live around here?'

'I live here. Here is home.'

Puzzled, she raked for a few minutes then stopped again, brushing a stray strand of hair out of her eyes.

'But where did you live before here?'

'Nowhere. This is where I grew up. My parents worked here as part of the staff. I'm here on scholarship. I've never lived anywhere else.'

'Your parents are teachers?'

Still working, he answered her without looking up. 'No. My parents were part of the staff.' He emphasised *were* and *staff*.

'So,' Allie worried the grass with her rake, 'they don't work here any more?'

'No.' His voice was cold. 'They don't let you work here after you're dead.'

Allie froze. He worked furiously; she could see the muscles move under his shirt.

Here lie Mr and Mrs West. At peace.

'Oh God, Carter. I'm sorry. I didn't know.'

He kept raking. 'Of course you didn't. How could you? Don't worry about it.'

Dropping her rake, she walked over and touched his arm.

'I'm really sorry.'

Jerking his arm away, he glared at her. 'Don't be. And, seriously? I don't want to be here all day, so would you help?'

88

Stung, she picked up her rake and walked a few graves away. For twenty minutes they worked in silence. Allie's back and arms ached, but she'd made several impressive piles of leaves and grass. She looked over at Carter several times, but he never stopped.

Gradually, the awful buzzing of the garden equipment declined, and after another ten minutes or so it stopped altogether as the last grass trimmer was turned off and returned to Mr Ellison, who was carefully organising the returned supplies.

'I think we're done here.'

Allie was so lost in her work that Carter's words startled her and she dropped her rake. As she picked it up, the strand of hair escaped again, and she brushed it back again absently.

'Here,' he said, 'turn around.'

She looked at him doubtfully but after a moment's hesitation did as he asked. Standing behind her, he smoothed the errant lock, gently winding it into her clip. She stood very still. His light touch on the nape of her neck gave her goosebumps. After a few seconds the touch stopped, but he said nothing.

When she turned around, he was walking to the chapel carrying both rakes. She hurried after him, tripping over a tuft of grass.

'Here you go, Bob,' Carter said, handing the rakes to Mr Ellison.

'Thanks. You in trouble again, Carter?'

'Always.'

Mr Ellison had a deep chuckle that Allie liked instantly. She smiled up at him, and stuck her hands into her pockets.

'I hope we did an OK job, Mr Ellison.'

He smiled at her kindly. 'It looks great, Miss Sheridan. Thanks for your help.'

As they walked down the path he called after them, 'Don't let Carter get you into any more trouble.'

Without waiting for her, Carter strode across the churchyard and then out the gate.

Briefly Allie wondered whether she should try and catch up with him, but she decided against it. Instead she walked at a leisurely pace hoping he'd get far ahead of her.

A few minutes later, though, as she rounded a bend he was standing on the path, kicking a stone. Avoiding his eyes she walked past him quickly, without a word.

'Allie, wait!' She could hear him running to catch up with her, but she didn't turn around. When he reached her he began walking alongside her, backwards so that he could see her face.

'Here's the thing,' he said, 'I seem to have behaved like an arse again.'

'No worries,' she said coolly. 'At least you're consistent.'

She was surprised to hear him laugh.

'OK, I deserve that. I'm sorry I snapped at you. I'm just really sensitive about . . . some things.' His eyes darkened and he kicked a rock off the path.

Allie thought about Christopher and how sensitive she'd been about his disappearance.

'It's cool,' she said. 'I'm over it.'

'You sure?' he said.

'Totally.'

Clearly satisfied, he turned around and walked beside her.

'Have you recovered from last night, then?' he

asked.

She looked over at him, surprised. 'How do you know about last night?'

'Nobody has any secrets at Cimmeria,' he said. 'I heard Jo got hurt running in the dark.'

Allie wondered how honest she should be. She wanted to talk about it with somebody, but she was afraid Carter would make fun of her.

'It was scary,' she admitted.

'What exactly did you see?'

'Nothing,' she said. 'I mean, it was too dark. We just heard . . .'

She didn't know how to explain it.

'What did you hear?' His dark eyes were hard to read.

'I heard something growl,' she admitted, 'like a dog. But I heard footsteps, too. The human kind.'

'What do you think it could have been?' she asked. 'I mean, do people have dogs here? Like teachers or . . . staff?'

'No dogs,' he said shortly.

'Well, somebody has a dog,' she muttered. 'Or somebody growls.'

He stopped so suddenly she nearly tripped into him.

'Honestly?' he said. 'I think it was some of the guys teasing you. Trying to scare you.'

For some reason she hadn't expected that.

'Why?' she asked. 'That's stupid.'

'Because they're childish,' he said. 'And bored. And you're new. They did it for fun.'

The idea that a gang of boys would make fun of her did seem plausible. And it hurt, though she tried not to show it. As they walked down the path she stared at her feet, swallowing hard. But

91

something about his explanation didn't ring true. Because what about Jo? She'd been there, too.

As she thought it through, she decided there were only two possibilities. Either the incident had been an elaborate hoax, in which Gabe and Sylvain had both participated. Or Carter was lying to her.

She glanced up at him from under her eyelashes—he was staring straight ahead.

'You know, Gabe and Sylvain rescued us,' she said casually. 'Were they in on it?'

Carter's mood darkened. 'Oh, they rescued you, huh? How heroic.' He turned to look at her. 'What's going on between you and Sylvain, anyway? You've only been here a few days, but I hear he's already staking a claim.'

She couldn't resist rising to the bait.

'That's ridiculous. Nobody's claiming anybody. Sylvain's just been nice to me. He seems like a nice guy.'

'Sylvain? Nice?' Carter scoffed. 'I doubt that very seriously.'

She glared at him. 'You know what? Sylvain has been nothing but nice to me since I got here. Unlike just about everybody else.'

Grabbing her arm, he turned her to face him. 'Just . . . be careful, Allie. Things aren't as straightforward in here as they are out there.'

His expression was intense and he looked sincere, but she yanked her arm loose angrily. Before she could reply she heard Sylvain's silken voice.

'Allie. There you are. I was just coming to find you.'

He appeared out of the shadows, walking down the path from the school. Carter gave her a warning look and she shot him a glare.

'Carter. Of course. I should have known you'd have detention today. You always do.' Sylvain's tone was light and joking, but there was something serious underlying his words.

'And you, Sylvain, never do.' Carter's voice was laced with contempt as he shoved past Sylvain and stalked away towards the school.

With concern in his eyes, Sylvain turned to Allie. 'Did something happen? You look upset.'

'It was nothing,' Allie said as Carter disappeared around a bend. 'He's just a bit of a tosser, isn't he?'

'I think that describes him perfectly.' When Sylvain smiled his eyes were cat-like. 'So how was detention? Awful?'

'It wasn't too bad. Just one blister.' She held up her right hand, where a white bump had formed on her palm at the base of her ring finger.

'Tragic.' He lifted her hand up to his lips and lightly kissed it. Allie shivered. Goosebumps again. 'I have decided you should never do manual labour,' he said. 'It's not your style. You should have servants feeding you, while you wear silk . . .'

The absurdity of the idea made her laugh. 'Yeah, they could peel me grapes while I count my diamonds . . .'

'You joke, but it could happen.' He still held her hand, and now he pulled her with him down the path. 'Regretfully, this is not merely a social call. I have come for you at the request of Isabelle. She would like to see you.'

Allie's stomach muscles tightened. She wasn't really surprised that the headmistress would want to see her, given that she'd already been given detention. But she was so hoping not to be in

93

serious trouble for a change.

'OK,' she said. 'I guess that's not a surprise.'

As they walked she turned to look at him. 'About last night . . .'

'Ah yes,' he said. 'The brutal attack in the garden.'

His tone was teasing but Allie was serious. 'Who was that? I heard footsteps, and, like, a dog or something.'

'I think the footsteps you heard were probably Gabe and me,' Sylvain said. 'And what you thought was a dog was probably a fox.'

'A fox that growls?' Allie asked dubiously.

'It could have been trapped in one of the sheds and distressed,' Sylvain shrugged. 'It is not unusual.'

Allie studied his face closely. 'Carter said he thought it was some boys making fun of me.'

Sylvain frowned. 'That is ridiculous. I would know if that had happened. It is bizarre to me that he would say such a thing.'

For some reason, Allie was relieved to hear him say that. 'Yeah,' she said. 'That's what I thought, too.'

As the path reached the school's grassy lawn, Allie had a thought. 'Why did Isabelle send you to get me rather than one of the junior students?' she asked.

'Oh, I was at a prefect meeting and we were chatting,' he said. 'It's not unusual. She knows we are . . . friends.'

She glanced at him in surprise. 'I didn't know you were a prefect.'

'Didn't you?' he said, pulling her closer. 'Well now that you know, you must do everything I say.

Because I am the boss.'

Laughing, she pulled free of him. 'Oh is that how it works? Well, we'll have to see about that.'

She ran ahead with Sylvain on her heels, and when he caught her at the door she was helpless with laughter. But as she reached for the handle the door swung open and Zelazny stepped out.

Allie's giggles evaporated.

'Miss Sheridan.' It might have been Saturday but the history teacher still wore a suit and tie, and his voice oozed disapproval. 'I'm gratified to see that you are taking your morning of detention so seriously.'

I've been arrested by less grumpy men, Allie thought.

But before she could speak, Sylvain stepped in front of her. 'It is my fault, Mr Zelazny. I have been trying to cheer Allie up because she was so sad when I found her on the path after her difficult morning of detention. Please do not judge her for my actions.'

Zelazny marched past them. 'Detention she richly deserved,' he muttered.

'Of course,' Sylvain said, smoothly steering Allie through the entry hall as she struggled not to laugh out loud.

When they were out of earshot Allie doubled over with laughter, but Sylvain shushed her. 'Not here, *ma belle* Allie,' he whispered. 'His hearing is exceptional.'

She covered her mouth with her hands, stifling her own giggles.

'I do not want to see you trapped in detention for an entire week,' Sylvain said. 'August is very . . . sensitive.'

'August?' she asked.

'Mr Zelazny. That is his first name.'

'Oh.'

'And now,' he said, 'I must leave you. Isabelle will be waiting in the first classroom on the right. Good luck.'

Bending over he kissed her hand.

Allie wasn't quite sure how to respond.

'Bye!' she said too brightly, before hurrying into the silent and empty classroom wing.

The first door on the right was closed, and Allie knocked lightly.

'Come in.' The headmistress' distinctive voice answered immediately.

Inside, Allie found Isabelle sitting at the desk, surrounded by stacks of papers. A laptop was open beside her and she closed it before Allie could see anything on the screen, but she looked at its top longingly.

Modern life still exists.

'Please, have a seat.' Isabelle gestured at a chair near her. 'You must excuse me—I'm doing the accounts and it always seems to involve filling a village hall with papers, so I choose to work on it in the spacious environs of a classroom.'

Pulling off her glasses, she stood up and stretched before moving to the seat next to Allie. 'How was detention this morning?'

'Fine, I guess,' Allie shrugged. 'I mean, it was hard work but it was fine.'

Isabelle smiled at her kindly. 'I think August was too stern with you, and I've told him so. I wanted you to know that. I didn't want to undermine him by removing his punishment but I don't think it was fair.'

Her words were so unexpected that Allie couldn't think of anything to say—nobody had ever apologised to her for injustice before. She didn't even know it was possible.

'Thank you,' was the best she could come up with, but Isabelle seemed to see on her face how much it meant to her.

'August is known for his strictness, so I don't want you to feel singled out,' she continued. 'He sees to it that a week never goes by without at least a few students working in the gardens or organising the old store rooms. But I've asked him to give you more time to adjust before he includes you in his punishment rota again.'

She studied Allie curiously. 'And the incident last night—we should talk about that. Sylvain said some sort of wild animal frightened you in the garden?'

'Well, we don't know what it was,' Allie said. 'It crashed through the garden and . . . chased us, I guess. We thought we heard it growling, or something. What do you think it could have been?'

'Sylvain suggested it could be foxes. We do have rather a lot of them around,' Isabelle said.

Frowning, Allie tilted her head to one side. 'We have foxes in London, but I've never heard one of them growl or seen one chase people.'

'Well, this is the country,' Isabelle said. 'Foxes are wilder here—the ones in London are practically tame. A vixen can be very protective of her cubs. I've asked the ground staff to look out for any other sort of animal but I can't think of what else it could have been. I'm very glad you are both OK.'

She sounded sincere, and Allie was gratified that she hadn't made her sound like an idiot.

Isabelle was moving on to other issues now, though.

'How are you, really? Are you making friends? Sylvain tells me you're doing well, and that you and he are getting along famously, and I'm glad to hear that. He is one of our best students.'

Allie blushed. It was weird to think that Sylvain, who flirted with her constantly, discussed her with the headmistress.

'I'm OK,' she said, sliding down in her chair a bit. 'I'm friends with Sylvain and Jo, and I've met a few other people. Everybody's been sort of nice except . . .'

She bit her lip, and Isabelle looked at her encouragingly. 'Except who? It's OK to tell me.'

'Oh you know.' Allie crossed and uncrossed her ankles. 'Katie Gilmore? She's a bit bitchy.'

Isabelle sighed. 'I will be honest with you, Allie. Sometimes I think Katie is one of the trials I was put on this earth to deal with. She's been spoiled her whole life—I fear I'm being very unprofessional telling you this, but I think I can trust you. Because of her childhood, she has a hard time interacting with students who are not as privileged as she is— she's been too sheltered by her family's wealth. However, she is not immune from punishment, no matter how powerful her parents, so if she goes too far tell Jules or me.' Isabelle polished her glasses with a clean cloth. 'I wouldn't mind seeing her working in the garden for a week. It would do her a world of good to get her hands dirty.'

Thrilled that the headmistress was being so honest with her, Allie giggled at the image then stopped herself. But Isabelle chuckled too so she knew it was OK.

'Anything else aside from that?' Isabelle grew serious again. 'Your coursework is looking fine. You're certainly doing very well in my class. Any problems academically?'

Allie shook her head. It was true the work was hard, but it was more interesting than the work at her last two schools and she found that, actually, she enjoyed it.

'What about home life?' Isabelle asked. 'I've noticed that you haven't asked to phone your parents since you arrived. Would you like to phone them? I'm happy for you to talk to them.'

Again Allie shook her head—more vigorously this time. 'I don't want to talk to them right now,' she said, avoiding Isabelle's eyes. 'I want some time without them.'

When she glanced up, Isabelle's expression was hard to read, but something told Allie she understood.

'Of course,' she said, adding, 'but if you ever change your mind, come to me.'

The conversation had now skated onto thin ice for Allie, who fidgeted in her seat, hoping she'd soon be released.

Nothing escaped the headmistress' attention and she stood up with another weary stretch.

'Well, I suppose I should free you to have lunch and enjoy the rest of your weekend.'

Needing no more invitation, Allie leapt to her feet and headed for the door but Isabelle's voice stopped her just as she was about to open it.

'Please, Allie,' she said, 'don't ever be afraid to come to me with any problem, however small or large. I am here to help you. I am absolutely not here to get you in trouble. You are safe with me.'

Her words seemed heartfelt and Allie smiled shyly. 'I will,' she said before hurrying out.

She could feel Isabelle's knowing eyes following her down the hall.

*   *   *

'Oh God. Please make the torture end.' Jo fell face down onto her biology book.

Sitting across from her at the table in the library, Allie threw a pen at her.

'Yep,' Gabe said, closing his book, 'we need a break. I've still got a bit more to do, but nobody's saying I can't do it later. It's Saturday afternoon, it's a beautiful day—who wants to go outside?'

Without raising her head from her book, Jo stuck her arm straight up in the air. 'Me,' she said, her voice muffled by biology.

'Allie?' he asked, stacking his books.

She shook her head. 'I've had enough of the great outdoors today, thanks. I think I'll explore the building.'

Jo's head popped up; her blonde hair stood on end. 'The building's cool. Ask Eloise to show you the study chambers. They're wicked.'

She seemed largely recovered from the night before; the cut on her cheek was closed with two flesh-coloured butterfly stitches, and there were no other visible wounds. Allie hadn't yet had a chance to talk with her about what had happened—she was dying for a few minutes alone but Gabe had scarcely left Jo's side all day. Now he stacked her books with his, and the two stood up to leave.

'See you at dinner if not before?' Allie asked hopefully.

100

'Defo,' Jo said, smiling.

When they were gone, Allie stretched and looked around. The room was mostly deserted.

She walked towards the librarian's desk. Behind the high, polished wood counter Eloise was filing in an old-fashioned library card file.

'Uh . . . hi?' Allie's voice was hesitant.

'Oh Allie. How wonderful to see you again,' Eloise said, straightening. 'How are you?'

The librarian's dark hair was pulled back in a loose style from which tendrils escaped; purple-framed glasses perched at the end of her slender nose.

'I'm fine, thanks. I was studying, over there,' Allie pointed in the general direction of her table, 'and I just thought I'd come say hello.'

'Are you here for those books I told you about?' Eloise set the card file down. 'I've set them aside for you.'

Reaching under the desk, she pulled out a stack of books with a card on top reading 'For Allie'.

'I believe it's extra reading for your English class,' Eloise explained.

Allie had already forgotten about the books the librarian had mentioned that morning and, frankly, she thought she had enough to read already.

But still . . .

'Oh good,' she said politely, putting the books in her bag. 'But actually, I was just going to explore the building and Jo said there were some cool study rooms or something in here?'

Eloise looked blank for a minute, then brightened. 'You must mean the carrels in the back. They're quite something. Let me get the keys.'

She removed a crowded key ring from a hook behind the front counter. Allie followed her along what seemed like hundreds of years' worth of Oriental rugs, and past endless rows of shelves.

'This place is huge,' she said, looking up to the ceiling.

'Just be glad you don't have to dust it,' the librarian replied chirpily. 'Mind you, if you get detention again you might get that chance.'

Allie couldn't help but laugh. 'Please, no.'

'Don't worry.' Eloise smiled. 'If you're good it'll never happen.'

They turned a corner and the room changed slightly. There were fewer bookshelves in this section, and more tables and leather chairs.

'This area is reserved for advanced students,' Eloise explained, choosing a key from the ring in her hand.

'Here we go.' The walls were panelled with elaborately carved dark wood. Eloise inserted the key into a lock so skilfully hidden in the woodwork that Allie couldn't see it at all, and a door that until then had been virtually invisible opened silently.

'Wow,' Allie said. 'A secret door.'

'Wow indeed.' Eloise looked at her over the tops of her glasses. 'These study rooms are in the oldest part of the building. We're not at all certain what their original purpose was. But, well, take a look.'

She clicked a light switch and stepped back. Allie walked into an illuminated room about eight feet wide by six feet long. Inside the windowless space was a desk with a lamp, a leather chair and a small bookcase. Dominating it all was an elaborate mural covering the walls. Stepping into the centre of the room, Allie turned a slow circle to take it all in. The painting seemed to tell a story: men and women armed to the teeth and fighting in a field, overlooked by enraged cherubs under a stormy sky.

The scene was chilling, Allie thought.

'How does anybody study in here?' she asked. 'I'd spend the whole time ducking for cover.'

'It doesn't seem to bother anyone.' Eloise looked at the swinging swords, her eyes unreadable. 'But I can't say I disagree with you.'

She stepped out of the room. After a last glance around, Allie followed, and Eloise locked the door behind them.

'Are they all like this?'

The librarian nodded. 'They're very similar. The paintings in each room tell a different part of the same story. This is the main battle painting. It seems to be the last in the series.'

She walked down to the end of the panelled wall and unlocked another hidden door. Turning on the light, she gestured for Allie to follow and they stepped into the small study room. This room's paintings showed the same people, the men in hats and formal attire, then women in elaborate long dresses. They appeared to be talking in a circle, in front of what looked like a smaller version of the building she was in now.

'We think this is the first in the series,' Eloise said.

'Is that Cimmeria?' Allie asked.

'Before the expansion,' Eloise said. 'The painting is of that time—early eighteenth century.'

'What's it all about?' Allie asked. 'Some kind of war?'

Eloise was studying one of the faces. 'Nobody really knows any more. The school lore is that the

103

building was originally built by a single family. Some kind of disagreement divided them, and they essentially went to war with one another—the winning side kept the school. But none of that is recorded in the school records, and let me tell you, if it was I would know. I'm the school historian.'

As they walked out of the room, Allie was lost in thought.

'Weird,' she said. 'I mean, how could something so important just get lost?'

'Things do,' Eloise said. 'Especially if nobody wants to remember it.'

'I really do not want to study in those rooms,' Allie said firmly.

'Luckily, you've got another year before you're advanced enough to sit back here.' Eloise gave her a bright smile. 'So you're safe for now.'

CHAPTER SEVEN

As Allie walked out of the library and down the hall to the classroom wing she was still thinking about the strange library paintings. With classes out, the rooms were empty and silent as she idly climbed the staircase past the familiar lower rooms and up to the second floor. Only advanced classes were held up here and she'd hoped it would have some air of mystery, but she was disappointed to find that it looked exactly like the lower levels—a wide hallway with a polished wood floor and classrooms on either side. With the lights off, it was lit entirely by daylight filtering through classroom windows.

Her rubber-soled shoes rendered her footsteps nearly silent as she peeked through open doors at empty classrooms where desks waited in patient, ghostly rows.

She wasn't sure when she first heard the voices—perhaps midway down the hall. It was a low murmur that caught her attention only when it momentarily grew louder.

She stopped walking.

Someone shouted and there was a crashing sound, followed by a concerned wave of voices that seemed to be trying to calm things.

Allie was poised to turn back when a door at the end of the hall opened and a figure stepped out of the shadows.

Instinctively she ducked into the nearest doorway and hid in the shadows behind the door, listening. At first she could hear nothing but the sound of her own breathing, then, after a moment, she could hear the faint sound of footsteps heading her way. She counted her breaths.

. . . ten, eleven, twelve . . .

The footsteps paused.

She stopped breathing.

'Allie?' Carter whispered, his voice harsh. 'What the hell?'

He reached in and grabbed her arm, pulling her roughly towards the stairwell. She was too surprised to protest and stumbled alongside him. He hustled her down the stairs to the first floor landing, where he turned her to face him.

'What were you doing up on the second floor?' His fingers dug into her upper arm.

'Exploring,' she said, trying to free herself. She tried to appear calm but she knew she sounded defensive.

'Exploring what? The classrooms?'

Feigning nonchalance, she shrugged. 'Yeah. Sort of. It's not off-limits or anything, is it?'

'Allie, did you ever actually read the information you were given when you started here? Do you think rules are just optional for you?' Sarcasm dripped from his voice, and now Allie could feel anger growing in the pit of her stomach.

What is wrong with everybody at this bloody school?

'I read enough to know it was boring,' she snapped. 'Now will you just stop being a psycho and let me go?'

'The second floor is for advanced students and Night School only,' Carter said, as if he were talking to a child. 'You could get into serious trouble if they catch you there. You must *never* go up there.'

She wrenched free from his grip. 'Bloody hell,' she said, rubbing her shoulder. 'Overreact much? You'd think I killed someone.'

His expression did not change. 'Seriously, Sheridan. I'm starting to think you like getting in trouble.'

Turning on her heel she stomped down the stairs, firing over her shoulder, 'Well, from what I hear about you, West, that's a bit pot, kettle.'

He didn't reply.

*　　　*　　　*

Allie waited outside the dining room that evening, fidgeting as she watched the students stream in. Katie passed by, glowing ethereally. She whispered

106

to the cluster of acolytes who always surrounded her and they all giggled. Allie saw Jules among them, unsmiling.

Unable to help herself, Allie crossed her eyes and stuck out her tongue at them, but they only laughed louder.

'What an idiot,' she heard Katie say, and she flushed.

A few minutes later Jo and Gabe appeared, bright stars in a constellation of friends. Jo was laughing at some unheard joke. Allie waited to be noticed, trying not to care whether or not they saw her. But a few seconds later Jo looked up and gave her an enormous smile. She bounded down the hallway and grabbed her hand, dragging her into the group.

'Allie! There you are. Come with me—you need to meet everyone.'

At the table, Allie sat on Jo's left, Gabe sat on her right. In the raucous rumble of pre-dinner conversation, Jo raised her voice enough to be heard.

'Everybody, this is Allie. Allie, this is everybody.'

'Come on, Jo, you could be more specific.' The heckler was about Gabe's age, and sat across the table from Allie. His glossy light brown hair was just long enough to fall fetchingly over his right eye. He smiled flirtatiously. 'I'm not everybody. I'm Lucas.'

The others hooted derisively, but his smile was contagious and she couldn't help but smile back.

One by one the others at the table laughingly gave their names. There was a slim girl named Lisa, with long, straight fair hair and a hesitant smile. Ruth was athletic and unsmiling with messy shoulder-length, dark blonde hair. She sat next to Phil, who was cool looking with very short dark hair and trendy glasses. Allie got the feeling Ruth and Phil liked each other.

There was an early excited buzz of conversation ('been hearing all about you . . .' 'What do you think of Cimmeria?' 'Isn't Zelazny a . . .' 'Shhh! Careful, he's right over there . . .' 'Do you like it here?') before everybody moved on to other subjects.

Distracted by the day's events, Allie played disinterestedly with her food, which wasn't, she thought, very good tonight. She could just make out the sound of rain against the windowpanes. The weather had gradually turned grey, and now it was pouring down. She was so deeply entangled in a complex net of her own thoughts that bits of the conversation floated by her like flotsam.

'Twenty pages by Tuesday!'

'Most amazing smile . . .'

'What is this meat, anyway?'

'Mystery meat.'

Laughter.

'I heard a teacher say it's supposed to rain for the next three days.'

A chorus of groans.

Allie looked up.

'It's so boring here when it rains,' Jo explained. 'The common room will be packed. We should get there early.'

As soon as they'd finished they hurried out and down the hall. Jo claimed a sofa in the middle of the room, kicking off her shoes and tucking her feet underneath her. Allie sank into a deep leather chair across from her. They were just settling down when Gabe walked up.

He, like Allie, had seemed distracted that evening. 'I can't stay,' he said now, looking at Jo apologetically. 'It's this stupid project.'

He kissed her, whispered something in her ear that made her smile, then hurried out.

Finally, for the first time since the previous night, Allie and Jo were alone.

'What should we do now?' Jo asked. 'Do you want to play Trivial Pursuit?'

'Not right now.' Allie scooted forward in her chair and leaned towards Jo, lowering her voice to a whisper. 'Jo, what *was* that last night? What does Gabe think?'

'Well, there was some sort of crazy fox or something . . . I don't know,' Jo said. 'It all happened so fast.'

Disappointed, Allie leaned away from her. 'That's what Sylvain said, but it didn't sound like a fox to me.'

'What do you think it sounded like?' Jo asked.

Allie shook her head. 'I don't know. Something with teeth.'

'A bear?' Jo suggested impishly. 'A dragon? A *wookie*?'

'Jo, seriously!' Allie was frustrated. 'What happened last night was real. Gabe and Sylvain took it seriously. They didn't seem to think we were being silly. They were . . . well, not scared, but like, really nervous. Now I feel like everyone's trying to make us think we were hysterical. Or like it was some big joke. But I think there was something out there.'

Jo made a soothing gesture with her hands.

'Look, Allie, something definitely happened,

109

but it was dark, and I don't think anybody knows whether or not it was really dangerous. We could have just scared ourselves. Gabe says some people went out last night looking for whatever it was, but they didn't find anything.' She smiled. 'I can tell you it's pretty unusual. It's not like we usually get attacked by wild growly things. So don't get too freaked out.'

Allie wasn't convinced but she didn't want to appear obsessed, so she nodded reluctantly.

'You're right. I'm sure you're right.'

'Right, so. Back to what to do tonight,' Jo said. 'If not Trivial Pursuit . . . backgammon? Something else? Monopoly? Noughts and crosses?'

Allie tried to summon interest in board games for Jo, but she found them dull at the best of times.

'Have you ever played chess?' Jo asked, finally.

Allie's expression must have given her away because Jo's face took on a determined focus.

'Seriously? That's outrageous. Well, I'm about to take care of that right now.'

Jumping off the sofa, she knelt beside the table in front of them and pulled a shoebox-sized wooden box from underneath it. From it she began to pull out glossy pieces. Setting the black pieces on her side, she handed Allie a white knight.

Allie held it up and made a neighing sound. Jo gave her a withering look.

'Pony,' Allie said weakly.

'Get serious, Allie. So you hate board games. Fine. Chess is not a board game. Chess is only sort of a game, because really chess is war.'

When Allie made a face Jo added firmly, 'So chess is exciting.' She pointed at the piece Allie still held. 'That is not a pony. That is a knight that kills.'

Pointing at a square she said: 'Put it there.'

Trying to look serious, Allie placed the knight where she was told but, shooting Jo a rebellious glance she murmured 'good horsey' under her breath.

Jo ignored her and picked up a pawn.

'These are your foot soldiers. They have the least freedom and the least power, but because they're willing to sacrifice themselves for their betters you can't win without them.'

She set down the little round-headed piece and pulled out a piece shaped like a castle tower.

'This is your rook—the king's fortress. It is the only piece on the board that can legally take the king's place at any time. Its role is to confuse the enemy. It goes here.'

Setting it down she picked up two more pieces. In her right hand she held a piece shaped vaguely like a minaret. 'The bishop. Slick and dangerous, he has huge power. I think of him as the queen's bit of rough.' Now she waved the tall, regal piece in her left hand. 'The king. Almost always weaker than you'd think—all the pieces protect him but he almost never helps anyone else, because if he does he could die.'

Allie cupped her chin in her hand. 'This is like Shakespeare, only . . . lamer.'

Now Jo picked up a slender, crowned white piece and handed it to her. 'The queen. She's a complete bitch. But if you want to win, you have got to work with her.'

'Great,' Allie said. 'What happens next? And at what point do I begin kicking your arse?'

Jo handed her the white pieces. 'If you practise and work hard? Maybe by your twenty-seventh birthday. I've been playing chess since I was five. Set yours out the way I've done mine, then I'll beat you for the first time.'

Allie arranged her pieces as a mirror image of Jo's.

'So, tell me a bit about your friends,' she said, picking up the queen. 'Lisa and Lucas seem nice, but Ruth and Phil I couldn't really tell . . .'

Jo nodded. 'I think you'll really like Lisa—she was my first friend at Cimmeria. Ruth's cool but she's kind of, I don't know, intense, I guess. So you have to be in the mood to deal with her. Phil's OK—he tells terrible jokes when he loosens up. But he's kind of shy around new people.'

At that moment, Ruth ran into the room, breathless, her clothes soaked and her wet hair dropping beads of water.

'Jo.'

She stood in front of them, panting, her hands clutching her sides as if she'd run very quickly. Water puddled on the floor at her feet.

Allie froze, the queen still in her hand. Jo seemed speechless, but Ruth didn't wait to be asked.

'It's Gabe.'

CHAPTER EIGHT

Jo jumped to her feet sending chess pieces scattering across the floor.

'What . . .' She looked confused, fearful.

'He's hurt. Phil too. It went wrong.'

Allie stood up and moved to Jo's side. 'What

112

happened? Where are they?'

Ruth gave her an appraising look; Allie thought she saw Jo nod.

'The summerhouse,' Ruth said.

'Let's go,' Allie said, taking Jo by the hand and pulling her towards the common room door. Ruth didn't follow them.

The two of them dashed through the grand entry hall where they skidded to a stop on the stone floor and shoved the heavy wooden door open. Outside the rain was pelting down. Allie dashed out without hesitation, but at the foot of the steps she stopped and turned to Jo.

'Which way?' She shouted to be heard above the noise of the storm as thunder rumbled above them.

Jo pointed past the west wing. They hurtled down the drive, then onto the wet grass and out towards the woods. Allie could hear her own ragged breathing ringing in her ears, the sound of rain . . . and nothing else.

A few minutes later she saw an elaborate Victorian gazebo through the trees. It was empty. They ran up the stairs and looked around, panting. Allie bent over with her hands on her knees trying to catch her breath.

Jo pointed into the woods. 'There.'

Allie peered into the rainy gloom, but could see nobody.

Then she heard a shout that seemed to come from far away, deep in the forest. Allie looked at Jo to see if she'd heard. She was staring off into the trees, her lips slightly parted as she listened.

'Did you hear that too?' Allie whispered. Jo nodded, her eyes still fixed on the forest.

'It's Gabe,' she whispered back.

They stood still, watching. More shouts, but they could see nothing. Then, after a few minutes, shadowy figures came into focus, walking out from between the trees. Allie could make out Carter and Gabe. They seemed to be holding somebody up between them. She couldn't see who it was.

'Oh my God.' Jo was still whispering.

As the boys walked up the stairs to the summerhouse, Allie could see that they were wounded. Carter had a cut on his forehead that was bleeding heavily. Gabe had blood on his hands and shirt. He glared at Allie.

'What the hell are you doing here?'

Carter turned to Gabe. 'Not right now, man. We've got enough problems.'

Gently, they laid down the person they carried. Allie didn't recognise him, but Jo gasped.

'Phil. Oh no.'

Gabe looked up at her, his eyes worried. 'I think he's going to be OK. Sylvain's gone to get help.'

Allie pulled at Gabe's arm, turning it over to reveal a cut on his wrist bleeding freely.

'Gabe,' she breathed, colour disappearing from her face.

What the hell is happening? Allie thought, looking at the disaster scene in front of her. *And why isn't anybody else asking that question?*

On his knees beside Phil, Carter tore a strip from the end of his shirt and tied it tightly around the unconscious boy's leg. Then he tore another one and held it up to Jo. 'Tie this around Gabe's wrist.'

But Jo seemed unable to move. She held the white fabric as if she didn't quite know what it was.

Seeing Jo's fear, Allie stepped over. 'I'll do it.'

As she reached for the fabric, Jo let it fall from her hand.

The makeshift bandage fluttering, Allie turned to Gabe. 'Hold out your hand.'

Gabe lifted his arm and Allie wrapped the strip expertly around his wrist and hand, weaving it into a tight bandage, then tucking the end in so the fit was snug.

'Hold your hand above your heart until the bleeding stops,' she intoned automatically.

Turning back towards Phil, she saw that Carter was watching her.

'You're bleeding too,' she said.

'I'm OK.'

'I can see that. Someone should look at that cut.'

Hearing footsteps running across the grass, Allie looked up to see a group of people running their way. As they neared she saw that Sylvain was in the lead, Zelazny and Jerry right behind him. Zelazny glanced at Allie with irritation.

'What is she doing here?' His tone was accusing.

Sylvain's eyes met Allie's for a second then he returned his focus to Zelazny. His voice was soothing. 'We'll find out later—first we must deal with this.'

'How bad is it?' Jerry asked, checking the tourniquet.

Carter looked worried. 'Not good. He needs a doctor. He's bleeding a lot.'

'What about you?' Jerry asked.

Blood dripped down Carter's face and onto his soaked white shirt, but he didn't look up. 'I'll be fine. I just need a couple of stitches.'

'OK, you and Gabe get to the nurse. Sylvain, help me with Phil. Everybody else, get back inside.

Now.'

His tone was firm and on his last word they all moved at once. He and Sylvain carried Phil by draping his arms across their shoulders, and Zelazny hurried ahead of them. As if she'd been shaken awake, Jo turned to Gabe and hugged him.

Allie walked over to Carter and slipped her arm around his waist to help but he wrenched himself free.

'I'm fine,' he insisted roughly.

Flushing, Allie moved away from him.

'If this is how you look when you're fine, I'd hate to see you when you're bad,' she muttered.

He snorted derisively but walked alongside her, an arm's length away.

'What the hell was that all about, Carter?' she asked, as soon as they were out of earshot of the others. 'Why was everybody all Ninja all of a sudden? It was freaky.'

'It was nothing,' he said. 'An accident. It happens.'

'It *happens*?' she asked, her voice disbelieving. 'An accident in the woods in the pouring rain in which half the student population ends up bleeding to death . . . happens?'

The dark look he shot her was made even more murderous by the blood streaming down his face.

'Has anybody ever mentioned you've got an exaggeration problem?' he said.

'No,' Allie replied. 'Anybody ever mention you've got a dickhead problem?'

After that, they didn't speak.

As the rain pounded down on them, she cast a sideways glance at him from underneath lashes so covered in raindrops it was like looking through a

116

waterfall. He was staring ahead, his jaw set.

When they reached the school steps, Isabelle stood at the top in a long white raincoat. The rain made a dull plastic sound as it pounded against the hood.

'Carter. Allie. Are you OK? Carter, you look horrible.'

'I'm fine,' Carter insisted. 'I just need a couple of stitches.'

Isabelle scrutinised him, then turned to Allie. 'And you? Are you hurt?'

Allie shook her head and water poured onto her nose.

'Good. Carter, get to the nursing station. Allie, would you come with me, please?'

Without waiting for a reply, she walked back inside briskly.

As Allie turned to follow her, Carter grabbed her elbow. She thought he looked like a victim in a horror film.

'Come find me before curfew,' he said. 'I'll be in the great hall.' Then he sloshed into the school, leaving a trail of water in his wake.

Frowning, Allie's eyes followed him down the hall.

'As if,' she muttered before hurrying after Isabelle.

They walked past the common room and then through a door so neatly hidden in the wood panelling that Allie had never noticed it before. Inside was a spacious, windowless office with a fireplace, its carved mantelpiece topped with unlighted candles. One wall was entirely covered in a tapestry—a knight with a sword, and a damsel by a white horse. Isabelle handed her a soft white towel, and Allie rubbed the water roughly out of her hair and then wrapped it around her shoulders, shivering. Now that she was inside she felt cold.

'Please sit down.' Isabelle gestured to two leather chairs across from her desk. She perched on the edge of the desk, watching her. Allie was conscious of the low timbre of classical music playing from hidden speakers.

'You're sure you're OK?' Isabelle asked. When Allie nodded she continued. 'Good. I just want to talk to you for a minute, then I'm going to send you off to get some dry clothes. You're not in any trouble, but I just need to know what happened tonight.'

Allie looked at her, puzzled. 'I don't . . .?'

'I mean what were you and Jo doing out at the summerhouse? Tell me what happened from the beginning.'

Allie wrapped the towel more tightly around her shoulders and thought quickly. Was someone in trouble?

Am I in trouble?

'We were just . . . looking for Gabe,' she said carefully. 'Jo wanted to surprise him by sneaking up on him but we couldn't find him. We went to the summerhouse to get out of the rain, and then we saw the boys coming out of the woods.'

She felt uncomfortable lying to Isabelle but the whole thing felt wrong. When Ruth had come to get them, she'd looked frightened. She'd been white as a sheet. Allie's instincts told her to cover for Ruth, even though she didn't know her very well.

Ruth wasn't supposed to tell us anything.

Isabelle watched her closely. 'Then what

118

happened?'

'We knew right away that something was wrong, but nobody would tell us what happened.' The last bit sounded self-pitying, but really, why was everybody being so secretive?

'Is that everything?' The headmistress gave no indication at all that she didn't believe her, so Allie decided it was time to ask some questions of her own.

'Do you know what happened?' she asked. 'Carter refuses to tell me and everybody else acts like I've done something really wrong.'

Isabelle leaned forward. 'I'm sorry about that, Allie. They shouldn't behave like that. You're new, and there's no way for you to know. I'm not quite clear yet as to what happened or how the boys got hurt, but I intend to find out.'

'It's just,' Allie said, 'it looked really bad.'

Isabelle stood up. 'I think it looked worse than it was. I'm told nobody was seriously injured, and sometimes games just get a little too rough. It's nothing for you to worry about. I will speak with those involved.'

Isabelle dropped her hand to Allie's shoulder and squeezed it lightly as she walked by her to the door, which she held open for her.

'Thank you, Allie. I'm glad you're OK. You don't need to worry about Phil—he's already being seen by medical staff. And it is clear to me that Gabe and Carter's wounds are superficial.'

Though Allie felt as if she should have demanded more answers, Isabelle's explanation did make sense. Boys did always get into trouble—she'd seen Mark and Harry hurt themselves plenty of times. They'd both ended up in A&E on more than one occasion after a night of tagging had gone wrong.

But what could have happened to them all out in the woods? And why won't anyone tell me?

Back in her room she changed into a dry skirt and jumper, dumping her wet clothes on the floor. She wanted to get back downstairs before curfew and find out how everyone was doing.

As she dabbed on pale pink lip gloss in front of the mirror, though, her hand stopped. *Should I go and meet Carter?*

It wasn't that she really wanted to meet him— he'd been a complete arse. She was just curious. Why did he want to meet her alone? And why in the great hall? She hadn't been in there since Isabelle showed it to her the day she arrived.

She checked the clock. It was only ten. There was still plenty of time until curfew.

She dashed down the stairs then tiptoed down the corridor towards the great hall.

'Allie.' Sylvain's silky accent caressed her name and she spun around to find him right behind her. 'I was hoping to run into you. I was concerned—are you OK?'

He pulled her into a hug and, after hesitating, Allie hugged him back. His fingers delicately traced a line down her back to her waist.

Goosebumps.

He stood back to look at her. 'You're still wet. I'm so glad you're not hurt.'

'I'm fine.'

She tried to think of an excuse for what she was up to. There's no way he would be happy to know she was on her way to meet Carter. But what he didn't know, she reasoned, wouldn't hurt *her*.

120

'I was just looking for Jo . . .' she said.

'I believe she is with Gabe.' His fingers were under her chin now, tilting her face up so that she looked at him. She could feel his breath on her cheek. He smelled of cool juniper.

'What were you and Jo doing in the summerhouse anyway?' His tone was casual, but something about his manner sent off warning signals. 'Zelazny was very cross to see you there.'

Is he investigating me?

'It was before curfew,' Allie argued. 'I don't see why everybody cares that we were outside. We just wanted to go out. So we did.'

'In the pouring rain.'

Allie was tired of being questioned. 'We thought it would be fun,' she said. 'And, you know what? I could ask you the same question. What were *you* doing outside in the pouring rain?'

He studied her curiously, as if he saw something new in her he hadn't noticed before.

'Fair enough, *ma belle*.' For the first time she heard cool distance in his voice. She'd touched a nerve.

'How's Phil?' she asked, trying to move to safer ground.

'He is going to be OK—but he lost some blood so it will be a couple of days. It was a bad fall.'

As she opened her mouth to ask what had happened out there, he spoke again.

'You should have something warm to drink,' he said. 'Come with me. There's hot chocolate in the kitchen.'

'No.' Allie's response was more panicked than the situation called for and Sylvain raised one eyebrow in surprise as she fumbled for a reason.

'I . . . There's something I need to do. Let's talk tomorrow? I have to . . .'

Her explanations fading, she dashed past him to the library. It was deserted—even the librarian's desk was empty. Running across the soft rugs down to the stacks, Allie disappeared into the shadows between two tall bookcases.

Behind her she heard the door open and close again. He called her name twice, softly. After a minute, the door opened and closed again. To be safe, Allie stayed where she was a few minutes longer. When she'd heard nothing while counting slowly to two hundred, she stepped out of the stacks, opening the library door to peek out into the hall. Sylvain was nowhere in sight. She sighed with relief.

The great hall door swung open without a sound when she pushed it. The lights were off but she could see a faint glow at the far end of the vast, empty ballroom. She walked in that direction hesitantly.

'Carter?' she whispered.

A voice made a ghostly 'woooo' sound that echoed around her.

'Cut it out, West.'

He chuckled.

As she neared the light, she saw that he was sprawled in a chair with his foot propped up on a table between a couple of lighted candles. His forehead was neatly bandaged. He was holding a book, which he now dropped lightly on the floor.

There was another chair next to him, and he gestured at it.

'Sit.'

'Don't tell me what to do,' she muttered, as she

122

sat.

He smiled darkly. 'Sorry, I thought I was being polite.'

She ignored that. 'How's your head?'

He waved the question away. 'I'm fine.'

There was a moment of silence.

'So, what's up?' Allie asked to break the stillness. 'Why did you want to meet me here? In case you're hoping, I don't dance.'

He shrugged. 'I like it here. I'm always here. They never check it, I don't know why.'

Lifting his foot from the table, he turned to face her. 'I just want to know how you and Blondie ended up in the summerhouse tonight right when everything went down. Gabe left you both safely in the common room on the verge of a girly conversation about . . . shoes or lipstick or whatever girls talk about. Fifteen minutes later, you're at the summerhouse in the pouring rain tying bandages. How did that happen, Allie?'

She dodged his eyes. 'Jo just wanted to look for . . .'

He cut her off. 'Oh, give it a rest, Allie. I'm not Isabelle.'

Surprised by his vehemence, she fumbled for something to say. 'I . . . uh . . . Well . . .'

He sat still, studying her.

The same instinctive worry that stopped her from telling Isabelle told her not to tell Carter either. But she had to find out what was going on around here, and if anybody would know, he would.

'Ruth. She came and got us.'

In the candlelight, his eyes were fathomless. She stared into them for a long, silent moment looking for a reaction, but saw nothing.

123

When he spoke, his voice was cold. 'What did she say?'

Allie crossed her arms across her torso, visualising Ruth standing in front of her, water streaming from her hair and dripping onto the floor. Fear on her face.

'She said Phil and Gabe were hurt. And something weird. I think she said "It went wrong."?'

Carter came out of his chair so fast that later she couldn't remember seeing him do it. Holding her by her shoulders he seemed to tower over her. Allie recoiled.

With his lips a few inches away from hers he spoke in a harsh whisper. 'You must never tell anybody else what Ruth did. Swear it.'

Allie stared up at him, and her lips moved for a second before any sound came out.

'Yeah, sure. OK, I won't tell anyone. Jesus, Carter.'

As if he'd just realised what he was doing, he let her go.

'You're freaking me out,' Allie said, rubbing her shoulder. 'What is your malfunction?'

Trying to look casual, he leaned against a pillar.

'Sorry. But Ruth shouldn't have done that and people might be pissed off if they knew. I don't want her to get in trouble, so you really can't say anything.'

'Hey,' she said icily. 'No worries, mate. And while we're all about honesty maybe you could tell me what tonight's performance was about? How did you all end up cut to pieces in the middle of the forest?'

Crossing his arms, he looked at her coldly. A

long silence fell.

'Well, thanks for the inquisition and the threats and everything. It's been really great. But I should probably be going.' Allie affected her most bored expression.

Carter stared at her as if there was something else he wanted to say. In fact, she could almost pinpoint the moment when he decided not to say it.

'You make a good bandage,' he said instead. 'Where'd you learn to do that? Crimea?'

She thought about just getting up and walking out. But she stayed. She wasn't sure why. Maybe curiosity.

'London,' she said. 'First aid class. Girl Guides.'

He raised one sardonic eyebrow. 'You were in the Girl Guides? No way.'

She couldn't figure out why they were having this jovial conversation after he'd just gone all Hannibal Lecter on her but she decided to go along with it.

'Yes way. I was a kid then but that stuff stays with you. Bandage-tying. Butterfly-catching. Jam-making. I can do it all.'

He barked a short laugh but Allie didn't smile. 'What's really going on around here, Carter? I mean, what happened to you tonight? Did you guys get in a fight? It looked really bad.'

If he'd closed a door in her face it couldn't have been more clear. His eyes went blank.

'Just let it go,' he snapped. 'And don't ask anybody else either. Nobody will tell you a thing and people will get angry if they know you're asking.' He looked at his watch. 'It's nearly eleven. We have to go.'

He blew out the candles and the room plunged into darkness.

125

As she walked towards where she thought the door might be Allie tripped over something in the darkness. Carter caught her. For just a second they stood face-to-face. Though he was wreathed in shadows, Allie thought he looked almost sorry.

But I'm probably wrong about that.

'This way,' he said, leading her by the hand through the dark room with the confidence of somebody who'd done it many times. His fingers felt warm and strong against hers, but she really didn't want him touching her right now—she moved stiffly beside him.

By the time they emerged blinking into the lights of the empty hall his face was studiously expressionless.

'It's eleven, Sheridan. You should hurry. You don't want detention again.'

'Yeah, sure,' she said sarcastically. 'Blood and gore we can have. But Allie out after curfew? That would be a disaster.'

'Good night, Sheridan,' he said, firmly.

She turned for the stairs.

'Whatever, Carter.'

*   *   *

'You have to trust me, Allie.'

Carter's eyes looked into hers intently but she resisted.

'Why would I trust you? You don't trust me.'

They were standing in the great hall. It was filled with lighted candles—they glittered on windowsills, table tops, and in hugely tall candelabra. The heat they gave off was intense.

Carter's eyes glittered in the light. 'But I can

126

help you . . .'

Someone banged on the door loudly. Threateningly. Allie felt her heart pound.

'They're here,' he said.

The banging came again, more insistent this time. The noise was almost deafening and Allie covered her ears.

'Who is it? Who's here, Carter?'

His voice was urgent. 'You have to trust me. Do you trust me?'

Over his shoulder she could see the door was cracking under the strain of the pounding.

'Yes!' Allie cried, reaching out for him. 'Yes! I trust you.'

*   *   *

Gasping, Allie sat up in bed clutching the duvet in tight fists.

A loud bang made her jump but it was only the wooden shutter thrown against the wall by a stiff breeze coming through the open window.

Climbing up on top of the desk to look out the window, she saw a storm had blown up during the night—the trees swayed, and leaves, freed from their branches, rode the wind high above her.

The air smelled fresh as she latched the window tightly into place and climbed back into bed.

Pulling the covers up she muttered aloud, 'Get out of my *head*, Carter West.'

CHAPTER NINE

When classes resumed on Monday, Allie had the discomforting sense that none of the weekend's events had actually occurred. Everyone took their normal seats in class at the normal time. And Jerry and Zelazny treated her exactly as if they'd never seen her wrap a bandage in the pouring rain.

Sylvain wasn't in English class, but Carter arrived late as usual and just smirked when Isabelle gave him an exasperated look. If he hadn't still been wearing a bandage on his forehead she might have thought she imagined the entire thing.

Between classes, she met Jo in the library and they talked in whispers about what had happened after they'd parted. Jo told her Gabe hadn't even needed stitches in the end, and that the nurse had commented approvingly on Allie's bandaging technique.

'Now Gabe really wants to know how we ended up at the summerhouse, but . . . since you told me not to say anything about Ruth, I haven't. Why don't you want me to tell him?'

Allie leaned closer. 'I can't . . . It's just . . . important that you don't.'

In fact, she'd been up half the night trying to decide what to tell Jo. She would not lie to her only real friend at Cimmeria, but she'd promised Carter not to tell.

'I don't know how to explain it. I just heard that Ruth could get into trouble or something.'

She watched Jo's face as she considered this explanation.

'OK, but if I don't tell him the truth, what reason do I give him for us being there?'

Allie twirled a pen anxiously between her fingers so that it spun without stopping between every finger on her right hand until it reached the pinkie.

'We could say that we were playing Truth or Dare, and kind of spying on them. Or that I wanted to go for a run in the rain and you tried to stop me.'

Jo tilted her head to one side. 'Of those two very poor options, the first one is slightly less crap.'

Allie smiled. 'Thanks Jo.'

Over the next few days, rumours were rife about what had occurred down in the woods that night. Everybody knew that several people had been hurt, but there was widespread confusion over just what had happened. Students were forbidden from going out onto the grounds, and that only made the gossip worse. Nobody seemed to know that Allie and Jo had been there, and the most common rumour was that the boys had run afoul of the same fox Jo and Allie had encountered, although everybody seemed to think it very unlikely.

Phil didn't return to class that week, but Ruth said he was feeling better and would be back soon.

Given the fact that they were all, as Allie saw it, under house arrest, at least the weather was terrible. Throughout the week the rain was unrelenting. It was not as heavy as it had been on Sunday, but it was steady and the days were grey.

The teachers seemed to be amped up on educational adrenalin and that soon became the main topic of conversation at meals and breaks. The students discussed with increasing dismay the amount of work being assigned. Allie and Jo were in the library every evening until curfew, trying to keep up.

By the time Allie ran into Sylvain on Thursday evening as she came out of the library in search of a cup of tea, she was exhausted. He fell into step with her as she headed towards the dining room.

'Well, well. Hello, *ma belle* Allie. How are you? I haven't seen you since the weekend.'

Allie felt her heart beat faster but she tried to sound like seeing him was no big deal. She hoped he wouldn't ask where she'd disappeared to when she ran away from him. 'I'm good. Just trying to keep from being so buried in homework that I'm never seen again.'

He nodded. 'I know. The teachers are suddenly very busy making work for us.'

She turned to him. 'And what's up with that? Are they always this evil?'

He smiled and his eyes sparkled. 'No, this is unusual even for Cimmeria. I think it's possible they are keeping everybody too busy to try to sneak outside.'

Allie tried to hide her surprise.

'Because of the other night?' she asked.

'Perhaps.'

She looked longingly towards the front door. 'I'd love to go outside . . .'

'Are you bored, *ma belle*?' Moving so quickly she didn't have time to react he took her hand and pulled her closer to him. 'I could read your palm. Perhaps that would amuse you. And I would see into your soul.'

'You can read palms?' Her voice was doubtful but she liked the feeling of her hand in his.

'Of course,' he smiled. 'Can't you? It's easy.'

Turning her hand over, he ran his finger along

the shallow lines of her hand with a touch as light as a cat's whisker.

'You have a very long life line,' he murmured tracing a line from her wrist to the middle of her palm. 'And your heart line is strong. See this line here?' He ran his fingertips along a line that ended between her thumb and index finger. She shivered at the delicacy of his touch. 'Do you know what that tells me?'

Mute, Allie shook her head.

'It tells me you are in love with someone. Or maybe that you will be soon.'

Her body tingling from his touch, Allie tried to think of a witty reply but before she could speak the library door swung open.

Jo said, 'Hey Allie, don't forget the . . .' When she saw Sylvain her voice trailed off. 'Oops, oh dear, I think I forgot my . . .'

Improvising badly Jo ducked back inside. A moment later the door opened again and a group of students walked out chatting. Allie could hear Jo whispering at them 'No, wait a second . . .'

Sylvain dropped Allie's hand with a regretful smile. 'I should like to explore that topic further with you sometime,' he said.

'Yes,' she said, flustered. 'Let's . . . do.'

'Perhaps we could meet after dinner on Saturday to . . . talk?' he said.

'Sure,' she said, trying not to sound breathless.

He smiled. 'Good. I'll find you in the dining hall. See you then.'

'See you then,' she parroted back inanely.

*   *   *

Throughout the week the pace of schoolwork never let up. To make things worse, on Friday all students were given research papers to complete over the weekend. When assignment slips were handed out in history class, Zelazny's neat handwriting glared at Allie from the page:

3000 words on the socio-economic impact of the English civil war on the agrarian society of the day
Due Monday. No exceptions. No excuses.

The library was so crowded on Friday afternoon that, once every seat was taken, students spilled out into the hallway where they sat on the floor in small clusters, their books and papers spread out around them.

'We look like refugees,' Jo muttered, as she and Allie carried armloads of books out to a free spot near the school's front door.

'It's mad. How long can they keep this up?' As she spoke, Allie was balancing a china cup of tea on a century-old history book and lowering herself to the floor.

'Good question,' Jo said, snatching the cup from its precarious perch before it could crash to the stone floor.

'Thanks.' Allie settled down with her back against the wall.

Jo took a sip of Allie's tea. 'I should have got one of those. Now I'll just end up drinking yours.'

'And we definitely should have got biscuits.'

'We're idiots.'

Allie shuffled her books, a frown of concentration creasing her forehead. 'Where's

Gabe today? I've hardly seen him or Sylvain all week.'

Jo was choosing a notebook. 'Dunno. He said he had something to do and would do his paper later.'

'Weird,' Allie said. 'The teachers are being so tough but Sylvain and Gabe don't seem to mind.'

Jo shrugged. 'Nobody's telling me much about what's going on. Gabe and I had a row about it and we never row.'

'Boys are rubbish,' Allie said, opening her book.

Having finally found the right notebook, Jo was now focused on finding something it contained, and she rustled through its pages as she spoke absently. 'All I know is all the Night School guys are out every single night, and I'm sure it has something to do with the other night. But it's top secret.'

Allie stopped and stared at her, a brittle, yellowing book page still gripped between her fingers.

'Wait. You know who's in Night School?'

Jo froze, guilt spreading across her expression. 'No. Not really. I mean, I kind of . . . guessed. Anyway, a few are pretty obvious about it.'

'Like who?'

'I don't know, really,' Jo said carefully. 'I mean, just guessing, it could be Sylvain, and Phil, maybe Lucas, and, possibly Gabe and Carter, I mean, but who knows?'

She was lying so badly Allie would have laughed if she hadn't been so surprised.

'You mean, you think your own boyfriend is in it, but you're not sure?' she said.

Jo looked around to make sure nobody was paying attention to them, then leaned towards Allie and lowered her voice to a whisper. 'Look, it's

133

really super-secret, you know? You get in a lot of trouble if anybody finds out you've said anything about it. I mean, a *lot* of trouble.'

'So, we really shouldn't be talking about it now?' Allie whispered.

'No,' Jo hissed.

Allie returned to her book, turning one slow page after another, but her mind was still whirling around what Jo had told her.

She leaned forward again. 'No girls?'

Jo gave her a significant look.

'Maybe Jules,' she mouthed. 'And Ruth.'

Allie's eyes widened. 'No way,' she said, disbelieving.

Jo raised her right hand. 'Swear to God.'

For half an hour after that they worked in silence, save for the sound of notes being scribbled and pages turned. Then, without warning Allie's head popped up.

'That explains the way Carter reacted last Saturday,' she said, as if their conversation had never paused.

Jo looked intrigued. 'Why? What? And . . . when?'

Allie explained about Carter chasing her away from the second floor.

'Interesting,' Jo said when she finished. 'I didn't know they actually ever met in the building, though. And during the day? That's kind of weird.'

Allie twirled her pen again, getting ink on the side of her hand. She rubbed at it futilely. 'What exactly is it that they do anyway?'

Jo didn't look up from her book. 'No idea.'

Allie was still rubbing at the ink on her hand. 'I've always had the feeling that Carter knew what was really going on. So this would explain why.'

Jo gave her a look.

'What?' Allie asked, cocking her head.

'Nothing.'

Allie picked up her pen, but Jo was still looking at her.

'*What?*' Allie said again, giving her a light shove. They both giggled.

'Well, it's just . . . You know. You and Carter.'

Allie stopped laughing. 'What about me and Carter?'

'I don't know. He just sort of always picks on you.'

'Yeah, I've noticed,' Allie said dryly. 'That would be because he's a psycho.'

'No. I mean . . . I don't know. Something about how he picks on you interests me.'

Allie frowned. 'Jo, what the hell are you talking about?'

'Oh it's nothing. It's just that I thought for a little while there he liked you, and I know you liked him, and now it's like you two hate each other.'

Allie shrugged. 'It happens.'

'Hmm . . .' Jo's voice was doubtful.

'There's no hmm about it,' Allie said. 'All he does is order me around and tell me what to do and not do. He's good looking and everything, but I don't like him.'

Jo drew a squiggly line on her notepad and then drew over it again until it was bold. She gave it a forked tongue.

'You know, all that stuff Gabe and I said about Carter?'

Allie nodded.

'Well it was true. But he's been different since

135

you came here. I haven't seen him with any girl since then.'

Allie smiled broadly. 'What? In two whole weeks? I mean, seriously. What restraint! He must be totally in love with me.'

They dissolved into a fit of giggles.

'Anyway, in more sane news, Sylvain asked me to meet him tomorrow night after dinner,' Allie said. 'I think it's kind of a date.'

'Ooh, a real date,' Jo smiled. 'Seriously, forget everything I said about Carter. I'm just being silly. I'm so excited that you're the one who's going to bagsy Sylvain. All the girls will be so jealous of you.'

'I'm sure that will make them all be very nice to me.' Allie's tone was sarcastic but Jo arched an eyebrow knowingly.

'If Sylvain's your boyfriend they won't dare be anything but nice.'

Before Allie could ask what she meant she said, 'Right, enough frolicking. We need fifteen hundred words before dinner, which is in . . .' she checked the delicate gold watch on her wrist, 'just over three hours.'

'Fascist,' Allie said.

But she was already writing.

*　　　*　　　*

At dinner that night all discussion centred on rumours that the school grounds were now opened to students 'within reason'. The problem was, nobody knew what that meant.

'Does it mean we can go outside again without dying?' Lisa asked, flipping her long hair over one shoulder.

'Nobody died, Lisa.'

Allie thought Gabe's tone was unnecessarily sharp.

Lisa just shrugged and nibbled her salad.

'I'll bet it's perfectly safe,' Phil said, his voice deliberately measured, 'but I was just thinking of going to the common room.'

'Same here,' Gabe said quickly.

'Not me. I'm going out. I've had just about enough of inside.'

Jo's voice was emphatic but she didn't meet Gabe's eyes. He was staring at her intently, but she just looked around the table pretending not to notice.

'Jo . . .' His tone was ominous, but she just shot him a warning look.

'What?'

Throwing his napkin down, Gabe shoved his chair back and stood up, muttering, 'I'm not hungry any more.'

He stormed out without looking back.

There was a brief awkward silence while everybody pretended not to notice what had happened right in front of them. Allie saw Phil and Lucas exchange a look.

Ruth tried to distract everyone by launching into a story about a science experiment, but her voice gradually trailed off.

'Right, well, I'm pretty much done. Jo?' Allie said loyally.

Jo gave her a grateful smile and followed her out. Allie waited until they were far enough away from the table to be certain they wouldn't be overheard.

'What was that about?'

137

Jo was hurrying down the hall, and for a second she didn't answer; when she did, her tone was bitter. 'Well, obviously Gabe doesn't want me to go outside because it's not safe. And obviously Gabe wants to act like I'm a child and he's the parent and can tell me what to do. Which I *hate*. I've already got two useless parents, thanks. I don't need another.'

She moved through the ornate entrance hall so quickly that Allie was nearly running to keep up by the time they reached the front door. Jo shoved it open impatiently and they both stopped, side by side at the top of the stairs.

'Well,' Allie said, looking up at the innocent blue evening sky. 'It looks perfectly safe to me.'

'I hope it isn't,' Jo said. 'Last one to die loses.'

Laughing, she dashed down the stairs with Allie right behind, and they hurtled onto the empty grass. For a few minutes they danced on the lawn, twirling circles in the freedom of the fresh air.

'Wait,' Allie said breathlessly, reaching for Jo's arm. 'Where are we going?'

They slowed to a more leisurely pace.

'Good question. Some place where Gabe won't find me and drag me back inside like a caveman.' She thought for a moment. 'Have you ever been in the chapel?'

Allie made a face. 'No, but I've raked its grass.'

'Oh yeah. I forgot that detention thing. It's actually pretty cool. There's some ancient poetry on the walls in, like, a million languages. It's super-old.'

The chapel was out in the woods, and Allie glanced in that direction uncertainly—Jo's manic behaviour was starting to worry her.

'Is it safe to go right now?' she asked. 'I mean with all that's been happening?'

'Probably not,' Jo said, smiling wickedly. 'Are you coming or what?'

Without looking back, she headed off across the grass towards the trees.

CHAPTER TEN

The sun glinted off Jo's bright blonde hair as she sped across the lawn, and Allie hesitated for only a moment before speeding after her. As her feet carried her swiftly across the grass, she felt a rush of exhilaration so powerful that she laughed out loud when she caught up with Jo a few seconds later.

'Hurry up!' she shouted as she passed her.

Once they were in the forest, though, the blue sky disappeared, and with it the light. In the shadows, they slowed to a walk and some of Allie's courage left her.

'It's always so dark in here,' she said.

Jo didn't seem concerned. 'Forests are like that. You city girls just don't understand the countryside. There's only one thing to do in spooky forests.' She gave Allie a light, joking shove. 'Run.'

Jo ran ahead down the path with Allie right behind her. The ferns lining the path brushed softly against their ankles. Their laughter echoed hollowly off the trees. But Allie was still jumpy. The sounds of the forest—wind blowing through the trees, a bird call, a twig snapping underfoot— all made her nerves twitch.

Now that she thought about it, this didn't seem like a great idea.

'Maybe we should go back,' she said after a while. 'We could just play a game or . . . something. See what everybody else is doing.'

Jo didn't look back at her when she replied reassuringly. 'We're almost there.'

So, why am I so worried?

A few minutes later, though, Jo turned to smile at her. 'See? We're here already.'

The church wall was just ahead, and in the churchyard—fewer trees and more light. As soon as she walked into that glow Allie felt better, but Jo was already at the door, putting both hands inside the iron ring to lift the latch, and then shoving against it with her shoulder. It gave with a groan and they were inside. In the chapel the fading sunlight was fractured by yellow and red stained glass windows into shards of coloured light, and despite the natural chill from the stone floor and walls, the room seemed warm.

Standing just inside the door, Allie couldn't believe what she was seeing.

'Holy crap,' she whispered.

Jo watched her with a knowing look. 'Good, no?'

Allie tiptoed to the middle of the room and slowly turned in a circle. The walls were covered in paintings. Some were words—most of them obviously poems—others were images. The paint was faded to rusty red, ivory yellow and greying black, but it was clear, and it was easy to imagine how bright it must once have been.

'This one freaks me out.' Jo walked over to the back of the chapel, where a painting of simple figures showed a devil with a pitchfork prodding

140

naked suffering souls into a variety of horrible fates with the help of gleeful troglodyte-like demons.

Allie wrinkled her nose. 'Eeeuw.'

'Exactly. This is nicer.' Jo pointed at a nearby painting of a gnarled yew tree rich with fruit and birds. The roots twisted into the words 'Tree of Life'.

All around the painted images were words in ancient languages. Allie studied the Cyrillic letters of one.

'Do you understand any of it?' she asked Jo.

'A little. Some is Greek.' Jo gestured at a rood screen, then turned to a wall beside it. 'And that's some form of Gaelic. Most of it's Latin though.'

On the wall above the door a phrase was painted in elegant red letters. The colour was bright enough that Allie wondered if it had been restored. She stepped back to see it clearly.

'*Exitus acta probat*?' She sounded the words out and then looked at Jo quizzically. 'Do you know what that means?'

'The result validates the deed,' Jo replied without hesitating.

Allie looked back at the words.

'What's that about?' she mused. 'It seems kind of strange as a "Hey, welcome to church!" quote.'

'Buggered if I know.' Jo was spinning down the aisle in a dizzying dance.

Allie watched her for a moment with a puzzled frown then turned her attention to an elaborate painting of a dragon, whose tail twirled down nearly to the floor as a dove flew just out of reach of its claws.

'This is incredible,' she breathed.

'And now that you've seen it, can we go?' Carter

141

leaned against the door frame—his arms crossed loosely, his eyes watchful.

Allie jumped.

'Carter! Jesus. You scared me.'

But she felt unexpectedly relieved to see him. Jo was weirding her out, and now they could walk back together. Safety in numbers.

Still, she didn't want him to know that.

'You shouldn't sneak up on people,' she said tartly.

His eyes were cool. 'I didn't sneak. I walked. Isn't that how you got here?' When he turned to Jo his voice warmed. 'How's it going, Jo?'

She was at the opposite end of the chapel, pretending to study a painting.

'We're fine here, thanks Carter. You can tell Gabe I don't need his help.' Her voice was steady but she didn't meet his eyes and her jaw had a stubborn set.

He gestured placatingly. 'Hey, I'm not Gabe's minion. It's just about to get dark out there and I thought I might offer you ladies an escort. Why? Is Gabe looking for you?'

Jo gave him a withering look. 'Give it up, Carter. I know he sent you. He always sends somebody to follow me around.'

'Honestly, Jo, Gabe doesn't know I'm here,' he said. 'Have you two had a fight or something?'

Carter's face was so earnest that Allie was inclined to believe him, but Jo moved to the altar, as far away from him as possible.

'Something,' she said coolly.

Pretending she was studying the wall paintings, Allie made her way over to Carter who still stood by the door.

142

Staring intently at a delicate painting of a white rose she whispered, 'How did you find us?'

Just as quietly he replied, 'I followed you.'

Their eyes met and then they glanced away. Allie's skin tingled.

'What's up?' His lips barely moved when he spoke but his head inclined towards Jo.

'I don't know,' she replied. 'It's like she's not . . . her.'

'Whisper whisper whisper!' Jo's angry voice cut through their conversation, and they turned to see her standing at the altar, palms flat on the pulpit, glaring at them. 'Why don't you two just shag and get it over with?'

Allie stared at Jo with her mouth open. She felt like she'd been punched.

What the hell is wrong with her?

But she tried to keep the wounded tone out of her voice. 'Hey, that is so not cool, Jo. Look, it really is getting dark and I'd like to get back. Come with me?'

She held out her hand. Jo studied her for a moment, and then walked across the nave to her.

'Fine. Whatever. Let's go.' Her tone was reasonable and as she took Allie's hand she gave it a squeeze, but Allie had the uneasy sense that something still wasn't quite right. When they got outside the light was fading, and the woods looked darker and more ominous than before.

Jo balanced on her toes on the front step.

'Hey Allie, remember what I said about the only way to go through the scary woods?'

Allie gave her a puzzled look. 'What? Run?'

At that, Jo took off down the path at surprising speed as Carter and Allie stood in front of the church staring after her.

'What the hell?' Carter looked up at the sky like he hoped it held some sort of answer.

'I have no idea what is going on,' Allie said. 'I think she fought with Gabe and now she's just, like, lost it. Big time.'

'Oh great,' he sighed. 'I thought she was done with this stuff.'

Allie shot him a puzzled look. 'What? She's done this before?'

'She used to do her crazy act whenever anything went wrong, but she hasn't done it in a while.' He seemed exasperated. 'Now I've got to go and make sure she gets back to the school or Gabe'll kill me—will you be OK? I'll come back for you if you want.'

'You don't have to come back,' she said. 'I can keep up with you.'

They took off through the gate and at first she matched him step-for-step. But as they ran through the first stretch of darkened woods something occurred to her.

'We left the door open,' she said, slowing to a jog.

'What? At the church?' Carter stopped running. At first he looked doubtful but then he slapped himself on the forehead. 'Damn. You're right. I should go back and close it.'

But he didn't move. He looked ahead towards the school then back at the church as if he couldn't decide what to do.

Seeing his indecision, Allie knew what she had to do.

'I'll go back,' she said. 'I'll close it up. You go and catch up with Jo.'

144

'Are you sure?' he asked doubtfully. 'It's getting dark and it's nearly curfew.'

But Jo was not being rational and she was out there in the dark on her own. And while Allie wasn't thrilled about being in the woods by herself, she knew it was the right thing. But she had a feeling he wasn't going to let her, so she knew she'd have to convince him.

'We'll get in trouble if it's left open,' she pointed out. 'And I really don't think it would be great for Jo to be quizzed by Zelazny right now. Besides, what if a fox gets in and eats Jesus?'

He burst out laughing and for a second all the stress left his face.

'OK,' he said. 'But I'll double back for you as soon as she's inside.'

'Don't worry about me—I'm not afraid of the dark,' she lied. 'It's all good.'

'Thanks, Sheridan.' She could hear the relief in his voice. As he took off for the school, his final words floating back on the breeze. 'I'll come back.'

'Don't!' she shouted after him. He gave no indication that he'd heard.

As soon as he was out of sight, her bravery abandoned her. *I could just leave it open*, she thought looking down the path. *Maybe nobody would know it was us.*

Then she thought about how awful it would be if anything happened to that amazing chapel—what if it rained all night and the Tree of Life was ruined and it was all her fault.

She turned around and headed back through the gloaming to the church.

The pool of golden light that had illuminated the churchyard earlier was gone now, and as Allie walked through the gate, the chapel door loomed open like a leering maw.

Taking a deep breath, she hurried to the door and pushed her weight against it. It didn't move at all until she realised it was held open by a black metal hook that fixed it in place. Even after she'd freed it, though, the door was incredibly heavy. She gave it a good shove and it was closing with a reluctant creak when, just for a split second, she saw something move between the shadows inside.

Allie froze, staring into the darkness. Then, as the door continued to swing shut, she sprang into action, grabbing it and digging in her heels to try and hold it open. But the old door had a mind of its own now and nothing she did would stop it. It shut with a resounding clang that seemed to echo through the trees.

Allie's heart pounded and she stared at the closed door.

Bloody hell, what was that?

A sudden flutter of wings above her head made her jump, but it was only birds flying up into the darkening sky from a nearby tree.

With her hand on the heavy iron ring that served as a door handle, Allie considered her options. Someone was definitely inside—she'd seen them.

Unless it was a trick of the dark.

I should go. Get back to the school, she thought. *I'm just spooked.*

Then she imagined what Carter would have done if he were here. He would have opened that door without hesitating and demanded to know who was in there.

'But he's a psycho,' she muttered unconvincingly. It didn't really matter, of course. She already knew

146

what she was going to do.

She turned the ring.

Yanking the door open with effort, she leaned inside without actually stepping through the door.

'Hello?' she called. The room was so dark now that she could barely make out the drawings on the wall. 'Is anybody there?'

The only sound she heard was her own voice echoing back at her. But the silence that followed had a weight to it, as silences always do in ancient buildings, and she felt goosebumps rise on her shoulders. She was just about to step inside when she heard quick footsteps cross the churchyard behind her.

Spinning around, Allie crouched down as if to avoid a blow . . . there was nobody there.

There was no sound but the wind blowing in the trees.

Squinting, she peered into the thicket around the church. Every sound made her jump.

You know what? Fuck this.

Using all her strength, she shoved the door to. As the latch was still clanging shut she ran to the churchyard gate, slamming it behind her with a careless bang. Looking neither right nor left she ran down the path, speeding up as her muscles loosened until she was hurtling through the forest. But as she sped around a curve in the dark, she skidded on a stone and went sprawling, hitting the ground with such force that the breath was knocked out of her and she gasped for air, clutching her sides.

As her breathing steadied, she picked gravel out of a scrape on the palm of her hand while building up the courage to look at her knee. Blood oozed from a shallow wound and ran down her leg. She hoped it looked worse than it was.

Air hissing through her teeth, she pulled herself to her feet and experimented to see if her leg could hold her weight. It hurt, but it worked, and she limped down the path, cursing under her breath.

The path seemed endless, now. After what felt like hours, she stopped to rest her leg. It hadn't taken nearly this long to get to the chapel, had it? Had she taken a wrong turn?

A rustling noise in the trees stopped her fretful thoughts. She held her breath and listened.

'Carter?' she asked, tentatively.

After a second, she heard it again, but now it seemed to be on the other side of the path. Allie spun around to face it, squinting as she tried to see through the trees.

'Hello?' Her voice shook slightly; she tried to steady it. 'Who's there?'

Silence.

'If this is some sort of a joke, it's not funny,' she shouted into the dark.

After a moment, she hurried down the path, limping as quickly as she could.

. . . twenty-five steps, twenty-six, twenty-seven . . .

The sharp crack of a breaking twig behind her made her jump. She froze in her tracks. *That rustling sound again. But closer. Much closer.*

Now, ignoring the pain, she ran down the path, jumping over roots, feeling rocks skitter under her feet but keeping her balance. Her fists pumped the air beside her.

After a minute she turned to look over her shoulder—the path was empty. But when she turned back to the front, someone was standing right in front of her.

She screamed and skidded but Sylvain's hands caught her and pulled her close.

'Hey . . . hey!' He looked at her with concern. 'Are you OK? You're bleeding. What happened?'

Her words came out in broken phrases as she panted. 'There was . . . somebody . . . the church . . . in woods.' Her voice was breathless and frightened.

His hands tightened on her arms. 'Did someone hurt you?'

Allie shook her head. 'No . . . fell. But . . . could . . . hear someone . . . nearby. I think he was watching me. I heard him breathing.'

'You're shaking.' Sylvain pulled her into a hug. 'Come on, let's get out of here.' With his arm supporting her, she hobbled towards the school.

They both heard the footsteps at the same time.

'Do you hear that?' Allie whispered.

Sylvain nodded and looked in the direction of the sound, pushing Allie behind him. She peered over his shoulder as Carter stepped out of the woods. His face darkened when he saw Sylvain.

'I didn't know you were here.' Carter's voice was cold, and he looked at Allie. 'What's wrong? Are you OK?'

Stepping out from behind Sylvain, she nodded, feeling like an idiot. 'I fell. And I could hear something moving in the woods.'

'Must have been me. I took a shortcut. Or it could have been Ruth—I sent her back to get you.' Turning to Sylvain he said, 'We should get her back. Do you want me to take her?'

Sylvain considered this, then shook his head. 'No, it's fine. I'll take her. You have work to do. Make sure there's nothing out there.'

149

Allie could sense Carter's reluctance, but then Sylvain pulled on her arm and she walked with him.

Her leg hurt much more now and walking was increasingly painful. She said nothing, but when a tear trickled down her cheek Sylvain noticed.

'Is it your leg?' he asked, brushing the tear away.

'I'm sorry,' she said. 'I'm being a baby.'

'Don't be ridiculous,' he said, and without another word he scooped her up off her feet and carried her down the path.

'You can't carry me—I'm too heavy,' she protested.

'You weigh only as much as a girl,' he said. 'Put your arms around my neck.'

She did as he said. Now that she was off her leg the pain had lessened. *He's strong*, she thought, noticing that he wasn't breathing heavily from the exertion. After a second, she rested her head on his shoulder and enjoyed the oddly weightless sensation of being carried for the first time since she was a child.

They had been closer to the building than she knew, so it was only a few minutes before he was climbing the stairs. Someone opened the door for them and she lifted her head to see Zelazny standing in the lighted entry hall.

'What happened?' he barked.

'She fell in the dark,' Sylvain answered for her.

'Of course it was dark. It's after curfew,' Zelazny said pointedly.

'She fell before curfew,' Sylvain said protectively, and Allie tightened her arms on his neck.

'Take her to the nurse,' Zelazny said with obvious poor humour. 'Somebody else fell earlier—she's in the dining hall with them now. Join the queue.'

As he walked off she could hear him mutter, 'Ruddy clumsiness if you ask me . . .'

'I don't need a nurse,' Allie said, but Sylvain ignored her, taking her straight to the dining hall.

The nurse, who wore white scrubs with the Cimmeria logo, was wrapping the sprained wrist of a girl Allie didn't recognise as Sylvain set Allie down in a chair. ('Night tennis gone wrong,' the girl sighed when she left, her arm in a splint.)

Tutting at Allie's knee, the nurse cleaned the wound with an antiseptic liquid that stung so much Allie tried to get up and leave (Sylvain wouldn't let her), and then applied an ointment and bandages so gently she barely felt them at all.

Sylvain stood beside her the whole time, one hand resting on her shoulder.

'Don't run any marathons in the next few days, love,' the nurse chirped as Allie and Sylvain walked out the door, 'and you'll be right as rain in a few days.'

Allie thought it must be well after curfew by now—the halls were quiet as Sylvain helped her up the stairs to the girls' dorm.

'Do you want me to walk you to your door?' he asked when they reached the top, his sexy smile turning the helpful offer into something slightly more lascivious.

'I think I can make it from here,' Allie laughed. 'But thanks for rescuing me. Again. This is getting to be a thing with us.'

As she turned to go, he grabbed her hand and pulled her back. Before she had time to react he leaned down and kissed her. It was a long, deep kiss. When it ended, Allie stared at him, breathing heavily.

'You're welcome,' he whispered.

Surprised, Allie stepped backward too fast, stumbling over her own feet and colliding with the wall behind her. Colour flooded her cheeks as she righted herself.

'I . . . so . . . thanks . . . Well, good night.'

She could see Sylvain was trying not to smile as she turned to limp down the hallway.

CHAPTER ELEVEN

'So . . . what happened last night?'

It was Saturday morning. Allie sat in the quiet common room on the opposite end of a deep leather sofa from Jo. Each wore the same dark blue knee-length shorts and white, short-sleeved shirt, and each held a white mug of tea absentmindedly in her right hand.

They'd headed here together just after breakfast, where Gabe had not joined them.

Jo's clear blue eyes evaded capture, flitting around the room anxiously before finally coming to rest on Allie. 'Gabe can be a bit . . . controlling.' On the last word her voice was so low Allie leaned in to hear it. After a pause, Jo's left hand waved the thought away. 'And I hate that. Sometimes.'

She paused and Allie waited.

'So.' Jo sighed. 'Yesterday he was just acting a bit too much like my dad. Do this, don't do that. Don't question me. And if he thinks he can get away with that he's wrong. And . . . well, now we're not speaking. He was in the common room when

152

Carter and I came in . . .'

She interrupted herself, shooting Allie a worried look. 'By the way, Carter went back and got you, right?'

Allie nodded. 'That's a story too, but let's talk about this first.'

Jo sipped her tea. 'Gabe was there, and he was just so up himself. It was all the "I told you not to go out . . . You should've listened" bollocks that makes me just . . .' She balled up her right fist and shook it. 'So I told him what he could do with his advice and went to bed. Haven't seen him since. I hope you weren't too freaked out last night. I really didn't think Carter would leave you alone. That must have been a bit scary—you've never been out there at night alone.'

Allie felt a brief desire to blame Jo for her wounded leg, but shoved it back. 'It was fine. We were worried about you. I . . . wanted him to go.'

Jo set her cup down on the table and drew her legs up, wrapping her arms around her knees. 'So what happened after I took off? Were you OK? Carter was totally worried about you and really cross with me for making him leave you alone.'

'Was he?' Allie was surprised to hear it—he'd seemed so irritated when he'd come back for her. 'He did come back. But by then I'd run into Sylvain on the path. And the weirdest thing happened, Jo.'

Allie turned on the sofa so she was facing Jo, and crossed her legs. She lowered her voice to a near-whisper. 'Sylvain kind of ordered Carter away. He was like, "Go get back to work." What's that about? I could tell Carter didn't want to do it, but he did it anyway.'

Jo rolled her eyes. 'It's just some Night School

153

bollocks—Sylvain outranks him, I guess.'

Allie slid down the sofa so that her head rested on the back of it and her legs stretched out towards the table, revealing the clean white bandage.

'Oh babe, what happened to your knee?'

Allie smiled ruefully. 'I fell down on the path last night. Like a total klutz.' She held up her left hand to show the scrape on the palms. 'Scarred for life.'

'Oh God, it's all my fault. I'm so sorry I had a complete flakeout, Allie. Now Gabe's pissed off and you're wounded. Jesus. I'm such a mess.' She looked genuinely contrite.

'Don't be silly,' Allie said. 'It's nothing. It barely hurts.' Then she gasped and buried her face in her hands. 'Oh God. I can't believe I haven't told you yet. Sylvain kissed me.'

'He did?' Jo sat up straighter. 'When? And wherewhyhow?'

Her face still in her hands, Allie's voice was muffled. 'And he carried me down the path when my leg hurt.'

'Oh my God—he so fancies you,' Jo sighed. 'That's the most heroic thing ever. Tell me about the kissing.'

Allie peeked over her fingertips as she told her what happened.

'And it wasn't one of those friendly-on-the-cheek things either,' she concluded. 'It was a proper kiss. With tongues.'

Jo gave her a joking shove. 'So? Was it nice?'

'Yeah, I suppose.' Allie sank down further into the cushions, her cheeks bright red. 'OK. Yes. It was definitely very nice.'

'And don't you have some sort of date thing tonight?' Jo nudged her again as Allie nodded.

'Come to my room after and tell me *everything*,' Jo said.

Then she sat up straighter. 'Hey, that reminds me, the summer ball is in three weeks. Sylvain will probably ask you to go with him tonight! What will you wear? Tell me now.'

She was so irrepressible, Allie had to laugh at her. 'God, you're like a child. I don't know anything about this ball thing. What are you going to wear?'

'I bought the dress on my last trip home.' Jo brightened visibly as she described the slim-cut silver sequined minidress and matching sandals she'd found in a boutique in Bond Street.

She gave Allie an appraising look. 'Have you got a dress?'

Allie squirmed a bit. 'Well . . . not exactly. There are a couple in my wardrobe, and one vintage dress that I love. But I don't know what I'll do for sho . . .'

'You'll come to my room!' Jo interrupted her delightedly. 'I have—God I don't know—a million pairs of shoes. Problem solved.' She grabbed Allie's hand. 'We can do the whole girls-getting-ready-together thing. We'll do each other's hair and makeup. We'll be gorgeous.'

Allie hesitated, then confessed, 'Look, I've never been to a dance before. Not a real one. I mean, my schools just kind of didn't do that sort of thing.'

Jo waved her worries away. 'You'll love it. It's old-fashioned, but not . . . you know, stuffy. Everybody looks beautiful. Even the teachers. You wouldn't believe how some of them scrub up. It's really cool. When Sylvain asks you have to say yes.'

Allie, was now nearly flat on the sofa. 'But what will I do if he doesn't ask?'

155

They both sat in silence for a moment, pondering the true horror of potential datelessness.

'I could always go with Zelazny,' Allie said finally. 'He seems nice.'

They both dissolved into laughter.

*   *   *

That night as supper ended, Allie sat in the dining room with Ruth, Lisa and Lucas. Gabe had come to the table to get Jo a few minutes before and they'd all exchanged knowing glances as the two walked away. ('Massive make-up snogging session ahead,' Lisa predicted.)

'I think we should go outside,' Ruth said. 'It's hot in here and it's such a lovely night. We'll stay close to the building. We could just sit on the grass and talk.'

Lucas looked doubtful. He opened his mouth but the voice from behind Allie came first.

'I agree. It's a good night for croquet, don't you think?' Allie turned around to see Sylvain standing behind her.

Lucas looked at him and raised his eyebrow; Sylvain nodded very slightly. Lucas shrugged. 'OK then. Let's go.'

When Allie stood up Sylvain reached for her hand and they walked out side by side. He leaned towards her. 'I think you'll like it. Croquet seems boring during the day but at night it's much better.'

His breath tickled her ear and she shivered deliciously. She smiled up at him, then she raced forward coltishly, pulling his hand. 'Come on then. Don't dilly-dally.'

He laughed and ran with her. Outside, the

others were pulling supplies out of a small storage room near the front door. They all helped to put the wicket hoops in the turf. 'We need a sixth,' Lucas pointed out.

'I'll go and get Phil,' Ruth said, hurrying back inside.

Allie saw that Lisa was blushing—she was obviously happy to be Lucas' partner, but he hadn't noticed yet. Sylvain interrupted her reverie.

'While we are waiting for Phil, there is something I need to do.' His tone was businesslike, and he turned to Allie. 'Will you come and help me?'

'Sure.'

He glanced at the other two. 'We'll be right back.'

Taking her by the hand he pulled her around the side of the building so quickly she had to run to keep up. When they rounded the corner he stopped.

She looked around puzzledly. 'Where are we go—'

Without warning, he pushed her up against the stone wall and kissed her hard. In an instant, surprise turned to desire and she wrapped her arms tightly around his neck and kissed him back. He was, she thought, very good at this—she had never kissed anybody like this in her life and she didn't want it to end.

When he stopped, they were both panting, and looking into each other's eyes.

'I'm sorry. I couldn't wait one more minute,' he said breathing heavily, his blue eyes holding hers.

'Do it again,' Allie said, pulling insistently on his shoulders.

He smiled. 'If you insist.'

The second kiss was longer, and if possible, more passionate, as his lips travelled down her neck and his hands tightened on her hips.

'We should go and join the others,' he whispered regretfully after a few minutes, his breath warm against her throat. He brushed her swollen lips lightly with his thumb. 'Although I hate to say it. They'll be wondering where we are.'

'Stupid them,' Allie whispered.

He smiled and stepped back from her, although he still held her hand. 'Now we shall enjoy the croquet.'

'Yay,' Allie said weakly. 'Croquet.'

As they walked back around the corner she could see that everyone had been waiting for them, including Carter, who was talking to Lucas. His eyes told her that he knew exactly what they'd been doing.

'Allie! Sylvain,' his tone was mocking. 'This is great. What have you been up to?'

Surprised by his aggression, Allie flushed with anger. She thought they'd had a moment out in the woods when they understood each other and maybe they could be friends.

But now Carter seemed worse than ever.

Sylvain pulled her closer. 'Unfortunately, Carter, our teams are set already. We do not need another player.'

'I didn't come to *play*.' Carter put the emphasis on the last word. 'I came to see how Allie was doing after her fall last night.'

Allie could feel everyone's eyes on her. 'I . . . I'm fine, Carter. Thanks.' She faltered under his gaze which seemed to challenge her, as if she'd done something stupid.

'That's great. You do seem *much* recovered.' His words dripped sarcasm. 'Did you hurt your lips too? Or is that from something else?'

Allie's hand flew up to cover her mouth, as Sylvain took several steps forward.

'Why are you still here, Carter?' he asked icily.

Carter stared at him, unflinching. 'I just wanted to see if what I suspected was true.'

'Have you seen all you need to see?' Sylvain's voice was low and menacing.

'Hey, everybody,' Ruth stepped between them. 'Come on. Stay calm. Let's not get into something here.'

Carter ignored her. 'Oh, I've seen enough, Sylvain. You know what I'm going to say, right?'

Ruth sighed and stepped out of the way. They were now standing no more than a foot apart, glaring at each other. Allie wrapped her arms around herself.

'I have no idea what you're going to say, Carter,' Sylvain said.

'Leave Allie alone.' Carter took another step, bringing him just inches away from Sylvain. 'You know this is wrong.'

Sylvain smiled pleasantly. 'Thanks for your advice, Carter. Now I suggest you leave us alone to play our game.'

They stood glaring at each other for another moment, then Carter turned to Allie. 'Don't believe anything he tells you. He's a liar.'

Although she was thoroughly confused, Allie raised her chin defiantly. 'I don't need advice from you, Carter. I make my own decisions.'

She saw anger in his eyes, but without another

word he stormed off into the woods.

Allie's hands were shaking. *What is wrong with him?*

'Well, that was unpleasant,' Sylvain said, swinging a mallet casually. 'Shall we get on with the game? Allie, should we be blue?' Allie nodded mutely, her head still ringing with Carter's warning.

When she had a second she grabbed Sylvain's arm. 'What was Carter talking about?' she whispered.

He brushed her hair back from her forehead. 'I think he fancies you, *ma belle*. Perhaps he is jealous.'

As he walked off to take his shot she frowned. *Maybe he was trying to scare me away from Sylvain.* But, given how he talked to her, it was hard to believe Carter fancied her at all.

She couldn't imagine the evening being anything other than miserable after that, but in the end, it had been kind of fun. The hoops were treated with light-absorbing paint, which meant that, the darker it became, the more they glowed. The mallets had LED lights that you activated by clicking a button on the handle. The balls glowed whatever colour they were painted. This made the lawn gradually more colourful as darkness fell. In the end, they could hardly see one another, but they could follow each other's movements through the lighted mallets and rolling coloured balls.

Ruth was very good, and showed Allie techniques to keep the ball moving in a straight line. When Allie managed to knock one of Phil's balls off the playing area, Ruth laughed.

'I've taught you too well!'

By the time the game was over and they began

putting the equipment away, Allie found that she was laughing with Ruth and leaning comfortably against Sylvain, who had draped his arm casually across her shoulders. He caught her eye and she felt a tingling sensation of anticipation.

'You have the most beautiful eyes,' he said. 'They are translucent, like your soul.'

Turning, he said good night to the others and whispered in her ear: 'Walk with me?'

She nodded eagerly, her throat tightening.

They walked through the dusk around the back of the school. Near the back door he stopped and pulled her into his arms. He spoke softly, 'I've had a lovely evening, Allie. I'm glad Carter didn't upset you too much. He just wants you for himself.'

While Allie doubted his assessment she didn't let it show on her face. She smiled at him. 'I had a good time too.'

And she had, despite everything.

Then he pulled her close and nuzzled her neck before lifting his mouth to hers, and Allie felt all her concerns melt away. He could do the most amazing things with his lips. Her heart pounded and her breath came in short gasps as he kissed her ears, licking her earlobes delicately. Reaching her arms up, she twisted her wrists behind his head.

When Zelazny shouted 'Curfew!' from the back door a few minutes later, Sylvain lifted his head regretfully.

Allie wasn't ready for him to stop. 'Do it again,' she insisted.

He smiled, his hands warm on her waist. 'It's curfew. We have to get inside.'

'One more time?'

Tantalisingly he leaned over. She lifted her face

and parted her lips in anticipation, but he pecked her quickly on the cheek. 'Inside, young lady, before you get detention.'

'Curfew!' Zelazny shouted again. 'Last call!'

Sylvain draped his arm possessively over her shoulders. As they joined the crowd at the door they passed Katie and Jules. When Allie saw the venom in Katie's expression she smiled at her beatifically.

Allie: one, Katie: nil.

CHAPTER TWELVE

When Allie went down to breakfast the next morning, Jo was waiting impatiently outside the dining hall.

'How was it?' she asked without preamble, following Allie in. 'Tell me everything.'

As she piled scrambled eggs and toast on her plate, Allie laughed at her. 'You're so nosy.'

'He kissed you again, didn't he?' Jo said. When Allie nodded she squealed. 'He so fancies the pants off of you. Did he ask you to the ball?'

'Nope,' Allie said. 'So maybe he just likes kissing me.'

'He *will* ask you,' Jo said confidently as they walked to their usual table.

'Carter was totally weird last night, though.' Allie told her what had happened, and Jo frowned.

'That is . . . bizarre,' Jo said. 'Do you think he's jealous?'

'No way.' Allie was firm. 'He hates me. The way he acted last night . . . it was like I repulsed him.

And I don't know what was going on between the two of them but it was seriously intense. I thought for a second they'd get into a fight.'

'Carter wouldn't dare,' Jo said. 'He'd be in unbelievable amounts of trouble if he did. Anyway, who cares? Sylvain fancies you! And he's so going to ask you to the dance.'

*   *   *

Throughout the week the ball was the only subject of conversation—who was going with whom, what they would wear, how everyone was allowed champagne and there was no curfew at all.

Sylvain was involved in a major project, so Allie rarely saw him. But the way he looked at her each time they saw each other made it clear that Saturday night was not an aberration. He couldn't keep his hands off her. When they passed in the hallway he would pull her into a hug, or run his fingers down her arm. Every time the encounter left her slightly breathless, and hungry for more.

But he still hadn't asked her to the dance.

At the same time, Carter completely blanked her. Whenever she saw him he looked over her head. In class, their eyes never met. He treated her like she didn't exist, and by Friday, Allie was determined to find out what was really going on. She just wasn't sure how to do that.

After class that afternoon, she ran to the library in hopes of finding an obscure book of poetry for Isabelle's English class. When she pushed the door open it slammed into someone heading the other way.

'Sorry,' she said, then stopped. Carter glowered

at her in the doorway.

When he started to walk by her without saying another word, she'd had enough. 'Hey!' she whispered sharply. 'What's wrong with you?'

'Nothing.' His voice was distant.

'Oh really?' she said. 'Then why are you so broken?' Shoving her way past, she walked into the library. She heard the door close behind her. Then he grabbed her arm and turned her to face him.

'You do not get to call me broken,' he hissed in a stage whisper.

She could see how angry he was but she couldn't have cared less. 'I can call you whatever I want, Carter,' she said, shaking his hand off her arm. 'And the way you've been acting lately is not normal. It's totally lame.'

'What is normal, Allie?' he whispered angrily. 'Define normal for me. Is Sylvain normal, for example?'

She felt a chill run down her spine. 'What kind of question is that? What's he got to do with the way you treat me?'

'Nothing,' he said, but his eyes said differently. His dark brows were lowered, and she could sense the tension coiled within him before he spoke again. '*Everything*. How can you be so stupid? I thought you were clever, but you're just another stupid girl. You don't know the first thing about him, or about this school, and yet you'll make a public spectacle of yourself snogging him.'

Her eyes widened. 'I'm not—'

'Not what?' he interrupted her. 'Not falling for Sylvain's well practised lines? Really? Because to me it looked like you are.'

He was so angry that she felt panic rising as

she tried to reason with him. 'Carter, I don't understand—so I'm seeing Sylvain now. So what? Why do you care? You hate me anyway.'

He stood so close to her that she could feel his breath on her cheek. He smelled of spice and coffee. 'You think I hate you?' Those deep, dark eyes held hers. 'I don't. I just thought you were smart.'

When she opened her mouth to argue he put his finger lightly over her lips. Her eyes held his for a long second. She could taste the salt of his skin on her tongue. Then he swore under his breath, turned on his heel and walked away.

*　　　　*　　　　*

'The question of the day, Allie, is should you wear your hair up or down?' Holding a wide-tooth comb, Jo studied Allie's head intently. It was Saturday morning and they were in Jo's room. Allie sat in front of a mirror. They were surrounded by the gowns from Allie's wardrobe and shoes from Jo's limitless supply. Jo had insisted that they needed to 'practise'.

Allie twisted a strand of hair around her finger and then released it. 'Does it matter? The dance is in two weeks and Sylvain still hasn't asked me to go with him. I might as well dye my hair green and shave it into a mohawk.'

Jo held one pair of shoes up to a dress, considered it, and then tried another pair. 'Sylvain is going to ask you to go with him,' she said. 'I have it on the best authority.'

Allie looked at her hopefully. 'Really?'

'Really.' Jo pointed a kitten heel at her

accusingly. 'So get serious. Hair up or down?'

'Um . . . I don't know.' She picked up a brush and ran it through her hair. 'So . . . who's Lucas going with?'

'Lisa of course.' Jo's voice was muffled as she pulled out another pair of delicate shoes.

'And Carter?'

'I hear he's asked Clare.' Jo set down the shoes. 'I think up would be best.'

'Up is fine. Who's Clare?'

'Small, blonde, pretty. In our biology class. Third row over. I think she's in English with you too. He pulled her last year and then dumped her. Everyone was furious with him, because she's so sweet. Seems like they're getting back together.'

Allie studied herself in the mirror. *Why should I care who Carter goes with?*

She pulled her hair up with her hands. 'What a complete bastard. Yes, I think you're right. Up could work.'

Jo smiled. 'Excellent. Once we choose a dress I'll know what to do with it.' She spread the three dresses out on the bed and studied them critically. 'Right. Strip and try them on. Today we decide.'

The first dress Allie tried was black and fitted. It brushed her ankles, had a high neck in the front and was backless. It was incredibly sophisticated.

'Lovely,' Jo said, studying the line of the dress. 'But it's a bit too old for you.'

'Totally. I look, like, thirty.' Allie pulled it over her head, dumping it back on the bed. The next dress was white, with a long straight skirt and spaghetti straps.

'Gorgeous!' Jo pronounced. 'Summery. Virginal.'

Allie wrinkled her nose, then twirled in front of

Jo's mirror. 'It's a bit clingy,' she said doubtfully. The dress hugged every curve, leaving little to the imagination.

'But you pull it off,' Jo said. 'It looks amazing with your colouring, and I have the perfect shoes for it.'

The last dress was Allie's favourite. Dark blue silk and knee-length, it had a full skirt with a built-in organza petticoat. Its low beaded V-neck plunged just far enough in the front, and the back was high. The sleeves were tight and ended just below her elbow. It fit like a glove.

When Allie pulled up the side zipper and turned around, Jo gasped dramatically, her hand to her heart. 'You look *amazing*. That is a dress you should wear every single day of your life. Except at the summer ball.'

'Why not?'

'It's a winter dress. Everybody else will be in light summer frocks and you'll be sweating in heavy silk. Save it for the winter ball. It's much more important than the summer ball anyway. Hide this dress away until then, though. This will be what you wear the night you blow everybody away.'

Jo seemed so certain Allie couldn't see the point in arguing with her. She knew little enough about clothes, having always been a jeans-and-trainers kind of girl. On the rare occasions when she'd dressed up for weddings her mother had chosen her outfits. But she had to admit the white dress suited her.

Jo held up a pair of silver sandals with low heels. 'What do you think? Are they perfect or are they perfect?' she asked, beaming proudly.

Holding her hands up in surrender, Allie

laughed. 'I guess they're perfect.'

'Now, for your hair . . .'

Jo led her back to the chair and sat her down. She ran a comb through the thick waves of her hair and pulled it up into a loose ponytail. With no access to the henna she'd used at home to colour it bright shades of red, Allie's hair was gradually fading to its natural dark brown.

Jo worked in silence for a while, but Allie could see she was thinking. After a moment she said, 'So, why do you care who Carter takes to the ball?'

Allie squirmed uncomfortably. 'I don't really care . . . I just wondered. How do you know for certain that Sylvain's going to ask me?'

Jo twisted a strand of her hair into a glossy loop and pinned it into place. 'A little bird told me. A very knowledgeable bird.'

'I wish he'd get on with it,' Allie muttered, watching her hair take stylish shape. 'Everybody else already has a date.'

'There.' Jo stepped back and smiled at her in the mirror, obviously pleased. 'Sylvain would be lucky to have you.'

Allie's usually unruly hair looked sleek and shiny, loosely twisted with white silk ribbon into a chignon. A few curly strands framed her oval face, drawing attention to her grey eyes.

'That's amazing,' Allie breathed, looking at herself in astonishment.

'That's how you'll wear your hair,' Jo said, adding modestly, 'if you like it.'

Allie hugged her. 'I love it. Where did you learn to do all this stuff?'

'Girl school,' Jo said blithely as she gathered up shoes from the floor. 'Which I think you're now enrolled in, too.'

Allie was quiet for so long that Jo, who was busy putting shoes away, stopped and looked at her worriedly. 'Are you OK? I didn't mean anything by that.'

Allie smiled at her. 'I'm fine, don't worry. It's just that I had the weirdest thought.'

'What's that?' Jo had returned to organising her shoes.

'Even with everything that's going—even with Carter being an arse, and Sylvain not asking me, and classes being super-hard—with all that, I think I'm sort of . . . happy.'

'That's because you're crazy.' Jo laughed.

'No, I mean it. I'm really happy. For the first time in a long time. You know, I thought I'd hate this place. I was ready to hate it. And the old me would have hated thinking about dresses and dances and shoes and having my hair done and worrying about how I look. But I don't hate it. I . . . kind of like it.'

Kneeling by the wardrobe arranging shoes, Jo looked up at her. 'And that's a good thing, right?'

'Yeah,' Allie said, thoughtfully. 'I guess it is.'

*　　　*　　　*

An hour or so later, Allie carried the dresses back to her room, and tucked them away in the wardrobe. She fixed her hair back into a ponytail, carefully saving the ribbons in the top drawer of her desk. Glancing at the clock she dashed out— only twenty minutes left before they closed the dining room after lunch.

'Hey Allie.' At the sound of the voice behind

her she turned to see Jules walking in the same direction.

Great. Just what I need right now.

'Oh. Hi Jules.'

As ever, Jules' blunt-cut blonde hair was perfectly smooth and she wore her cute pink Birkenstocks. Allie thought again how unfair it was that she got to wear her own shoes.

'I was just wondering,' Jules said, 'are you going to the ball? You really should. I know you're new, but it's an experience you really won't want to miss. You don't have to have a date.'

Allie bristled a bit at the last line. 'Yes, I'm planning on going,' she said.

'Oh great! You know, you might never be here for summer school again, so it would be such a shame not to see the summer ball.'

Allie frowned. 'Why would I never be here for summer school again?'

Jules looked puzzled. 'Oh, I didn't mean anything by it. It's just that, you know, it's usually only for the top students. I understand that you're here for . . . other reasons.'

Allie felt as if she'd been punched. 'What do you mean? What reasons?'

'Oh, didn't you know?' Jules looked increasingly uncomfortable. 'Isabelle made special arrangements for this one term. After that, I assume you'll join the other . . . you know, regular students.'

Allie straightened her shoulders and took a step forward. 'What are you trying to say, Jules? That I don't belong here?'

'Oh, of course not!' Jules took a hurried step back. 'I hope I haven't off . . .'

170

'Offended me? Yes, Jules, you've offended me.'
She turned and ran down the hallway, her fists
clenched so tightly her nails dug crescent moons
into her palms.

At the foot of the stairs she turned and skidded
around the corner nearly colliding with Sylvain,
who caught her easily.

'Don't you ever just walk anywhere?' he laughed,
holding her up.

'Only when appropriate,' she said, her voice
more brusque than she meant it to be. She took a
deep breath and tried to calm down.

'What's the matter?' He studied her face with
concerned eyes. 'Is everything OK?'

She shrugged. 'I just ran into Jules. It's . . . Oh,
it's not worth going into. She's just a bitch.'

He looked amused. 'Oh, she can be rather . . .
difficult. But I wouldn't take her too seriously. She
means well.'

He had this way of smiling with his eyes that she
simply couldn't resist, and after a second she smiled
back. 'You're right. I shouldn't let her get to me.'

'I've been hoping to run into you, to be honest.'
He leaned against the wall, and taking her hand,
pulled her closer to him so that their conversation
felt more intimate.

He's so cool. How does he do *that?*

'I wanted to ask if you have a date for the ball
yet.'

Allie felt her cheeks go red as her heart began to
pound. *I must look as calm as possible.*

She shook her head. 'No, not yet.'

His eyes still held hers. 'I was hoping you'd agree
to go with me.'

Go to the ball? I want to fall in love and marry

171

you. Have babies, buy a house, live in France . . .

'That would be great,' she said calmly.

'Fantastic. I cannot wait.' He gave her a sleepy, sexy smile.

They stood for a moment as if loath to leave each other, then he lifted her hand, kissed it lightly and let it go. 'You'd better go and have lunch before they close up.'

She nodded. 'See you later.'

'*À bientôt.*'

Allie floated into the dining room on a cloud of happiness and almost didn't see Jo waving at her from their usual table. She was eating a green salad as Allie walked up.

'Nothing but salad for me until the ball or I won't fit into that dress—what happened?' Jo moved so quickly from the statement to the question and Allie was so drunk on romance that for a second she just stared at her.

'You look like something happened. Tell me— what happened?' Jo demanded.

Allie smiled dreamily. 'Sylvain asked me.'

Leaping from her seat Jo screamed and danced around the table, pulling Allie into a hug. 'I knew it! Didn't I say? I'm, like, omniscient.'

'You are a genius,' Allie laughed. 'And I guess I better have salad too, if I'm going to wear that white dress.'

Back in her own seat, Jo passed her the salad bowl. 'This is going to be the best summer ball ever.'

But as Allie served leaves onto her plate, she looked up to see Carter staring at her furiously from a nearby table. When he realised she'd seen him he stood up and stalked from the room.

CHAPTER THIRTEEN

The two weeks until the dance seemed to last months, and Allie felt that the entire school was in a state of suspended animation. Classes dragged. Teachers refused to give in to student apathy and distraction so coursework piled up, but, for the first time, the library was largely empty in the evening.

'If I get behind this week . . . so be it,' Jo pronounced, the drama of her statement somewhat undermined by the fact that she was sitting on her bed and waving a tiara. 'I'll catch up next week.'

'Hear hear!' Allie was lying on her stomach on the floor, flipping through a beauty magazine and contemplating hairstyles. 'Maybe I should get my hair cut short?' She held up a picture of a pixie-ish model.

Jo tilted the tiara in her direction. 'A new haircut lifts your spirits, young Allie. Never forget that. But that's too short for your face shape, FYI.'

Allie turned the page. 'Wise words, Josephine. Wise words.'

Back in her room, the white dress hung tantalisingly from Allie's wardrobe door, with Jo's shoes arranged neatly on the floor beneath it. Every morning when she woke up that was the first thing she saw, and each night she ticked another day off a mental calendar.

While Allie was trying to keep up with her classwork, she was finding it nearly impossible to concentrate. So a few days before the ball, when she found herself reading the same paragraph in her history book for the fifth time, she gave up on the entire enterprise. Standing up from her desk she stretched, then stood looking out the window at the sunshine.

I've got to move.

She pulled on her running clothes and gathered her hair into a ponytail. As she slipped down the stairs she passed only one other student and on the landing, when she leaned over to look down at the main floor, she could see nobody at all. Outside, the sun beat down on the soft green grass. From the front steps she could see a number of bodies baking on towels and blankets spread out on the lawn, but she never could understand the attraction of just lying in the sun. Instead, she struck out for the summerhouse, jogging at a brisk pace. Movement had always helped to calm her down, and now she threw herself into it, running faster down the footpath. She counted each footstep quietly under her breath.

'Two hundred and ninety-six. Two hundred and ninety—'

'Why do you do that?'

The voice seemed to come from nowhere, and it startled Allie so much that she tripped and nearly fell down, and had to grab a tree branch for support.

Carter stood on the edge of the path, his hands on his hips. Panting, she bent over to rest her hands on her knees while she caught her breath.

When she stood up, she tossed her ponytail over her shoulder. 'What? You're speaking to me now, Carter? I'm honoured.'

Ever since their altercation in the library Carter had avoided her, and she'd been happy to let him.

He acted as if she hadn't spoken. 'That counting

174

thing. I've heard you do it before. Why do you do that?'

'It's none of your bloody business, you stalker. Now get lost.'

Turning back down the path she took off running again, but he easily matched her stride.

'It was a simple question.'

Allie gave a frustrated squeak and sped up, anger propelling her. But he didn't fall behind, and finally she shouted at him in short bursts.

'You don't. Ignore somebody. For weeks. And then. Ask them. Personal questions. You. Arsehole.'

'Temper.'

'Whatever.'

Silence fell as she concentrated on not speaking to him.

'Allie, don't trust Sylvain.'

'I'm ignoring you.'

'I can't go into why. But he's not who you think he is.'

She slowed down and glared at him. 'What's that supposed to mean?'

He started to speak, then stopped. Shaking her head in disgust she ran away down the path—after a while she couldn't hear his footsteps behind her any more.

When the summerhouse roof appeared above the trees, even through her rage, Allie gasped. She hadn't been able to really see it properly that night in the rain. It was beautiful—a fanciful construction, with a narrow, pointed roof rising twenty-five feet high, covered in brightly coloured Moorish tiles in an intricate design.

Six delicately carved pillars supported the vivid

roof. She climbed up the steps into the shady, open air interior, where a stone banister and benches circled the edges. Sitting down on the cool seat she rested her chin on her arm as she looked out into the woods. Carter was nowhere to be seen.

What was he going on about? Was it just jealousy? Or was he serious?

He sounded serious.

She tried to think of anything Sylvain had done to make her doubt him. He'd always been there for her when she was in trouble. He'd protected her from Zelazny. Yes, he was slick, and yes, apparently he was super-rich, but he didn't act like a snob. He seemed kind. Carter on the other hand had been difficult, pushy, judgmental and threatening.

It was obvious who she should trust.

I just don't understand why Carter cares so much.

*   *   *

That night at dinner, when Allie arrived at the table Jo, Lisa and Ruth were talking animatedly in low voices.

'You have to do it, Lisa,' Jo said. 'It's tradition.'

'I'm going to do it, and you know I hate this sort of thing,' Ruth said.

Clearly reluctant, Lisa stirred food around her plate, her long, straight hair swinging forward around her face. 'I don't know. It's just a bit weird.'

'What's weird?' Allie asked pulling up a chair. 'What's for dinner tonight? I hope it's lasagne.'

'The Summer Splash!' Jo's eyes were bright with enthusiasm. 'It's always the night before the summer ball, and Lisa doesn't want to do it. But

176

she has to. And I thought you were only eating salad.'

'Oh balls,' Allie said. 'I'd forgotten about the salad thing. And what the hell's a Summer Splash?'

She poured herself a glass of water from the jug on the table.

'Oh, crikey. I completely forgot to tell you about it.' Jo let go of Lisa's arm and turned to Allie. 'It's a tradition. Sixth formers sneak out at midnight the night before the ball and go swimming in the pond.'

Puzzled, Allie looked at Lisa. 'What's wrong with that? Can't you swim?'

Raising her chin, Lisa shot an accusing look at Jo. 'Not just swimming. Tell her the whole truth.'

Jo rolled her eyes. 'OK, fine. Skinny-dipping. Must you be such a prude, Lisa? It's going to be awesome!'

Allie choked on her water. 'What? All of us? Guys and girls? Naked?'

Ruth pounded her on the back.

'It's dark, Allie.' Jo was beginning to sound exasperated. 'And it's no big deal. You just dive in and then jump out and put your clothes back on. It's not a porn movie. It's good, clean, wholesome fun and it's a tradition and you have to do it because I don't want to do it alone.'

Allie leaned towards her. 'Let me make sure I'm getting this—you, me, Ruth, Lisa, our dates for Friday night and a bunch of strangers are going to get naked in a pond. Together. For fun.'

'Exactly!' Jo said brightly. 'And we're all going to be there, right?'

Lisa looked nauseous.

'Surely Allie's not invited.' Katie stood by their table, as beautiful as ever. 'She's too new. This is for Cimmeria students.'

'Oh bugger off, Katie. Seriously.' Jo glared at her.

Katie stood her ground. 'I'm serious, Jo. I really don't think it's fair. I'm going to speak with Jules about it.'

'You can't speak with Jules about it you moron,' Jo said. 'It's unofficial. She can't do anything about it.'

'Jo,' Allie said, her jaw set, 'when did you say this splash thing happens?'

'Midnight Thursday,' Jo said with a wicked glint in her eye.

'Great. I'll be there.'

Katie gave her a chilling look. 'If you do this, Allie, then don't go crying to Isabelle if anything happens. Just remember I warned you.'

As Katie walked away Allie muttered under her breath: 'Yeah, and you care because you're my *best friend*, Katie.'

Jo snickered. 'Forget her. I'm glad you're going to do it. I've been looking forward to this since I got to Cimmeria. If Lisa and Ruth come too we can just all do it together, and it will be even better.'

Looking miserable, Lisa stared at her empty plate. Allie smiled at Jo, but her heart sank. Already she regretted her rashness in agreeing to go. Still. How bad could it be?

'But how do we get out of the school without getting caught?' she asked. 'I mean, do the teachers just let you go and dive naked into a lake in the dark?'

Jo's face told her the answer before she said a word. 'They do whatever they can to stop us. I mean, imagine the wrath of parents if one of us got

178

hurt.' She smiled cheerfully. 'Getting out is half the fun.'

As the kitchen doors opened and the staff walked in carrying platters of lasagne, Allie groaned. 'I'm not sure which is worse, being forced to skip lasagne, or swimming naked with Katie Gilmore.'

'Gabe and I have a plan for getting out,' Jo said. 'Let's talk about it after dinner. Come to my room at eight and we'll plot.' She began filling her plate with salad. 'I love plotting.'

*   *   *

At ten past eight that night, Allie stood in the hallway outside Jo's door. Hearing voices inside, she raised her hand to knock . . . then put it down again. After a moment she straightened and tapped on the door then turned the handle and stepped inside.

Jo, Lisa, Ruth, Gabe and Lucas were sitting in a circle. Allie took a spot on the floor between Ruth and Lucas, and, pulling her feet up, wrapped her arms around her knees. Gabe was pointing at a small area on a map.

'. . . so, given all of that, I think the only safe way out is through the classroom wing.'

Lucas looked sceptical. 'Hang on, all we know is that all the other doors will be watched. Why wouldn't they guard that one too?'

'Two reasons,' Gabe said. 'First, because The Rules say we can't go in that wing outside of class hours under any circumstances—so the amount of trouble we'd get in if we were caught is pretty serious. Second, because it's marked as an alarmed fire door.'

'What will we do about the alarm?' Allie asked.

Gabe's reply was simple. 'There is no alarm.'

There was an uproar, and Gabe, who seemed to enjoy their astonishment, held out his hands for silence. 'There are no alarms anywhere in this building at all. Any sign that says "alarm" is a lie.'

Lisa's quiet voice broke the stunned silence. 'Why?'

'I don't know,' Gabe said. Watching him closely, Allie got the feeling he was lying. He knew precisely why. He just didn't want to say.

No fire alarms. No burglar alarms. Nothing to warn anybody about anything.

'So,' Jo brushed aside the alarm conversation, 'how do we get into the classroom wing without attracting attention?'

'I know that one,' Lucas said. 'Here's what we do . . .'

CHAPTER FOURTEEN

'Ouch!' Hopping up and down in the dark, Jo grabbed her toe.

'Shhhh.' Though Jo couldn't see her, Allie held a finger to her lips and they both froze.

It was eleven-thirty Thursday night, and they were standing on the stair landing in the dark, the polished wood floor cold against their bare feet. They'd worked on the plan until late Wednesday night, and talked about it half of the day today. Allie had decided that getting out of the building was definitely going to be the best part.

Now they listened for any sounds, any sign that they'd been noticed, but the old building was silent. After a moment they began feeling their way down the stairs again, each holding her shoes in one hand and clinging to the banister with the other. Lucas had reminded them that the third from last step creaked, so they carefully stepped over it. When they reached the bottom, Allie looked towards Isabelle's office—no light shone under the door.

Her eyes were adjusting to the dark—she could see a little better now.

As they stealthily tiptoed down the wide hallway to the classroom wing door, Allie stopped.

'Did you hear that?' she breathed, her lips barely moving.

Jo shook her head, but at that moment they both heard the sound. Footsteps. Nearby.

Allie spun around looking for a place to hide. Thinking fast, she ran behind a stone column, pulling Jo with her. A few seconds later, a lithe shadow flitted down the hallway. Allie pressed back against the wall, but Jo leaned forward, squinting into the darkness. Before Allie could stop her, she dashed after the shadow.

'Jo!' Allie whispered, but there was no reply. She hesitated for a moment, deciding what to do, then stepped out after her. At first she could see nothing, then she bumped into Jo, who was standing just down the hall with Lisa.

'Found her!' Jo whispered, clearly delighted.

Lisa looked less thrilled, and Allie wondered why she'd come. She'd been so reluctant in every conversation about it. Now she seemed unable to stand still, hopping nervously from one foot to another like an anxious dancer before a show, her eyes enormous in her delicate face. Allie gave her a sympathetic look, and then pointed at the door to the classroom wing.

Jo nodded.

'What about Ruth?' Allie whispered.

'She's late—we can't wait.'

Allie turned the handle. If the door creaked, they were dead.

It swung open silently on hinges Gabe had oiled that afternoon.

They slipped through and then ran as fast as they could down the long corridor. The door at the end was marked with ominous, official-looking signs that warned of alarms and security; there were numbers to call in case of emergencies. Allie wondered if she dialled them, who would answer.

Standing still for one brief moment, they exchanged a look in the shadows, then one at a time they each put a hand on the door, and at Jo's nod, they pushed it.

The door opened without a sound.

Rushing through, they tumbled onto a path covered in gravel that cut into their bare feet. They all hopped around in comedic fashion pulling on their shoes and trying not to cry out. Thinking how ridiculous they must look to anyone watching, Allie stifled a giggle.

'GoGoGo!' Jo whispered, and they ran recklessly into the night, reaching out for each other until all three held hands.

By the time they reached the treeline, Jo and Lisa were winded, and they stopped for a moment to catch their breath. Allie was anxious—they were still too close to the school.

'Which way from here?' she hissed. Jo nodded

towards the right, and Allie motioned for them to move. They continued on at a slower pace.

At first, the woods were almost completely silent, but gradually Allie began to notice rustling noises and the sound of snapping twigs. Reaching out for Jo, she squeezed her hand and nodded in the direction of the sounds. She could see Jo's white teeth in the darkness as she smiled.

'The others,' she whispered.

As they put distance between themselves and the school, people were less careful, and soon they could hear other sounds: muffled giggles, occasional whispered oaths as somebody tripped, fake bird calls followed by more smothered laughter. Allie felt the tension between her shoulder blades begin to ease.

Jo stopped so suddenly that Allie and Lisa nearly tripped over her.

'We're here,' she whispered, and disappeared behind a shrub. Peering around in the darkness Allie couldn't see a pond—just trees and brush. But she and Lisa followed Jo into a hiding spot.

'Why are we hiding?' Lisa whispered.

'Nobody can know who's here until midnight,' Jo said. 'It's tradition.'

'How do you know all this?' Allie asked.

'My brother told me all about it when he was here,' Jo explained.

Jo had a watch with a glow-in-the-dark dial, and the three stood looking at it as the minute hand moved inexorably to midnight.

'Where's Ruth?' Allie asked.

Jo held out her empty hands. 'She was supposed to meet us either in the school or along the way, so I presume she's here already somewhere.' She checked the watch.

'Nearly,' she whispered, grinning widely. 'Get ready.'

Allie could feel Lisa trembling. She longed to comfort her but she was too scared herself. She took a deep breath and looked out towards where she presumed the pond must be.

Am I really going to do this? I mean, who skinny-dips anyway? Isn't that something that only happens in films?

At that moment, a deep male voice rang out in the silence making her jump. 'It's time, kids. Drop trou.'

As Allie and Lisa hesitated, Jo started undoing her shorts, but when she saw that they hadn't moved she paused and gave them a warning look.

'You may as well,' she said. 'At this point, it would be worse going back without doing it.'

Lisa and Allie exchanged a look of dread. 'I will if you will,' Lisa said finally.

Allie could now hear people splashing into water and screaming with laughter. She sighed heavily.

'Oh, what the hell.' As she pulled down her tracksuit bottoms, Jo cheered and ripped off her shorts. In seconds they were all naked. Lisa and Allie crossed their arms protectively across their breasts, but Jo grabbed their hands.

'If you're going to do it, do it proudly,' she said, pulling them out onto the path.

In the dark, Allie saw only flashes of skin as people jumped into and out of a pond she couldn't quite make out in the gloom.

'On three,' Jo said, giggling. 'One. Two . . .'

They leapt into the dark water, hitting with an icy splash. Allie, who could only barely see the pond in the black night, heard the loud shrieks of laughter around her muffled into silence as she sank below the surface. She was surprised by how deep it was—she'd never been a strong swimmer. As she splashed towards the surface a sudden flash memory came to her: a hot sunny day. She was seven, and Christopher was teasing her for sinking like a stone in the pool. 'You run like a rabbit, but you also swim like a rabbit . . .' he'd laughed while she paddled wildly.

When she came up for air now, sputtering and shivering, she couldn't see Jo or Lisa anywhere.

'Jo?'

How had she lost them in seconds? But the pond was crowded with laughing students—none of whom looked familiar. As she thrashed in the cold water looking for a familiar face, Allie grew increasingly panicked. She was alone and naked in a lake full of strangers. Hot tears of fear and shame burned her eyes. Suddenly she realised she was struggling to breathe. She hadn't had a panic attack in weeks, but now she wheezed three laboured breaths in a row as she fought to stay afloat.

I can't . . . breathe . . .

She went under for just a second, and kicked hard to find the surface again. Under the water, somebody's foot hit her shin hard and pain shot through her leg. She didn't cry out—she didn't have enough air left.

Again the cold water closed over her head, and again she tried to make her way up. But this time two strong hands grabbed her shoulders and pulled her to the surface. Gratitude rushed through her, but then she saw who was helping her and she struggled to free herself while trying to cover her breasts with her hands.

'You're OK, Allie. Look at me,' Carter's voice was calm and commanding, and his eyes were locked on hers. 'Breathe slowly through your nose. Don't look away. Breathe slowly.'

She tried to explain to him that she was dying but no words would come out.

'Breathe in,' he said, demonstrating, his eyes willing her to try. 'And now out.' He blew air out forcefully.

When she tried to do what he asked she only wheezed ineffectually, and she felt a wave of fear. She wasn't going to make it.

But that's OK, really. If I can just rest for a second . . .

Her eyes fluttered shut and darkness seemed to blanket her.

When Carter slapped her face it startled her so much that she took a sharp reflexive breath, that burst of oxygen revived her hope.

'You can do this, Allie. Breathe with me.' She could sense that he was trying to keep his voice steady, and it struck her that she really could die.

He took a deep breath, and she tried to do the same. This time a little air entered her lungs.

'Good!' he said. 'Again.'

A deeper breath, and she could feel the tightness in her chest begin to loosen. He urged her on but she was trembling violently now and on the fourth successful breath she burst into tears.

'You're OK, Allie,' Carter said, putting his arms gently around her shoulder. 'Just keep breathing.'

Shielding her body with his, he led her out of the water to shore. She could hear people laughing and splashing around them, but she didn't know or care if they were laughing at her.

His voice was gentle. 'Where are your clothes, Allie?'

'I don't know,' she whispered hoarsely.

He half-smiled. 'Why am I not surprised to hear that?' He helped her off the path into relative privacy behind a large tree. 'Stay here. I'll find something for you to wear.'

As he walked into the shadows, she watched the muscles move in his hips and back, and forced herself to keep breathing.

He's beautiful, she thought.

When he reappeared a few minutes later he'd put on a pair of shorts. In his hands he carried a guy's shirt and a pair of girls' shorts.

'This is the best I can do,' he said apologetically.

Since he was shirtless, she had a feeling the guy's shirt he'd brought was his own.

She turned away as she pulled on the shorts, then turned back towards him and held out her hand for the shirt. He handed it to her wordlessly. She couldn't see his face in the darkness, but as she shrugged on the over-sized shirt she felt her heart pound in her chest so loudly that she thought he must surely be able to hear it.

'Ready?' She noticed his voice shook.

'Yes.'

Reaching for her hand, he helped her out of her hiding place and onto the path. The warmth of his hand was comforting—his fingers were strong, and she clung to them.

'I couldn't find any shoes for you,' he said anxiously. 'This might be hard on your feet—do you want to wear mine? Or I could carry you?'

Though the sharp pebbles cut into her feet, she

shook her head. 'I'm OK,' she said.

As they walked away from the lake the noise and laughter faded behind them. After a few minutes, the only sound they could hear was their own breathing. Carter still held her hand.

When she was certain they were alone, Allie stopped and looked up at him. 'Carter . . . Thank you.'

Dropping her hand, he looked down at the ground. 'It was nothing.'

'No, Carter.' She grabbed his hand back. When he looked at her, his eyes were so vulnerable she couldn't tear hers away. 'It was *something*.'

They stared at each other for a long moment but just as he started to speak . . .

'Allie! Carter!' Jo's voice broke the spell as she raced up the path towards them with Gabe and Lisa right behind her.

Grabbing Allie by the shoulders Jo gave her a worried shake. 'Where have you been? Are you OK? I looked for you *everywhere*.'

Even as she nodded, Allie felt the unwanted tears begin again.

'I couldn't find you. Carter helped me . . .' She turned to look at him, but he was gone.

'. . . out,' she whispered.

*   *   *

Breakfast the next morning was a muted affair—the students who'd spent much of the night in the woods were easily identifiable by their bed-hair and the circles under their eyes. Jo and Allie sat in near silence with Lisa yawning beside them. None of them was hungry. Allie clutched a steaming cup of tea as if it were the only thing keeping her alive, while Jo shredded a piece of toast into minute particles.

Allie had spent the night on the floor in Jo's room after they'd crept back into the school unnoticed using the same door through which they'd departed an hour earlier.

They'd talked until four in the morning, after which she told Jo she felt better, but she didn't really.

I mean how do you get over having a naked panic attack in front of half the school?

At least she now knew what had happened after they jumped into the pond. During the night, Jo told her the whole story. How Gabe and Lucas had been in the water and had spotted the girls as they ran to the water. That Gabe had grabbed Jo as soon as she'd hit the surface and pulled her over to where they were swimming near a tree. How she'd managed to hold on to Lisa and pull her along even while Lisa tried to hide from Lucas. And how in all the commotion she'd lost Allie.

'The pond filled up with people so fast and it was so dark, when I went back to where we started, or where I thought we'd started, I couldn't find you anywhere,' Jo said. It was Jules and Ruth who eventually told her that they'd seen Allie with Carter, and that Allie looked ill. 'Ruth had gone with Jules in the end, because Jules didn't want to go on her own. And Jules thought we'd been drinking and that that's why you were ill, and she gave me a bollocking, which is why it took me ages to find you.'

'I never saw Sylvain there, but then I didn't see anyone, really,' Allie said.

189

'I don't think he was there,' Jo said. 'But just about everybody else was.'

Allie, who had prepared a bed of coats and sweaters on the floor, buried her face in Jo's spare pillow. 'I wonder how many people saw me freak out?'

Up on the bed, Jo stretched out flat and yawned. 'Not many, that's for sure. It seemed like nobody saw you all night except Jules.'

'But she'll tell everyone.'

'She won't. She's a prefect. She has, like, a duty to support you, or something,' Jo said. 'Anyway, what exactly happened?'

Allie explained about the panic attack and how Carter had rescued her. She didn't talk about the way she'd felt when he pulled her from the water and helped her breathe. Or about watching him walk away in the moonlight. Instead she'd focused on how calm he was, and how coolly he'd handled the crisis.

Jo thought for a moment, and when she spoke her answer was carefully phrased. 'People here have a weird thing with Carter because he acts like he's better than everyone, and because he has really upset a lot of girls over the years—pretending he likes them and then suddenly not liking them any more. And, you know, he does his own thing. I'm actually kind of surprised he was down at the pond at all tonight, or last night . . .' she looked at the clock. '. . . this morning. Whenever. Because that's the kind of scene he usually avoids. So people think he's standoffish. But he can be a good guy—he really can.'

She yawned widely. 'Lots of people know he doesn't like them or that he thinks they're shallow.

190

He makes it obvious.'

'That's what I like about him,' Allie had murmured, closing her eyes. 'He's so honest.'

'Honesty can be good,' Jo said, turning out the lamp. Her last words floated out of the darkness, disembodied. 'But it can be bad, too.'

Now, as they sat stirring cereal around their bowls, nobody seemed to have anything to say. Lisa was the most cheerful of them all—she'd survived the splash, and Lucas had walked her back to the school building afterwards. She thought he was starting to like her. But even she was tired.

'God, I'm so going to need a nap before tonight,' she said, resting her head on her hand. 'I'm a wreck.'

'I feel like arse,' Jo said succinctly, reaching for the sugar. 'Who knew sleep mattered?'

'Arse about sums it up for me too,' Allie said, sipping the scalding tea and yawning. Nobody had said anything to her about last night, and there'd been no whispering when she walked in the dining room. Maybe Jo was right and it had been so dark and crowded nobody'd seen her losing it last night.

By tradition, classes ended at noon on the day of the summer ball. Through her morning classes Allie fought to stay awake, taking notes that would later make no sense to her at all.

Carter studiously ignored her in biology, and in English she dozed off while waiting for the class to start and never saw him come in. When she looked up, he was there but not looking at her. It was just as well. In eight hours she was going to the dance with Sylvain. This really wasn't the time to be thinking about standing in the water with his arms around her. Naked.

She straightened the papers on her desk and pulled her textbook out of her bag.

No—not the time at all.

Isabelle had taken her place at the edge of the circle of desks.

She glanced around the room knowingly. 'My, some of you look very tired. Didn't you sleep well?'

They shifted uncomfortably in their seats. Somebody snickered.

'I heard there was a kerfuffle at the pond last night. I do hope you weren't disturbed.' More nervous laughter. The headmistress' expression was enigmatic as she pulled on her glasses.

'I'm sure that most of you are daydreaming of dancing in the arms of your dates but we must get through today's class nonetheless,' she said, opening her book. 'So I thought we would talk about romance today. Let's open with a beautiful poem about secret love. "Silentium Amoris" was written by Oscar Wilde, who you probably think of more for his humour, but this is a straightforward and simply beautiful story of love.'

She read the first two stanzas in her rich, powerful voice. Lost in the flowery prose, Allie almost instantly tuned out, drawing a sleepy butterfly on her notebook. She was giving its wings elaborate decoration when she heard her name.

Confused, she sat up straighter. Everyone was looking at her. 'Sorry?' she said, flushing.

'Good morning,' Isabelle said tartly as the class tittered. 'I said, would you mind reading the third stanza for me.'

Standing, Allie picked up her book and cleared her throat and began reading—she started quickly, but slowed as the words began to take shape.

'But surely unto thee mine eyes did show
Why I am silent, and my lute unstrung;
Else it were better we should part, and go,
Thou to some lips of sweeter melody,
And I to nurse the barren memory
Of unkissed kisses, and songs never sung.'

An unaccountable wave of sadness washed over her. She thought for a second she might cry, but fought the urge.

What the hell is wrong with me?

'What does that poem say to you, Allie.'

Horrified to find Isabelle was still focusing on her, Allie tried to think of what to say.

Her voice was nearly a whisper. 'He's afraid to tell somebody how he feels about them, but it makes him sad that the other person doesn't know how he feels.'

'And why would he be afraid to tell this other person of his feelings?' Isabelle said.

'Because she might not feel the same way he does.' Somehow, the fact that it was Carter who answered that question didn't surprise Allie, who dropped her eyes to her notebook as her pen drew small, interlinking circles around the butterfly. 'So he thinks it's better never to find out if that's the case.'

'Now it's worth pointing out that this poem could well be a he writing about another he, but for the sake of conversation we can discuss it in more conventional terms. So why would he think that's better?' Isabelle mused, strolling across the room to lean against an empty desk. 'She might feel the same way, but if he doesn't ask he'll never know.'

193

'He's afraid of being hurt,' Allie whispered, adding another swirling circle to the chain she'd created.

Isabelle looked from her to Carter curiously.

'That would explain it,' she said. 'Now, speaking of being hurt, I have another poem for you in a somewhat different vein by the American writer Dorothy Parker . . .'

The rest of the class seemed to take for ever. The minute it was over, Allie was up from her desk and heading for the door with her head down, determined not to make eye contact with anyone.

Especially Carter.

She was the first one to the stairs and her feet pounded on the stair boards as she hurried up, counting to herself.

. . . thirty-one, thirty-two, thirty-three . . .

Inside the sanctuary of her own room, she closed the door behind her and leaned her back against it staring at the neat familiarity of the space.

What just happened? Was Carter trying to tell me he fancies me? Or am I reading into it? Is Sylvain right?

She was so tired, she didn't trust herself to think about serious things right now. And the bed she hadn't slept in last night seemed to call to her. Dropping her book bag on the floor, she set the alarm for six, and pulled the shutter to, closing out the dazzling sunlight. She paused only long enough to kick off her shoes before climbing into bed fully clothed. It felt wonderful to be alone, and in the cool darkness she wondered once more about Carter, before forgetting about everything and falling asleep.

CHAPTER FIFTEEN

When Allie arrived at Jo's room at half past six, Jo and Lisa had already draped the room in dresses and cluttered it with shoes. Allie was feeling much better—more normal. Somehow, sleep had settled her. Whatever might happen tomorrow, tonight she was going to have a good time. Just enjoy the dance. So last night had happened. So what? She'd been through worse. She didn't care what anybody thought before she came to Cimmeria, and she wasn't going to start caring now.

Lisa, who was going to the dance with Lucas ('just as friends, you know?') was flushed with excitement. 'I just think it's the perfect dress.'

Her excitement was contagious and Allie instantly felt more positive about everything. 'It'll be beautiful, I'm sure of it.'

'Frankly, it'll be great just to spend some time with Gabe.' Jo sighed. 'I've hardly seen him in days.'

'Any clue as to what's going on?' Allie asked, hanging her silky white dress on the wardrobe door.

Jo shook her head. 'Not a peep. Just "working on the project . . . ?"?' She deepened her voice and made it mildly defensive, which sounded so much like Gabe that Lisa and Allie giggled.

'Yeah, Sylvain is more like, "Eet ees amporTANT wot we are doEENG",' Allie said, and they all collapsed in giggles again.

A silver tray of sandwiches cut into triangular quarters dominated Jo's desk, along with jugs of juice. Jo insisted that they all must eat something before leaving the room. ('Last year I nearly fainted at the ball because I was too excited to eat all day.') Slim as a daisy stem, Lisa nibbled delicately at the edge of a cucumber sandwich before setting it down on a napkin. Jo shot her a warning look.

'Eat it, Lisa.'

'But I'm not hungry . . .?' Lisa said, pushing the sandwich away.

Allie, who had skipped lunch to sleep, grabbed a cheese sandwich and took a huge bite. 'Oh my God, how can you not be hungry? I'm starving. To *death*.'

Lisa, still undecided about how to wear her hair and beginning to panic, wordlessly held up a magazine, which was opened to a picture of blonde starlet with an elaborate up-do.

'I wish you'd just let me work my magic and stop worrying about it,' Jo said. 'I can do better than that. In fact, Allie, I'm going to do your hair right now. I have a feeling Lisa's will take for ever.'

Allie stuffed the rest of the sandwich into her mouth. 'Mmph,' she said agreeably as she climbed into the chair.

'Exactly.' Jo brushed her hair and then began twisting it gently with the ribbon.

'I love having my hair done,' Allie said, closing her eyes. 'It's like having a head massage.'

'If this whole expensive education thing doesn't pan out for me I'm definitely opening a salon in Mayfair in London,' Jo deftly twisted a lock up and pinned it into place. 'I'll call it MayHair.'

Allie laughed up at her. 'You've really thought about this. Well, fine then. If your expensive education doesn't take, I'll be your first customer.'

As Jo predicted, getting ready took for ever. Lisa's hair alone took ages. In the end, and after much disagreement, she had it twisted into a simple chignon that made the most of her long, slender neck.

'It's perfect.' Lisa smiled at herself in the mirror. 'Jo, you're a genius.'

'I know,' Jo said, smoothing her own hair into a flattering gamine style. 'But guess what time it is.'

Allie looked at her watch and groaned. 'Step it up, ladies, we've only got ten minutes.'

They grabbed their dresses.

'I knew this would happen,' Jo said, slipping her silver minidress over her head. Allie zipped up the back for her.

'Yes you did. For all the good it did us.'

While Allie pulled on the long white dress, Jo slipped on her strappy sandals and turned around to help.

Allie gazed at her admiringly. 'You look like a film star.'

'Darling, I might, but you look like a princess in a fairy tale.'

Lisa wore a silvery blue silk dress with delicate straps and a matching silk wrap she draped loosely across her back. When she finally pulled her shoes on, Jo and Allie applauded their sardonic approval.

'You look gorgeous, but good lord it takes you for ever to get ready,' Jo said.

Lisa picked up her clutch bag and smiled without rancour. 'Everybody says that.'

'Wait! Nobody gets out of this room until I've taken a picture.' Jo waved a small camera at them.

She pulled Allie and Jo over to the full-length

mirror, and they squeezed close together, giggling. When they were all reflected, Jo held up her camera and snapped the picture.

'Perfect,' she said checking the image. 'We look amazing.'

'We'll probably never look this good again,' Lisa said sombrely. Allie and Jo stared at her for a second and then burst out laughing.

'You're impossible, gloomy guts,' Jo said hugging her. 'Don't make me mess your hair up.'

They walked out the door together at eight o'clock on the dot. When they reached the top of the stairs, a noisy crowd of boys had gathered at the foot of the staircase, all clad in white tie.

The girls stood still for just a second as the crowd looked up at them and fell silent. To Allie the moment felt unreal—dreamlike. She'd freaked out and nearly drowned naked in a pond last night and yet here she was only hours later, in a beautiful dress, with good friends. It felt like she was living someone else's life.

Sylvain, Lucas and Gabe stood in the crowd below, although there was no sign of Carter.

She stood straight and sucked her stomach in. Jo caught her eye and gave her a wink, then held out her hand. Allie took it, and then reached out to Lisa with her other hand. They walked down the stairs together in a butterfly's fluttering of silk.

Focused on not losing her balance in Jo's borrowed kitten heels, Allie kept her eyes on the steps ahead. When she glanced up, Sylvain was in front of her, smiling. She dropped Jo's hand.

Sylvain admired her openly as he lifted her hand, kissed it, and placed it on his arm. 'You look beautiful,' he said.

She saw warmth and desire in his eyes. Her stomach fluttered.

Raising her chin she smiled up at him. 'So do you.' And he did. He belonged in that dark, perfectly tailored suit. Its fit emphasised his muscular shoulders and chest. He smiled his perfect smile.

She felt a sudden flash of doubt. *Is this the right thing to do? Is Carter telling the truth?*

As if the thought showed on her face, Sylvain brushed his fingers lightly across her brow smoothing an invisible hair. 'I can't wait to dance with you. Let's go in.' His voice was so reassuring, and his moves so sure, she squared her shoulders and walked in with him.

As they joined the stream of beautifully dressed students flowing into the great hall, staff in tuxedos stood by the doors holding trays of tall champagne flutes. They each took a glass as they walked in.

Inside Allie expected to find a disco. Instead, an elegantly anachronistic scene unfurled in front of her. A small orchestra had set up in one corner where it played a waltz. Everywhere candles sparkled on tables, in the chandeliers, in wall sconces, in the fireplace. Vases filled with white flowers topped every surface. The tables were covered in white linen, and the chairs were draped with white silk ribbons. The scent of jasmine floated on the breeze.

Isabelle appeared in a flowing white chiffon gown cinched at the waist with a gold rope belt. Allie glanced down at her own dress and thought that, compared to Isabelle, she looked like a little girl. She reached out and tugged Jo's hand to get her attention and nodded in Isabelle's direction.

Jo smiled knowingly. 'What can we do? Our headmistress is hot.'

Gabe led them to a table in a corner, and they stood around it for a moment a bit awkwardly.

'What are we waiting for?' Allie whispered to Jo.

'You'll see.'

After a moment, Isabelle tapped a silver spoon against a champagne flute, and the room fell silent.

'Welcome to the 223rd Cimmeria Summer Ball.'

Everybody clapped enthusiastically, and she waited for the applause to quieten.

'Every year, this is a very special occasion when we gather to celebrate the school, its history, and all of you; for you are Cimmeria's future. Many of your parents attended this ball years ago, and many of your grandparents and great-grandparents before that. You stand now where they stood then. Young and hopeful as they were. You are now part of the circle. Unbroken.'

She raised her glass. 'To the summer ball. And Cimmeria Academy.'

'To the summer ball,' they chorused. 'And Cimmeria Academy.'

'Enjoy!' she called out, laughing at their raucous applause.

When Sylvain pulled a seat out for her she was surprised by his formality, but then she noticed Gabe and Lucas had pulled out Jo and Lisa's seats as well.

Tradition, I guess.

Allie, who had only ever had small sips of champagne at Christmas, thought it tasted a bit like the cider she used to drink with Mark and Harry. She stopped and stared at the glass. *How long has it been since I thought about Mark and Harry?*

She wondered what they were doing. If they were still getting into trouble. Whatever they were doing, she thought, looking around the room, it isn't anything like this.

She raised her glass again. The second sip of champagne was better.

At that moment the orchestra began playing an extraordinary song. It sounded exotic, but Allie couldn't place it. Hungarian? Turkish? As soon as it started she could feel the excitement in the air—it was electric. A few couples began dancing in a complex pattern that seemed to involve circles within circles. It was dizzying to watch and after a moment she turned away, feeling light-headed.

'It's a traditional Cimmeria song.' Sylvain had been watching her. 'It was written for the school itself a long time ago by an Egyptian composer who went to school here.'

'I've never heard anything like it,' Allie said.

She would have asked for more information, but at that moment waiters walked by with trays of hors d'oeuvres, and Gabe, Sylvain and Lucas all took several. Jo and Allie each took one, but Lisa waved the tray away. Jo frowned at her and Lisa shrugged innocently.

'Everything is so beautiful,' Allie said, biting a fried prawn.

'They've been working on it since yesterday morning,' Jo said. 'I could hear them in here hammering away this morning too.'

'It's all perfect,' Sylvain said, smiling at Allie. 'I think we should definitely dance. But you must finish your champagne first.'

Obediently, Allie took another sip, wrinkling her nose at the pleasant feeling of the bubbles in her nose. 'It really grows on you, champagne,' she murmured half to herself. The others laughed at her.

'Yes,' Gabe said cheerfully. 'Champagne definitely grows on you.'

'Don't drink it too fast,' Jo cautioned, shooting Sylvain a warning look.

Allie dismissed her with a smile. 'Remember, Mum, I used to drink quite a bit.'

Jo didn't look placated. 'Cimmeria champagne is pretty strong, Allie.'

'She'll be fine,' Sylvain said. Standing up, he held out his hand. 'May I have this dance?'

She tingled at his touch. 'I have no idea how to dance to this music, Sylvain. I predict humiliation if we do this.'

'Oh, I don't think it will come to that.'

His face was so confident she almost believed him. They walked to the edge of the dance floor where the couples were still swirling in their intricate circles. They moved with impressive speed and practised perfection and Allie watched them in awe. She saw Isabelle moving gracefully in the arms of a handsome, dark-haired man she'd never seen before. She was incredibly elegant, and Allie sighed enviously.

'How do they all know how to dance like this?'

'Most of us have had dance lessons since we were children.'

'How weird that people still do that.'

'Is it?' He pulled her into his arms and lifted her chin so that she looked into his bluer than blue eyes. Then he held her tightly, his right hand in the small of her back pulling her close to his chest, her right hand in his left. 'It seems strange to me that anybody wouldn't do that. Tonight I will teach you one dance, a simple one. Just follow me. We'll start very slow. It's left right left left right. Like this.'

He demonstrated, and she followed carefully. At first she looked down at her feet and stepped on his toes, but then he lifted her chin with his index finger so that her eyes met his.

'Don't ever look down. Just watch my eyes, they will tell you where to go next. And it's left right left left right, over and over again. Ready?'

'No.'

He laughed, and twirled her out onto the dance floor.

'Left right left left right . . . Left right left left right . . .' Allie murmured the directions under her breath as she moved, but kept her eyes on his face. They twirled three slow circles without a mistake. Then four. Five!

Allie couldn't believe it.

'How are you doing this?' she laughed incredulously. 'Seriously, Sylvain, I don't know how to dance.'

He held her eyes with his, rising and falling with the steps. 'We can do it because you're trusting me. I'm leading. You're following. It's very simple.' He smiled. 'Also, we're moving very, very slowly . . .'

As they spun and she gained confidence, he gradually increased their speed until they were moving seamlessly around the floor.

When she was moving with confidence, he lightly kissed her neck just below her ear. All of her senses tingled. He whispered, 'You look so lovely tonight, Allie. Thank you for coming with me.'

She felt the blood rush to her face, and her body responded to him as he pulled her closer. All the while they spun in a smooth and constant series of circles. Allie was growing dizzy—the rest of the room was a watercolour blur. She and Sylvain were completely alone.

'This is incredible,' she whispered.

After what felt like only a few minutes, the circles led them to the edge of the dance floor, and he guided her back to the table, his arm tight around her waist.

Allie's head spun, and she held onto him for support. 'I feel dizzy.'

'It's the dancing. You're not used to it.'

She looked back at the dance floor and watched the dancers spin. A few of the couples were less than perfect in their moves and the others swirled past them, like water flowing around stones.

With one hand, Sylvain lifted two glasses off a passing tray. 'What you need is more champagne.'

Allie accepted the glass he passed her with a grateful smile. 'Thank you. I'm so thirsty.' The wine was cold and refreshing, and she gulped it down. 'You know, I'm starting to really like champagne.'

His chuckle was warm, and he was so close to her she could feel it in her own body. 'So you've said.'

Allie looked for Jo in the crowd of dancers. Her very short dress made her easy to spot—it was definitely the tiniest dress in the room. She and Gabe were twirling around the dance floor with assurance. She saw Lisa's dress swirling a short distance away as she and Lucas spun easy circles.

She barely noticed when Sylvain took the empty glass from her hand and replaced it with a full one.

Looking around the room, she saw Ruth and Phil walking towards the dance floor holding hands—Ruth wore a pretty pale pink silk dress that showed off her athletic figure. Nearby Jerry sat talking comfortably with Eloise from the library; she was in a sexy little black dress with a low back, and her long hair was loose.

'She's not very old at all,' Allie said, surprised.

'Who?'

'Eloise. I always thought she was old. Or at least, you know, older.'

Sylvain smiled. 'Yes, I think she wants people to think she's older. If they knew she was so young, nobody would take her seriously. She was at school here six years ago.' He gave the librarian an appraising glance. 'Very sexy, Eloise.'

Allie punched his arm lightly. 'Hey! Watch it. Remember who your date is.'

His smile was wicked. 'I could never forget. And in fact, I think it's time for my date to dance with me again. Come on now, bottoms up.' He finished his own drink then waited until she'd emptied her glass before holding out his hand.

As they headed back to the dance floor she felt a little unsteady on her feet, and reached for Sylvain's arm to steady herself. At that moment, Carter stepped in front of them. Their eyes met and, remembering that morning's English class, Allie felt a spark of electricity. Then she noticed he had his arm around a small girl in a blue taffeta dress. She was pretty, with long, curly blonde hair. Before Allie could say anything to him, he turned away very deliberately and smiled down at his date, whispering something in her ear that made her giggle.

Allie flushed and must have tensed because Sylvain looked over to see what had caught her

205

attention. When he saw Carter, his eyes narrowed, and his arm tightened around her waist.

'Is everything OK?' he asked her coolly.

Forcing a smile she pulled him onto the dance floor.

'Everything is perfect.' But she noticed she'd slurred the last word, and she frowned with concentration as she tried to figure out why.

Bloody hell—am I drunk? Already?

'You look,' he said as they took their first steps onto the dance floor, 'like an angel.'

Carter was right there at the edge of the dance floor, Allie was sure of it. He was probably watching them. With his date.

Fine, then. She'd give him something to watch.

She pulled Sylvain closer. 'I don't feel like one.'

He threw his head back and laughed as they picked up speed. This time the dance steps were easier, and at first Allie relaxed into the movement and the music and let Sylvain decide where they went on the floor. Her head felt light and pleasantly dizzy. She gave into the feeling with a soft sigh, leaning back against his arm and letting him support her completely. She felt the air rush around them.

He pulled her closer until his lips were against her ear; as he nibbled sharply at her earlobe she gasped and would have tripped were he not holding her so tightly.

After that, he was silent for so long that she glanced up at him worriedly.

'Is everything OK?'

'I'm sorry,' he said, his voice taut. 'You are irresistible.' His expression was so intense it made her nervous.

He swirled them to the edge of the dance floor and led her hurriedly out of the room. Feeling a bit woozy, Allie clung to his hand as he rushed out into the dark night, past a small crowd gathered near the back door, then around the corner to a quiet empty spot, out of view.

She tried to talk without slurring her words. 'Where are we . . .?'

He shoved her roughly against the wall, and she cried out at the impact, although she felt it as if through a cushion of cotton wool.

'Stop! Sylvain, you're hurting me.'

His eyes were luminous in the moonlight and she saw something like ferocity in them.

'Not one more second.' He kissed her so hard that her head hit the wall and she bit her tongue. Tears filled her eyes from the blow. She struggled to get away, her fists pounding at his chest, but it was all a bit hazy and after a second she couldn't quite remember why she was fighting.

A vague memory of Carter's warning filtered through her confusion: *Don't trust Sylvain. He's a liar.*

Then Sylvain tilted up her chin and kissed her neck. For a second she liked it, but then he nipped at the skin so hard it hurt and she gasped, her body moving involuntarily against his as she tried to get away. But she couldn't move—he was pressed hard against her. His hands moved up from her waist to her breasts and she started to panic in earnest. A tear ran down her cheek as she shoved against his chest but it seemed to have no effect on him.

'You want me,' he whispered. His left hand moved up to her throat, holding her so tightly she found it hard to breathe.

'Stop!' Her voice was just a whisper.

She clawed at his wrists but he was too strong.

'Say it,' he said again, pressing harder. 'Tell me that you want me.'

'Ask yourself a question, Sylvain. If you force somebody to want you, do they really want you?' Carter's voice came from right behind Sylvain.

Sylvain's hold loosened enough for Allie to breathe but he didn't let go as he turned to face Carter. As she breathed in, his smile was feral.

'Oh do go away, Carter.'

Carter stood his ground. 'What are you trying to force her to say, Sylvain? Spell it out for me. Like I'm simple.'

'This is none of your business, Carter. Your jealousy is pathetic.'

'Tell it to Isabelle. And while you're at it, tell her what you were about to do to Allie. And then you can have a long talk about The Rules.'

Dizzy and bewildered, Allie struggled to free herself as she looked from one boy to the other. She licked her lips and tried to speak clearly. 'Carter, what is going on? I don't understand . . .'

He kept his attention on Sylvain. 'No. But Sylvain does, don't you Sylvain?'

Their eyes met in an icy clash and for a second Allie thought Sylvain would not back down, and she wondered what Carter would do. But then without warning Sylvain let go and stepped away from her.

'Fine Carter. Be the hero. Save the girl. But we both know you're pathetic. And it's me she wants.'

Tensing his shoulders and curling his hands into fists, Carter took a furious step forward but before he could pounce, screams split the night air. Carter and Sylvain froze.

Carter turned to Allie, the rage gone from his expression. Now he looked alert—on guard.

'Allie, stay here. Don't move.'

Sylvain didn't look around at her as the two of them ran back around the building.

Trembling, Allie stood right where they'd left her. When she reached to touch the back of her head she could feel a lump under her fingertips.

How did I get so drunk? And what the hell just happened?

She wrapped her arms tightly across her chest. She was sore all over—she knew she'd have bruises on her arms in the morning and her head really hurt. Sylvain had been out of his mind but she hadn't fought properly. She hadn't stood up for herself.

Too drunk, she thought disgustedly. *Or . . .* her expression changed, *did he put something in my drink?*

She wasn't an inexperienced drinker and she'd never got drunk on one can of cider either. And she'd only had three glasses of champagne. As the idea took shape, a horrified look crossed her face.

Would Sylvain do something like that?

Before she could complete the thought, piercing screams. The sound was close—just around the corner. She jumped back into the shadows, pressing her back against the wall.

She heard crashing; sounds of fighting. Then, silence.

She held her breath.

After a moment, in the darkness, footsteps. Running towards her. Fast.

'Carter?' she said, her voice tentative.

The footsteps stopped.

With a gasp, Allie realised her mistake. The rush of adrenalin cleared the haze of alcohol, and she pressed back against the wall, the rough brick cold against her skin. She made herself as small as possible. Although she could see nothing, someone was there—she could sense them watching her. Frozen, not breathing, she counted her heartbeats.

. . . ten, eleven, twelve . . .

Footsteps moved towards her again. Slower this time.

Flinging herself from the wall, Allie raced around the corner towards the school entrance. The footsteps followed—fast.

She sped up to evade them, then tripped over something soft on the ground. Screaming, she lost her balance and pinwheeled to the ground.

On the cool, damp grass, she curled up into a ball and covered her head waiting for the attack. But none came. Instead she heard footsteps running away, gradually fading into the night.

Allie stayed still for a moment until she was sure she was alone. Then she sat up cautiously and peered around her.

Her hands were covered in something wet and sticky. As her eyes adjusted, she saw that she'd tripped over a girl in a pale dress, lying prone on the ground. She touched the girl cautiously but she didn't move. With her hands on the girl's shoulders, she rolled her over onto her back.

'Hey, are you OK?'

Then she saw. She sucked in her breath.

The world seemed to go silent.

She scrambled back away from the girl, staring at the shape in the dark.

Numb, she stumbled to her feet and walked with slow steps to the back door. Inside the lights had gone out and the hallway was dark and chaotic. It smelled of smoke. People were shouting and running past her. Allie felt disembodied— distanced from everything around her. She looked straight ahead, her bloodied hands out to either side.

Over and over in her head she thought the same words: *None of this is real. It cannot be real. None of this is real. It cannot be real . . .*

As she made her way back towards the ballroom the smoke grew thicker, bringing tears to her eyes. The grand room—so beautiful earlier that night with its sparkling candles and white flowers— was on fire. The only light came from the handful of torches held by teachers, and from the fires themselves. In that half-light, boys in tuxedos beat flames with wet tablecloths while girls in gowns carried water using anything they could find: ice buckets, punch bowls, flower vases. The floor was littered with abandoned high-heeled shoes and broken champagne flutes.

The fires were small and already beginning to go out—it was clear the students were winning the battle. But the intense smoke was the biggest problem—it was hard to breathe.

'Open a window!' somebody shouted.

'Don't!' came a firm reply. 'It'll make the fires worse. Get out if you need a break.'

Zelazny's familiar stern voice was somehow comforting to Allie, who stood stunned in the middle of the room unable to take it all in.

'Allie! Are you all right?' Jo appeared at her side, her face smeared with soot, an empty vase in

211

her hand. 'Jesus. Where did the blood come from? Are you hurt?'

Dropping the vase, she grabbed Allie's bloody hands and turned her around looking for obvious wounds. Allie shook her head but for a second she couldn't find her voice. Her lips moved, but no sound emerged.

'Allie, you're scaring me.' Tears sprung to Jo's eyes. 'Please, please, please tell me you're OK.'

Her words jarred Allie and suddenly the truth burst out of her as she gripped Jo's hands so tightly it must have hurt. 'Oh my God, Jo. There was screaming, and . . . There's blood . . . everywhere.'

Jo's cornflower-blue eyes were wide with fear— her hands squeezed Allie's so hard it hurt. 'Allie, please try to explain—where is the blood from?'

Allie stared at her hands. 'Jo, this is Ruth's blood. She's out back. Her throat is . . . it's cut. Badly. I think she's dead.'

Swallowing hard, Jo whipped around calling urgently: 'Jerry!'

Allie watched through the dark and smoke as Jo ran to the teacher who had been beating smouldering embers with a soaked tablecloth. His face was black with soot. Eloise stood nearby, her long hair tangled down her back. She'd taken off her heels and stood barefoot spraying foam from a fire extinguisher.

Jo spoke quickly, her face panicked. Allie couldn't make out her words.

Jerry and Eloise exchanged a look. Eloise handed the extinguisher to another teacher and the two ran out of the room.

When Jo returned to her side, Allie looked around. 'Where's Lisa?'

Jo bit her lip. 'I couldn't find either of you anywhere.'

'So you haven't seen her at all?' Allie could hear the hysteria in her own voice but was helpless to stop it. 'Jo, she could be hurt! She could be . . . like Ruth.'

Tears filled her eyes and she fought them back as Jo grabbed her bloodied hands.

'Stay calm, Allie. I haven't had a chance to really look for her.' She glanced around the room. 'It looks like most of the fire is out now. Let's look for her together.'

Moving quickly, Jo headed across the room pulling Allie with her. They walked through the lingering smoke, checking everybody they could find.

Nothing.

'Out front.' Jo was moving swiftly now, and Allie was right beside her. They headed for the front door and then skidded to a stop. In the entrance hall a frail body in a silvery blue dress lay still on the stone floor, a long, filmy wrap stretched out on either side of her, as if blown on a breeze only she could feel. A tall wooden candle holder lay across her body.

'Oh no.' Jo's words were a whisper as they rushed to Lisa's side.

Allie crouched beside her and picked up Lisa's hand. 'She's alive,' she said.

Jo pulled the candle holder off of her and threw it to one side. Lisa's hair had fallen across her face and Allie gently smoothed it back, revealing a deep gash across her cheek. Jo gave a small cry and her hand covered her mouth, her eyes filled with tears.

'Lisa? Lisa, wake up. Can you hear me? We

213

really need you to wake up.' Allie said the last word with such force that it seemed to reverberate.

She saw droplets fall on Lisa's dress and it took her a moment to realise that she was crying. Burying her face in her hands she sobbed, as Jo cried beside her.

'Wake up.'

CHAPTER SIXTEEN

In the chaotic hours after the attack, teachers herded the students into the darkened dining room and attempted to calm the panic. Staff carried in boxes of torches and handed them out, while nurses set up a triage in one corner. The injured queued to have their wounds bandaged, burns assessed and broken or sprained ankles splinted.

The room was generally clear of the choking smoke that lingered in the hallways, but the air was filled instead with the stifled weeping of students and the brutally efficient conversation of medical staff.

'Hand me those bandages.'

'This ankle needs an ice bath, you got one free?'

'Antibiotic by injection.'

Lisa remained unconscious, and was carried away to the nursing ward by two silent members of staff. At first Jo and Allie insisted on going with her, fluttering around the stretcher like shrill birds. But Eloise convinced them to stay.

She had a smear of soot across one cheek, and still wore her little black dress. Although her shoes were long gone, her eyes were bright and tireless.

'I promise you she's going to be OK. She needs to rest. And we really need your help down here. Please tell me I can count on you.'

They nodded reluctantly, and she sent them upstairs to wash off the blood and change clothes.

As they climbed the stairs, the fearful rumble of the aftermath gradually faded into the pitch black silence of the dormitory wing. Jo held Allie's hand. Allie's head pounded, and her stomach was churning. She thought she might throw up.

When they separated at the top, Jo said, 'It's safe up here, right?'

'She wouldn't have sent us here otherwise,' Allie replied, but her voice was uncertain.

'OK. Be really, really fast. I'll meet you in the bathroom.'

Allie opened her bedroom door slowly and flashed the light around to verify its emptiness. In the dark it felt foreign—as if it had no attachment to her at all and her belongings had been placed randomly. Hurrying across the room, she rifled through the dresser, grabbing whatever clothes came to hand.

Later, in a dark, cold shower lit only by a torch propped up against Jo's borrowed silver kitten heels, she scrubbed the blood off her body fiercely. The cold and the water cleared her head, as if she were washing the whole night away. Jo waited for her by a sink, swinging her light around the room. Occasionally they called out to each other for reassurance.

'You still alive?'

'Yep. You?'

'I think so.'

When she was finished, Allie left the ruined

215

white dress and the sparkly silver shoes in the shower changing room.

She and Jo hurried downstairs where the air of panic had transmuted into grim efficiency.

Torch beams bobbed down hallways as students carried scorched furniture out of the ballroom. Outside the back door a generator rumbled steadily, and thick black cables snaked down the corridor to the great hall where the Klieg lights they powered gave the still-smouldering space an unearthly glow.

Teachers armed with clipboards orchestrated the work. Some stood on chairs and called out instructions while others were sequestered in small, whispering groups around the walls.

Jo and Allie stood side by side, surveying the room.

'Well, I guess we should find Eloise,' Allie said, her voice shaky.

But instead of the librarian they found Isabelle perched perilously atop a rickety wooden chair, issuing orders calmly to the teachers and students who milled around. Her white dress was smudged with soot but otherwise perfect, although her hair had escaped from its clips and flowed in waves over her shoulders. She looked relieved to see them—especially Allie.

She crouched down to take her hands and pulled her closer. Speaking so quietly only Allie could hear she said, 'I'm so sorry that you had to see that. Are you OK?'

As she looked into Isabelle's concerned eyes a flood of conflicting emotions swept over Allie. She wanted to cry for Ruth and for herself. She wanted to hug the headmistress for caring. Instead, she

216

willed her tears back and nodded to show she was fine. Giving Allie's hands a final squeeze, Isabelle stood up again.

'OK, you two,' she said, businesslike again. Handing them a clipboard with a pencil connected to it with string, she continued, 'I need to be sure that we know where everybody is. There are fifty-two students here this term altogether. Identify everybody you can find. Search the central ground floor—not the wings, not upstairs. Do not go outside under any circumstances.'

A group of teachers approached her, and she turned away to deal with them.

At first Allie and Jo were overwhelmed—it was so dark and people rushed by them in the haze. But then they came up with a system, ticking off names of everybody they'd already seen, then starting on students they didn't recognise.

The work steadied their nerves. They wandered from room to room checking names off their list as the number of missing students dwindled. After about an hour electricity was restored, making their chore easier. The bitter burning smell lingered, but the air gradually cleared.

Throughout it all, Allie had a strange sense of distance—of watching herself on television as she moved around the school doing what had to be done. She couldn't even feel her own exhaustion. Her body moved but she felt disconnected from its actions.

By the time the sun came up, about twenty-one students were still not ticked off their lists. These included Gabe, Carter, Sylvain, Jules and Lucas.

'Where do you think they are?' Allie asked.

'Night School.' Jo's voice was weary as she

rubbed her forehead. 'They're all Night School. We've looked everywhere—this is all we're going to get. Let's go and turn it in.'

After searching the dining room and the library, they found Isabelle with Jerry and Eloise in the empty great hall. The stench of scorched wood and plaster was thick and nauseating. The electricity was still out in here, and the generator had been turned off, so it was dim and hard to see. Faint ambient light coming in from the hallway shimmered on the smoke particles still dancing in the air. They looked, Allie thought, like tiny black crystals. She could see that one wall was entirely blackened as far up as the ceiling. Small piles of rubble still smouldered here and there. But otherwise, the room was less damaged than she'd expected.

Isabelle scanned the list quickly and handed it to Jerry who looked it over and nodded.

'Thanks, you two,' Isabelle said. 'You did a brilliant job.'

'But so many are still missing!' Allie protested.

Isabelle had circles under her reddened eyes. She looked so tired Allie felt guilty for bothering her.

'We know where they are, and they're fine,' she said, putting her arm around Allie. 'Don't worry about them.'

'It's all the Night School guys, right?' Jo's arms were crossed tightly across her chest.

'You know we can't talk about Night School with you, Jo. But I expect you also know the answer to your own question.' Eloise's voice was sharp.

Jo held her ground. 'I'm sorry, Eloise, I just think it would be good if we were all a bit more

218

honest right now than we usually are.'

Isabelle squeezed Allie's shoulder gently and let go before turning to Jo. 'And a lot of teachers would agree with you,' she said, to Allie's surprise. 'But right now, we just have to get through the next twenty-four hours.'

'How many people were . . . killed?' Allie's voice was small.

'One, Allie.' Isabelle's voice was filled with sympathy. 'And I'm so sorry you had to see that. If you want to talk about it with any of us—we're here any time.'

Allie, who thought she could feel nothing, was surprised to feel a tear run down her cheek.

Where did that come from? she wondered, dashing it away.

As they walked away, Jerry squeezed her arm, and Eloise wrapped her in a warm hug.

'Hang in there, lovely,' she whispered.

When they'd gone Jo turned back to Isabelle. 'How's Lisa? Can we see her?'

'She's not awake yet. The doctor said she needs to rest.' Isabelle looked at them with concern. 'There's some food in the dining room. I'd really like you to take a break and get something to eat. I'll come find you there if we need you.'

Although it was hard to even imagine eating, at her insistence Jo and Allie headed down the dark hall. The dining room had a hushed, exhausted feel. It was early morning now, and light streamed with inappropriate cheeriness through the big windows. Tired, dirty students sat or slept at most tables—plates of half-eaten food in front of them. At one end of the room a buffet table was piled high with sandwiches, and big copper urns held steaming coffee and tea.

They stood in front of it, staring at the food. It just seemed weird to care about eating right now, but after filling their plates they found an unoccupied table; pushing aside the used cups and saucers to make room. For a while they ate in tired silence. Jo sat lotus-style, her white-blonde hair fluffed around her head in a disarrayed halo. Allie bent her leg to pull one foot up onto her seat and leaned her elbow on her knee. At rest, her face looked pale and worried. She finished a sandwich and pushed her plate away.

'What did you see?' She asked the question with no warning.

Jo looked puzzled for a second, then widened her eyes. 'Last night?'

Allie nodded.

Jo put down her cup of tea, and her face clouded over. 'Oh Allie it was crazy. Where were you, anyway? At first, everything was beautiful, you know? Gabe and I were dancing, and then suddenly there was a noise—like a big bang—and the lights went out. Then it all got really confusing because it was totally dark, everyone was running to where they thought the door was, and people were screaming that they couldn't get out, and then a table got knocked over and the fire started, and the smoke was . . . awful. Just awful.

'Gabe and I got down on the ground so that we could breathe, and made sort of air masks out of napkins. We got to where we were far from the fire, and then he said he had to go and see what was going on—like, why people weren't getting out of the room. And then he was . . . gone.'

Allie waited for more, but Jo stopped and tore

220

the crust of her sandwich into little pieces.

'What happened then?' she prodded.

'It was dark. I could just . . . hear screaming, and the smoke was really bad. I think the door was locked or something, because suddenly there was a crashing sound and then there was fresh air, but that made the fire worse. Then people started putting the fire out with water and fire extinguishers, and people could get out, and then you walked in.'

Jo sighed and took another bite of her sandwich, but Allie could see she was now forcing herself to eat.

'Have you seen Gabe since?'

Jo shook her head and a tear traced down her cheek. 'I'm trying not to be stupid. Eloise says everyone's fine, so he's fine. He just . . . left me there. In a fire.'

She hid her face in her hands, and Allie could tell that she was crying.

'Oh babe.' Allie reached out to squeeze her arm and tried to think of something to say. 'He made sure you were safe first, right? That was the very first thing he did. And, you know what? He has faith that you're tough, and you can take care of yourself. And that's kind of cool.'

Jo nodded, although she was clearly still unconvinced, then she closed her eyes and leaned on her elbow. 'I'm so tired.'

Allie scooted her chair closer and pulled Jo's head onto her shoulder. 'Me too.'

In a few moments, they were both asleep, their arms wrapped around each other.

*　　　*　　　*

221

The sound of movement woke them a short while later. The Night School group had returned.

Gabe was the first one through the door. The second she saw him, Jo flew across the room and flung herself into his arms. They disappeared out the door talking in whispers.

Sylvain wasn't far behind Gabe. Allie, who felt that she hadn't had time yet to process what had happened between them last night, wasn't ready to see him yet. She slid down low in her seat and stared into her empty teacup and hoped he wouldn't notice her.

She hadn't had a second to think about what had happened between them last night. And how she'd got so drunk so fast.

As she thought about last night, she ran her fingers absently across the lump on the back of her head. It was smaller now, but it still hurt.

When Carter and Lucas walked through the door a few minutes later she felt a surge of relief. They both looked tired and filthy—dirt smeared their faces and their hair matted with sweat.

She was still keeping her head down, so Carter didn't notice her as he filled his plate and grabbed a coffee. But Lucas saw her immediately.

'Any word about Lisa?' he asked.

She shook her head. 'Nothing yet.'

His lips tightened. 'I feel so awful about . . . I just wish I'd been with her.'

Seeing how worn out and defeated he looked, Allie hugged him. 'Isabelle says she's going to be OK, and I believe her.' He nodded against her shoulder. 'I think you should go and crash, Lucas. You look awful.'

He managed a smile. 'Thanks Allie. You sound like Carter—he was just telling me the same thing.'

As Lucas walked off, Allie looked around for Carter. He was sitting alone at one of the furthest tables—with his legs sprawled out. He was eating with mechanical thoroughness; his eyes were fixed on his plate as if he really didn't want to see anything else.

She waited until he'd eaten before walking over to him. Weariness made his face so vulnerable that her breath caught—he looked like a little boy. But the guarded look returned almost immediately. Pulling out a chair, she didn't wait for him to invite her to join him.

'Hey,' she said.

'Hey back.' His voice was distant.

She studied his face. 'Are you OK?'

'I'm good.' He looked up at her. 'You OK?'

She shrugged. 'I'm alive.'

'I heard about Ruth . . .'

She held up her hand reflexively. 'I don't want to talk about that.'

'Sorry,' he said.

'It's not your fault.' She willed dark images of Ruth's body out of her mind. 'I just . . . can't talk about it right now. I'm not ready.'

'OK.' He sipped his coffee.

Silence fell between them.

She waited three breaths.

'Carter?'

'What?'

'Have you seen Phil? Is he OK?'

He shook his head. 'Not OK. He's devastated. He blames himself for not being with her when it happened, the poor bastard. He's going home for a

223

while.'

Allie absorbed this information, before speaking again. 'About last night . . .'

'Allie . . .' He shot her a warning look, but she ignored him.

'Was I drunk? Or, I don't know . . . drugged? I mean, I've been drunk before, and I know how you get drunk, obviously. But I just had *three* glasses. And I was . . . Well, I don't really know what I was.'

'I don't know what you were either, Allie.'

His tone was accusing, and she leaned away from him, stung. 'Hey. That's not fair.'

'You want to know what I think?' His dark eyes flashed with repressed anger. 'I think you drank too much and you trusted Sylvain. I tried to warn you.'

'I know! I know you did.' She was angry too, but her anger was directed at herself. 'It's all my fault. And I'm sorry I didn't listen. I was stupid. I'm a dumbass, OK? Will you forgive me now?'

His expression softened. 'Look, Allie, it's just . . . I've told you before. You haven't been here long enough to understand how things are here. Just be careful, OK? Things are not what they seem. People aren't always who they seem to be.'

Even though his tone was kinder, his warning chilled her.

What kind of school is this, anyway? Who are these people? Worry burned her stomach. *Can I trust anybody? Even Carter? He's always been such a pain in the arse, but has he ever lied to me?*

She studied his serious face, then reached out and put her hand on his arm. 'Thanks, Carter.'

Surprised, he raised one eyebrow. 'For what?'

'You kind of rescued me from my own stupidity last night. That's twice in twenty-four hours you've

224

saved me. In some countries, I'd owe you my life, or my first-born child or something.'

He half-smiled, but she thought his eyes still looked guarded. 'Just . . . believe me next time, OK?'

She nodded fervently, but all she said was, 'OK.'

As he leaned back in his chair and took a sip of his cooling coffee his eyes narrowed and he stared hard at something behind her. Allie turned. Across the dining room Sylvain sat alone, his eyes boring into them. She could feel anger radiating off him like heat.

Carter returned his glare, unflinching.

'Oh bollocks,' Allie muttered.

'You're going to have trouble with him,' Carter told her, turning to face her. 'He is powerful around here, and he's not going to be happy if he doesn't get what he wants. And what he wants is you.'

Staring fearlessly back at Sylvain, Allie said, 'Well that's too bad. Because he can't have me.'

Pushing back her chair she stood and stalked over to where Sylvain sat at the front of the room. His expression was intimidating but she was sober now. She leaned over until her hands rested on the arms of his chair and her face was just inches from his.

When she spoke her voice was a threatening whisper.

'That was the worst date I ever had. And we. Are so. Over.'

She waited just long enough to clock the surprised look on his face, then she walked to the door. Out of the corner of her eye she saw Carter smile.

As she climbed the stairs to the girls' dormitory she counted every single step. When she reached her own room sixty-one steps later she opened the door.

All was as she'd left it hours ago—dresser drawers were still open and clothes strewn on the floor from her hurried late-night search for something to wear.

Taking a deep breath, she took the sixty-second step into the room and began the process of making it feel safe again. First she picked up the clothes and put them away, then she straightened the already straight desktop and closed the wardrobe door. Finally, when everything was perfect, she closed the shutter over the window to block the daylight, kicked off her shoes and lay down on top of the duvet. She was completely exhausted. But she was also far too wired to sleep.

For half an hour she tossed and turned as last night's events swirled through her head like the dancers at the ball. *Who killed Ruth? . . . Carter must think I'm a complete slapper . . . Was I drunk? Jo said the champagne was strong . . . But Ruth was . . . She was . . .*

Dark and cloudy images of Ruth's bloodied body made her retch and she sat bolt upright. Her heart was pounding and her hands dripped with sweat.

She couldn't breathe.

Air. I need air.

Springing from her bed she scrambled up onto her desk and flung the window open. Daylight poured in and she took a strangled breath of warm,

226

fresh air . . .

'Ouch!'

The voice outside her window startled her so much she nearly fell off the desk as she scrambled backwards. Clutching the chair as if it would protect her, she wheezed breathlessly.

'Who . . .?'

'Allie? What's the matter?'

'Carter?' she wheezed. 'What the . . . hell are . . . you . . .?'

Ignoring her question he reached through the window and pulled her closer—her body slid easily along the polished wood of her desktop; she didn't have the strength to resist.

His dark eyes were serious as he watched her struggle to breathe. 'Remember what you did the other night? You need to do it again. Breathe in through your nose. Slowly. And out through your mouth.'

She tried to process what was happening. 'Were you . . . spying . . .?'

He glared at her. 'Bloody hell, Allie. Will you just shut up and breathe?'

With her eyes on his, and his hands gripping hers, she breathed in sync with him, raggedly at first, but gradually more easily. When she seemed to be breathing normally, he let go and the questions burst out of her.

'Are you a total *pervert*? How on earth did you get up here? And how did you find my room? And . . .'

Sitting on the ledge outside her window, Carter laughed and held up his hands. 'Come on, Allie. I've lived at this school my whole life. I know every inch of it. Including the roof. Which is, by the way,

227

super-easy to get up on and I'm kind of surprised you haven't tried it yet.'

Allie looked for any sign that he was lying to her but saw nothing but exasperation.

'Did you come here from your room?' She paused, looking around. 'Where is your room anyway?'

He pointed across the building. 'Look, the guys' dorm is on the top floor of the main building. My window is the third one there on the top floor, do you see it?'

She counted the dormer windows and nodded.

He turned back towards her. 'It's easy to get here from there.'

Suddenly she had a flashback to a few weeks ago. She stared up at him.

'You've been here before.' Her voice was accusing. 'When I first came here, I thought I heard somebody outside my window late one night. It was you, wasn't it?'

He had the grace to look embarrassed. 'Oh balls. I didn't think you heard. Sorry about that.'

'You freaked me out, Carter,' she said. 'What were you doing here?'

He squirmed uncomfortably. 'I was . . . actually on my way to see somebody else and you opened your window and nearly knocked me off the roof. I'm not a peeping Tom or anything.'

Remembering Jo's warning that he broke girls' hearts, Allie wondered who he'd been going to see. She studied him speculatively.

Who the hell are you anyway, Carter West?

Having him on the defensive made her feel more in control, and she crossed her legs and rested her elbows on her knees. 'So, why are you here now,

Carter? On your way to see some other girl again?'

He leaned against the window frame, avoiding her eyes. As he did it, he dislodged a pebble from the ledge, and she could hear it clicking its way to the ground three storeys below.

'No. Of course not. It's not a big deal or anything. I was just . . . worried about you, I guess,' he said finally. 'It's been a pretty terrible night and you get these panic attacks, so I just . . . you know . . . worried.'

They held each other's gaze for a moment, but his eyes were so limitlessly dark they seemed to summon images of last night's awful events. She covered her face with her hands to block them out.

'I keep seeing Ruth and remembering . . . It was bad, Carter. Really bad. It was dark but I could see that her throat was cut. There was so much blood . . . And then the footsteps. I thought I was next.'

'What footsteps?'

When she looked up he was staring at her. For the first time it occurred to her that in all of the chaos she'd never had a chance to tell anybody about what happened outside.

When she filled him in, he kept returning to the footsteps she'd heard. 'You're quite certain the footsteps came from within the school and then headed away?'

Allie nodded—she could see that his mind was working.

'How many footsteps did you hear? I mean, how many people do you think there were?' he asked.

'One, I think, but I'm not certain. I was too frightened. Carter, who could have done this? Do you think it could have been a student? Or . . . a teacher?'

229

Until now, the idea had not occurred to her, but suddenly it all seemed appallingly possible. She hoped he'd laugh at her, or tell her she was being stupid. But he didn't.

Instead, he rubbed his eyes. 'I don't know. I don't think so—but I don't know any more.'

'Why didn't they kill me too?' Her voice was plaintive as she finally said the words she'd been avoiding since last night. 'Why am I still alive?'

Carter looked out over the school grounds. He didn't speak for a long moment. When he did, his voice was rough. 'I don't know, Allie. But if it's possible the killer saw you, and maybe thinks that you saw him . . . Well. You need to be very careful from now on.'

It was a warm morning but Allie shivered. She lowered her voice to a whisper. 'Carter, what is going on?'

His eyes locked on hers, and she could feel how much he wanted to tell her something, but the moment passed and he shook his head.

'I can't, Allie. I just can't.'

She was so tired she couldn't bear to argue— she'd had almost no sleep in two days. Resting her head on her hand and closing her eyes, she yawned.

'I want to stay awake and fight off murderers but I'm too tired,' she murmured. 'It really sucks being alone right now, Carter. I wish you could stay.'

A long silence passed between them, but she'd dozed a little and didn't notice until Carter spoke again.

'Scoot over,' he said.

She made room for him on the desktop and he climbed lithely through the window then closed it behind him.

A sudden rush of adrenalin made her feel very awake. 'We'll be so busted if Jules finds out,' she said, although she didn't really care.

'Oh, I can handle Jules,' he said. Sitting on the floor beside the bed he stretched out his legs with a groan of pleasure—his lanky frame had been compressed on the window ledge, and he'd probably been running all night. 'Besides, everything's crazy today. Nobody will notice. Get into bed and let's both try to sleep.'

After a second's hesitation, Allie climbed off the desk and onto the bed. Feigning nonchalance, she pulled the blue blanket off the footboard and handed it down to him. But when their fingers touched as he took it from her they both froze for a second.

'Do you need a pillow?' she asked, forcing her voice to be steady.

'Thanks—no, this is good.' He sounded calm but she could see how tight his jaw was as he unfolded the blanket.

Allie stretched out and tried to relax but her body was rigid—every muscle tensed as if for flight. She put her hands over her face.

'I can't do this. I'll never sleep.'

Carter lifted one of her hands off her face and held it. 'Did I ever tell you that I used to have panic attacks?'

Surprised, Allie rolled onto her side so that she could see him. 'Did you? When?'

'A few years ago.' He was lying on his back, staring at the ceiling. 'I was going through a rough patch and I started having these . . . episodes. A good friend helped me through it. And one thing he taught me was to stop thinking about what was freaking me out, and to concentrate instead on things that made me feel safe. Even . . . happy. To force better thoughts into my head. What makes you happy, Allie?'

She thought hard. *Christopher, alive and well and normal. Being part of a normal family. Being here. Until last night anyway.*

'I don't know,' she whispered.

Carter was quiet for a while, holding her hand against his chest. When he spoke again, she could feel the rumble of his voice through her fingertips.

'Imagine . . . we're somewhere else. Somewhere really beautiful. Maybe on a beach with white sand and blue water.'

She tried to see herself sitting with Carter in the shade of a palm tree, sand between their toes.

'You're safe here,' he said, his voice low and steady. 'Maybe later we'll snorkel and watch the fish swim. Bright colourful fish. Can you see them?'

Focusing on his words, she thought she could see them—flashing by in the blue water. She began to hear the rhythmic rumble of waves. His voice was so calming, her shoulders relaxed at last as bright shoals of tiny blue, red and yellow tropical fish scattered across her imagination. Her breathing became more steady. She felt herself sinking into the warm water—slowly and deliciously.

'It's beautiful.' Her voice was thick with sleep.

'Yes it is,' he said, still holding her hand.

In her mind she surfaced, and saw a ship on the horizon, sails unfurling as she fell asleep.

CHAPTER SEVENTEEN

When Allie woke some time later, she was alone, but she had the not unpleasant feeling that Carter had been with her most of the time. She'd half-woken several times from bad dreams and in her exhausted daze thought she'd heard him whisper: 'It's OK. Sleep.'

Sitting up, she looked at the alarm clock. It was just before seven o'clock.

Morning? Or night?

A glance out the window revealed a summer evening. She'd slept all day.

As she stretched her tired muscles, her stomach rumbled so loudly at first she didn't know what she was hearing.

'Starving,' she announced to the empty room.

Jumping out of bed, she headed straight for the door then skidded to a stop when she caught a glance of herself in the wall mirror. Her hair stood on end, her face was smudged with soot and she still wore the same clothes she'd put on in the middle of last night, now almost unrecognisably wrinkled.

She made a face at herself. *Oh balls. Even* I *can't go out looking like this.*

Grabbing a hairbrush off the desk, she forced it through the tangled waves, then quickly changed clothes, hopping up and down on one leg and swearing under her breath when her skirt caught on the shoes she'd put on first.

Still buttoning the waistband, she rushed out of her room, stopping briefly at the mirror to wipe the soot off her face, and headed down the empty hallway to the landing, where she stopped.

It was quiet. Unnaturally quiet.

An awful thought crossed Allie's mind: *What if everybody left while I was sleeping, and they just forgot me?*

Even though she knew it was absurd she felt a rush of fear as she raced down the stairs, hearing only the rubber patter of her shoes on the steps. As she neared the ground floor, though, she saw crowds of students moving in a subdued hush to the dining room and she slowed her pace. She felt ridiculous.

Of course they hadn't left.

You're losing it, she scolded herself, before taking a calming breath and joining the throngs.

The smell of food mingled unpleasantly with the acrid scent of scorched wood and plaster. As she looked around for a familiar face, she noticed that several of those around her had visible bandages. One hopped on crutches.

In the dining room, the night's chaos had all been cleared away, but the tables had not been reset for supper with the usual crystal and china. Stacks of plates stood on every table, and students were handing them around to each other. No candles glimmered (after the fire she was glad of that). Everyone sat quietly as if nobody knew quite what to say.

She noticed with relief that Jo, Gabe and Lucas were at their normal table and she headed straight for them, but then Carter walked up beside her.

'Hey.'

As she turned to look into Carter's dark eyes her stomach flip-flopped. Suddenly shy, she shoved her

234

hands in her skirt pockets.

'Hey back.'

'Did you sleep OK?'

He'd showered and changed—his cheeks were still rosy from the water, and his hair was damp on the ends. The tiredness was gone from his face.

She nodded, trying to stay cool, as if boys slept in her bedroom every day. But heat rose in her cheeks, betraying her. 'Did you? When did you leave?'

'An hour or so ago.'

He had a way of talking so quietly that she was forced to lean closer to him in order to hear. It made even ordinary conversations like this one feel intimate.

'I needed to change,' he continued. She was hyper-aware that her arm was rubbing against his. 'I didn't want to wake you—it took you so long to fall asleep.'

The tension between them was unbearable. One of them was going to have to look away, but Allie didn't want to be the one.

What's happening to me? she wondered. *I can't fancy Carter. I just . . . can't.*

'Yeah,' she said breathlessly. 'I mean . . . I had to change too.'

Looking around, Carter noticed that most of the room was seated. 'We better go or Zelazny will start shouting.'

He steered her to the table and waited until she was seated then, to her surprise, pulled out the chair next to her. He never sat with her group at meals, and she tried not to show on her face how pleased she was.

Gabe had no such qualms.

235

'Carter!' he said, leaning back in his chair with a teasing smile. 'You do us an honour.'

Carter shrugged. 'Oh, you know how it is, Gabe. Sometimes I just need to be close to you.'

Jo, who still looked tired, leaned towards Allie. 'Did you sleep?'

'Eventually,' she said. 'You?'

'Not really.' Jo gave a weary smile. 'But I think I might be starving. Does that make me a bad person?'

'I hope not,' Allie said. 'Turns out death and destruction can really negatively impact a low-calorie diet. Who knew?'

'Any news on Lisa?' Carter asked.

Lucas was the one to answer. 'I tracked down Eloise an hour ago and she said Lisa's awake and doing OK. We should be able to visit her soon.'

Allie felt herself smile for the first time since last night. The mood lightened, and for a while conversation buzzed in an almost normal way.

Then Lucas' voice rose above the hum. 'Hey, did everyone hear about the announcement?'

Allie glanced around the table, but she could tell nobody knew what he was talking about.

'What announcement?' Carter asked.

'Isabelle's making some sort of big announcement tonight about what happened. There's a rumour that they're sending everybody home, shutting the place down for the rest of the summer.'

'No!' Jo sounded stricken and Allie glanced over at her, surprised by her vehement tone. Gabe put a hand on her arm and she looked up at him with wild eyes. 'They can't send us home. They *can't*.'

'I'm sure they won't.' Gabe's voice was soothing

236

and Allie looked away as he tried to calm her.

The doors at the end of the dining room opened and the staff emerged in their usual orderly black-clad ranks, carrying steaming bowls and platters. Even though she was ravenous, Allie watched with strange disinterest as they set food on the table. Eating seemed so pointless, somehow, after all that had happened.

Sensing movement, she glanced down to see Carter serving stew onto her plate. He caught her eye and smiled guiltily.

'Mmm . . . Delicious stew,' he said lamely, and she surprised herself by laughing.

He slipped vegetables on her plate next, but when he handed her a roll she held up her hands in surrender. 'All right, all right. Stop. I'll eat. I promise.' She took a dutiful bite, chewing with false enthusiasm. 'OK?'

Now busy clearing his own plate, Carter ignored her sarcasm. In fact, that first bite had tasted pretty good and Allie found the second went down even easier. In the end she emptied her plate and sopped up the last of the gravy with the roll, then sat back in her chair with a satisfied sigh.

'You really were hungry,' Carter observed, amused.

'My brother always says I eat like a boy . . .' Allie said without thinking, and her smile faded as suddenly as it arrived. She never talked about Christopher.

The low hum of conversation in the room gradually increased as rumours spread about the impending announcement, and Allie was relieved that things felt, if only momentarily, slightly more normal. But as she glanced around the table she

237

noticed that Jo looked wan and worried as she picked at her food. Before she could say anything to her, a voice spoke from the front of the room.

'Can I have your attention, please?'

Dressed neatly in pressed black trousers and a pale blue cardigan, Isabelle stood still until the room quieted. The man she'd been dancing with the night before stood a few feet behind her, his hands folded in a position of calm. His alert eyes seemed to miss nothing. Then Allie felt her heart pound—Sylvain walked through the door and stood nearby, as if he were part of a triumvirate.

What's he doing?

Isabelle's face was sombre, but Allie marvelled at how normal she looked.

'I know many of you were up all night, and I appreciate how tired you are. We are all so grateful for your efforts in putting out the fire.'

Allie glanced over at Carter and saw that he was watching Isabelle with a slight frown.

'What happened last night was unprecedented in the history of Cimmeria,' Isabelle continued. 'It is disturbing and will require considerable work on our part to set right. The fire alone has damaged ancient walls. Bits of our history are gone for ever. But we will restore this school, have no doubt, and it will continue as it has always done.'

Faltering applause from the students seemed to take her by surprise, and she waited for it to fade to silence.

'I am very sorry the events of last night occurred. It was upsetting for all of us. Our hearts go out to those of you who were close to Ruth Jansen—she was a lovely, if disturbed girl, and we will all miss her terribly. Her suicide came as a horrible shock.'

Allie gasped and covered her mouth with her hand. *Suicide? What is she talking about?*

'We know that some of you might have problems dealing with her death, we are all—the teachers and myself—ready to help at any time if you need counselling or just someone to listen.' Isabelle's eyes were suffused with understanding. 'You don't have to suffer alone.'

A murmur swept across the room and Allie noticed that some students were weeping. Turning to catch Jo's eye, she saw that she was biting her lip and trying not to cry—Gabe had his arm around her.

'A memorial service will be held at the chapel next week. I'm sure those of you who knew her well will want to attend.'

After waiting a moment for all of that information to be absorbed, Isabelle continued in a brisker manner. 'Some students injured in the fire will be leaving us tomorrow to recuperate at home, and we wish them all the best. We hope to see you all back in the autumn term. For those of you remaining—the work to repair the damage done by the fire should take about a month, and I fear there will be some disruption in the meantime—it's annoying but necessary. The great hall is, of course, off limits for now.'

She took a step back. 'For your safety, curfew is early tonight—we'd like everyone to be in their rooms by nine o'clock—and you are all to remain indoors at all times for at least the next forty-eight hours.'

As soon as she finished speaking, the teachers clustered around her and the students began trooping towards the door in a low rumble of hushed conversation.

Spinning around to face Carter, Allie whispered, 'What the hell . . . ?'

Tight-lipped, he shook his head.

Looking up towards Isabelle, Allie stood up. 'I need to find out when we can see Lisa. I'll catch up.'

Carter grabbed her arm, his eyes contained a warning. 'Allie . . .'

'I can handle it,' she said, shaking off his hand. 'I promise I won't freak out. I really want to know about Lisa.'

'I'll find you after,' Carter said, hurrying after Gabe and Lucas.

Standing at the edge of the group of teachers, Allie waited for a break in their conversation. They were clearly agitated, but they were whispering so quietly she could only make out a phrase here and there.

'Too dangerous . . .'

'Send them home!' (Said with great force by Jerry, who was shushed.)

'. . . about Nathaniel.'

Then Eloise noticed her. 'Can we help you, Allie?'

Everyone fell silent as they all turned to look at her. Allie crossed one ankle behind the other in an unconscious gesture of nervousness.

'I was just wondering if we can see Lisa?'

Isabelle stepped through the crowd and put her arm around her. 'She's doing OK, Allie. She's awake but she's groggy. You can see her tomorrow.'

Allie held Isabelle's eyes challengingly. Up close she looked more anxious than she'd seemed from a distance—she had dark circles under her eyes. But she didn't back down under Allie's gaze.

'Is there something else you need, Allie?' she asked evenly.

For just a second Allie imagined saying, *'Yes. Why are you pretending Ruth slit her own throat from ear to ear?'*

But something told her this wasn't the time or place to challenge Isabelle.

'No . . . Thanks,' Allie said, hurrying to the door.

Just before she reached it, she heard the whispers begin again.

*   *   *

Outside the dining hall Jo stood alone, leaning against the wall. She looked less pale than she had during dinner but Allie didn't like the way her hands clenched and unclenched. She seemed to cheer up briefly when Allie gave her the good news about Lisa, but something was still not right.

As the two climbed the stairs towards the girls' dormitory wing, Allie glanced over to see Jo staring down, near tears.

'What is it, Jo?' she asked. 'What's going on?'

'It's nothing, Allie.' Jo didn't meet her eyes and Allie knew she wasn't telling the truth, but she didn't think pursuing the issue would help.

When they reached Jo's room, Allie walked in with her, suddenly afraid to leave her alone. Something was terribly wrong. Jo sat down on the bed, kicking off her shoes in her usual way, but she was wringing her hands.

Allie leaned back against the desk. She spoke in calm tones. 'Jo, is there anything I can do?'

'I need to talk to Gabe,' Jo said, then she repeated the phrase in different ways. 'I just . . . I have to talk to Gabe. I need to see Gabe.'

'But we just left Gabe,' Allie said, puzzled.

Jo shook her head. 'I need to talk to him alone. I'm freaking out. He'll know what to do.'

Studying her pale face, Allie made a quick decision. 'OK, don't worry. I'll go and find him. Do me a favour and just rest for a while, OK? You're wiped out. Have you slept at all today?'

'But I'm not tired,' Jo said, sitting down on the bed. 'I'm way too wired to sleep.'

'I was too,' Allie said. 'But try, OK? Just lie down and I'll stay here until you're asleep. I'll find Gabe, I promise.'

'I need to talk to him.' Jo's voice was blurred with exhaustion, and her eyes fluttered shut, even as a tear slipped down the side of her face. Finally, she leaned back against the pillows.

'Just rest for a second,' Allie said softly. She stood by the open window—the breeze was still cool. 'I'll find Carter and get him to send Gabe back.'

'How will you find Carter?' Jo's voice was drowsy.

Looking out the window at the lengthening shadows on the grass below, Allie said, 'I can always find Carter.'

*　　　*　　　*

When Jo's breathing was regular and steady, Allie quietly closed the window and shutter, then tiptoed out, closing the door behind her with a nearly silent click.

Downstairs, she found the ground floor mostly empty. All the students who had been milling around had disappeared to their rooms. She wasn't sure where to start looking—she'd never been to the guys' dorm, and she wasn't even sure how to get there aside from going across the roof, which didn't seem like a great idea right now.

At that moment she heard a slapping sound down the hallway and looked up to see Jules walking purposefully, a clipboard held against her chest. The sound came from her pink Birkenstocks hitting her heels with every step.

She remembered Jo's words when she'd asked her if any girls were in Night School. '*Maybe Jules . . .*'

Allie stepped into her path. 'Hey Jules. How's it going?' She used her friendliest tone, and Jules looked a bit startled.

'Hello Allie.' She slowed her pace but didn't stop and Allie swung into step with her.

'Do you know where Gabe and Carter are?'

'Why?' Jules asked suspiciously.

Allie attempted a friendly but exasperated approach. 'It's a long, crazy story, but Carter has something of mine and I really need it, and Jo thought he might be with Gabe. Do you know? Like . . . where they are?'

Jules studied her face.

'No,' she said crisply, hurrying her pace.

Cursing silently, Allie rushed after her.

'Look, Jules. It's super-important. I wouldn't ask otherwise.'

Jules stopped and turned to face her. 'They're in a meeting in the classroom wing where you're not allowed to go, OK? But if you hang out near the

243

door you'll probably catch them as they come out. On the other hand, I don't have any idea how long they'll be.'

By now, Allie wanted to shake her, but she was not giving up.

'So,' she said, dragging one toe in a straight line on the floor, 'where are you headed right now?'

Tucking the clipboard under her arm, Jules affected exaggerated patience. 'What's your point, Allie?'

'Just that, if you're going to that meeting, could you please send Carter back here. Now? Or just tell him I'm waiting here and I need to speak with him. It's really important.'

Looking like she couldn't believe what she'd just heard, Jules began walking again. 'Of course, Allie. And would you like me to get you some tea and chocolate while I'm there? Because I've got nothing better to do today than to be your messenger girl.'

Dropping behind her, Allie raised two fingers at her back.

'No thanks,' she said, her voice cheerful and steady. 'I can get my own tea.'

Jules' voice floated back to her as she turned the corner. 'How lovely.'

'Thanks,' Allie muttered when Jules was out of earshot, 'and you have a great day, too, Jules.'

Leaning against the wall with her arms crossed over her chest and the rubber sole of one foot propped on the antique wood panelling behind her, Allie waited. After ten minutes, she slid down the wall and sat on the floor, crossing her legs. In this spot she was hidden by the baroque, marble-topped occasional table next to her, so Isabelle didn't see her when she walked by with her dancing partner a few minutes later.

'. . . she needs to know that Nathaniel is out of control.' Her voice was icy with rage. 'Last night was unacceptable. She's got to do something about it. At least pick a side. My God, Matthew, people got hurt. *Children* got hurt. This can't continue.'

Matthew murmured something in reply that Allie couldn't make out.

'Well then you will just have to go and see her personally,' Isabelle snapped as the two walked out of earshot.

Isabelle's words had an electrifying effect on Allie, who leaned forward to peer around the heavily carved mahogany legs of the table.

So it wasn't a teacher or a student after all. She drew her knees up close to her body and wrapped her arms around them as a strange feeling of relief washed over her. At least the murderer wasn't somebody she thought of as a friend.

More footsteps.

Allie leaned forward again to see Carter standing nearby, looking up and down the wide corridor.

She scrambled to her feet. 'Carter.'

'Allie! Has something happened? Jules said you were looking for me.'

Allie almost smiled. *I can't believe it. She did tell him.*

She stepped closer and lowered her voice. 'Is Gabe in that meeting you were just in?'

He nodded.

'He needs to go to Jo's room—she's freaking out,' Allie said.

Carter didn't seem surprised. 'I'll tell him. I

could see something was wrong at dinner—he didn't want to leave her, but . . .'

Allie's eyes were worried. 'She's being very strange, Carter. Not like herself.'

'I told him that would happen.' There was a pause while he seemed to come to a decision. 'Allie, we need to talk.'

'Sure. What's up?'

He looked around. 'No, I mean, in private. Can you meet me at the chapel in twenty minutes?'

She looked at him dubiously. 'We're not supposed to leave the building on pain of wrath-of-Isabelle and it's after nine already.'

'It's the perfect time,' he said. 'Everybody's in meetings or gone to their rooms for curfew. The teachers are all distracted.'

Allie thought about saying no. The last thing she needed was detention. But Carter looked so determined. She hoped that whatever he had to say would explain some of what was going on.

'OK, but if I get expelled I'm so grassing you up.'

Even though his lips curled up in a smile, his eyes were serious. 'Good. See you there. Give me a ten-minute head start so that I can let Gabe know about Jo. Then run fast.'

As he walked away Allie muttered under her breath: 'Run fast? I thought you said everyone would be too busy to notice.'

She paced impatiently (*three hundred and ninety-one steps*) while waiting for ten minutes to go by. At the eight-minute mark, she began walking towards the front door (*thirty-three steps*) with casual nonchalance. The entrance hall was quiet, but as her hand touched the door handle she heard voices coming down the hall.

Aside from large candle holders and tapestries there was little in this space save for one wrought-iron table draped in heavy fabric. Allie darted behind it just as Eloise and Zelazny rounded the corner.

'Will this take long?' Eloise was asking as their footsteps approached. She sounded irritated.

'I hope not.' Zelazny opened the door. 'But it depends on what we find.'

'Where do you want to start?'

As they walked out the door Allie heard Zelazny's reply: 'Where we found Ruth's body.'

The click of the latch echoed in the empty, stone entry hall.

In her hiding place, Allie frowned. *What are they looking for?*

At first she thought there was no way she could get out of the building with Zelazny and Eloise now outside, but then it occurred to her that Ruth's body had been found at the back of the building. The chapel was in the woods across the front lawn. Although she hadn't heard all that Zelazny was saying, if they were starting at the back, she should have plenty of time to get to the shelter of the treeline before she could be seen.

To give them time to get away from the front, she counted to one hundred before opening the door. It swung silently on its hinges and she peeked outside.

Not a soul in sight.

Stepping out into the late evening light, she carefully closed the door behind her.

It was just after Isabelle's nine o'clock curfew, and the sun was thinking about setting at the end of the long summer day. Standing on the top step, illuminated in the golden glow, Allie looked upward for a long minute as if she were trying to absorb the light into her soul. Then she darted across the lawn and hurled herself towards the forest.

Once she'd made it safely to the treeline (*ninety-seven steps*), she slowed a bit to catch her breath, then jogged down the path through the darkening shadows. All was silent and dim. When she reached the churchyard gate five minutes later the quiet was oppressive.

If Carter's in there, I certainly can't hear him. The metal clang the latch made when she opened the gate seemed to ring out in the peaceful glade.

Instinctively she headed to the yew tree where they'd sat talking on detention day. As she neared it she saw a foot clad in a dark shoe dangling down. Reaching up, she grabbed it and it was instantly retracted.

'Hey—you made it.' He was sitting on the same broad branch, his back against the tree trunk. As he leaned down to help her up she marvelled again at his strength—he lifted her easily into place next to him. She shifted herself back onto a smooth spot and sat facing him, her knees bent and her feet flat on the branch between them.

'So . . . what's this all about, Carter?' she asked, cocking her head. 'Why did you want to meet all the way out here in detention-land?'

'Because I didn't want to be overheard, and this is about the only place I know of where I can be a hundred per cent sure we can talk safely.'

Something in Carter's posture looked uncomfortable. He seemed to have trouble deciding what to say and she couldn't catch his eye.

'It's just . . .' he said, then stopped. After a moment he tried again. 'There are some things you need to know.'

Thank God for that, Allie thought. *Some answers at last.*

She didn't wait for him to start. 'Carter, what do you know about all of this? Why are they pretending Ruth killed herself? Her throat was . . . There is no way she did that to herself. And there were others there. I heard them. And Isabelle knows about them.'

Carter had started to interrupt her before she mentioned Isabelle. Now he stopped and stared at her. 'What makes you think Isabelle knows?'

Quickly she told him about overhearing the teachers and then Isabelle talking about someone named Nathaniel, and the implication that he was involved in what had happened.

Carter raked his fingers through his hair. 'So, they don't think anybody at the school had anything to do with Ruth's death but they're going to tell everyone she killed herself.'

Allie leaned forward. 'Why, though? Won't the police be able to take one look at her and know it wasn't a suicide?'

He met her gaze. 'What police?'

She gaped at him. 'Are you serious? You think they haven't called the cops?'

'Haven't. Won't.'

'But . . . how . . . ?'

His reply was immediate. 'The police haven't been here because the police have no idea what's going on here and nobody's going to tell them. They will never know Ruth died here. Her body will turn up in an alley somewhere and her parents, who spend most of their time in France, will tell the cops she was a runaway. And the cops will believe them because her dad's an investment banker and her mum wears designer clothes and those kinds of people don't lie, right?'

Allie couldn't believe what she was hearing. 'Are you serious? Carter, are you saying this will all be covered up?'

'Of course it will, Allie. There's a reason you'd never heard of Cimmeria before you came here.' His tone was bitter. 'Don't you get it yet? Don't you know where you are?'

Allie didn't know what to say. She searched for the right words. 'Carter, what is going on here, really?'

'That is what I'm trying to figure out,' he said, staring out over the churchyard. 'Look, Cimmeria is a very unusual, tightly knit place. Everybody knows everybody. Everybody is here for a reason. Remember when we had that sort of argument, when we first met? You thought I was saying that you didn't have a right to be here?'

Flushing at the memory of her humiliation, Allie nodded.

'We don't get new students here in the middle of summer term who don't have a strong connection to the school. Like their parents are on the board. Or their whole family studied here. Something like that,' Carter explained. 'All I was trying to find out was which one of those you were. But you're none of them. You don't have any connections to the school at all.'

He met her gaze directly. 'That just doesn't happen.'

Clinging to the branch with her knees, Allie

250

chewed on her thumbnail as she tried to process what he was telling her. Evening was encroaching on the summer sun, and it was getting harder to make out his features in the fading light.

'I don't know what to tell you,' Allie said. 'My parents said the police recommended Cimmeria—or at least,' she stopped to think, 'they sort of said that. But they were all top secret about it before we came here. They wouldn't even tell me where the school was. I still don't know the name of the nearest town. The whole thing was all rushed and weird and James Bond-y.'

Carter shook his head. 'The police in London wouldn't have recommended this school because they wouldn't ever have heard of this school. So your parents lied to you. Now, why would they do a thing like that?'

Feeling her heart pound crazily, Allie tried to breathe normally and not panic. (*Five breaths in, four breaths out.*)

'You know what, Carter?' Her voice was tight and she swallowed hard. 'You're right. I really don't know where I am.'

'Then you need to find out,' Carter said. 'And you need to decide pretty fast who you're going to trust.'

CHAPTER EIGHTEEN

This was all too much for Allie to handle. Shivering now, she wrapped her arms around her torso. 'Carter, if you're trying to scare the crap out of me? You've totally succeeded. So, can you stop now?'

For a long minute he said nothing, then he sighed heavily. 'I'm sorry to dump all this on you. And I really don't want to scare you. But I do want you to realise this is all serious.'

'I knew this was serious the second I fell down in a puddle of Ruth's blood,' she snapped. 'I get it, OK? I freakin' get it. We're in a lot of trouble. Something messed up is going on. People are dying. This school is really weird. And I don't belong here.'

Carter slid along the branch until he was so close to her their knees touched, and pulled her into a hug. At first she tried to push him away, but he held her tight.

'I'm sorry. I shouldn't be doing this to you. I just don't want you to get hurt,' he said.

Taking a tremulous breath, she allowed herself to relax in his arms. The warmth of his body felt like security.

Letting her go, he leaned back far enough to see her face. 'I was trying to freak you out, but only because I'm worried about what might happen. The thing is, I came out here today to convince you to go back home.'

Surprised, she looked up at him as he continued, fumbling now with his words. 'I figured they'd let you go because of, like, mental stress or whatever.'

She opened her mouth to argue, but he continued before she could speak. 'Only, I decided that I really didn't want you to. Go, I mean. What I mean is . . . I really hope you'll stay. We'll figure out what to do.'

'I think we'll have to,' Allie said simply, 'because I haven't got any place to go any more.'

In the darkness, Allie couldn't see his eyes when

252

he replied. 'Then you're just like me.'

Carter looked up at the sky where the last light was now fading away. 'We better go in. It's getting late.'

Jumping down from the branch with athletic grace, he turned and put his hands around her waist to lift her down. She held onto his shoulders as he set her on her feet. His eyes held hers for a second, then he turned towards the gate.

'Step on it, Sheridan,' he said, his voice rough.

'I'm right behind you.'

As they hurried back down the wooded path the sun disappeared entirely, and with the dark came disquiet. Allie looked around as they jogged in the gloaming, trying to sense movement or danger in the forest around them. The breeze blowing through the tops of the pine trees made a mournful hum. She could tell that Carter was hyper-aware of every sound—his eyes were watchful—and she stuck close to his side, matching him stride for stride. Neither of them spoke until they reached the treeline and the school came into view. They stopped to catch their breath at the edge of the school lawn.

Even though Allie knew nothing was safe any more, she was still glad to see the school, with lights shining through its leaded windowpanes, and her spirits rose just a little.

'OK,' Carter said, panting after their rush through the woods, 'here's what we do: I think the front door is the least likely entrance to be watched right now. Sprint as fast as you can across to it. I'll be right behind you.'

Allie gave him a challenging look. 'Like you could pass me.'

He couldn't repress a smile. 'Fine then. I'll race you.'

'What does the winner get?' Allie asked, raising an eyebrow.

Carter chuckled. 'I'll think of something.'

'Or maybe I will. OnetwothreeGO!' Allie caught him off guard as she took off, her arms pumping and her legs powering her across the lawn; he scrambled to react before she gained too much ground.

'That's . . . cheating,' he panted behind her.

'Deal with it,' she replied, speeding up.

She had to admire his power—despite her head start they reached the steps at almost the same time. Fighting to be the first to the door, they sparred for space and grabbed the door handle at the same time, Allie's hand on top of his. Playfully, they shoved at each other to be the one to open it.

'Shhh!' Carter hissed suddenly, and they both froze, listening.

Then she heard what he'd heard first: footsteps inside. She didn't dare move. They were all tangled up—his arms wrapped around her grabbing for the door, while she had one hand on the door and the other on his arm. The muscles in his arms and chest were hard against her body. Her heart pounded as she inhaled his distinctive scent of coffee and spice. She felt him tremble, and looked up to find that he was watching her, his eyes as dark as the night above them.

'I think they're gone,' he whispered, his eyes still locked on hers.

She nodded, not daring to speak.

'Ready?' he asked.

'Yes.' Her whisper was almost inaudible.

Tearing her eyes from his she turned to face the front, pressing back into the warmth of his body for just as long as it took to turn the handle. Then the door swung open silently—the entrance hall was empty.

'Act cool,' Carter hissed, giving her a light shove into the room.

The push seemed to bring her back to reality.

'Always,' she replied, raising her chin and sauntering across the stone floor.

He latched the door behind them and they strolled down the hallway.

Allie was still recovering from whatever had just passed between them but Carter talked in his usual laconic fashion as if nothing had happened at all.

'You're fast,' he said.

'I've always liked running.' She tried to strike the same casual tone. 'I like knowing I can get away.'

A smile played on his lips. 'Somehow, that doesn't surprise me.' They were near the staircase now. 'Right. I'm off to the guys' dorm. You OK from here?'

'Totally,' she replied.

'All right,' he said, holding up his fist. 'See you later, then.'

She bumped her fist against his and then turned towards the stairs. But as he disappeared down the wide hallway, she whispered after him so quietly there was no way he could hear: 'Good night, Carter.'

*   *   *

Sun poured through the windows on the main staircase as Allie bounded down the next morning, her hair damp on her shoulders. She'd been so worn out the night before that she'd fallen asleep within minutes. She must have slept soundly, because she had no memories of nightmares, or any dreams at all for that matter. Now, after a hot shower, she felt like herself for the first time since the summer ball.

The dining room was busy, if less raucous than normal, but neither Jo nor Gabe were anywhere to be seen, so she sat down next to Lucas.

'Hi,' she said, barely glancing at him as she focused on the scrambled eggs and bacon piled high on her plate.

Lucas barely waited for her to sit down. 'Gabe and Jo have been MIA since last night. Is something up?' Lucas asked.

Chewing enthusiastically she shook her head. 'Haven't seen them today,' she said, swallowing with effort. 'Seriously, I'm so hungry.'

'Have you been to see Lisa yet?' he asked.

'No, have you?'

He nodded. 'This morning. She's pretty beaten up, but she's awake and talking.'

For a moment, Allie was so relieved that she forgot to eat. 'Oh Lucas, that's great! I'll find Jo after breakfast and we'll go and see her.'

After rushing through the rest of her breakfast, she hurried back upstairs to find Jo, moving so fast she was nearly running when a door opened right in her path. She had to skid around it as Katie stepped out, blowing on her nail varnish.

'Will you watch where you're going, Allie?' she snapped, holding a hand tipped in perfect pale pink up out of harm's way. 'You're always thundering down this hall like a herd of wildebeests.'

'Sorry bi . . . I mean, Katie,' Allie said keeping her voice sweet as she walked by at a slower pace.

But Katie followed her. 'Where are you going? Are you looking for Jo?'

Allie didn't turn around to look at her. 'Why, Katie? Are you her press officer?'

'Don't be stupid. I was just . . . worried about her.'

She didn't sound at all worried, and Allie felt her nerves tingle. Warning signs flashed in her mind. Stopping in her tracks, she turned.

'Why are you worried about her? What's happened?'

Katie blew on her nails with deliberate languor. 'Nothing's happened. I just saw her this morning looking upset. You know, I'm no expert, but I thought she looked like she was on something.'

Allie's stomach tightened. 'What do you mean "on something"? Jo doesn't do drugs.'

'And I thought you two were friends,' Katie said. 'Well, if she hasn't told you, then I guess she doesn't trust you. So I better not say any more.'

Curling her hands into tight fists at her side, Allie turned back towards Jo's room. 'Whatever, Katie. Go peddle your evil gossip to Jules or your other stupid friends. Just leave me out of it.'

'With pleasure,' Katie replied, walking in the other direction. 'But you are going in the wrong direction. The last time I saw Jo she was going into your room. Not hers.'

Allie refused to react and continued on to Jo's room, but she moved in a quick staccato rhythm as Katie's words rang in her ears. Why would Jo be in her room? She knocked twice on the door before opening it without waiting for an answer.

The room was empty.

The shutter was open but all the lights were out, and the bed was rumpled but didn't look slept in. Clothes were piled on the floor in an uncharacteristically messy fashion. Her desk drawers were half open, as if Jo had been in a hurry and looking for something.

Determined not to listen to anything Katie said ever, Allie sat at the desk and waited for a moment in case Jo was nearby and might soon return, but after a while she was forced to concede Jo wasn't coming back.

Heading back down the hall to her own room, she moved more slowly. As she opened her own bedroom door she felt a vague sense of dread.

Nothing was as she'd left it. The light was on, and the room was a wreck. Her desk drawers had been thrown open and ransacked—pens, books and papers littered the floor.

Allie looked around cautiously before taking a step inside, but the room was empty. As she walked across the room she picked up her scattered belongings numbly, stacking papers and gathering books in a neat pile. By the time she reached her desk she realised that what she was holding was her copy of The Rules, which had been torn apart.

Someone had scratched a thick line across the front page and scrawled on it:

THIS IS BOLLOCKS!!

Flipping it over, she saw a note on the back. The angry scrawl was hard to read, but she knew it was from Jo even before she read the message.

A

Everything's ruined. Everyone's lying. You need to know the truth but nobody will tell you. Come talk to me: I'm on the roof. DON'T TELL GABE where I am.

J

'Shit.' Even as Allie breathed the word she noticed the window above her desk was wide open.

She ran back across the room and closed the door. Her mind was whirling. *What should I do? What should I do?*

Climbing up onto her desk, she looked out the window. The dormitory rooms were just below the attic. She leaned over and looked down to the ground below.

It was a long way down.

But Carter had done it and he said it was easy. If he could, then she could. Taking a deep breath, she cautiously eased herself out until she was sitting on the ledge where he'd perched the other day, resting her feet on the old Victorian gutter beneath it.

'Jo?' she whispered tentatively.

There was no response.

Far below her she could hear voices and the crunching sound of people walking on the gravel drive.

Holding tightly to the window frame, she tested the strength of the gutter she was standing on. It was solid. She turned around so that she was facing the wall and, clinging first to the window, and then to slate roofing tiles, she slid along the edge of the gutter for about two yards until she reached another ledge and hoisted herself up onto it, finding finger holds in the brickwork. Once there she stopped and breathed heavily, looking around.

'Jo?'

A rustling sound above her head made her look up, but she could see nothing. Then she heard a bitter giggle.

'Finders keepers.' Jo's voice sounded angry.

Grunting with the effort, Allie pulled herself up onto the next ledge; from there she could see the roof. Jo was sitting on the very top, leaning against a chimney stack. Her hair was a tangled mess and Allie could tell she'd been crying.

'Jesus, Jo. How'd you get up there? And how will we ever get down?'

Jo waved her hand dismissively. 'Don't be such a coward, Allie, for God's sake. Take a chance now and then, why don't you?' Then she leapt to her feet and stood up fearlessly, balancing on the very tip of the peaked roof.

Holding her breath, Allie began looking for a way to get up there. She spotted a jagged section of roofing tiles where she figured she could get a grip and pull herself up, and cautiously made her way over to it. Once she'd begun the climb, she saw how the tiles formed a natural series of hand- and footholds.

On the last stretch though, her foot slipped. As she felt herself slide she tried to scream but no sound came out.

Her fingers grabbed a chunk of masonry, and held on. Once she had a solid grip, she felt along the wall with the toes of her shoes until they located a jagged tile.

As soon as both feet connected to the roof, she pushed herself up with a mighty shove, sprawling onto the roof in an ungainly heap.

Leaning back against the broad chimney stack, Jo—who had made no move to help her—clapped sardonically.

'Hooray for Allie. She climbed to the very top of the Cimmeria ladder of success in no time at all. I think she deserves a drink. Don't you, audience?'

Reaching down she pulled a bottle of vodka from behind her feet and held it out to Allie. It was half empty.

'Have a drink. The audience and I think you should.'

Angry now and still shaking from her near-fall, Allie ignored the bottle. 'What audience, Jo? What the hell are you talking about? And what are you doing up here?'

Shrugging, Jo pulled the top off the bottle and took a swig, making a face.

'You know, this just does not get better with time,' she said, putting the top back on the bottle. 'I really question Isabelle's choice of vodka. You'd think she'd have Grey Goose or Absolut, but no. Just this nasty Russian stuff.'

How can she be drunk at eight o'clock in the morning? Allie wondered.

'Jo, have you been drinking all night?'

'No! Don't be ridiculous. Just for the last few hou . . . What time is it?' She turned her arm over to look at her watch, spilling vodka on the roof. 'Oops!'

Allie tried to look calm. 'Please sit down, Jo, and talk to me.'

'Of course Allie!' Jo smiled at her as cheerfully as if they were in the dining hall chatting after lunch. 'I want to talk to you. But I've been sitting for ages. It feels great to stand up and stretch.'

Spinning around on one foot, she wobbled wildly. Gasping, Allie covered her mouth with her hands, but then Jo caught herself and laughed. 'That was a close one!'

Allie's heart was pounding so rapidly she feared she might have a heart attack. 'Please, Jo. Please sit down and talk to me. I'll drink your vodka. Just . . . sit down.'

As if it had only just occurred to her, Jo slowly lowered herself until she was sitting on the roof. The smile had disappeared from her face. Now she looked mournful and tears slipped silently from her eyes.

'Nobody understands me, Allie. Not even you. You're my best friend and I can't tell you the truth. That makes me so sad.'

Sniffling, she picked up the bottle and took another drink. Then she swiped her arm across her eyes, and handed the vodka to Allie. Allie tilted the bottle back and pretended to take a drink, then she held onto the bottle carelessly, as if she'd forgotten she still had it.

She leaned towards Jo. 'Oh, honey, I'm so sorry you're sad. Has something happened?'

Jo looked at her as if she were mad. 'Of course something's happened, Allie! Ruth's dead! She's dead. And nobody will tell the truth about what happened. Everybody's a liar.'

Swinging her arm up she pointed at Allie. 'And you don't know anything. Everybody's keeping you in the dark because they don't know why you're here. Or who you are. Who are you, Allie Sheridan?'

Allie held up her hands. 'I'm just . . . me, Jo. I'm nobody.'

Shaking her head vehemently, Jo looked increasingly angry. 'No, no no! That's not true either. You don't know anything. You really don't know. And that's . . . stupid. And nobody will tell you. Nobody will tell you.' Suddenly she looked up and met Allie's eyes in what felt like a parody of complete clarity. 'I know things and I won't tell you.'

Allie swallowed hard. 'What do you know, Jo? Do you know who killed Ruth?'

Jo narrowed her eyes slyly. 'Everyone knows what's going on, Allie. Everyone except you.' She added in a sing-song voice, 'But I won't tell you . . .'

'Jo, you have to tell me.' Allie's heart was pounding, but she struggled to keep her expression blank. 'It's really important. The police have to know.'

Shaking her head back and forth Jo looked tearful again. 'My parents don't want me around, did you know that Allie? They don't care about me at all.'

Allie tried to keep up. 'I'm sure they do, Jo. They must do. They're your parents. But tell me about Ru—'

'No they don't!' Jo shouted. 'My parents love money, and they love St Tropez and Hong Kong and Cape Town. But not me. Not me.'

She was sobbing now. While she was distracted Allie scooted across the roof closer to her—close enough so that she could, if necessary, grab her.

'Oh Jo. I didn't know.' Jo had completely lost it, but she had to get her to talk about Ruth. 'Tell me who hurt Ruth, Jo. And then we can talk about your family some more.'

Jo glared at her. 'Don't try and trick me, Allie.'

263

As she spoke, Allie heard movement just below them. Before she could react, Carter appeared nearby, climbing nimbly up onto the roof beside her.

'Hey ladies.' His voice was studiously casual. 'How's it going.'

Through her tears, Jo beamed at him. 'Carter West! I love you Carter West. You're so handsome and you have those deep dark eyes. I would have chosen you if I hadn't chosen Gabe.' Then she looked confused for a second. 'No, I would have chosen Lucas if I hadn't chosen Gabe. But if that didn't work out I'd choose you. Definitely. Or maybe Sylvain.'

Carter didn't hesitate. 'And I'd have chosen you too, Jo. Because you're the prettiest girl at the school.'

Smiling shyly, her face red and puffy, her hair standing on end, Jo said: 'Really? That's the nicest thing anybody ever said to me. Give me a hug.'

Jumping to her feet without warning she wobbled wildly, her arms pinwheeling. Allie gasped and reached out for her, but Carter was at Jo's side in an instant, wrapping her in a bear hug and laughing with her.

'Careful Jo, we're up a bit high here.'

She ignored his words. 'I love you Carter West. You're much nicer than Gabe.'

He gently lowered her down to a sitting position again, his eyes on her all the time. 'You know Gabe loves you, right? Would you talk to him if he came up here?'

'Gabe doesn't love me. He doesn't tell the truth about anything. He's a liar like everybody else.' She gave Carter an appraising look. 'But I'm not sure if you're a liar too.'

She rose unsteadily to her feet, brushing Carter's hands away when he tried to stop her. 'Carter, you know what Gabe is. Allie doesn't know anything. But you do.' She turned to Allie. 'Gabe is important—much more important than me or you or Carter. He's in Night School—do you know what Night School is, Allie?'

Carter was frozen, staring at Jo as if he didn't know what to do. Allie shook her head. 'No. What is it, Jo?'

'It's a bunch of boys and girls pretending they're knights or soldiers or gods, or something. They think they'll be kings of the world.' Jo pointed at Allie. 'They don't like you, did you know that? They think you're dangerous. I keep telling them they're wrong, but they won't listen! Where's my bottle?'

Spotting the bottle at Allie's feet, Jo took a quick step towards her. Climbing to her feet, Allie picked up the vodka and looked wordlessly at Carter but before they could decide what to do, Jo lunged for it.

Carter reached out for her but it all happened too fast; a loose tile caught her foot, and she lost her balance. Falling out of control, she rolled down the steep slope of roof, and with a piercing cry, disappeared.

The vodka bottle fell from Allie's nerveless hands, rolled off the roof and hit the ground below with a crystalline crash. In the awful moment that followed Allie could hear a voice screaming far away and realised it was her own.

Carter stared at the space where Jo had been, his face empty. And one second seemed to stretch beyond the limits that physics allow.

Then they both heard a scrabbling sound from the edge of the roof. Before Allie could react, Carter had thrown himself to his stomach and begun inching down the steep roof to the edge. Allie followed suit, and they both saw bloodied hands trying to hold on. They lunged for Jo at the same moment. Carter grabbed Jo's left wrist, and a few seconds later Allie had her right hand. Over Jo's shoulder, Allie could see the steep fall down to the ground.

Now she could hear a high-pitched whining sound from below the rooftop, as if Jo were too frightened to cry. The blood on her hands made them slippery and as Allie struggled to hold her Carter shouted tersely, 'Get her wrist.'

By now, Allie had Jo's arm in her grip, but because she was facing down the steep slope of the roof she had to use all of her strength to hold onto Jo without falling off herself. Pulling her up was impossible. Carter's face was purple with effort, but at this angle even he was having difficulty.

'OK, let's try something different. Let go of her arm,' he said, panting. 'I'm going to try and swing around so that I'm sitting up. Then I can get some traction to pull her up. Grab me around the waist and hold on.' Catching her eye he added, 'Don't let us fall, Allie.'

So frightened she couldn't breathe, Allie nodded her understanding. Holding Jo's arm in an iron grip, Carter swung himself into a sitting position with a groan of effort. As soon as he was ready, Allie let go of Jo's arm and, moving as quickly as she could, scrambled into position behind Carter, bracing her feet hard into the roof tiles. As Allie wrapped her arms around his waist, he shouted, 'On three, pull me back as hard as you can. One, two . . .'

At three, Allie dug in her heels and heaved.

Jo's torso appeared over the edge of the roof.

Carter and Allie scooted back and then, 'Again!' Carter shouted. 'Pull!'

This time, Jo was fully on the roof, and they both reached for her arms to pull her to safety.

Relieved tears burned Allie's eyes. Panting from the exertion, she crawled over to Jo. 'Are you OK?' She grabbed Jo's hands to see her injuries, and winced. 'Oh Jo,' she said. Several of Jo's nails had torn clean away, and she had a deep cut to the palm of her left hand that was bleeding freely.

'Allie? Jo? Are you up there?' Gabe's voice came from below them.

Carter and Allie exchanged a look. But it was Jo who answered. 'Gabe,' she cried out, sobbing, 'Gabe, help me!'

'Jo?' he shouted, fear in his voice.

Allie could hear him climbing fast up towards them, apparently taking the same path Carter had earlier.

Leaping onto the roof, he stood staring at them for a second, astonished, before rushing over to Jo.

'What the hell happened? What's wrong with your hands?' When she didn't answer he turned towards Carter. 'Carter?'

Carter's voice was dull with exhausted tension. 'She fell off the roof. I think she hurt herself trying to hold on. We need to take her to the nurse.'

'Jesus Christ.' Gabe wrapped his arms around Jo and lifted her up so that she was on her feet with him supporting her. Looking at Carter over her shoulder, he mouthed, 'Vodka?'

Carter nodded. Although Gabe looked saddened, his voice was calm. 'I've got you, babe. I'm going to get you down. Carter, can you help me?'

Turning to Allie, Carter said, 'Stay here, OK? *Do not move*. I'll come back and show you the safe way down.'

Beyond speech now, Allie nodded, and Carter hurried after Gabe. She listened to them lowering Jo down to the ledge, and then manoeuvring her through the window. There was a low murmur of conversation that she couldn't make out, and then the sound of Carter returning.

Still sitting on the roof with her arms wrapped tightly around her body, she rocked back and forth, counting every movement. (*One hundred and seventeen, one hundred and eighteen, one hundred . . .*)

'Are you OK?' He'd crouched down beside her so that his face was even with hers. She could see the worry in his eyes as he wiped a tear from her face with his fingertips.

Straightening, she nodded.

'Then let's get off this crazy roof,' he said.

He helped her to her feet and then led her past the spot where she'd climbed up earlier to a section where the roof sloped more gradually down towards the ledge. It was easy from there to make her way down to a sturdy ledge, and then walk the short distance to her bedroom window.

From the windowsill, she climbed through onto her desk, banging her head hard on the top of the window frame in the process. Inside, she reeled around the room, clutching her head as he slipped

268

gracefully through the window and looked at her in amazement.

Despite what they'd just been through, she saw him try not to smile. 'Allie, what have you done to yourself now?'

She pointed at her head.

'Come here.' He grabbed her arm and pulled her over to him, and examined her head briefly. 'Seriously, if you survive Cimmeria, you're going to end up with no brain cells at all.'

He kissed the wounded spot, his lips as light as a wish. 'There. I think that's all the medical treatment you need.'

It was probably a coincidence, but her head *did* feel better.

'How did you find us?' she asked.

'Jules said there might be a problem. I came looking for you. You weren't here but I saw that.' He pointed at the note on her desk. 'Then the open window, and I put two and two together.'

'Thank you, Carter.' Her voice was fervent. 'I think you saved Jo's life.'

'I'd rather you two just didn't get into trouble in the first place,' he said, but he smiled. 'Now, should we go and find Gabe and Jo and make sure she's OK?'

Allie nodded, astonished to find herself smiling back. 'Thanks.'

'You're welcome,' he said. 'Now try not to hurt yourself walking down the hall.' She punched him on the arm as she opened the door, and then jumped back.

Isabelle stood in the hallway outside, her hands on her hips.

CHAPTER NINETEEN

Allie and Carter walked down the hallway with Isabelle and Matthew flanking them. Allie had the feeling they were being marched. There had been no discussion. Isabelle had said, 'Carter, Allie. Come with us please.' And off they'd gone.

They walked quickly to Isabelle's office. She held the door open for them, and then walked in last, before sitting in the chair behind her desk, Matthew next to her, one hand resting on the back of her chair. She did not introduce him.

'I've called you here because I want to know if I've made a mistake.' Isabelle fixed her eyes on Allie.

'What . . . what do you mean?' Allie replied warily.

'I broke a lot of rules to let you into this school.' Isabelle's voice was clipped with anger. 'Was I wrong?'

As Allie felt fear uncurl in her stomach there was a quick tap at the door.

'Come.' Isabelle's voice was a command.

Sylvain stepped into the room. He glanced around, avoiding Allie's eyes, then shut the door behind him and leaned his back against it.

Her heart sinking, Allie turned back to the front. 'I don't understand,' she said. 'What have I done?'

'I gave explicit instructions that students were not to go outside, and I find that not only have you been sitting up on the roof drinking with Jo Arringford, you've also been to the chapel. I ask you, what am I to think, Allie, except that you are

270

insubordinate?'

Allie stared at her, mouth agape. *How did she know about the chapel?*

Carter leaned forward. 'Hang on, Isabelle. She went to the chapel because I asked her to. I was with her all the way. She was safe.'

'And Jo was very upset,' Allie said. 'I was afraid she'd get hurt. I was just trying to help her.'

Isabelle's glare was icy. 'A bottle falling off the roof missed a student by inches. If he'd been hit we would have been liable. Glass, and might I add, vodka, are scattered around the front door.'

Allie was so stunned and angry she had to drop her eyes so Isabelle couldn't see the rage in her expression. *Ruth dies, the school burns, and she's worried about being sued over broken glass?*

Isabelle shifted her attention to Carter. 'And why, may I ask, were you with her all the way? You know the rules.'

'After what happened with Ruth and Lisa, Allie was upset. She was thinking of leaving the school,' Carter explained. 'I wanted her to be able to talk freely without fear of being overheard.'

Impressed at how smoothly he used truth to, well . . . lie, Allie shot a glance at Isabelle to see how she was taking it. She didn't look impressed.

'I appreciate that Allie was upset, but there are places where that conversation could have happened in this building, Carter,' she said dryly. 'And I do not like it when my rules are blatantly ignored, particularly when they have been set out so clearly, and so recently.'

Carter held out his hands, palms up. 'Well then I should apologise, not Allie. I was the one who suggested the chapel. At first she even refused to

271

go because she didn't want to break your rules, but I convinced her. If anyone was insubordinate it was me. But I did it for reasons I thought were right.'

Carter's voice was surprisingly confident, Allie thought. His tone was more like that of a son placating an angry mother than a student addressing a headmistress.

'May I, Isabelle?' Sylvain looked at the headmistress enquiringly, and she gave him a brief nod.

'Carter, you not only disobeyed Isabelle's instructions, but mine as well,' he said, his elegant French vowels curling around each word. 'And in doing that you put Allie in danger, and that is unacceptable.'

For the first time in this conversation Carter looked tense. Allie saw him clench his hands into fists and then very deliberately relax them in his lap. He said nothing.

Isabelle sighed. 'Enough. Carter and Allie, this was a serious infraction of the rules I set out last night. I understand that you're both still upset because of what happened on Friday night, otherwise you would both face detention and written warnings. Instead I am telling you now that another such infraction will not be permitted.'

'What's going to happen to Jo?' The question burst from Allie's lips before she could stop herself.

Isabelle shot her a sharp look. 'Let's start with what exactly happened on the roof this morning, Allie, shall we?'

Allie told her about finding the note, noticing the open window, and then climbing up to find Jo on the roof, and of all that transpired.

'I really didn't know what else to do, except to

help her,' she explained. 'Is she OK?'

'Four of Jo's fingernails were torn off,' Isabelle said, 'and one hand has a deep cut. She's badly bruised. All of these wounds were presumably incurred when she fell. She is also drunk. As her wounds are largely superficial and drunkenness is temporary, she's been treated by nurses and sedated. She will remain in the infirmary until we decide her punishment. Her parents will be notified.'

'Will she be . . . expelled?' Allie gripped the arms of her chair so tightly her knuckles paled.

Isabelle looked disapproving. 'I will not discuss disciplinary actions regarding other students with you, Allie.'

Matthew leaned over to whisper something in her ear. When he finished, Isabelle turned to Allie. 'You may leave now, Allie. I would like to speak with Carter in private for a moment.'

Allie glanced at Carter, but he was looking straight ahead as she walked from the room. She noticed that Sylvain and Matthew both stayed behind.

Not all that private, then.

Closing the door behind her, she leaned against it trying to listen but could hear nothing through the solid wood.

Turning, she ran up the stairs to the girls' dorm, stopping at room 335.

She knocked, then jumped back when the door opened almost instantly.

Jules was, as ever, immaculate—her uniform crisp and her hair perfect. 'Allie. What can I do for you?'

If she was surprised to see her, she didn't show

it.

'I want to visit Lisa,' Allie said, 'but I don't know where the nursing ward is and I figured you would.'

'I heard she woke up at last,' Jules said. 'Go to the ground floor and all the way through the classroom wing. Then up the staircase at the end. It's on the first level you'll come to. You'll know it when you see it.'

Allie hesitated, wishing she trusted Jules enough to really talk to her. When she didn't move the blonde prefect raised her perfectly arched eyebrows and asked, 'Is there something else?'

'It's just . . .' Allie twisted the hem of her shirt around one finger, 'Carter told me you gave him my message last night. And I wanted to thank you for doing it. You didn't have to.'

Jules crossed her arms loosely. 'You're welcome. Although I'd feel better if you'd told me the truth about why you wanted him. And now, with all that's happened with Jo Arringford I'm wondering if I should regret my decision.'

'But all I did was try to help Jo!' Allie burst out in protest. 'I didn't give her vodka or take her up on the roof. I just tried to save her life. I don't see why that's so awful.'

'Well, why didn't you come and get me first?' Jules asked.

'Why would I do that?' Allie replied. 'You'd only try to get her in trouble.'

Jules looked exasperated but also, Allie thought, a little hurt. 'You and Jo are my responsibility while you're on this floor, Allie. You should never put yourself in danger like you did today. And Carter told me about your panic attacks—why didn't you ever tell me? I'm not here to get you detention or

274

yell at you. I'm here to help you. But no matter what I do you treat me like I'm your enemy.'

This came as such a surprise that for a moment Allie was struck speechless. 'I just . . . I thought you hated me,' she said at last.

'I've never hated you,' Jules said. 'You just always seemed intimidated by me and angry, and I didn't know how to make you see that I'm not the enemy.'

'But you're friends with Katie Gilmore, and she really does hate me.'

To her surprise, Jules gave a brief laugh. She held up her hand apologetically.

'I am friends with Katie and, yes, she does hate you, but she's just jealous. She likes Sylvain and Sylvain likes you, and that hurts her feelings and makes her mean. She's used to getting what she wants. But you should know that has nothing to do with me. I tell her all the time she needs to grow up and leave you alone, but,' she shrugged, 'she's her own person.'

Her expression grew more serious. 'Don't judge me by her behaviour. Judge me on my own.'

Sheepish now, Allie rubbed the toe of one foot against the other. 'I'm really sorry, Jules. I've been a complete arse.'

'It's OK,' Jules said. 'I should have sat you down and talked with you before. I'm the prefect, and I should know how to handle this sort of thing. But I'd really like it if we could put that stuff behind us.'

With a challenging look she held out her hand. 'Friends?'

After a split second of hesitation, Allie took it. 'Friends.'

'All right, now go to Lisa—she's probably lonely

over there by herself,' Jules said, stepping back into her room, adding in her more normal officious voice: 'And no more rooftop excursions, please.'

*　　　*　　　*

As Allie hurried along the route Jules had described to the nursing ward, she replayed her conversation with Jules in her head.

How could I have been so wrong about her? Was I that wrong, really?

She remembered Carter and Sylvain both laughing at her for not liking Jules—they seemed to think she was great, although Sylvain had agreed she could be difficult.

But difficult isn't bad.

It used to bug her that they defended her, but maybe if she'd completely misjudged Jules it all made sense.

She tried to remember the things the prefect had said that upset her, and suddenly all she could remember was her baffled expression when Allie got angry or upset.

But still, it seemed odd that Jules suddenly wanted to be her friend. Jo's drunken words from the rooftop rang in her ears: *'They don't like you . . . They think you're dangerous.'*

The lights were turned off in the classroom wing, and she felt along the wall for a light switch. When she failed to find it, she walked quickly. Her footsteps echoed as she half-ran down the corridor past the doors opening onto vacant classrooms, where empty chairs and desks sat in ghostly rows and circles.

At the end of the hall, an unmarked door had

a frosted glass window through which daylight poured.

That looks promising.

She pushed it open.

Behind it a narrow, utilitarian staircase climbed upward, brightly illuminated by windows on every floor. The first level she came to was a mezzanine between the ground and first floors. Stepping off the staircase she immediately entered a corridor where the low ceilings and linoleum floors contrasted with the soaring spaces and polished wood elsewhere in the building. On one side of the corridor a row of closed, white doors each had a frosted glass window subdivided by a neatly painted blue cross. The other wall was lined with windows through which light and fresh air streamed.

'Hello?' Allie called tentatively.

Her voice echoed in the empty hallway.

It was so quiet she felt unnerved as she walked down the sunny hallway. She knocked hesitantly on each door she passed and tried handles. Nobody answered, and the first three she tried were locked.

But the fourth opened.

The room was dark, all the curtains drawn. The room was tiny, with just one bed.

Allie could just see a bright puff of blonde hair on the pillow.

'Jo?' she whispered, taking a tentative step into the room. 'Are you OK?'

There was no response, but something told her Jo was awake. Leaving the door open, she tiptoed across the room to crouch beside the bed. Jo's eyes were closed, but her breathing was uneven.

'Hey,' Allie whispered, 'are you all right?'

A tear escaped from Jo's eye and trickled down

the side of her face. She wiped it away with hands mummy-wrapped in bandages.

'I don't want to talk right now, Allie.' Her voice was hoarse and dull.

Wounded, Allie thought about arguing, but instead she walked to the door. As she opened it, she looked back—Jo was lying on her back staring up at the ceiling as if she were already alone.

Back in the hallway, Allie tried the other doors. Two doors down from Jo's room, she peeked in to see a sunny, white-painted space in which two rows of four hospital beds were separated by white curtains fluttering in a light breeze that whispered in through a half-open window. Only one bed was occupied.

Lying under a white duvet on a white bed against a white wall, Lisa was pale and her eyes were closed—her thick lashes made shadows like bruises on her skin. Her silky, long hair was strewn across the pillows, and a large bandage covered one side of her face. One arm was in a splint.

Allie was struck by how thin she was. Did she ever eat? She looked so . . . breakable.

As she sat down in a wooden chair at the edge of the bed, it made a faint creaking sound and Lisa opened her eyes.

She smiled drowsily. 'Allie.'

Allie smiled back, but worry lines clustered between her eyes. 'Hey. How are you? Are you OK? I heard you were awake.'

Lisa pushed herself back against the pillows. She had a plaster on her wrist where an IV had been connected at some point, and dark purple bruises stained her upper arms.

'I'm OK. I'm pretty drugged up, I think. I just

278

don't know how long I've been here.'

Her fragility made her eyes look enormous and childlike, and Allie felt a surge of unexpected protectiveness.

'Not long.' Allie had to stop and think about it. 'I mean, it's . . . What day is it? Sunday, I think.' She flushed at her own confusion, but Lisa seemed satisfied.

'Good. I thought it was longer.' She looked out the window and a shadow crossed her face. 'But it's going to get dark soon, isn't it?' She looked so fearful that Allie took her hand and squeezed it.

'Don't worry. You're totally safe in here.'

Lisa didn't look convinced, but the drugs seemed to affect her ability to hold onto a thought, and a moment later she seemed relaxed again.

'Lisa, what happened to you?' Allie asked. 'Jo said she lost you when the lights went out, and she didn't see you again until we found you . . . well, you know, in the entrance hall.'

Her eyes darkening, Lisa frowned with concentration. 'It's all really hazy. I remember dancing with Lucas. Then we decided to go for a walk and get some air. We were going to go out the front door because the back was crowded. But then the lights went out. At first it was no big deal—in fact it seemed kind of fun. The candles were lit in the entrance hall, so we could still see and everything. But then people started screaming.

'Lucas told me to stay there, that he would come back for me. And he ran back to the great hall to see what was happening.'

She stopped and looked up at Allie with empty eyes. 'And that's it. I don't remember anything else. It's just a big, giant blank.'

279

Allie patted her hand. 'Isabelle says you're fine—have you got a concussion or something? My brother had one once and he couldn't remember falling down until two weeks later.'

'Yes, the nurse said I hit my head on something when I fell, and cut myself somehow—I have twelve stitches.' She touched her bandage unconsciously.

'What about your arms?' Leaning closer, Allie carefully pushed up Lisa's short hospital gown sleeves so she could see her skin better. 'Those bruises—they look like . . . like handprints.'

Looking looked down at her arms, Lisa said: 'Do they? I have no idea how they got there. And I sprained my wrist when I fell, I guess.'

'Did they . . .' Allie faltered and started again. 'I suppose they told you about Ruth?'

Nodding, Lisa looked as if she might cry. 'I don't believe it though,' she whispered. 'How could she . . . kill herself? She never seemed sad or depressed. And she had all these plans for when she was older. She wanted to travel around the world, you know? I don't understand why she would do something like that.'

Allie contemplated telling her that she had doubts about the official story surrounding Ruth's death, but she didn't feel like Lisa was the right person to confide in. It wasn't that she didn't trust her, but more that she didn't want to worry her.

For a while after that they sat quietly, and Lisa dozed, but when Allie shifted in her chair, the creaking sound woke her up again.

'You're still here.' Lisa's drowsy voice sounded pleased.

''Course I am,' Allie said. 'You shouldn't be alone all the time. It's too boring. Where are the

280

nurses anyway?'

Lisa glanced around as if she expected to see them jump out from behind a cupboard.

'I don't know. It's weird, they were here a lot yesterday, but I've hardly seen them today.' She yawned. 'Tell me what's going on out in the real world? What's been happening?'

Allie wondered how much to tell her. Then she decided that Lisa knew Jo even better than she did.

'Not much. Everything just feels kind of weird. And . . . Lisa, Jo kind of freaked out this morning, and now she's seriously busted.'

Lisa looked more alert. 'What do you mean? Why is she in trouble?'

Allie told her what happened that morning on the roof. When she finished, she expected Lisa to look shocked, but instead she just shook her head.

'Oh poor Jo. She must be so upset. I wish I could go and talk to her.'

'Lisa, Carter told me she's done this kind of thing before . . . ?'

Lisa nodded. 'You know Jo,' she said. 'She's absolutely lovely. But her parents ignore her. They always have. I think she used to do this sort of thing to get them to notice her. Then it just sort of became a habit, I guess. They got tired of it and sent her here. But she's happy here, so it hasn't happened in a long time. The only thing I can think is, what happened at the ball was too much.'

She looked sorrowful. 'She really liked Ruth, you know?'

Allie nodded. 'I guess it makes sense. I've just never seen her like that before. I didn't know what to do.'

Lisa reached out for her hand and squeezed

it. 'Poor you. You must think Cimmeria is a madhouse. It's really not you know. Not usually anyway.'

'I'm OK.' Allie put her hand over Lisa's. 'When are they letting you out?'

Lisa shrugged. 'Nobody's said.'

Glancing at her watch, Allie stood up. 'I should probably go and see what's happening out there. Things have been so weird. I feel like if I'm not there the whole school could just . . . blow up. It's freaky.'

She leaned over to hug Lisa, who felt so bony in her arms she barely dared apply any pressure at all.

Lisa smiled up at her. 'Thanks for coming to check on me.'

'I'll come back,' Allie promised. 'If you feel well enough to see her, Jo is two doors down. But give her some time to sober up first.'

As Allie shut the door, she heard Lisa say: 'Don't forget about me . . .'

CHAPTER TWENTY

'Hey Allie!'

The voice came from the common room as Allie walked back across the school building from the medical ward, and she turned to see Lucas waving her over.

'Hey, I was just with Lisa,' Allie said. 'She looked good.'

'Great!' he said. 'I know she wanted to see you. Did Jo go, too?'

Allie shook her head. *Does he still not know*

what's been happening?

'Have you talked to Gabe lately?' Her tone was cautious.

'No, I haven't seen Gabe, Carter or Jo. Do you know what's going on?'

She lowered her voice. 'There was a thing this morning.' She told him briefly about what happened up on the roof.

Lucas rolled his eyes. 'Oh God. Not this again.'

Allie stepped back in surprise. 'What do you mean "again"?'

'Jo used to do this sort of thing all the time. It's why her parents sent her here in the first place. She just snaps sometimes. Drinks too much, does drugs, then nicks someone's Porsche, gatecrashes a stranger's wedding . . . You know. The usual Mummy-doesn't-love-me thing.' He didn't look sympathetic. 'It's why I broke up with her. All that drama queen crap. It gets old.'

'Do you think they'll kick her out?' she asked.

Lucas laughed as if she'd made a joke. 'No way. Her parents are so connected and so loaded. She could kill somebody and they'd still let her stay until graduation and throw her a little party on her way out.'

Before Allie could respond he continued, 'Anyway, at least that explains where Jo and Gabe are—she's in trouble again and he's trying to help, poor sod. But where's Carter?'

Allie gave him the short version of how she and Carter had broken curfew the night before. 'I hope he's not in too much trouble,' she said as she finished the tale.

'Oh Isabelle will get over it, don't worry. She pretends he's just another student but everyone knows she loves him like her own child.' He glanced at her appraisingly. 'So, what's up with you two anyway? Are you an item now?'

Blushing, Allie shook her head. 'No, of course not. We're just mates.'

'Mm-hmm.' Lucas didn't seem convinced. 'Mates who sneak out after curfew to be alone in the woods. The best kind of mates.'

His tone was teasing, and Allie felt her colour rise further.

'Don't be daft,' she said. 'Anyway, I don't know where he is now.'

'I hope Sylvain isn't giving him a hard time. He'll be so jealous about you spending time with Carter now that you've dumped him.'

Allie had been staring at the floor to hide her red face, but now her head shot up. 'How do you know I've dumped him?'

Lucas smiled again. 'Allie, there are no secrets at Cimmeria—especially when it comes to relationships. Katie Gilmore's been annoyingly happy ever since Friday night, and she's telling everyone that Sylvain dumped you,' Lucas said. 'Given that he's being a miserable git we all assumed that, actually, you dumped him. I'm guessing we're right?'

Allie nodded.

'Good. He can be a complete dick. That's what happens when your parents are billionaires and you're their only son.' Lucas smiled wickedly. 'He's not good enough for you. Carter's much cooler.'

As Allie tried again to insist that she and Carter were only friends, he laughed and talked over her. 'Listen, I've got to go. I'm going to see if Carter's made it back to the guys' dorm. Or Phil or anybody, really. I'm so bored. I might be forced to study if something doesn't happen soon. Total nightmare.'

As he was saying goodbye, though, a tall, graceful girl walked over. 'Did I hear you threaten to study, Lucas? Please don't. The earth might stop turning and we're having pasta for dinner tonight. I don't want to miss it.'

'Fine then,' Lucas replied. 'I'll find something else to do—wouldn't want you to miss your spaghetti.'

Allie and the girl looked at each other expectantly for a moment before Lucas noticed. 'Oh, sorry. I didn't realise you two didn't know each other. Allie Sheridan, this is Rachel Patel. Rachel meet Allie. You should talk. You might like each other. You're both freaks.'

'Arsehole,' Rachel said affectionately.

Feeling left out of their friendly teasing Allie studied her shoes, but after Lucas walked away, Rachel turned to her with a wide smile that showed off perfect white teeth and dimples. 'Lucas is cool. He's that guy I'm such good friends with that we can never date. Have you got one of those?'

She had golden-brown skin and almond-shaped eyes, and her long, curly dark hair was held back with a thin, braided silver band. Her smile was irresistible and Allie found herself smiling back easily.

'I guess everyone does,' she said, thinking about Mark back in London.

'Totally. It's like a rule of nature.' Rachel studied Allie for a moment. 'So at last I meet the famous new girl everyone's been talking about.'

Allie liked her voice—it was almost honeyed, with the faintest hint of a northern accent.

'Nobody talks about me,' Allie said, embarrassed.

''Fraid they do. You're actually in my history class, you know,' Rachel said.

Allie tried to remember seeing her there, and summoned up a vague image of a serious girl who always knew all the answers to Zelazny's questions. 'You wear glasses,' she said, her tone inadvertently accusing. 'And you're super-smart, right?'

Rachel pulled a pair of stylish, dark-framed glasses out of her skirt pocket just long enough for Allie to see them. 'Guilty. I'm a total geek. I can't help it. And I only wear these to see the projections.'

She paused, then said, 'People really do talk about you, you know.'

Allie made a face. 'Oh good. What do they say?'

Her brow wrinkling with thought Rachel went down the list, rapid-fire. 'Oh you know, first that you were going out with Sylvain, then that you weren't; that you're friends with Jo, and then that Jo went crazy; that you're the one who found Ruth's body the night of the ball . . .' She paused. 'Which sucks, by the way, if it's true.'

Allie dropped her eyes and Rachel's breath hissed between her teeth. 'Blimey.' She glanced at her watch. 'Where were you headed anyway? Are you busy?'

Allie shook her head.

'Let's go and get lunch,' Rachel said as they walked down the hallway. 'I want to know everything. Along with the whole Ruth thing, I want to know what's up with Jo Arringford. What happened? Did she really throw herself off the roof? The gossip on this is unbelievable . . .'

286

Sitting in a quiet corner of the dining hall with cups of tea and sandwiches, Allie found herself telling Rachel everything. All about finding Ruth and then Lisa, as well as the entire story about what happened on the roof. Rachel hung on every word as her sandwich sat uneaten in front of her.

Why she could tell her things she hadn't told anyone else, Allie didn't know. *Maybe I just need someone to talk to who isn't a guy and isn't going to throw herself off a roof*, she thought. Whatever the reason, she couldn't seem to stop herself from talking and talking.

There was something inherently honest about Rachel. She seemed both knowledgeable about Cimmeria and critical of it. She knew everything about everybody at the school, and yet she clearly kept her distance from most of them. Lucas seemed to be her only good friend, but when Allie asked why she didn't sit at the table with him, Gabe and Jo for meals she made a face.

'That's just not my scene,' she said.

Rachel didn't just listen, though. She proved to be a veritable gossip columnist of Cimmeria intrigue.

'How do you know all of this?' Allie asked at one point.

'I just listen,' Rachel said. 'You'd be amazed how much you can learn if you sit quietly and pretend to mind your own business. Maybe it's in my blood. My dad's a sort of investigator.'

'Like a cop?' Allie asked.

'Kind of like a cop.'

As the room had emptied and the two of them were alone, Rachel issued a challenge. 'Name anybody at this school and I will tell you everything about them—known or suspected.'

'Seriously?' Allie laughed.

'Seriously.'

'OK . . . Katie Gilmore,' Allie said.

Rachel smiled. 'Good choice. Unbelievably rich. Her father's an investment banker, lives in Kensington, shags the housekeeper. Buys the kids off with holidays in the Seychelles and buys off their mum with a black AmEx,' she poured herself a glass of juice. 'Her brother finished here last year, now goes to Oxford where he is learning to mint money like his daddy.'

'Impressive,' Allie said, with a look of respect. 'What about Jules?' she asked.

Rachel nodded. 'Jules Matheson—very clever, perfect school record, perfect looks—perfect everything. It's a bit scary. Her dad's a QC. Her brother went here a few years ago, just graduated with honours from Cambridge in ancient history. Nothing tawdry there. Want to know about Jo?'

Swallowing hard, Allie hesitated before she answered. This felt just a little bit like betrayal. But Jo never told her much about herself, really. And after what had happened . . .

'Yes,' she said.

'Jo Arringford,' Rachel reeled off. 'Daughter of banker and former government minister Thomas Arringford, who is now an executive with the International Monetary Fund living in Switzerland, with homes in Knightsbridge, Cape Town, St Tropez . . . you name it. Her parents are divorced. Daddy has a new wife who is six whole years older

288

than Jo. Mum lives in the St Tropez house most of the time. A brother, eight years old, is at Eton. Jo's very bright—with perfect scores. She's had three breakdowns, and one suicide attempt . . .?'

'Stop!' Allie said, too late.

'. . . a year and half ago,' Rachel finished.

'Jo tried to kill herself?' Allie whispered.

Rachel nodded sombrely. 'Christmas break. Her parents . . . neither of them asked her to come home. She stayed here . . . took some pills.'

Allie felt sick. 'How did they . . .?'

'Lucas found her—they'd only been going out a couple of months. He'd stayed here to spend Christmas with her. When she didn't come down to dinner on Christmas Day he went up to her room to check on her, and . . . Happy Christmas, everyone.' She sighed. 'They pumped her stomach, made her see a shrink. Lucas stuck by her side every inch of the way. When she was better he broke up with her. She started going out with Gabe three weeks later.'

'No wonder . . .' Allie's voice trailed off.

'What?' Rachel asked.

'After Jo . . . you know. Lucas didn't seem surprised.'

'Yeah, well. He wasn't,' Rachel said dryly.

'But why is everybody—why is *Lucas*—still her friend?'

'You've met her,' Rachel said. 'Ninety-nine per cent of the time she's the sweetest, kindest girl you've ever met. People forgive her the one per cent. Besides, she's one of them.'

'One of them?' Allie asked.

'You know, her family's wealthy, her parents went to school here, some of them knew her when she was little. She's Cimmeria all the way,' Rachel said.

As Allie sat still for a moment, thinking, a somewhat horrible thought occurred to her.

'What do you know about me?'

Rachel looked doubtful. 'Are you sure you want to know?'

Allie nodded. 'I can take it.'

Obviously uncomfortable, Rachel thought carefully before answering.

'OK, I know very little about you and I consider what I do know to be unsubstantiated.' She paused, looking apologetic. 'But here goes. The name Sheridan is unfamiliar to everybody, so you're not legacy unless it's on your mum's side. You're an only child as far as everyone knows. Your parents have government jobs of some sort. You grew up in south London. You have a criminal record. Your parents sent you here as punishment. You're on scholarship. You found Ruth's body.'

Allie swallowed hard. When it was all reeled off like that . . .

'God, I sound like such a loser.'

'Hey, I didn't mean it that way.' Rachel looked worried. 'I don't really know much about you. I don't think you're a loser.'

Allie considered this, then shot Rachel a challenging look.

'What about you?'

'What about me . . . what?' Rachel said, puzzled.

'Tell me the gossip about you.'

Rachel smiled. 'Fair enough. OK. Let's see. Rachel Patel, daughter of Rajesh and Linda Patel. Born in Leeds. Father Asian, mother not. Father was a scholarship student at Cimmeria, now an international security expert; works for a couple of governments. Top secret stuff. On the Cimmeria Board—*very* influential. Rachel has one sister, Minal, who is twelve. Rachel's mother has two PhDs—overkill if you ask me—and runs a private medical research firm not far from here, where the family has a palatial home on several acres. Rachel has perfect scores in most things, especially science, and wants to be a doctor when she grows up. OK?'

Allie smiled, but her eyes were serious. 'OK.'

They were even.

* * *

Jo didn't show up in biology Monday morning.

Unable to handle not knowing what was going on, Allie stayed after class to ask Jerry where she was.

'Jo broke The Rules quite seriously, as you know, Allie.' He took off his wire-framed glasses. 'So she's been given what we call in-house suspension as punishment.'

'What's that?' Allie asked.

He wiped the lenses with a clean white handkerchief. 'It means, once she's released from the infirmary, she must stay in her room. Her meals and classwork will be brought to her there, but she cannot take part in any normal activities.'

Allie twisted the hem of her white shirt around her fingers as she considered his words. 'How long will she be . . . suspended?'

Jerry perched his glasses back on his nose. 'Just a week, as long as she abides by the restrictions, keeps up with her work and doesn't break any more rules.'

'Am I allowed to see her?'

He shook his head. 'No contact, I'm afraid, Allie. She is meant to use this time in isolation to reflect and study.'

Allie stared at the floor while he spoke but then she looked up at him, her face filled with concern. 'Is she better? She wasn't . . . you know . . . her normal self yesterday.'

Behind the sparkling lenses his brown eyes were kind. 'I'm afraid I haven't seen her. Ask Eloise or Isabelle—they're overseeing her punishment. But I'm sure she's fine.'

Allie nodded. 'Thanks Jerry.'

So, Jo is busted but not expelled, Allie thought as she walked down the hallway. *Lucas was right.*

She wondered if Jo was still crazy or whether she was back to normal, and then felt disloyal for wondering. But she couldn't pretend that what happened the day before had not made her doubt whether she really knew Jo after all.

Talking to Jerry had nearly made her late for English, and when she walked in, most students were already in their seats. She sat down next to Carter, who was doodling on a corner of his notebook.

'Hey.'

'Hey back.' He looked up to smile at her for a second, then returned to his drawing.

'Where have you been?' Allie asked, pulling books out of her bag. 'I haven't seen you since yesterday morning.'

He gave her a significant look. 'You know. Stuff.'

She raised her eyebrows but let it slide.

'Jerry says Jo's under house arrest for a week,'

she said, flipping through the pages of her book.

'Serves her right,' he said, adding as an afterthought: 'A straitjacket wouldn't hurt either.'

'Good morning, class.' Isabelle's voice saved Allie from thinking of a riposte. 'Recently we read works by T.S. Eliot, and last week I asked you to read a work that influenced his writing heavily, the *Rubáiyát of Omar Khayyám*, translated quite famously by a man named Edward FitzGerald. We discussed Mr FitzGerald on Friday . . .'

After all that had happened that weekend Allie had no memory of Friday's class at all. She decided she'd have to take Isabelle's word for it.

'Let's start with my favourite passage, Stanza LXIX. Clare,' she turned to the pretty blonde girl, 'could you read it for us please?'

Allie felt a rush of jealousy tinged with guilt— Clare had been Carter's date to the ball, and Allie had been avoiding her ever since. She remembered the look in Clare's eyes when she looked up at Carter with a kind of adoration. But Carter had been looking at Allie at the time.

Standing, Clare read in a sweet, bell-like voice:

''Tis all a Chequer-board of Nights and Days
Where Destiny with Men for Pieces plays:
Hither and thither moves, and mates, and slays,
And one by one back in the Closet lays.'

'Thank you, Clare,' Isabelle said.

As the student took her seat, she cast a hopeful look at Carter but his eyes were on his notebook.

What a mess, Allie thought, drawing a black heart on a clean notebook page and then stabbing an arrow through it.

Isabelle leaned against a desk. 'Now this is an almost existential piece of writing—most of you will remember the basic theories of existentialism from earlier this term, if you do not, get ye to the library as this will be on your test—that I love both for its bleak view of life and its dark humour. The balance is quite unique. So, what do you think he's saying?'

When Allie read the passage on Sunday, she'd had a flashback to Jo's abortive chess lesson a few weeks ago. But before she could raise her hand, Carter's voice surprised her—she didn't think he'd been paying attention.

'I think he's saying we're pawns. And that fate decides what happens to us—who we marry, when we die. But what about personal choice? Don't we make decisions? Isn't that power?'

'Precisely,' Isabelle said. 'On the other hand, isn't our personal choice affected by what fate throws at us?'

'But that's absurd.' Sylvain's distinctive voice came from the back of the room, and Allie turned in her seat to see him. 'Everything is up to us. We have all the power. Fate does not exist. How can it?'

'Typical,' Carter muttered.

Sylvain glared at him. 'What is that supposed to mean, Carter?'

Before Carter could reply, Isabelle stepped between them. 'I'm glad you're both taking poetry so seriously, but I've never had an argument in my classroom over Omar Khayyám before and I'd rather not have one now. Now, then, I think we've exhausted my favourite passage. The next passage I'd like us to look at . . .'

294

*   *   *

Throughout the next week, the school returned to a kind of battered normality. The smell of smoke gradually disappeared, and work began in the great hall. A skip appeared outside the west wing, and students were regularly asked to avoid the main hallway between the great hall and the skip. The distracting percussion of hammers and drills soon became a tedious part of daily life.

Lisa was sent home to recover from her injuries, and without her or Jo around, Allie found that she spent most of her time with Rachel. This meant she spent most of her time in the library, as that was where Rachel appeared to live. So Allie was not at all surprised when Rachel suggested they go to the library to study after class on Friday afternoon. Lucas came along reluctantly, on the grounds that he had a paper due on Monday and he hadn't yet even looked at the coursework.

Rachel had proved to be an ideal study companion for science homework, since she knew everything.

'You really are a science geek,' Allie marvelled, making a face as Rachel explained the biological structure of tapeworms, her eyes fairly glowing with interest.

Looking up from his books, Lucas said: 'Why do you think I hang out with her? It's not like she's fun or anything.'

Rachel elbowed him in the ribs and turned to Allie. 'Science is my thing, but you can help me with French. French is definitely *not* my thing.'

'Don't mention French to Allie,' Lucas warned

her. As they both looked at him blankly he mouthed 'Sylvain'.

'Oh don't.' Allie buried her face in her hands.

'Too soon?' Lucas asked.

Allie nodded, but Rachel was struggling not to giggle.

'What?' Allie asked.

'It's just,' Rachel snickered, 'you broke up with *Sylvain*. That's like breaking up with, I don't know, God or something.'

She and Lucas were both now giggling uncontrollably. 'Just about every girl in this school wants to go out with him and you just dumped him.'

Allie felt her face redden, and she looked around to make sure nobody had heard them.

'Will you shut up?' she hissed. 'Seriously!'

As they tried to control themselves, with Rachel wiping the tears of laughter from her eyes, Allie turned the pages of her book, frowning. 'Well, he was a wanker,' she muttered defensively.

That set them off again only this time Allie found herself joining in. It was, she had to admit, kind of funny. In an awful way.

That night after dinner, bored of the library, Allie retreated to the common room to read her English assignment. Even after a week of trying to catch up, she was still behind on her work. Despite the fire and Ruth's death, teachers had been ratcheting up the pressure, and she had mountains of chapters to read. But by nine o'clock, she was half-asleep, curled up in a deep leather chair near the unplayed piano in one corner of the room with her head resting on one hand and the words on the page in front of her starting to swim. When a piece of paper folded into a tiny square was shoved in front of her, it took her a moment to absorb what was happening.

'Your mate Carter asked mc to give it to you,' Lucas whispered, putting a sarcastic emphasis on the word 'mate'.

'What? Where is he?' Allie asked, sitting up and looking around her.

Lucas shrugged. 'I passed him in the hall a few minutes ago. I gotta run. We're playing cricket out front.'

Glancing around to make sure nobody observed her, Allie unfolded the piece of notebook paper. Carter's neat handwriting filled only a few lines at the centre of the page.

Allie
We need to talk.
Come and find me at 9:30, in the library. I'll be in the ancient Latin section in the back left corner. Don't let Sylvain see you looking for me.
C

Allie's heart beat faster. As soon as she finished reading the words, she folded the note in half to hide its message and slipped it between the pages of her book.

The next twenty minutes went by slowly as she tried to read but found it impossible to concentrate. Finally, at nine twenty-five, she gathered her things and, stretching theatrically to indicate how tired she was in case anyone was watching, she rose from her chair.

'Well, I guess I'm off to bed,' she said to nobody

before heading for the door.

Once out in the hallway she stopped and flipped through her papers, waiting to see if anybody followed her out. When nobody came out after her, she headed for the library, stopping to look over her shoulder before opening the door.

Inside, the room was full but hushed, and as she walked across the soft rugs she flipped through the pages of her notebook as if looking for something. Occasionally she peered at book numbers on shelves, then as if she hadn't found what she sought, moved on.

I should be an actress, she thought. *So convincing.*

Gradually she made her way past the wall of elaborate panelling where the senior student study cubicles held their strangely violent murals, and then on to the section on ancient languages. The further back she went the fewer people she saw. By the time she reached the bookshelves lining the back wall there was nobody around at all.

Unsure where the Latin books were kept, she moved aisle by aisle, pulling heavy books off the shelves to determine the language. But although she found rows of dusty leather-bound books in Greek and entire stacks in Arabic, she found no Latin.

'Why have they hidden the Latin books?' she muttered. 'Is this some sort of clever joke? Like, if you want to read Latin you have to go the . . .'

'Allie.'

The whisper that cut off her random thoughts came from somewhere ahead of her, in the very back corner of the room.

'Carter?' The lighting was dim. As Allie squinted to see who'd spoken a hand reached out of the shadows and pulled her into the space between two towering bookcases.

'Jesus,' Allie said. 'A simple "Hello" would do.'

Carter didn't smile. 'I'm sorry, I just wanted you to get back here before everybody in the library wondered what you were doing hanging out in the ancient languages section talking to yourself.'

'A paper on ancient Rome for history class.'

Allie was delighted with her cover story, but Carter didn't look impressed. 'We're studying Cromwell.'

'I'm working ahead,' she said defensively. 'We must study Rome at some point.'

'Very convincing.'

As she took in his humourless face, her heart sank. 'What's wrong, Carter? What's with all the intrigue? Why didn't you just come get me in the common room?'

'Look, we have a problem.' Crossing his arms, he leaned back against a bookcase as if he was trying to put distance between them.

'Right,' she said. 'What's our problem?'

'From now on, if anybody asks you what you saw Friday night, you tell them that Ruth killed herself, OK?'

Allie opened her mouth to protest, but he held up his hand and kept talking. 'Because as far as everyone's concerned she did, OK? She killed herself.'

Silence fell as she thought about what he was saying. 'But I know that's not true,' she said.

'Do you?' he said. 'How do you know? Because of your background in forensic science? It was dark, Allie. There was a lot of blood. You got freaked out. But there is no way you know

299

whether or not Ruth killed herself. So stop playing detective.'

'Did Isabelle send you to tell me this?' she asked angrily.

'Nobody sent me.' She locked her eyes on his, looking for any sign of evasion, but he did not look away.

He reached out for her hand. 'I'm on your side, Allie. I really am.'

'Then I don't get it!' she said, yanking her hand free. 'Why are you doing this? I saw what I saw.'

He stepped closer to her. 'Look, Allie, word is getting around that you were with her when she died.'

'That I . . . What?' Allie stared at him.

'And that you were the last person to see her alive and the only person to see her dead body.'

She shook her head. 'I don't . . .'

He chose his next words carefully.

'Allie, there's a rumour going around that you had something do with Ruth's death.'

CHAPTER TWENTY-ONE

The next morning, Allie walked down the stairs at six forty-three precisely. Her hair was pulled back snugly in a ponytail that bounced with every step. She looked drawn, but resolute.

When she'd left Carter the night before, she'd gone to the bathroom and splashed cold water on her face. She'd stayed there for some time, staring at herself in the mirror, replaying their conversation in her head.

'How can anybody think I had something to do with Ruth's death?' she'd asked him, aghast. 'That's insane. I hardly knew her. Why would I want to hurt her?'

'It's a set-up, Allie.' His face had been grim. 'They're also saying that you got Jo drunk up on the roof, and that you've got . . . mental problems.' She opened her mouth to protest and he held up his hand. 'Whoever is spreading this stuff knows it's not true. They're messing with you.'

'But why? Why would anybody want to do that?'

'Some people feel threatened by you.'

'How am I threatening?' she asked plaintively. 'I'm nobody,'

'I've told you before, I don't think that's true,' he said. 'And neither does anybody else.'

'I don't get it.' She ran her hands through her hair, pressing her fingers hard against her temples. 'My parents are civil servants. They're not rich. Most of the people here are millionaires' kids. How can they be threatened by me?'

'That's what we have to find out,' Carter had said.

After that she couldn't sleep. Restless, she climbed out of bed at two o'clock and opened the window for fresh air. Then closed it an hour later because she was cold. Once she heard footsteps pass her door, then silence again.

More than once the thought passed through her mind: *Could it be Rachel? I trusted her. She's the only one who knows everything. I didn't tell anyone else. She loves gossip. But she wouldn't . . . Would she?*

She thought that perhaps she'd dozed off at around four, but not for long. When the alarm

301

went off at a quarter past six she was wide awake, staring at the ceiling.

And now she had to get through breakfast.

* * *

By going down to the dining hall as early as possible on a Saturday, Allie hoped to avoid most people. She and Carter had decided she should go about her day as usual. But she didn't really want to deal with, for example, Katie Gilmore right now.

When she walked in, nobody seemed to pay any undue attention to her and as she filled her plate with cereal and toast she allowed herself to feel relieved. *Maybe this whole rumour thing isn't going to be a big deal.*

She looked around the room for her usual dining companions, but she was so early nobody was there.

'Hey Allie. Come sit with me.' Rachel was sitting alone at a table to her right.

For a moment, Allie hesitated, her thoughts from last night swirled queasily. But it would look weird if she didn't sit with Rachel.

She's the most gossip-aware person in the school. If she doesn't mention the rumours about me, I'll know it's her.

She made her way over and set her food down. 'Thought for a second I was going to have to sit by myself.'

'I'm always here this early,' Rachel said. 'My dad kind of beat the whole early riser thing into me when I was little, and now I guess I'm stuck with it. Abusing children is just wrong.'

Rachel had created a toast, egg and cheese

302

sandwich, and as she poured milk into her cereal Allie had to admire how she was systematically demolishing it. 'Your breakfast looks better than mine,' she observed.

'Most important meal of the day, girlfriend,' Rachel said, chewing. 'Hey, did you know people are spreading a really sick rumour about you?'

Allie froze, her spoon halfway to her mouth. 'I've heard something about that,' she said cautiously. 'I heard it's something crazy.'

Rachel nodded. 'The whole "Allie's a psycho-killer"? That's the one I heard anyway. I got it from Sharon McInnon, do you know her?'

Allie shook her head.

'Well,' Rachel said taking a bite of her sandwich, 'I told her to go fuck herself.'

A wave of relief washed over Allie. *It wasn't Rachel after all. I knew it wasn't.*

'How'd she take that?' she asked.

'She was OK with it,' Rachel said. 'I think she's used to me telling her that because she's such a bitch.'

Now they were both giggling, but Allie's worries wouldn't let her relax for long.

'Who's saying these things, Rachel?' she asked. 'They're such horrible lies—who would do that?'

'I've been trying to figure that out all morning,' Rachel said, frowning. 'Don't worry. I'll get to the bottom of it.'

She raised her cup of tea. 'With you on my side, Rachel, they don't stand a chance.'

But for some reason, Allie still felt uneasy.

As she walked down the hallway after breakfast she was lost in her worried thoughts.

I can trust Rachel now. Right?

She'd nearly made it to the stairs when Katie's straight-razor voice sliced the normal Saturday morning quiet.

'Hello Killer! How are you feeling this morning?'

Allie spun around to face her. 'Fuck off, Katie.'

'Language.' The redhead's perfect lips curved into a vicious smile. 'We should have known if they let you into the school everything would go to hell.'

Her circle of glossy acolytes giggled around her, whispering to one another while waiting for Allie's response.

'What are you talking about, Katie?' Allie fought to keep her voice steady, despite the anger coursing through her. While she was trying to think of the best way to handle the situation, the overwhelming desire to punch Katie in the face was winning out. Her hands curled into fists.

As her internal battle raged, Katie took a step towards her. 'I hear you have anger issues,' her voice was low and malicious. 'Is that what happened to Ruth, Allie? Did she upset you? Make you angry?'

Allie felt her fist go up before she knew what she was doing, but before it made contact with Katie's pert nose someone grabbed her from behind and pulled her back so quickly her feet briefly left the ground.

'Katie, shouldn't you be bingeing and purging?' Sylvain's silken voice asked as Allie struggled in his arms.

Katie stared at him in disbelief. 'You can't be serious, Sylvain. What are you doing? Why are you defending the little nobody? What on earth do you see in her?'

Allie had stopped fighting now, but he still held

her firmly. The warmth of his body against hers brought back unwelcome memories.

'I see somebody with more class than you will ever have in your miserable life.' His clear blue eyes swept her group of friends. 'And that goes for all of you. Now you can all go on with your business, please.'

After a brief fluttering of indecision, the group began migrating to the dining hall. Katie led the way, her head high.

Only when they were completely out of sight did Sylvain drop his arms and step back.

'I wish you'd have let me hit her,' Allie said ungratefully.

'The thought did cross my mind,' he said.

'She's so horrible. I just . . . Anyway.' Allie scuffed at the floor with the toe of her shoe and didn't meet his eyes. 'Thanks.'

'You are welcome. But I am afraid that you will have many problems now. These rumours they are . . .' Sylvain swirled his finger around in the air, 'everywhere. And she will use them against you.'

'I know,' Allie said. 'I just wish I knew who was saying these things.'

He looked at her seriously. 'When everybody is saying it, I think it no longer matters who said it first. But I believe the first rumours were spread by somebody who is known to be jealous of you.'

Allie glared at the dining room door. 'Like Katie.'

'Like Katie,' he said.

'Is she behind it all, Sylvain?'

'I do not know for certain. But it is something I have . . . heard. I will ask around. And if I find out, I will speak with Isabelle.'

Allie didn't want to be beholden to him, not after what had happened. *But if he could stop this from getting worse . . .*

'That would be good, Sylvain.'

'Don't worry about it. As you British say, I owe you one.' She flushed but he continued, his accent thickening as he talked. 'I have to say this, Allie. The night of the ball—I am sorry about how rough . . . I hurt you, I know. It was wrong of me. You are different from the girls I have been with before. I know that I cannot treat you like them.'

Allie's cheeks burned, but she faced him squarely. 'You shouldn't treat any girl like that, Sylvain. Ever.'

To her astonishment, he lowered his head. 'You are right. *Absolument*. Please accept my apology.'

'I . . . I'm just . . . Sylvain, don't,' she stuttered. She didn't want to forgive him. She wanted to stay angry at him. But then a thought occurred to her.

'I have to know one thing,' she said. 'Did you put something in my drink that night?'

He looked horrified, and at that moment she knew the truth.

'My God. Of course not. What do you think I am?' he said.

'I'm sorry,' she said. 'I just had to know. Because things all got so blurry.'

'Cimmeria wine is strong,' he said. 'If you're not used to it and you drink it too fast it will go to your head. And I let you drink too fast, that much is true. And I did try to use that to my advantage. That was wrong of me.'

His humility and apparent honesty left her with no choice.

'I accept your apology, Sylvain,' she said. 'I'm

over it.'

Before he could reply, she added, 'Look, I'm going to run away before anybody else calls me a murderer or apologises for practically date-raping me, OK? I can't take any more excitement before nine o'clock.'

Just before she turned to run for the stairs, he said, 'Be careful, Allie.' His eyes were intense. 'There is real danger around you at the moment.'

'Oh good,' she said wearily. 'I was hoping you'd say something like that.'

*   *   *

Allie would never have used the word, but she hid in her room for much of the morning. By lunchtime, though, she'd finished all of her homework and was looking around for something to do. And she was hungry.

Unable to face another meal in the crowded dining hall, she sneaked down just before most students arrived for lunch and grabbed several sandwiches, packing them away in her book bag with bottles of water and an apple.

But as she walked down the hallway to the front door, a group of younger students passed her and she heard one of them whisper, 'There's the murderer'. Some giggled and others gawked at her fearfully.

What could she do? She couldn't fight them all. So she pretended not to hear, and kept going.

When she walked down the front steps a few seconds later, though, one of Katie's friends passed her and made a wide circle around her as if she were toxic.

'Gross,' the girl said, looking her up and down before hurrying away.

Her chin up, Allie kept going. But the lawn was crowded with students stretched out in the sunshine and she imagined that she could hear whispers and laughter all around her. Before long she was running across the grass and into the treeline.

Away from them all.

At the summerhouse she stopped to catch her breath. It was completely empty—she could see nobody at all. Sitting on the steps, she dropped her head to her knees and breathed slowly until she calmed down.

Why did this always happen to her? For a brief moment she'd thought she'd found a place where she could just . . . be. Where she was safe. Where she was almost accepted.

But it was always the same.

Everybody turns on me. Everybody leaves me.

She wanted to cry but she couldn't. Staring into the trees, she allowed herself to think about Christopher. He hadn't just gone. First he'd shut her out. Treated her like there was something wrong with *her*. Like he didn't love her any more.

Now it was happening again. Only this time it was everyone.

Well. Almost everyone.

She had Carter. And maybe she should trust Rachel. There was something inherently good about her. And at least for now she still had Lisa, too. And maybe even Lucas.

So . . . she wasn't alone this time.

After a while, she realised she really was starving. Relishing the peace in the glade by the

308

summerhouse, she spread her blanket on the grass and ate her sandwiches in the warm sunshine—completely alone. No whispers, no laughter, no craziness. Later, she stretched out with her head on her bag. She was asleep within minutes.

When she woke up, the summer sun had moved lower in the sky, and she was now in the fast-cooling shade.

Gathering her things she headed back up to the school building with some reluctance. Her afternoon of peace had been so pleasant, she wasn't ready to deal with the situation she was in.

Nearing the building she realised it was later than she thought—the lawn was empty of sunbathing students and in the hallway she could hear the buzz from the dining hall. It must be after seven; everyone was at dinner.

Climbing the stairs to her room she felt a pang of hunger, then remembered that she'd thought to set aside a sandwich and some biscuits for dinner.

I won't have to face anybody until tomorrow morning.

She knew she was being cowardly, but she didn't care.

As the evening wore on, though, the flaws in her plan became clear. She hadn't spoken to one person since eight o'clock that morning. She had no television, computer or video games. She'd been reading all day and she'd slept for hours. By eleven-thirty she was sitting on her desk staring out the open window, wide awake and very bored.

Lights had been coming on in dorm rooms around her for the last hour as students returned from the games she'd heard them play on the lawns. Half an hour ago, she'd heard Zelazny's

309

gruff bellow of 'Curfew!' followed by the low rumble of voices and footsteps in the corridor outside her room.

Now, sliding across the desktop to the windowsill, Allie climbed out onto the ledge, less timidly than the last time. Her skirt fluttered against her thighs in the cool evening breeze. Following the path Carter had showed her the previous weekend, she had to pass a few windows to make her way along the ledge to the spot where the roof sloped at a gentle angle, and she could pull herself up. From there, she would make her way safely across the rooftop to the main building. There a similar sloping spot made a natural exit onto a ledge that led past the boys' windows.

But some students were still up—light poured from the two windows she had to pass before she could make it to the relative safety of the roof.

When she reached the first window she peered cautiously through a corner of the glass. The lights were on, but the room appeared empty and she scuttled past it, exhaling only when she was well beyond it.

The next window was wide open. As she neared it she could hear voices and laughter. Peeking inside she saw three girls talking. One—a pretty girl with olive skin and straight, dark hair that swung just above her shoulders—sat on the bed facing the window. Allie recognised her as one of Katie's acolytes.

The other two sat on the floor, their backs to her. Even from behind, the familiar short blonde hair made Jo impossible to miss. The girl next to her had a distinctive, vivid auburn ponytail.

Katie.

What is Jo doing hanging out with her? I thought she was still in the infirmary.

Astonished, Allie hung on to the bricks and tried to decide what to do. The girls looked relaxed and they could be planning to talk for hours. There was no way she could pass the window without the girl on the bed seeing her. But she couldn't pull herself up onto the roof from here. She was trapped.

Her fingers were sore from holding on to the bricks and she was trying to find a way to shift her position on the narrow ledge to get more comfortable, so she wasn't really paying attention when Katie's words floated out the open window and it took her a moment for her to realise who she was talking about.

'. . . and I think something needs to be done,' Katie was saying. 'Isabelle has no right to let somebody like her loose among us. We don't know anything about her. First Ruth and then . . . well. She could have killed you up on that roof, Jo. It's a miracle you survived.'

Wait. What is she saying?

She waited for Jo to tell Katie she was crazy.

'I used to think she was my friend,' Jo said. 'But now I don't trust her at all. That scene up on the roof was so scary. I could have died.'

I saved your life! Allie glared at the wall in front of her as if she could cut through it with her eyes.

'Of course you could have,' Katie said. 'Just look at what happened to Ruth. It's no coincidence that Allie didn't go to get help first. She came up there so she could be alone with you when you were vulnerable. God knows how you survived.'

'Carter was up there too,' the acolyte said, sounding surprisingly reasonable.

311

'Yes, Carter did help me . . .' Jo said uncertainly.

'But why didn't he stop her from pushing you off?' the acolyte asked.

Pushing who off? Nobody was pushed!

'Because he's in love with her.' Katie's voice rang with contempt but Allie felt her heart skip a beat.

He's in love with me? She smiled stupidly at the old brickwork in front of her. *Really?*

'He's done here, too,' Katie finished.

Allie stopped smiling.

'We should never have accepted him in the first place,' Katie continued. 'I've never understood Isabelle's obsession with him. He doesn't belong here. He's not legacy any more than she is. Standards are really slipping here. I'm going to tell my father—he needs to intercede.'

Her caustic tone seemed to amuse the acolyte. 'That should scare Isabelle,' she giggled.

'It better. He's on the board,' Katie said. 'And Jo, you need to write to your father too. He's incredibly influential. Tell him what happened on the roof, how some crazy new girl tried to kill you and Isabelle won't lift a hand to protect you.'

Allie held her breath, waiting for Jo to tell her this was a stupid idea. That she wouldn't have anything to do with it. That she knew Allie and she deserved to be here.

'OK,' Jo said.

OK? Allie thought, betrayed. *OK? You spoiled little . . .*

Someone knocked on the door.

Allie leaned around to peek through the edge of the window. Jules stood in the doorway.

'Katie, Ismay, can you come with me for a moment? I need to talk with you.' Jules sounded stern, Allie thought, but Katie just rolled her eyes.

'Seriously, Jules?' She stood up and walked past the prefect, her every stride conveying irritation. 'This is so boring.'

I wonder what that's about? Allie thought, watching them go.

The acolyte, who Allie now knew must be Ismay, was right on her heels. Jo trailed behind them.

Though she was overwhelmed with the desire to throw herself into the room and demand an explanation from her ex-best friend, Allie waited right where she was. As soon as they were out of sight she shot past the window like a Fury. A few seconds later she was climbing across the roof to the main building and then skidding down the slope to Carter's open window.

He was sitting at his desk working, and he didn't notice her right away.

She studied his face—taking in his fair skin and slightly mussed straight dark hair. The way his long lashes cast feathery shadows against his cheeks. She liked his hands—his fingers were long but strong; his nails square and neat.

She felt an unexpected warmth spread through her as she watched him.

He really is lovely . . .

As if he'd heard her thoughts, Carter looked up and their eyes met.

With a startled cry he leaped from his chair so quickly it fell over. Allie tried not to giggle out loud as he slowly returned to his desk and peered out the window.

'Allie?' He looked embarrassed and cross, although she thought the latter was probably just to hide the former. 'What the hell . . . ?'

'Hi,' she whispered. 'I can't sleep. Want to come out and play?'

He opened the window. 'You're mad. Get inside before you kill yourself.'

'Katie is such a *bitch*,' she complained as she clambered across his desk.

Carter raised his eyebrows. 'No argument.'

'You don't understand.' Allie paced the floor. 'I heard her talking through a window. She's trying to "finish us" and she hates us both and she's planting awful thoughts in Jo's head about me—that I tried to kill her on the roof. I think she's behind these horrible rumours about Ruth.'

As she ranted, he closed the window behind her, then picked the wooden chair up off the floor and propped it under the handle of his bedroom door, testing it for stability.

Finally he turned back to her. 'What exactly did you hear?'

She told him what had happened that morning—with Katie and her friends, and how Rachel had known all about the gossip by seven in the morning. His eyes narrowed when she mentioned Sylvain's intervention, but he said nothing. As she told him about what had transpired in Katie's room his face darkened. She could see he was trying to stay calm.

'OK, so there are two possibilities,' he said. 'Either she didn't spread the first rumour and she's just taking advantage of it to spread more rumours about you and Jo, or she did spread the first rumour and this new rumour is just part of her evil plan.' He punched his right fist into his left palm. 'That socialite bitch.'

'What should we do?' Allie asked. Then for the first time she paid attention to where she was. 'And why is your room bigger than mine?'

He had two bookshelves to her one, and space for an extra chair in the corner. While the walls were whitewashed like hers, all the fabrics in the room were dark blue, giving it a more masculine feel. Allie noticed that all of his shelves were filled with well-thumbed books. And that a battered football rested on the seat of the spare chair. She pointed at the neatly made bed and he nodded. She sat down and stretched out her legs.

'I've been here longer,' Carter said absently.

He pulled out the desk chair and sat across from her. 'These rumours are intended to cause the most damage possible, even to get you to leave the school. This feels like a campaign to me. To get rid of you.'

Allie slid forward on the bed until her knees nearly touched his.

'OK, Carter. Enough with secrecy, and all that bollocks. It's time. Tell me about this place.'

'Allie . . .'

He leaned away from her, but she ignored the warning look he gave her.

'Uh-uh. Not this time. Someone *died*. And somebody else is trying to ruin my life here. For all I know, whoever killed Ruth could go after me next. You know things. You are allegedly my friend. So tell me everything. Now.'

He walked across the room and stood against the wall, his previously relaxed posture now tight insecurity, his arms crossed.

'You don't understand, Allie. I can't. If I did— and if anybody ever found out . . .' He shook his head. 'It's just bad. Trust me.'

'How can I trust you if you won't tell me the

315

truth?' she asked. Under her breath she muttered, 'Maybe I should just go and ask Sylvain . . .'

Carter's cheeks reddened. He stalked back over to where she sat and leaned over her. 'Do you want to know what you mean to Sylvain? Well I'll tell you. Every year he picks a pretty new first-year girl, shags her and dumps her. It's his thing. And each one thinks she's *so* special. The last one left school afterwards because everybody was making fun of her. But when her parents withdrew their offer of a generous donation to Cimmeria Isabelle warned him never again.' He spat the words out at her as if it sickened him to say them. 'So, that's who you are to him, Allie. His newest, naive conquest. Who thinks the gorgeous rich boy chose her. Just her.'

'Stop it!' Allie shoved him away and jumped to her feet. She and Sylvain had just made up, and he'd seemed so sincere.

'If that's true, why didn't you tell me before, Carter?'

They stood inches from each other, both furious. She could feel his breath against her face.

'I tried,' he said. 'I just . . . didn't think you'd believe me.'

But she wasn't letting him off that easily.

'From what I hear, you're a bit of a lady-killer yourself. How is what Sylvain does any different from you?'

He winced but didn't look away. 'The difference is, Sylvain does it to be mean. I don't want to hurt anybody. I'm just looking for the right person.'

'People say you're into one-night stands,' she said accusingly.

'Are these the same people who say you killed Ruth?'

316

She hadn't thought of that.

'Point taken,' she conceded. 'So, you tell me. Is what they say about you a lie?'

His eyes locked on hers. 'Yes, Allie. It's a lie. Or at least an exaggeration. I got this . . . I guess, reputation . . . because if I go out with someone and I can tell they're not the right one for me I break up with them straight away. And they're never the right person.' His eyes seemed to hide nothing from her—she saw only vulnerability. 'I don't want to hurt anybody, Allie. I really don't. I just want the right girl.'

Standing so close to him she fancied she could feel the warmth of his body crossing the space between them, and without really knowing why she was doing it, she held her hand up, her palm facing him, her fingers spread.

'OK. I believe you. I'm sorry.'

He pressed his palm against hers. 'Thank you,' he said softly.

'For what?'

'For believing.'

He glanced at their hands quizzically. 'Is this some sort of London thing?'

As Allie laughed he entwined his fingers with hers. Instantly she felt goosebumps.

'You big city kids have all these crazy traditions,' he said.

'Yeah,' she whispered, her throat tightening. 'You country kids don't know what you're missing.'

'I've heard that. And, you know, someday,' he pulled on her hand until she took a step towards him, 'I'd really like to find out.'

Their faces were so close now it was inevitable— when he brushed his lips very lightly against hers she gave a little gasp then reached her hands behind his neck and pulled his head down.

The warmth of his mouth exhilarated her as, with a groan of surrender, he wrapped his arms around her, his lips moving in delicate butterfly kisses along her chin.

'I've wanted to do this,' he whispered in her ear, 'for so long.'

Her entire body tingled and she pulled him harder against her. Heat spread through her body. His kisses were more insistent now, as if he would devour her.

Suddenly he wrenched himself away with obvious effort, walking as far away from her as he could get within the room's limited boundaries. He stood against the far wall, his eyes dark and his hair rumpled where her fingers had tangled it.

He was breathing heavily and she knew what he'd say before he spoke. 'God I hate to do the grown-up thing, but we should . . .'

'No, you're right.' They stared at each other for a moment. 'OK,' she said. 'So. There's that.'

'Yes. There's absolutely that.' Carter laughed—a warm, intimate chuckle. 'You just . . . stay over there for a minute, if that's OK. Now, what were we talking about before we were so . . . interrupted?'

His smile had almost as strong an impact on her body as his kiss—she felt like she was the only girl in the universe. It was hard to focus on his words.

'I was . . . I think I was asking you to tell me everything,' she said.

His smile faded. She was sorry to see it go but the conversation needed to happen.

'There are reasons why I haven't told you everything, Allie. It's not just that I'm a wanker who wants to keep things from you.'

'I get that.' They were calmer now, and she felt like he was really listening. 'But I think I need to know where I am. What this school is about. People are getting hurt. I don't want to get hurt, Carter.'

He looked troubled. 'If I tell you, I'm breaking a vow. I keep my word. It's the one thing you can say about me.'

'But aren't you starting to wonder just who you made a vow to?' Allie asked. 'Tell me, Carter. Tell me about Night School. And I swear I will never tell another living soul.'

Carter's eyes searched her face as if he were looking for a sign telling him the right thing to do. Finally he sat down in the chair, gesturing at the bed.

'You may as well sit down,' he sighed. 'This could take some time.'

CHAPTER TWENTY-TWO

'The first thing you need to know is that I don't know everything,' Carter said. 'I'm a new initiate as of last term. There's a full year of training before they accept you.'

'OK.' Allie sat on the bed with her arms wrapped around her knees, her eyes watching his intently. 'But you grew up here. You must know something.'

'I know what they've told me,' he said. 'And it's pretty serious stuff.'

He leaned his elbow on the back of the chair. 'This is the first step to a larger organisation. Kids are recruited to Cimmeria specifically to join Night

319

School, because people in this bigger organisation want them for life—does that make sense?'

Allie looked confused. 'Kind of . . .'

'OK, what I'm saying is, you start Night School at Cimmeria, then you continue it at Oxbridge— and if you're in Night School, you will get in to Oxford or Cambridge or LSE, without doubt. And you're a member of a club there. Then, when you graduate from university, you go and work for a company run by a member of the organisation. And eventually you run a company that hires people who started in Night School. And you do what you're told. What I'm saying is, this is *for life.*'

Frowning, Allie tried to process what he was telling her. 'What is this bigger group called?'

He shook his head. 'I have no idea. I'm not sure it has a name. It just . . . is.'

'So . . .' Allie was still trying to understand. 'You're in Night School now, and when you finish at Cimmeria you'll go, let's say, to Oxford, where you'll be in the university-level version of it, then you'll go to work and get really rich . . . I don't get it. Wouldn't that happen anyway? What's the point?'

Carter lowered his voice to a whisper.

'I can only tell you what they tell us, Allie. And what they tell us is that Night School runs the world.'

'Runs the . . .' Allie stared at him, 'what do you mean?'

'I mean presidents, prime ministers, MPs, CEOs, journalists—the people you see on TV, the people you read about in newspapers, people who run the world—Night School is everywhere.'

As Carter ticked the professions off, she looked

320

doubtful. 'What? All of them?'

'No. But a lot of them. And at all levels. Night School runs newspaper corporations. Television companies. Government departments. Militaries. Everything. It's everywhere.'

'And it all starts here?' she asked doubtfully. 'Carter that's impossible.'

'I don't know if it's just here, though. We have exchange students all the time from schools in other places—like Sylvain.'

'So, it's like a giant, kind of . . . conspiracy?'

'Yes.'

Stunned, she searched his face for any sign that it was all some elaborate joke. But there was nothing.

'How does it work?'

He shook his head. 'That goes beyond what they tell the neos.'

'Neos?'

'Neophytes,' he explained. 'It's what they call us the first year.'

'How embarrassing,' she said dryly. 'So what *do* they tell you?'

'We get the big marketing pitch—the whole "society of power" speech—and a fancy dinner with a bunch of rich guys in tuxedos who used to be us,' he said.

'OK, but what do you do?' she asked, wrinkling her brow. 'I mean, here, at Cimmeria. All this training you all do, what is it?'

He took a deep breath. 'God, it's hard to explain. They've got all these theories of war and strategy being the basis of everything so, I know it sounds weird, but the first thing they do is teach us how to play chess. We play chess for *days*. While they feed

321

us all this stuff about how knights are warriors and pawns are foot soldiers . . .'

'Wait, I've heard that before.' She stared at him. 'Jo said those exact words to me a few weeks ago. Is Jo . . .?'

'In Night School?' He looked uncomfortable. 'Not exactly. Her dad is, and he's insisting that she should be too, but Isabelle thinks she's not ready. She has these . . . problems, you know. So they've given her like introductory to introductory training, and Gabe keeps an eye on her.'

'What? Her own boyfriend?' Allie was horrified. 'Is, like . . . spying on her for these guys?'

'No!' Then he paused. 'Well, sort of, I guess. But it's not like he's pretending to like her.'

'No,' she said sarcastically. 'He would never do something like that.'

He held his hands up in surrender.

'So,' she continued, 'after chess, it's like . . . what? War games? Is that what you're doing out in the woods at night?'

He nodded. 'More or less. Combat training, techniques in subterfuge. That kind of thing.'

'Crazy. Why are they teaching you that? You're just kids.'

'War is a strategy for life and for business. And some of us will end up running militaries. And governments.' He shrugged as casually as if he were talking about a maths test. 'Look, this is what Cimmeria is about, to an extent. And everybody at this school is connected to it in some way.'

He gave her a direct look. 'Except, apparently, you.'

'Except me,' she said.

'So,' he said, 'what are you doing here?'

Allie sat still, staring at him for a long moment. Then she slid to the edge of the bed, poised to bounce off of it.

'I don't know. But I'm ready to find out. Are you with me?'

'In theory . . .?' he said cautiously, 'yes. What do you have in mind?'

Her face was animated with a mixture of excitement and determination. 'You know how yesterday in the library we decided I should pretend nothing was going on and nobody was talking about me, while you tried to find out what was happening?'

He nodded.

'Well, bollocks to that. Whatever is going on here, the place to find out is Isabelle's office. Let's go there. Now.'

'No way!' He looked shocked. 'That's insane, Allie. If we got caught in Isabelle's office they'd kick us out. No question. We'd never get into a good university. It would ruin everything.'

'But I know how we can avoid all of that,' Allie said, jumping to her feet.

'How?'

'By not getting caught.'

She headed for the door.

'Allie . . .' She ignored his warning tone and opened the door, but he reached past her to close it again. 'Hang on a minute.'

He lowered his voice to a whisper. 'What exactly are you looking for? What do you think you'll find?'

'Two things,' she said. 'Why Ruth died. And why I'm here.'

When he didn't appear convinced, she raised

her chin defiantly. 'I'm going Carter. I'm doing this now. I'm not waiting for later, or for someone to maybe someday decide to tell me this information out of simple human kindness. That's not going to happen. OK? So are you coming with me? Or is being the future president of Cimmeria Incorporated really that important to you?'

He stared into her eyes for a long minute, then seemed to make up his mind.

He opened the door.

CHAPTER TWENTY-THREE

'Is that your foot? Or somebody else's?' Allie's whisper was so quiet it seemed to fade into the inky darkness around her.

'Of course it's mine,' Carter whispered. 'Who else's foot could it be?'

They were tiptoeing down the grand hallway from the staircase towards Isabelle's office. Around them the old building was unnaturally quiet—it didn't creak or settle. It was as if it held its breath.

Carter had explained that, as part of their training, Night School students patrolled the hallways of the school at night, but not constantly. So on the way down, they'd hidden in an alcove on the first floor and waited until a pair of shadows walked by, silent as death.

After that, Carter figured they had more than an hour before the patrol would be back again. So they'd slipped down the stairs, skipping the creaky step near the bottom.

Now they stood outside Isabelle's nearly invisible

office door, waiting until they could be certain that the headmistress wasn't inside.

'Why would she be in there?' Allie whispered. 'It's one o'clock in the morning.'

Carter shrugged, but the look on his face told Allie it was possible.

After hearing nothing through the door, he finally decided it was OK to go in. With his hand on the door handle, he held her eyes.

'Three,' he whispered, 'two . . . one . . .' He turned the handle.

The door was locked.

Carter swore under his breath and Allie stifled a giggle. 'Plan B?'

Reaching in his pocket he pulled out a twisted wire. 'Two minutes,' he said. 'Time me.'

Leaning down he pushed the wire into a lock Allie couldn't see, and moved it gently with his fingertips until without warning, the door gave way.

'Whoa. Less than two,' she said admiringly. 'Where did you learn to do that?'

He gave her a look. 'Where do you think?'

'Church?'

He smiled and pushed the door. It swung open with a sound like a sigh. 'Yeah, right.'

'So,' Allie whispered walking into the office, 'how does burglary make you a better future prime minister?'

Closing the door behind them, Carter took a cream-coloured cashmere throw off one of the leather chairs and pressed it into the base of the door. 'I have no idea,' he said.

Then with a click that seemed to echo in the quiet school, he turned on a small desk lamp. Standing beside the desk, the two of them looked around Isabelle's office, taking in the tapestry of the unicorn on one wall, the thick Oriental rugs, the shelves crowded with books and magazines, and the many neatly filled mahogany cupboards. An empty teacup with the Cimmeria seal sat on the desk amid stacks of papers. The air smelled faintly of Isabelle's distinctive citrus perfume.

'I feel like a criminal,' Allie whispered, suddenly unsure.

'Oh no you don't,' Carter said. 'We're here now. Let's get this over with.'

She knew he was right. It was too late to turn back now.

'Where do we start?'

Allie was mostly talking to herself, but Carter answered her immediately.

'I'll take the bookshelves. You start with the cupboards.'

For half an hour they worked in hurried silence. Carter started on the left side of the room and moved from shelf to shelf, looking for anything unusual. Allie sat on the floor, looking through the low cabinets.

The first cabinet held mostly maintenance records, phone records, receipts—nothing of interest. The second one held academic records, graded papers, and other bits of schoolwork from years past.

As soon as Allie opened the third cabinet, she knew she was on the right track.

'Bingo,' she whispered.

Carter looked up. 'What is it?'

'Student records.'

He stopped what he was doing and walked over. Looking for Ruth's records, Allie started to flip through the Js. Then stopped.

'It's not here.'

He looked puzzled. 'It has to be. Look again.'

'Jansen,' Allie muttered under her breath. 'J-a-n-s-e-n. No. It's not here.'

'It could be in the wrong place or something,' he said. 'Start at the beginning.'

Impatiently, Allie flipped through the neatly labelled manila folders, passing familiar names, as well as many she'd never heard of, until she reached one that stopped her.

'Found it?' Carter asked.

'No . . . It's mine.'

Her fingertips rested on a thick file with her name written on the top in thick black ink.

'Pull it.'

She could hear the tension in his voice.

'Do you think?' she asked.

'Two things, remember?' he said. 'We're looking for two things.'

With reluctance, she set her file aside and went through the rest of the records, lingering on the one labelled 'Carter West'.

'You want yours?'

Shaking his head, he said curtly, 'I know what it says.'

'OK.' Allie flipped through the last few files. 'Ruth's file isn't here.'

'They must have pulled it.' Carter walked over to Isabelle's desk. 'It could be in the desk—I'll start looking. You look through your own file.'

Allie sat on the floor, staring at the blank expanse of the folder cover, her fingers poised to open it. Now that the moment had come, she was scared.

Do I really want to know the truth?

Above her, she could hear the sound of Carter shuffling through pages and opening drawers. He was moving quickly—she knew she didn't have much time.

She opened the folder.

The first few pages were all the normal things: admission forms with no surprises, transcripts from her last two schools. Looking at her old grades, she winced and quickly flipped the page.

Then things got weirder. A copy of her birth certificate. Photos of her as a young child with her parents. A photo of her as a baby with a woman she didn't recognise, laughing at the camera.

A letter addressed to Isabelle in her mother's handwriting hurt her heart, and she held it up into the light to see it better. Then her breath caught. Words and phrases seemed to jump out at her.

'We need your help, Izzy' '. . . we don't know what to do' 'Christopher could have been taken . . .' 'We don't want to involve Lucinda but we think the time has come . . .' '. . . danger . . .'

'We need your help, Izzy?*' She calls her 'Izzy'?*

She turned the page. This one on thick, expensive paper contained a short note in elegant handwriting she did not recognise. It was dated July this year.

Isabelle.
Admit my granddaughter immediately under Protect Protocol. I will be in touch.
Lucinda

For just a moment, Allie stopped breathing.
Why is that note in my file? Who is Lucinda?

328

Increasingly anxious, she turned the page. The next few pages were photocopies of old Cimmeria school records, but they were not her own.

They were her mother's.

Her hands shaking, Allie flipped through them quickly, scanning each page and then turning it. Scanning and turning. Scanning and turning.

The last page was a note on yellowed card. She recognised the handwriting from the earlier note from Lucinda.

G.
So pleased to hear my daughter is doing well in Night School. Blood will out, as they say. I'd appreciate weekly updates on her progress from now on.
L.S.

Allie dropped the file, as if it could bite. But Carter's voice interrupted her whirling thoughts.

'Hey. You better come look at this.'

His tone was ominous, and she hurried over to where he stood at the desk holding a paper under the light. Allie peered over his shoulder to see it.

When she'd read the whole thing, she looked up at him, stunned.

'Oh my God, Carter. What are we going to do?'

*   *   *

After that, they didn't hang out for long in Isabelle's office. Allie quickly returned her file to its place in the cabinet, while Carter straightened the desk. He folded the throw back over the arm of the leather chair and then switched off the light.

They both leaned against the door, listening for what seemed to Allie like a very long time, then he opened the door and slipped outside while she waited. When he was sure the hallway was empty he came back for her. They closed the door behind them, standing frozen as the click of the latch sliding into place echoed in the preternatural hush like a shout.

It was half past one in the morning. If they were caught in the hallway now they'd have no excuses at all.

They'd only walked about twelve feet when, without warning, Carter stopped. Holding out his arm just as they rounded a corner towards the staircase, he held Allie back. After looking around, he dashed into the thick darkness under the stairs; he didn't need to say a word—she was right on his heels.

Pulling her up to him until her body was pressed against his, he whispered almost soundlessly into her ear.

'Someone's coming.'

With her head against his shoulder inhaling his scent of coffee and cinnamon, she nodded, then turned so she could see what was happening around them. His arms were wrapped around her protectively.

But now she could hear the footsteps too. Very quietly, someone was padding down the hallway towards them.

Allie held her breath and tried to make her heart beat more softly.

They watched as a shadowy figure walked past them to Isabelle's office door and tried the handle. Finding it locked, the figure paused for a moment

330

as if considering the options, before walking away.

When Allie looked up at Carter questioningly he pressed his finger lightly against her lips. They did not move for five minutes, then, after he'd stepped out to look around, Carter took her hand and they hurried up the stairs.

They made it unseen down the empty hallway of the girls' dorm into Allie's room, where she pushed the door closed behind them, then clicked on the desk lamp.

'Who was that?' she whispered.

'I couldn't see him,' Carter said. 'He wore a school uniform, though. So it's a student.'

'Do you think he saw us?' she asked.

He shook his head. 'He never looked our way.'

She relaxed a little. 'I guess we're not the only ones trying to figure out what's really going on around here.'

The adrenalin that had propelled her through the night's activities seemed to flood out of her body all at once, and she yawned hugely.

'We both need some sleep,' Carter said. 'Tomorrow's a school day after all.'

'But we need to talk about all of this.' Allie tried to force herself to feel more awake. 'My file and that letter . . .'

'After classes tomorrow—meet me at the chapel,' he said. 'And I'm going to breakfast at seven—go at the same time and I'll protect you from the gossipers. In the meantime . . . get some sleep.'

He opened the window, then turned back to her. 'One more thing. Earlier tonight? In my room?'

She blushed and waited for him to tell her it was a mistake.

'Was fantastic.' He smiled that sexy smile of his with his hair falling into his eyes, and climbed through the window.

A flood of warmth spread through her whole body. All the stress of what they'd learned tonight faded away and she smiled at the darkness.

'Right back at ya,' she said.

*   *   *

The next morning, Allie walked to breakfast at seven o'clock precisely. Carter stood waiting for her at the dining room hall.

'Is my lady ready for her escort?' he asked as she walked up.

'Your lady could murder a bacon sandwich,' she said.

'How ladylike of my lady.'

They walked into the dining room laughing but felt the chill in the room instantly.

'Whoa,' Carter murmured.

Intimidated by the sense that everybody was staring at her, Allie moved a little closer to him while they served their plates from the buffet. As they hurried to where Rachel sat with Lucas, Allie could hear the whispers and harsh laughter all around them.

Rachel and Lucas both looked worried.

'This sucks,' Lucas said as they sat down. 'What are we going to do?'

'I think Isabelle has got to step up,' Carter said. 'There's not much we can do, unless Allie wants us to follow her everywhere.'

'Isabelle wouldn't usually let this sort of thing get so out of control,' Rachel agreed.

'Maybe she's trying not to show favouritism,' Lucas suggested. 'Everybody knows she has taken a special interest in Allie.'

'Whatever.' Allie stacked her bacon onto her bread. 'All I know is I'm going to kick Katie's arse if she comes anywhere near me today.'

Taking a gigantic bite she looked up to see Carter shaking his head.

'What?' she said with her mouth full.

'Nothing,' he said.

'I think what he's thinking,' Rachel said, grinning, 'is that's our girl.'

'Could I have everybody's attention please.' Isabelle's voice rang out over the dining hall rumble. Silence fell.

Standing at the front of the room in a lavender cardigan open over a crisp white skirt and blouse, a silk scarf over her shoulder, she looked sterner than Allie could ever remember seeing her. 'I would like to remind all students that bullying is grounds for expulsion on a single offence. I trust I won't have to mention this again.'

As she turned and walked out, her footsteps echoed in the crowded room.

When Allie pointed at herself and mouthed, 'Is that about me?' Rachel, Carter and Lucas nodded.

Later, as they walked to class, they were divided over whether or not Isabelle had done enough to put an end to the gossip. Rachel didn't think so, but Carter and Lucas thought she'd done all she could for now.

Walking into biology class, she saw that Jo, freed from her house arrest, was already at their table— her pixie-ish blonde hair neatly combed, and her expression subdued.

Allie didn't know how she was going to handle this. She couldn't really let on what she'd overheard last night, because how could she explain hearing it? And she couldn't ask to move to a different seat—Jerry would want to know why.

The best thing to do, she decided, was take the high road.

If you can't say something nice, say nothing at all.

So she sat down next to Jo silently and turned her chair slightly so it faced away from her. Clearly Jo had decided to take the high road too, though, and they sat, side-by-side, without saying a word for seven long minutes until Jerry stepped up and began his lesson.

After class, Allie shot out of her seat and into the hallway. And she never looked back.

At lunch, Jo and Gabe avoided their usual table, sitting off in a corner of the dining room instead. Allie joined Rachel and Lucas, who, she observed, were sitting together more and more these days.

'Hey,' she said, dropping her bag. 'What's up with them?'

Rachel and Lucas exchanged a look she couldn't quite translate.

'The gossip,' Rachel said after a second, 'is that Jo was so drunk she now can't remember what happened on the roof. And so she has decided that she believes the gossip about what happened on the roof.'

'Oh brilliant,' Allie said, plopping down into a seat. 'So she now thinks I tried to kill her?'

They nodded in sync.

'This would be funny if it weren't happening to me.' Allie sighed.

'It's not happening to me and I don't think it's

334

funny,' Rachel offered.

'You don't believe her?' Allie asked hopefully.

'No way,' Lucas said.

'We know her too well,' Rachel said. 'Look, I'll try and talk to her later, see if I can talk some sense to her.'

'Or at least get her to remember what really happened.' Carter pulled out the chair next to Allie and sat down. 'Like how she got so trolleyed she nearly killed us all. If you ask me, it's pretty convenient that now that everybody knows something crazy happened that day she suddenly can't recall behaving like a lunatic on day release.'

'It's not like her not to remember,' Lucas said, frowning. 'When she's done this before she's always remembered what happened.'

The doubt in his voice gave Allie an icy stab of worry. *What if even Lucas and Rachel start doubting me? Then it would be just Carter and me.*

As if he knew what she was thinking, Carter brushed the side of her head with his lips.

'Don't let her get you down,' he whispered, and she found herself smiling at him in spite of everything.

She was aware that Lucas and Rachel were both watching them with dawning recognition, and that the whole school would soon know that they were together.

'I'm good,' she said, her voice firm. And she meant it.

*　　　*　　　*

For the rest of the day, Allie could not say she was bullied. Instead she was treated like a ghost—as if

335

she wasn't there at all.

Nobody outside of her immediate group of friends spoke to her. Even when she passed Katie in the hallway, she merely turned her head away and flounced by.

As Allie walked to her room after classes ended, Jules stopped her in the hallway. 'I just wanted to tell you that I'm sorry for how everyone's behaving,' the prefect said. 'I spoke with Isabelle about it yesterday, and she has given Katie and two of her friends written warnings about this.'

'You think Katie's behind the rumours, then?' Allie said.

'I've known Katie all my life, Allie.' Jules looked frustrated. 'But I've told her we can't be friends unless she fixes this. It is incredibly unfair to you. And it's just not going to happen on my watch. She knows how I feel, and I expect her to sort this out.'

'Thanks, Jules.' The gratitude in Allie's tone was genuine. 'It feels weird to have people say things about you that aren't true.'

'If anybody harasses you or bullies you, come to Isabelle or me,' Jules said. 'We'll deal with them. But, look, I know what happened between you and Katie yesterday and I'd rather this didn't end up in a fist fight.'

Allie flushed guiltily. 'OK, OK . . . I'll try to control myself.'

When Jules had gone, Allie put on her running clothes and headed outside. It was another unusually warm afternoon—the sun felt hot on her shoulders as she jogged out to the chapel, and she decided to go the long way, taking in the summerhouse as well. She enjoyed the run so much she was almost sorry when she arrived, but at the

336

same time . . . there was Carter.

As she opened the gate, she saw him immediately, leaning against the ancient wooden door of the church, watching her.

'Hey,' she said, running down the stone path.

'Hey back,' he said. 'Right on time. Look, before we go inside there's something that we need to get out of the way.'

Reaching for her hand he pulled her to him, and in the shadows of the doorway he lowered his mouth to hers. She smiled against his lips and pulled him closer until she could feel the warmth of his body against her. Spurred on by her response he kissed her more urgently, holding her so tightly her lungs felt compressed. When he stopped a minute later, she was flushed and breathless.

'I'm glad we got that over with,' she said.

'Me too.' He held the door for her. 'So now we can hopefully focus on all the bad, scary stuff without being distracted by the fun romantic stuff.'

His voice echoed off the cool stone walls as he stood aside to let her walk inside. As she passed him, Allie paused to run her fingers tantalisingly down his arm from his shoulder to the tips of his fingers. Goosebumps formed in their path.

'Uh-huh,' she said, laughing.

He tried to grab her but she danced just out of reach laughing. 'Not in church, Carter. We'll go to hell.'

'Then lead me not into temptation,' he said, following a few steps behind her.

'Fair enough,' she said, still just too far away from him. 'As long as you deliver me from evil.'

'Deal.'

She let him catch her near the pulpit and he

pulled her down giggling onto a dark wooden pew beside him, his arm around her shoulders.

'This place is amazing,' she said, looking around, as his thumb pulled up the short sleeve of her T-shirt and stroked the warm skin underneath. 'I've never seen anything like these paintings in my life.'

'I think lots of churches used to look something like this.' His lips were against her ear now, and she closed her eyes, feeling her body quiver. 'But they changed.'

'Sad for them,' she whispered.

'Isn't it?'

Their kiss was more passionate this time, and after a moment he lifted Allie up onto his lap. Pulling the band from her ponytail, he ran his fingers through her hair until it fell around his face in soft waves as she leaned forward to kiss him. Turning his head, he ran his lips lightly between her ear and the corner of her mouth. Her breath came in soft gasps.

After a few minutes, though, she pushed herself away. With a regretful sigh he let her go and she slid off of his lap onto the pew beside him.

'So much for getting that out of the way,' she said with a wry smile.

'I warned you about the leading and the tempting,' he said.

She laughed. 'How could I tempt you? I'm sweaty runner girl.'

He tugged a strand of her loose hair. 'Tempting.'

But after a moment he sighed. 'Right, so now we must destroy the lovely mood we've created and talk about what's going on.'

All the warmth seemed to leave Allie's body and she shivered. 'Yes, let's do it. You're sure there's nobody else here?'

'We're safe here,' he said with confidence. 'Let's start with your file.'

She nodded. 'It was strange. It had all the normal Allie-isn't-very-good-at-English stuff and then a lot of weird papers that weren't mine.'

He looked puzzled. 'Like what?'

'Like . . . my mum's school records.' She gave him a significant look. 'From here.'

'From here . . . as in, from Cimmeria?' His voice rose incredulously.

'Exactly. So, it turns out my mum wasn't very good at science either when she was my age. Oh, and she attended Cimmeria, a school she pretended she'd never heard of until the week I came here. In fact, she knows the place so well she called Isabelle "Izzy" in a letter.'

'Iz . . .?' Carter stared at her. 'What the hell is going on?'

'I have no idea. But there's more. There was also a note in my file from somebody named Lucinda to Isabelle dated a month ago. It *ordered* her to admit "my granddaughter" immediately, and "protect her".'

Carter let his breath out in a low whistle. 'I don't suppose you have a grandmother named Lucinda?'

'One of my grandmothers died before I was born. The other one died two years ago,' Allie said. 'Her name was Jane.'

'So . . .' Carter said.

'Who's Lucinda?' Allie finished the thought for him. 'Good question. There was also a note in Lucinda's handwriting to somebody with the initial "G", talking about how well her daughter was doing in Night School. It was very old.'

339

Carter pushed his hair back out of his eyes as he absorbed all of this information. 'Allie, did your parents tell you anything that was true, ever?'

She was surprised to feel tears burning her eyes.

'I don't know,' she said, forcing them back.

He squeezed her hand.

'OK, so let's sum this up.' He ticked them each off with a tap on the back of her hand. 'You're rubbish at English. Your mum probably went to school here. Lucinda is either your grandmother or thinks she is, and your parents forgot to mention her to you—for your whole life. And whoever Lucinda is, she's important enough that she can order Isabelle to do things.' He seemed to be finished but then he added, 'Oh, and Isabelle has a stupid nickname.'

Allie half-smiled up at him. 'That's about it, I think.'

'So . . . Not much then.'

'No,' she said feebly. 'Not much.'

'OK, so let's just leave that there for a minute, because it seems to me we'll need time to think about how to handle all of that.' He looked up at the old painting of the yew tree on the wall. 'Let's talk about the letter.'

The letter he'd found on the desk was from Nathaniel to Isabelle dated several days earlier. It had been short and angry. 'What happened on the night of the summer ball was just a taster of what I have to offer,' it said. 'Give me what I deserve or I will destroy Cimmeria with my own hands.'

It listed a date and time for a 'parley at the usual place'. The night was tomorrow, the time was midnight. But the place was never described.

'What's a parley?' Allie had asked at the time,

adding hopefully, 'It's just a couple of letters away from party.'

'Parley—it's a military term,' Carter had replied, flipping the paper over. 'It's a meeting of enemies to talk terms.'

'Oh,' Allie had said. 'So a really crap party then.'

Now, curled up on the church pew next to Carter she asked the question that had been eating away at her all day. 'Do we both think Nathaniel killed Ruth?'

He looked serious. 'I don't know. He all but said as much in that letter. But the main problem I have with that is, why? Why would he do that? What does he want that Isabelle won't give him? And why does he want it so desperately that he'd do something like that?'

She twisted a strand of hair around her finger as she stared at the yew tree on the wall. 'I read somewhere that most people who are murdered are killed by people who know them—like their family or boyfriends.' She dropped the strand of hair. 'God, I wish we could have found Ruth's file. I mean, what if Nathaniel's, like, her evil stepdad or something?'

Carter shook his head. 'If it was something like that, why would he be making demands to Isabelle, and acting like they have this long history, and she's done something bad to him at some point? It doesn't make sense to me.'

'None of this makes sense to me,' Allie said. 'The thing is, there's so much going on here that we don't know about—there's no way for us to figure out what's happening here unless somebody tells us.'

Carter stared at her. 'That's it, Allie! We'll get

them to tell us.'

'Um . . . like . . . how?' she asked, dubious.

He leaned forward, his cheeks flushed with excitement. 'Simple. Isabelle's meeting Nathaniel tomorrow night. I'll follow Isabelle to the meeting. Then I can listen to what they say and we can decide what to do next.'

'That's a great idea,' Allie said. 'I'll come with you.'

He glared at her. 'No you most certainly will not.'

'Yes, I most certainly will.'

'Allie . . .' His eyes warned her to drop it but she ignored it.

'Why should you go and not me? So much of this involves me and my family, and although I know more now, I still don't understand what's really going on.' He tried to speak but she held up her hand. 'This is my *life*, Carter. And I want to find out who's messing it all up.'

'It could be dangerous.' She could hear frustration in his voice. 'And you could get expelled. Allie, this is not a good idea.'

'It *is* dangerous,' she said. 'But I'm doing it. Look, there's one thing in my file I didn't mention. In the letter from my mother, she mentioned my brother, Christopher. And she says "what if he was taken".' She leaned forward intently. 'Don't you see, Carter? I could find out what happened to Christopher. I have to go.'

For a long moment his eyes searched her face. She could see the second when he gave in. 'OK,' he said, resigned. 'I don't like it. But I know if I don't let you go with me, you'll just go on your own and get in even more trouble.'

342

'Thank you!' She threw her arms around his neck.

'But I have one condition,' he said, holding onto her. 'We have to do it my way. Agreed?'

'Agreed!' Allie said, hugging him tighter.

'Now, how many hell points will we get if we desecrate this chapel?' he asked, breathing in the scent of her hair.

CHAPTER TWENTY-FOUR

Clinging to the ledge outside the girls' dorm rooms, Allie inched along towards the low sloping section of roof where she could make her way up and across to Carter's room.

It was just after curfew. The night was dark and clear—perfect sneaking out weather. And she'd already made her way past the first window—now there was only Katie's window to get by. Standing on her toes, she leaned across the window frame tentatively to peek inside.

The lights were on, but it appeared empty.

Stretching out her arm to reach the other side of the window she scuttled across.

Home free, she thought.

But as she took the next step she kicked something off the edge of the gutter—perhaps, she would think later, a roofing tile, or a stone that had rolled off the roof—and it clattered to the ground with the percussive impact of a tiny drumroll. Frozen in place, Allie couldn't decide whether it would be better to rush the rest of the way onto the roof—risking making more noise—or to stay right

343

where she was, as still as a corpse.

'Who's there?' The demanding voice came from about three feet from her right elbow.

Allie held her breath. She wore her running clothes—dark blue stretchy trousers and a dark blue T-shirt. Together with dark rubber-soled shoes, she figured she must be practically invisible.

Think Catwoman, she told herself.

'Jo? Is that you?' Katie's voice pierced the night. 'Or is it Allie, the crazed killer? If it's you, Allie, just so you know, I'm going straight to Jules to turn you in.'

Allie tried to breathe in time with the breeze so that the sound would disappear. After a few minutes—silence. She counted to one hundred, then raced to the sloping roof and climbed up, then hurled herself across to the boys' side. Practice was making her faster. She slid down the slope on that side until she'd reached a drainpipe, then slid across to Carter's room.

His window was open, the light was on, and he was standing across the room, waiting for her. She thought that his dark eyes grew lighter when he saw her.

As she climbed through the window, he walked across the room to lift her off the desk.

'Hey,' he whispered with that sexy half-smile that drove her crazy.

'Hey back.'

She'd already decided not to tell him what Katie had said about turning her into Jules—she knew it wouldn't take much incentive for Carter to insist that she stay at the school while he went out alone.

Instead, she reached up and pulled his head down towards hers.

A few minutes later, he lifted his head to look into her eyes. He stroked her cheek.

'We need to go and follow Isabelle now and find out who the killer is.'

'Quel drag,' Allie said, lifting her lips for another kiss.

'My German is terrible—what does that mean again?' he murmured.

She laughed against his cheek. 'It means why are you talking?'

After a minute he stepped away with a regretful sigh. 'Let's go do our spy thing before we forget what we're supposed to be doing.'

Allie straightened her clothing. 'OK. Let's go kick some arse.'

'Ooh, very convincing.'

'Thanks,' she said. 'I've been working on it all day.'

Carter opened the door and made sure the hall was clear before standing aside for her to pass. They slipped down the stairs, stopping on each level to listen for footsteps or voices.

At the backdoor, he again crept out first as she waited in the shadows, coming back for her when he was certain there was nobody around.

Perfectly in step, they ran around the east wing to the front of the building, following a course they'd chosen earlier that day. At the treeline they ducked down into the bracken, settling in with a clear sightline to the school building. As long as the meeting didn't happen somewhere behind the school, they were well positioned.

'Now,' Carter whispered, 'we wait.'

Above them, a full moon cast the grounds in a ghostly blue glow. In its light they could see quite clearly. So when a group of shadowy figures slipped out of the front door twenty minutes later they saw their every move.

After the figures made their way to the footpath that led to the chapel, Carter signalled her to follow, and they jogged slowly down the path, avoiding twigs that could snap underfoot and give them away. Carter ran about ten feet ahead of her, ensuring that their targets were just far enough away not to hear their footsteps.

They were nearly to the church when they heard voices. Dropping back, Carter grabbed her arm and they stopped in the shadow of the churchyard wall. Just ahead of them, the gate to the churchyard stood open and he crept through to look around, then motioned for her to follow him.

'These theatrics, Nathaniel, are tedious.'

Isabelle's voice. Allie could hear her clearly but could see nobody. *Where* was *she?*

Carter crossed to the yew tree, easily avoiding gravestones, rocks and other dangers, while she picked her way gingerly behind him.

'Hurry,' he whispered.

She frowned into the darkness. 'I *am* hurrying.'

He pulled himself up onto the big low branch, then leaned down for her hand and pulled her up beside him. Using that method they climbed the ancient tree one branch at a time, until they were sitting well above the fence top. Carter sat on one branch with Allie just below him. She couldn't actually see him without craning her head but she could still sense tension in his body. He was alert; poised.

Through the narrow and twisted branches around them, they could see the stream that ran

346

behind the church, down to the pond. The moon helpfully illuminated the scene.

A man stood on the far bank, meadow grasses up to his knees. A large German Shepherd dog sat beside him, still as a statue. Isabelle stood directly across from him on the near bank, her arms crossed. Allie could see irritation in her posture.

Leaning forward in her high perch, Allie studied Nathaniel with fascination. Wearing dark trousers with a black, short-sleeved shirt, he was neither particularly tall nor short. He had thick, dark hair and stylish glasses. In fact, he was ordinary looking in every way. But he exuded power; more panther than lion.

Tearing her eyes away from him, she looked across at the headmistress. Her clothes were unusual for her—a simple black tunic and leggings with knee-high boots. Allie got the feeling she was trying to look tough.

'All I want to know, Isabelle, is this.' Nathaniel's voice was a not unpleasant baritone, but something about it made Allie's skin crawl. 'Are you willing to do the right thing at last?'

Isabelle ignored the question. 'What set this off, Nathaniel? I thought you were satisfied with our arrangement.'

The wind picked up and for a moment Allie lost their voices in the rustling of trees. When she could hear them again, Nathaniel was speaking.

'. . . so I agreed to try to do things your way. I've been patient. Now it's my turn.'

For the first time, Isabelle moved, stepping towards the river, closing the gap between them. 'What you did the night of the ball was barbaric, Nathaniel. Why would anybody give you control of this school after that?'

'I did what I had to do,' he said. 'If you had just honoured our arrangement none of that would have been necessary.'

'What you had to do?' Her voice rose in anger. 'Killing one of my students in cold blood was something you had to do?'

Nathaniel arched one eyebrow. 'One of your students was killed? I had no idea. Perhaps you should talk to your staff. Nobody was killed by me or my people.'

Allie saw Isabelle's shoulders stiffen.

'A student's throat was cut from ear to ear,' she said. 'Are you telling me you had nothing to do with that?'

He had a predator's grin. 'Sounds to me like your school is a very dangerous place, headmistress. I wouldn't want my children to go there.'

She looked at him sceptically and he held up his right hand. 'I swear we had nothing to do with that. On my honour.'

'Your honour . . .' Isabelle's tone was disdainful, but something in her voice told Allie she believed him.

'Let me tell you what I think is behind all of this,' Isabelle said. 'I think you can see that the school is successful. That the tide is turning against you and your views. And that many of those on the board who once disagreed with me are now reconsidering their stance. But you're so arrogant that you still want to prove that your way is better.'

'Enough of this.' Nathaniel stepped closer to the water, the dog stayed where it was, its eyes fixed on Isabelle. 'Here are my terms, Isabelle. You will tell the board that you have changed your bizarre beliefs. That you realise how wrong you have been. And that you wish to turn the running of Cimmeria over to me.'

Every word dripped malice.

If Isabelle was surprised by any of this she didn't betray it. Instead, she sounded amused. 'Oh Nathaniel, don't be ridiculous. You know these terms are absurd. I reject them all.'

He took a step back. 'Then you will suffer the consequences.'

As he turned to leave, the dog right by his side, Isabelle shouted after him, 'Lucinda will know it was you, Nathaniel. She will deal with you.'

He disappeared into the trees without looking back. After a moment, Zelazny and Eloise walked out of the trees to Isabelle. They conferred briefly, and then walked back into the forest. When they reached the trees, two other shadowy figures joined them.

Her back pressed against the tree trunk behind her, Allie sat frozen, her thoughts in turmoil. When Carter looked down at her she could see from his expression that he was as confused about all of this as she was.

'Let's get out of here,' he said.

After climbing down from the tree they made their way through the gate; Carter latched it behind them then held out his hand.

'Ready?'

She nodded.

They began to run.

CHAPTER TWENTY-FIVE

The teachers had a few minutes' head start, but Carter took Allie on a different route back to the school. This path passed by a small stone cottage sitting quietly in a garden filled with flowers. The scent of jasmine and roses wafted to them on the breeze.

'Whose house is that?' Allie whispered.

'Bob Ellison's,' he said.

It was far behind them when he added, 'I grew up there.'

Allie stopped. 'That was *your house*?'

'Don't stop,' Carter said without looking back. 'We can talk about this later.'

The trees around them made ghostly shapes in the moonlight, but as they took up the same running pattern they'd used earlier—with Carter running ten feet ahead—Allie felt safe. Things that had frightened her in the past—a rustling in the undergrowth, the sound of a twig snapping in the distance—didn't bother her at all.

But when she heard Carter's voice, she skidded to a stop. He wasn't talking to her.

He'd got well ahead and around a bend in the footpath, so she couldn't see him or who he was speaking to, but something wasn't right. Acting on instinct, she ducked off the track and hid behind a tree surrounded by tall ferns. Once there she sank down on one knee and held her breath.

'. . . nothing at all,' Carter was saying.

Then the other voice—Gabe's voice: 'So you're just out patrolling on your own, even though it's not your shift?'

She could tell that he didn't believe Carter.

'Why, what's wrong with that?' Carter asked. 'I do this all the time.'

'Not tonight,' Gabe said. 'Didn't you hear Zelazny? We're only to go out on our own shifts after curfew. You better go and talk to him. He's not going to be happy.'

'Fine,' Carter said. 'See you later.'

Allie heard the sound of his footsteps disappearing in the distance. Then she could hear footsteps and voices heading her way—several people, she thought. She leaned over to peer around the tree. In the moonlight she saw Gabe talking to somebody, but his body hid whoever it was from her view.

'. . . such a screw-up sometimes, you know?' Gabe was complaining. 'He really needs to get it together. I don't know why Zelazny puts up with it.'

'Did you believe him?' the other person asked— Allie couldn't see who it was, and she didn't recognise the voice.

'I don't really care,' Gabe said. 'If he keeps screwing up it won't matter whether or not he's telling the truth.' He walked down the path. 'I never understood why Isabelle pushed us to let him in Night School in the first place.'

At that moment a crashing sound in the woods behind Allie made her jump. She ducked down low again, below the fronds of the bracken around her.

'Who's there?' Gabe asked. His voice sounded closer and Allie stayed very still, her heart pounding in her ears. In the moonlight she could see that he was standing on the edge of the path looking directly at her. She could hear him

351

breathing.

She knew Gabe. They'd always been kind of friends. But something was really wrong here. He sounded different. Angry. Even threatening.

All of her instincts told her to stay hidden.

Lucas' voice came from the woods nearby. 'It's me, dude.'

'Jesus.' Gabe sounded disgusted. 'Subtle, man.'

'Sorry! I tripped over a freakin' log. It's dark in the trees.'

'Whatever.' Gabe had returned to the path. 'We're moving on.'

After waiting until quiet returned and she was certain they were far down the path, Allie made her way cautiously back to the path and then ran at full speed towards the school.

She'd made it to the treeline when a figure stepped out of the bushes beside the path and into her way. Jumping back, she opened her mouth to scream, but a hand clamped over her lips and an arm wrapped around her as she struggled to free herself.

'Allie,' Carter whispered. 'It's me. Stop fighting.'

'Jesus.' She relaxed in his arms. 'You scared the crap out of me, Carter.'

'Did Gabe see you?' he hissed.

She shook her head. 'I hid.'

Obviously relieved, he pointed to their right. 'This way.'

Sticking to the shadows at the edge of the lawn, they looped around to the back door. From there getting back in was easy. They crept through the door, but the stealth wasn't necessary—the hallways were empty. They could hear raised voices from Isabelle's office but didn't linger to listen as they ran up the stairs.

*   *   *

'What the hell is going on?'

Carter paced back and forth across Allie's bedroom floor, raking his hands through his dark hair.

Perched on the edge of her desk, she didn't have any answers for him.

'Who is Nathaniel?' Carter muttered to himself. 'Why is he doing this?'

'A dog!' Allie said inanely.

Carter gave her a look and she explained. 'It was a dog Jo and I heard that night in the walled garden. Nathaniel must have been there.'

'Makes sense,' Carter said. 'But I still don't understand what's going on. Who is he?'

'OK, let's think about what he said. He talked about the board,' Allie said. 'He told Isabelle to go to the board.'

Carter glanced at her enquiringly.

'Well, why doesn't he go himself?' she asked. 'I mean, if he's so powerful. And if he can't go to the board, there has to be a reason.'

'Yes.' Recognition dawned on Carter's face. 'Because he's either been in trouble with them or they don't like him.'

'Or they don't know him.' She twisted up her face in thought. 'He could be a complete outsider. But I got the feeling he and Isabelle knew each other well. Like old friends gone wrong, or bad family or something.'

'Yeah. Or ex-lovers,' Carter said.

Their eyes met.

353

'Totally,' she said.

They thought that through for a minute—Allie swinging her foot, Carter pacing.

'And Lucinda.' Allie broke the silence. 'She said "Lucinda will know".'

'I heard.' He pivoted and paced.

'Lucinda again . . .' she murmured, watching him pace. 'Did you believe him? Nathaniel, I mean. Do you think he didn't kill Ruth?'

'I don't know.' His tone betrayed his frustration.

'I think Isabelle believed him.'

'Brilliant,' he muttered. 'This is just brilliant.'

'So that would mean . . .' Her voice trailed off. She didn't want to think about what that meant. Pulling her feet up onto the desk, she wrapped her arms around her knees.

'God this is a nightmare . . . What do we do now?'

He stopped pacing. 'I have no idea.'

*   *   *

For the rest of that week, Allie felt isolated. All the students were in their normal seats, and the teachers continued the lessons in the usual way, but to her nothing was the same. Something awful was going to happen—Nathaniel was going to do *something*—and out of all the students, only she and Carter knew about it.

Worse than that, she was still treated as if she were invisible by many students. She was ignored when she walked with them down hallways, passed them on the stairs, brushed her teeth next to them in the bathroom. And although she refused to admit it to anyone, it was getting to her. It was an

354

oddly disembodying experience to be treated as if she weren't actually there.

On Wednesday morning a girl she couldn't remember seeing before dropped a pen near her in French class, and when Allie picked it up and held it out for her, the girl acted as if she couldn't see it, even when Allie waved it back and forth in front of her. Eventually she let it fall back to the ground.

'Whatever,' Allie had muttered, turning back to her notebook.

On Thursday, Jules took her aside and told her she was doing all she could to get Katie to stop the campaign against her.

'I'm trying, Allie, I really am,' she said. 'But she's stubborn. I've tried talking to Isabelle about it but I've never known her to be so busy.'

Allie knew perfectly well why Isabelle was busy, but she couldn't tell Jules that.

'Jerry's spoken to the boys and told them they could all face punishment if they don't stop—so I think you'll see the guys getting back to normal soon. Of course, some may be more scared of Katie than they are of Jerry.' Jules looked uncomfortable. 'But with time this will all work out. The term ends in a few weeks and next term will be better . . .'

Or, next term, Katie poisons even more kids against me. And then this whole thing becomes impossible, Allie thought.

Jo was still avoiding her old friends—at mealtimes she either sat with Gabe or with Katie and her legions of minions across the room from her former table.

Allie thought she didn't look happy. *But I'm probably projecting.*

By Friday, though, she'd had enough. After her

last class ended she stormed down the hall to Jo's room, knocking perfunctorily before shoving the door open.

Jo sat on the bed reading a fashion magazine. 'You could knock,' she snapped.

'I did. And you could not be a bitch,' Allie replied.

Sighing heavily, Jo returned her attention to the magazine, flipping the page with a sharp, irritated crack.

'Look, Jo,' Allie said, leaning against the desk, 'we need to talk . . . Now.'

'Fine. Talk.' Jo kept flipping pages.

Crack. Crack. Crack.

'What can you remember about what happened up on the roof that day?' Allie asked.

Jo's normally sunny clear blue eyes were like chips of ice. 'I can't remember much, but I know that somehow I ended up nearly dying.'

Involuntarily, Allie glanced at Jo's hands where plasters still covered the tips of two fingers.

'It's the not remembering that's the problem here,' Allie said. 'Because I do remember. I remember everything. And what I can't figure out is why you never once came to me or Carter to ask what happened.'

Jo closed the magazine with exaggerated patience and looked at her.

'I didn't come to you because I don't trust you, Allie,' she said. 'See, the thing is, lying in my bed in pain with my hands wrapped up in bandages for a week, I had plenty of time to think about everything. And I realised that I have no idea who you really are or where you come from. All I know is what you've told me. And I also know that ever

356

since we met everything's just fallen apart.'

Colour flooded Allie's cheeks and she stared at Jo in disbelief. 'Are you telling me you think what's been happening here is my fault?'

'Think about it, Allie,' Jo said. 'Isn't it your fault, at least a bit? It seems to me bad news just surrounds you. Maybe Katie's right. Maybe you really are crazy.'

Her tone was venomous and her words stung. For a moment, Allie was speechless.

Jo was supposed to be her friend.

But then she lifted her chin and fixed Jo with a hard stare.

'You want to know what happened on the roof, Jo? Fine. I'll tell you. You drank half a bottle of vodka and you danced on the roof. You *danced*. You threw yourself around like a drunken fairy. You didn't know where you were and you didn't care who you took down with you. Both Carter and I risked our *arses* to save you that day. And right now, I've got to say, I'm kind of regretting that.'

Jo tried to speak but Allie talked over her. 'If you don't believe me, for God's sake believe Carter. You've known him for years. Or believe Jules, she's been trying to talk to you. Just don't believe people who are only using you to get at me. Because that's kind of pathetic.'

Her face red with anger, Jo threw the magazine at her. As it fluttered across the room Allie caught it easily.

'What I'm regretting right now is that I ever thought I could be your friend.' Jo spat the words out at her. 'Now get out.'

*   *   *

Fighting back tears, Allie stumbled down the hallway towards the sanctuary of her own room.

I will not let them see me cry.

But at that moment, Rachel stepped in front of her with an armful of books. She took one look at Allie's face and grabbed her hand.

'With me,' she said firmly, pulling her back into her room.

Dropping the books on the desk she sat down on the bed beside her. 'What happened?'

And that was all it took.

Her body shaking with sobs, Allie told her about confronting Jo and how she'd reacted. She added in the things she'd overheard Katie saying (although she left out the bit about being on the window ledge clinging to a wall at the time).

Rachel held her hand and listened, occasionally tutting sympathetically, but mostly just letting her pour out her heart.

'I just don't understand how she could say these things to me . . . or about me,' Allie said finally, as her sobs lessened.

Rachel waited for the tears to stop before responding.

'Jo has . . . problems,' she said diplomatically. 'She's fragile. Her home life is not . . . great. But she's good at heart. We all know that. She's being manipulated by Katie and her gaggle of hags to believe this rubbish about you. But that's not much consolation, I know. It hurts—I just wish there was something more I could do.'

She handed Allie a box of tissues. 'I think she'll come around. And when she does she'll be sorry she said those things.'

358

'Is this the reason you never really hung around with Jo and Lisa before?' Allie asked, drying her eyes. 'Because Jo's a little, what did you call it? Fragile?'

Rachel hesitated before replying. 'I had my own . . . encounter with Jo's group a long time ago. Do you remember how I told you once Lucas was the guy friend I could never date?'

Allie nodded.

'Well, that wasn't completely true.' Rachel looked down at her hands. 'I had a huge crush on Lucas when I first started here two years ago. He kind of took me under his wing. There aren't many Asians here and I was a bit self-conscious. But he made me feel completely welcome. I was just a kid and, well, you know how it goes. A fun, good-looking guy almost adopts you . . . I fell completely in love with him.'

Allie looked up at her in surprise, and Rachel shrugged. 'A few weeks later, a pretty blonde girl arrives late in the term, Lucas takes one look at her and . . .' She slapped her hands together and let them fall apart. 'Lucas became my best guy friend for ever.'

Allie looked at her, puzzled. 'But . . . they broke up, right?'

'Oh yeah,' Rachel rolled her eyes. 'They broke up. After she had a complete meltdown.' She sighed. 'But I guess some part of me could never forgive him for choosing her over me. And some other part of me could never forgive her for letting him make that choice. Or maybe that was all the same part of me.'

'That sucks,' Allie said.

Rachel smiled sadly. 'Yes, it does.'

For weeks now, Rachel had been Allie's rock. She seemed so wise and mature beyond her years—Allie had longed to tell her what she and Carter had learned. If anybody would know what to do, she reasoned, Rachel would. She had held off because she had promised Carter she'd tell nobody. But keeping all that information to herself was just about impossible. And there was nobody else to tell. And maybe she and Carter could use Rachel's help.

She looked at Rachel for a long moment as she fought an inner battle.

'What?' Rachel asked, puzzled.

Allie wiped the last tears from her eyes. 'There's something I have to tell you.'

*   *   *

'You did *what?*'

Carter's incredulous voice echoed in the summerhouse. It was after supper and the sun was dipping low in the sky, gilding the tops of the trees around them. They were sitting on a stone bench in a pool of warm sun.

Allie raised her chin stubbornly. 'I trust her, Carter. And it can't be just us dealing with this.'

'No, but we should both be involved in deciding who to tell, Allie. It's not going to be a secret for long if we go around telling people we think we can trust without talking about it first,' he said. 'I mean, I didn't just go off and tell Lucas.'

Allie thought about Lucas crashing through the woods.

'Don't do that,' she said quickly.

Carter shot her an exasperated look. 'Seriously,

Allie, how much do you really know about her? Have you, for example, ever wondered if she had anything to do with spreading the gossip about you finding Ruth's body?'

Allie thought her heart might have stopped.

'What? Are you saying she did?' she asked, fighting to stay calm.

'I'm saying I don't know and neither do you,' he said. 'I'm saying she loves to gossip. I'm saying it's a bloody big coincidence that you told her about it and suddenly everybody knows.'

'She wouldn't . . .' Allie faltered. Who could she trust any more, anyway? Why should Rachel be any different from Jo or Sylvain? Both of whom she'd trusted. Both of whom betrayed her trust.

'You don't know that, Allie.' Carter's voice was more gentle now. 'I don't know enough about her to know whether or not we can trust her. She's always kept to herself.'

'Like you,' Allie pointed out.

'Like me,' he conceded reluctantly. 'But her father is very big in Night School. He runs security for huge corporations, advises governments . . . He's an insider, Allie.'

'I know that. Rachel told me her dad was some bigwig on the board,' she said. 'But Rachel isn't in Night School, is she?'

'No, and that is unusual.'

'So it's possible she's not an insider like her dad,' she said.

'Yes. But you just took a pretty big chance on "possible",' he said.

She knew he had a point. 'You're right. I'm sorry. I'll be more careful.'

Mollified, he sat thinking for a moment.

'What did she say when you told her?' he asked.

'She didn't know what to think. But she was quite certain she'd heard her dad talking about some bloke named Nathaniel and complaining that he was causing trouble.' She looked over at him cautiously. 'She wondered if she should ask him about it.'

'*What?*' Carter nearly shouted the word and Allie ducked.

'She's not going to do it,' she hastily reassured him. 'She just wanted us to talk about the possibility. She thinks we can trust him.'

'Oh bloody hell.' Carter buried his head in his hands.

'What?' Allie asked innocently.

'This is how you keep a secret Allie? Seriously?'

'No . . . I mean, yes.' She shot him a look. 'I've only told *one* person, Carter. I think you're overreacting.'

'Al, we could get in a lot of trouble.'

'I know that,' she said defensively.

'Well then?' he said. 'Should we maybe try *not* telling people our secrets?'

She narrowed her eyes. 'So I guess you want me to tell Rachel you'd rather she didn't tell her father?'

'Yes, Allie. That's what I want.'

'Fine,' she said icily.

'Great.'

They sat in silence for a long minute.

'Did we just have our first fight?' Carter asked, looking up at her with that half-smile that always made her melt.

'No,' Allie said. 'I'm pretty sure we fought a lot before we got together.'

'True,' he said.

'Anyway,' she said, 'whether you like it or not, we now have somebody else to help us if and when we need help. And she happens to be very clever.'

'That could come in handy,' he conceded grudgingly.

'Yeah,' she said. 'That's what I thought.'

He lightly punched her shoulder. She tickled him back and before long they were both laughing. Draping his arm across her shoulder he kissed her temple.

'I'm sorry,' he said. 'I shouldn't be so pissed off. It'll be fine.'

'It *will* be fine,' she agreed, 'if we make it fine. Somehow.'

'Which reminds me, I wanted to tell you what I learned today,' he said.

Even though he sounded serious, she found it hard to focus on his words when she looked into those big dark eyes.

'OK,' she said, thinking dreamily: *He's really mine. Voluntarily!*

'Allie, this is important.'

'Sorry.' She untangled herself from him and sat up straight. 'Hit me.'

'Night School is starting late-night drills again.'

She frowned. 'What does that mean?'

'It means we've been given really weird instructions. We'll be patrolling the grounds in shifts all night, every night. Taking turns, so everybody gets some kip.' He looked off at the trees. 'We've patrolled the grounds before for training purposes but this is different. It's very intense. They're telling us it's a new training project to teach us what they call "protect and defend".

They're going to stage fake attacks that we have to fend off. They've even told us we can take time off from morning classes the day after our night shifts. This has literally never happened before. It starts tonight, and they've got us doing training all weekend.'

Watching his face, Allie could see the worry in his eyes.

'They're getting ready for Nathaniel to do something,' she said.

He nodded.

'I guess there's no way they'd call the police and ask for help?'

'Hah.'

'So . . . No more sneaking out at night?' she guessed.

'Absolutely not,' he said. 'The security is about to get intense around here.'

'OK,' she said quietly. 'So he's coming.'

'Oh yes.' Carter's eyes scanned the horizon. 'He's coming.'

CHAPTER TWENTY-SIX

For Allie, that weekend seemed to drag on for ever, slowed by a toxic mix of dread and loneliness. Carter and Lucas were both tied up in Night School, and Katie's anti-Allie campaign was still underway.

For the first time, she realised how much she'd come to rely on Carter. She rarely saw him, and even when she did there was only time for a quick hug. When she asked him how it was going out there, he said only: 'It's intense.' But his eyes told her everything she needed to know—he was tired. And worried.

She dealt with it all by not dealing with it. She spent most of her time in the library. Next week was the end of the summer term and she had essays to finish and exams to prepare for. In all the excitement of the last couple of weeks, she'd let herself get behind. After all she'd been through this summer, she did not intend to get poor marks.

Rachel was there all day every day so Allie always had someone to work with.

'Study buddies,' Rachel liked to say with inappropriate cheer.

But the seeds of doubt Carter planted still lived in Allie's mind. *Did Rachel spread rumours about me? Can I trust her?*

Rachel was so supportive and so open and honest about things, it seemed impossible. But Allie knew nothing was impossible.

The librarian's desk was manned by student volunteers, a fact Rachel observed with raised eyebrows.

'I guess Eloise is off playing war games,' she muttered, after the volunteers brought her the wrong book for the third time. 'I wish she could save it until the term is over.'

'Did you know Eloise was in . . .' Allie gestured vaguely.

Rachel nodded. 'She's an old friend of my dad's. I think he was one of her trainers or something when she was a student. Anyway, Eloise has no secrets from me.' Closing her book she added, 'I think, anyway. Who knows any more?'

'That's how I feel about everything.' Allie didn't

meet her eyes.

Rachel glanced at her watch. 'It's noon—want to take a break and get something to eat?'

Leaving their notebooks open on the table to reserve their place, they headed to the dining room. It was unusually quiet—many students were taking their sandwiches outside to the late summer sun. They chose a table in a quiet corner where they could talk without being overheard.

'Any news from Carter?' Rachel asked.

Allie shrugged. 'A little. He says it's all really intense, and they never get a break. What does Lucas say?'

'The same.'

Rachel bit into her sandwich, frowning. Allie could tell there was something on her mind but she waited until she was ready to talk.

'What are you going to do for your hols, Allie?' she asked at last. 'I know you and your parents have "issues".' She made air quotes around the last word. 'But are you going to go home?'

The question took Allie by surprise. With all that had been going on she really hadn't thought about what to do. She wasn't ready to go home to the uncomfortable silences and suspicious faces. The ticking clock and unspoken regret. But what else could she do?

'I'll go home, I guess,' she sighed. 'You know, I haven't talked to my parents since I got here. I was so angry at them for sending me here. Then I was angry at them for lying to me. I wanted them to notice I didn't call and to call me. Just to make sure I was OK.' She peeled the crust off her sandwich. 'They didn't call.'

Rachel leaned towards her. 'Here's the thing—

366

if you can't face it, you're welcome to come stay at mine. I spoke with Mum about it yesterday—I've told her all about you. She said for me to tell you you're welcome anytime, and you can stay as long as you like. We've got lots of room.'

That proves it, Allie thought. *She is genuinely my friend. She wouldn't invite me to her house otherwise, would she? That's what real friends do.*

But her paranoid subconscious had a counter argument: *What a great way to spy on me.*

Still, the idea was tempting. Spending a couple of weeks on a sprawling country estate with Rachel versus going home to her miserable parents to hash out family problems in their poky London house? It was really no contest.

But.

'Rachel, thank you so much. Can I think about it?' she said. 'I know I need to deal with my parents sometime. But right now I don't see the point.'

'I know.' Rachel's eyes were sympathetic. 'It's got to be hard.'

'Your family seems so wonderful,' Allie said. 'I think you won the family lottery.'

Rachel looked unconvinced. 'You've never met my dad. He wants me to go into his business. He's been harassing me to join Night School since I got here. It drives him crazy that I won't do it. And he is so not thrilled about me studying medicine. He hates doctors. Calls it "quackery". We row about it all the time.' She finished her sandwich. 'So, see? Nobody's family's perfect.'

Allie wasn't buying it. 'Yeah, but there's imperfect and then there's my family. We're imperfect like a ticking nuclear bomb is imperfect.'

Rachel laughed. 'You have a point. Clan

367

Sheridan clearly does not have it together right now.'

'Allie Sheridan?' A younger student Allie didn't remember ever seeing before stood at their table looking at Rachel.

'Her.' Rachel pointed at Allie.

'Me,' Allie said, looking at him curiously.

'Isabelle asked could you come to her office, please?'

She couldn't hide her surprise. 'What? Why?'

He stared at her blankly.

'Allie . . .' Rachel was trying not to laugh. 'What have you done now?'

Allie shrugged. 'She probably just wants to tell me how amazing I am. Again.'

'Uh-huh,' Rachel said. 'Well I'll be in the library all afternoon—come find me when you're free. If she doesn't throw you in the dungeon or something.'

'Thanks for that,' Allie said, gathering her things. 'I've got to say, at this point? If I found out there were a dungeon here, it really wouldn't surprise me.'

*　　　*　　　*

Isabelle's office was empty when Allie arrived, but the door stood open, so she sat in one of the chairs. As she waited she glanced around nervously as if even now she'd find that she and Carter had left something out of place that could give them away.

Isabelle strode in a few minutes later looking distracted, her glasses pushed up on top of her head.

'Would you like a cup of tea?' she asked, turning

on a kettle on top of a small refrigerator in a corner. 'I could really do with one myself.'

'Sure,' Allie said politely, although she didn't feel like tea.

The kettle rumbled to life as Isabelle rummaged about for an extra cup, then made sure it was clean. When it was ready, the headmistress handed her a cup, carefully turning the handle so that she wouldn't burn herself, then sank down in a chair next to her.

'That's better.' She sipped her tea reflectively, then focused her gaze on Allie. 'There is nothing wrong in the world that isn't made better by a good cup of tea. Thank you for coming, Allie. I don't want to take you away from your studies for too long. But with the term ending on Friday, I wanted to spend some time with you to find out how you are. You've now been with us for six weeks so you've had time to settle in. I know this has been an unusual term and I wondered if you wanted to talk about anything.'

For a moment, Allie was speechless.

Is she joking?

Isabelle was looking at her expectantly, and she knew she had to say something.

What should I say? 'Well, the murder was a little upsetting, and the fire did worry me a bit. I was nearly date-raped and my ex best friend is crazy. But, hey, at least I'm getting an A in History'?

'OK . . .' she said, cautiously.

She tried to think of something less sarcastic to say, but her head was full of things she couldn't talk about—things she wasn't supposed to know. And she knew Isabelle wasn't interested in how she was doing in biology, or why she was late with her essay last week.

As her silence stretched on, Isabelle raised an eyebrow and offered her a lifeline. 'You haven't had a panic attack in a while, I hear. I think that's progress.'

Until that moment, Allie hadn't noticed the stretch of time since her last attack. But it had been more than two weeks. And, actually, now that she thought about it, she hadn't been counting things much either.

'That's true,' she admitted. 'I guess I'm not . . . freaking out as much as I used to.'

Isabelle smiled. 'Well, things have been stressful here, but it seems to me you're handling stress better now. And I'm pleased to see that.' She set down her tea. 'Now, you and Jo . . .'

Allie winced. This was not a conversation she wanted to have.

'I've noticed that you're less close than you were, why is that?'

Hesitantly, Allie told her in basic terms what had happened. Dismayed, Isabelle closed her golden-brown eyes as she listened.

'I'll speak with Jo,' she said when Allie'd finished. 'She is going through a difficult time too. So you may have to be patient with her. But I know your friendship is important to her.'

'Was important,' Allie muttered, emphasising the first word.

'And will be again,' Isabelle said with confidence. 'If you're patient.'

She set down her teacup. 'Katie's little campaign is another issue I'm dealing with. I know Jules has talked to you—and I'm sorry I haven't had a chance to before now. I've been so busy. But I want you to know Jules has been updating me about this every single day, and she has been fighting your corner with Katie.

'You have been remarkably patient in dealing with her but I think we're at the point where I will have to consider suspending her if she doesn't stop,' Isabelle said. 'She knows The Rules perfectly well, as do her parents. I've written to them about this and they have not responded. So I'm giving her a final warning today. I very much appreciate your restraint.'

'Be careful!' Allie spoke before she could stop herself.

The headmistress looked at her curiously; Allie's voice faltered. 'I mean . . . Aren't her parents on the board? I think they're super-powerful; she's always bragging about it. They'd be . . . you know. Bad enemies . . . I think. If they're like her.'

Isabelle leaned forward. 'You're very sweet to worry about me, Allie. Don't worry—I'll be careful.'

Moving onto safer ground, they talked for a few minutes about her classwork. Isabelle praised her dedication and pointed out that all of her grades had steadily improved. Even Zelazny had praised her essay on the Civil War.

'So, actually, my only concern is what happens now,' she said finally.

'What do you mean?' Allie asked, puzzled.

'During the time you've been here I've spoken to your mother many times. She's worried about you. They both miss you.'

Immediately tears burned Allie's eyes, and she fought them back. She was surprised how much this hurt. She'd avoided contacting her parents because she was so angry at them. But she didn't know why they hadn't got in touch with her.

At the same time, she felt betrayed by what she'd found in her student file. Isabelle knew her mother well and had never told her. If her parents had betrayed her by not telling her the truth, hadn't Isabelle betrayed her too? In fact, hadn't they all lied?

Maybe now was time for truth telling.

'Do you know my parents well?' Allie asked.

Isabelle's expression changed instantly. She physically tensed.

'Why do you ask that question?' Her tone was cautious.

'Something my mother said when she brought me here has been bugging me,' Allie lied. 'She called you "Izzy" by mistake, and then corrected herself. As if she knew you. And then Katie and Jo both said something about everybody here being legacy. That made me wonder what I was doing here if I wasn't legacy.'

She stared hard at the headmistress. 'Am I legacy, Isabelle?'

Emotion flashed across Isabelle's face as she hesitated a second too long, but in the end her answer was simple.

'Yes, Allie. You are very much legacy.'

CHAPTER TWENTY-SEVEN

After leaving Isabelle's office, Allie stopped to splash cold water on her face before returning to the library. When she sat down, Rachel glanced at

372

her enquiringly.

'What? Was the dungeon occupied or something?' she asked with a teasing smile. But when she noticed Allie's reddened face her expression changed to concern. 'Hey, what's the matter?'

Allie smiled wanly. 'It's nothing, really. It just turned into an unexpected therapy session.'

'I hate it when therapy jumps out and surprises you like that,' Rachel said, but her eyes were still concerned. 'Want to take a break and talk about it?'

Her sympathy made Allie feel tearful again, and she nodded. She didn't want to cry in front of everyone.

Rachel led her to a quiet nook down the hall from the library, then went off in search of tissues, returning with a big box and two cups of tea.

'Tell me everything,' she said, settling down. 'Or at least everything you want to tell me.'

Allie started to speak, but then stopped. *If today is a truth-telling day, then why stop with Isabelle?*

She couldn't think of a good reason.

'Before I tell you, I need to ask you a question,' she said. 'It might hurt your feelings. But I hope you'll understand why I need to ask this.'

Rachel's almond-shaped eyes were wide with surprise, but she never lost her cool.

'OK,' she said. 'Ask me anything.'

'Have you ever gossiped about me?'

Rachel didn't even hesitate.

'Before I met you I did,' she said. 'Because I gossip about everybody. But as soon as I met you I stopped talking about you and I have never done it again. Ever.'

Watching her closely, Allie saw not a flicker of hesitation. Not the slightest sign that she was even uncomfortable with the question. She just seemed . . . herself. All of Allie's instincts told her she could trust her.

'The thing is,' Allie said, 'everybody seems to lie to me. My parents. Isabelle. Jo. I'm losing faith in . . .'

'Everyone?' Rachel finished for her. Allie nodded.

Rachel put her hand on her heart. 'I swear on my family, Allie, I'm not one of them. You can trust me.'

Somehow, Allie knew it was true.

Leaning forward, she pulled Rachel into a hug. 'I believe you. I'm sorry I had to ask.'

'I understand,' Rachel said, hugging her back. 'Maybe more than you know. Remember, I've been here a while. There's a reason I choose not to have many friends. Now, tell me what happened that upset you.'

Allie told her briefly about her meeting with Isabelle, and about asking her if she was legacy. When she told her Isabelle's answer, Rachel breath hissed through her teeth.

'She admitted it? Blimey O'Reilly! What did you say?'

'I tried to make her be specific,' Allie said, remembering the look on Isabelle's face—she'd seem torn.

'My mum went to school here, didn't she?' she'd asked the headmistress. 'You knew each other then.'

Isabelle nodded. 'She did. We were in the same class. She was one of my closest friends.'

Allie's brow creased. 'Then why have I never met you before? Or heard of this school?'

'It's a very long story, Allie, although I want you to know that your mother never fell out with me. She fell out with Cimmeria. And the people behind it.' She looked sombre. 'I think you should really talk about this with her. She wouldn't want me to be the one to tell you her story. It's not my place. But I can tell you that when she completed her education here she left all of this behind. I don't think she ever looked back. She hated it here. And I believe that's why she never told you about it.'

Setting her teacup down on a table, Allie had pulled her legs up, wrapping her arms around her knees. 'But she sent me here.'

Isabelle nodded.

'Why would she send me to a school she hated?' Allie's voice rose querulously.

'She couldn't handle you,' Isabelle said. 'And that's not your fault, it's hers. And she knows that. After Christopher . . . left, she wasn't herself. She worried herself into a place where she couldn't be a good mum to you any more.'

An unexpected wave of grief washed over Allie and she bent forward until her head rested on her knees, trying not to cry.

'Sending you here was one of the bravest things she's ever done in her life, Allie,' Isabelle said gently. 'She knew you were in trouble where you were. But to send you here she had to ask for help from . . . from people she'd left behind her long ago. And that was hard.'

Allie watched a tear fall onto her knee.

'Why didn't you ever tell me before?' she asked, her voice muffled. 'You and Mum are friends and neither of you ever told me. Isn't that like lying?'

Isabelle rested her hand on Allie's shoulder. Her voice was low and calm.

'She begged me not to tell you, and I had to honour her wishes because you are her daughter, not mine. I think she was wrong not to tell you the truth, and she knows I think that. But I couldn't betray her trust.' She sounded like she, too, was fighting tears now. 'But I didn't want to betray your trust either. And I'm so sorry I didn't tell you.'

Allie took a shaky breath. 'Are you keeping other things from me, too?'

There was a long silence.

'Adults,' Isabelle said carefully, 'can't tell young people everything they know. That isn't how things work. They tell them as much as they can to keep them safe. So, yes, I'm keeping some things from you until I think you're ready to know them. But please believe me that I will tell you when you're ready.'

Allie's grief was usurped by anger. *Why do adults always feel they're better suited to deal with important issues just because they're older? Why do they think that gives them the right to lie?*

But Isabelle wasn't done yet. 'And some of this—a lot of this—needs to come from your own parents. Not from me. You need to ask them these questions first, and give them a chance to be honest with you. If they won't tell you, or you think they're not being honest, then come to me. And I will tell you what I can.'

'How can I ask my parents anything?' Allie's voice rose. 'I haven't called them because I was waiting to see if they would call me. It seemed to me, if they missed me they'd call. Or at least write.

376

But they haven't. They're *useless*.'

'Your mother hasn't talked with you because she wanted you to have time to think.' Isabelle's voice was sorrowful. 'Time to decide whether or not you wanted to stay here. And whether or not you could forgive her. I know without a single doubt that she is sorry about how hard this has been on you. Because she is who she is, she can't tell you that.'

She added in a whisper, 'But I can.'

Allie buried her face in her hands so Isabelle wouldn't see her cry, but she felt the headmistress wrap her arms around her.

Later, when she'd quieted, Isabelle gave her a tissue, and put her teacup back into her hands.

'You need to understand, Allie,' she said, 'that you still have much to learn about yourself. Your family has a long and unique history. Your mother rejected that history, so she chose not to tell you about it. I think that's a shame. You have a most astonishing bloodline. Ask her about it.

'And I hope you will forgive your parents. They did what they thought was right.'

When Allie'd finished telling the story Rachel leaned back in her seat. 'Wow,' she said. 'That is so intense. And, I don't care what she says. Your parents are profoundly lame. But I'm super-curious about what she means about your bloodline.'

'It's got to be Lucinda,' Allie said. 'Whoever she is.'

'Your mysterious would-be-grandmother . . .' Rachel mused. 'No doubt—she's the key. You didn't ask Isabelle about her?'

'No. I got side-tracked with all that my-parents-are-rubbish rubbish.'

'It's driving me crazy,' Rachel said. 'Who is she?'

'I wish I knew.'

Rachel gave her a challenging look. 'You know what I'm going to say.'

Allie sighed. 'Your dad . . .'

'. . . knows everything,' Rachel finished for her. 'Let me tell him what's going on.'

'Carter doesn't want to tell anybody else—particularly not a board member like your dad,' Allie said. 'He's still cross with me for telling you.'

'Fine,' Rachel said. 'But it's not his family we're talking about here. It's yours and mine.'

She had a point.

'Let me think about it,' Allie said. 'I might need to work on Carter a bit.'

'OK,' Rachel said, 'but don't take too long to think. The term ends on Friday.'

*   *   *

By Monday, Allie still hadn't made up her mind what to tell Rachel about her dad, but when she walked to the dining hall at lunchtime all thoughts of the end of term, Lucinda and danger flew out of her mind when she saw Lisa standing in the doorway. She was pale and even thinner than before, but thc only visible reminder of the attack she bore was the red scar on her cheek.

'Lisa! Oh my God.' Allie ran over to hug her. 'When did you get back? How are you?'

'Hi Allie. I got here a couple of hours ago.' She smiled wanly. 'My parents didn't want me to miss my exams, and I was feeling better so . . .'

'That sucks,' Allie said. 'Well, welcome back! It's been all wrong without you. I'm glad you're here for, like, five whole days.'

378

'Thanks.' Lisa looked around the room, clearly puzzled. 'What's going on? Nobody's at our table. And Jo's off over there with . . .' She gestured at the corner of the room where Jo sat with Ismay and Katie.

Allie nodded. 'It's bad. Jo hates me now.'

'Get out.' Lisa looked at her doubtfully.

'No, I'm serious. A lot of stuff happened while you were gone. The group is pretty much over for now. Everybody's divided. I sit with Rachel Patel and Lucas most days if they're around, and Carter.'

'Why? What on earth happened?'

'Oh God, it's the longest story in the history of stupid,' Allie sighed. 'Just trust me: Jo hates me. But somehow I'm surviving.'

Lisa seemed lost. 'I have no idea where to sit now,' she said plaintively.

Allie's lips curved into a wicked smile. 'Well, you could sit with Jo and Katie Gilmore. Or you could sit with me and Lucas.'

'Lead the way,' Lisa said with a guilty giggle. They walked over to where Rachel and Lucas were already piling sandwiches onto their plates.

Over lunch they took turns filling Lisa in on all that had happened while she'd been home recovering. Allie tried to be fair in telling her side of things, but Lisa seemed to have no trouble believing the worst.

'Oh, Jo . . .' she said, shaking her head. 'Not this again.'

Lucas sighed. 'That's just what I said. It all seems a bit too familiar.'

'But blaming Allie, when we all know she does this stuff . . .' Lisa said. 'That's so mean.'

'Katie's taking advantage of her,' Rachel said.

379

'She's using her. And Jo must be pretty broken if she's falling for it.'

When Carter appeared late, his lips lightly brushed Allie's head before he slid into the seat next to her. Lisa's eyes widened, but Allie was smiling at Carter and didn't care that Lucas elbowed Lisa lightly in the ribs.

Aside from that, though, there were no sparks between Lisa and Lucas. In fact, at one point Allie noticed Lisa watching Lucas and Rachel with concern, and for the first time she realised how close they sat together and how companionable they seemed.

Maybe Rachel was thinking about forgiving him after all.

She didn't like the idea of finding herself in the middle of a Rachel-Lucas-Lisa triangle but, at the same time, she wanted Rachel to have the guy who made her happy.

A worried frown briefly lined her brow.

Why does love always have to be such a mess?

* * *

At eleven that night, Allie raised her head from her books.

'Sustenance,' she muttered. 'I must have sustenance.'

She was studying in the library with Carter, Lisa and Rachel, and had been since dinner ended. Library curfew had been extended to midnight for the week and even at this hour the place was packed.

'I'm going to get something to drink,' Allie said. 'Any takers?'

'I'm fine,' Lisa said, barely looking up from her book.

Rachel said, 'I don't want to be pedantic about this, but we *did* just take a break an hour ago.'

'Allie likes breaks more than she likes studying,' Carter observed.

'How is that not normal?' Allie said, getting to her feet. 'Fine. You stay here. I shall return when I've found food. And when you all faint from hunger later don't think you can just feed on me.'

Emerging from the room bleary eyed, she headed straight for a table stocked with power bars, bowls of fruit and carafes of tea and coffee outside the library doors. The hallway was lined with students taking study breaks, stretching, sleeping and chatting before diving back into their books.

'Coffee,' she mumbled, stumbling over to the table.

As she poured her coffee into a white china cup with the Cimmeria insignia in blue, she surveyed the food with dismay. 'Why are there no biscuits here?' she asked nobody in particular. 'And where is the chocolate? How am I supposed to work under these conditions?'

'I will bring you chocolate.'

Allie jumped and spun around, barely saving her coffee. 'Sylvain, bloody hell. You startled me.'

'*Désolé*— I didn't mean to frighten you.'

She wasn't convinced.

As he poured himself a cup of coffee, Allie turned to leave. 'Well, it's been really wonderful talking with you . . .'

He took a quick step towards her. 'Allie, wait. Please. I'd like to talk to you . . . really.'

'Oh God, do we have to?' Talking to Sylvain was

381

the last thing she wanted right now.

'No, of course not,' he said, looking wounded. 'But I'd appreciate it if you would give me just a few minutes of your time.'

She sighed. 'OK. As long as you promise not to apologise to me again.'

His blue eyes sparkled. 'I can't promise never to apologise again, but I want to talk with you about something else right now. However, I am very sor . . .'

'Right, that's it,' she said, heading away from him, but he grabbed her arm lightly, laughing.

'I couldn't resist, please do not go. I promise not to do it again.'

She didn't mean to smile at him but she did. 'OK, I give in. What's up?'

'Do you mind . . .?' He gestured down the hallway 'We should go somewhere else.'

'We're not allowed to go anywhere but here.' She pointed at the library. 'It's after eleven.'

'Oh, the rules are not so strict for me.' When she shot him a dubious look he added immediately, 'We will not go far.'

'Five minutes.' She held up her hand with her fingers splayed. 'Then I have to get back to work.'

'Agreed.'

Carrying her coffee cup she followed him down the hallway to the empty entrance hall. Their footsteps echoed in the spacious corridor.

As soon as they were alone, his demeanour changed. He seemed uncomfortable, and he looked around to make sure that nobody had followed them. His tension made her uneasy.

'So . . . what did you want to talk about?' she asked.

382

Without warning, he stepped close to her and pulled her into a hug. Before she could pull away he whispered into her ear.

'I am sorry to say, Allie, that you are in danger.'

'Sylvain,' she hissed, 'let me go.'

'Please, Allie, pretend we are talking like close friends.' His pleading tone startled her enough that she stopped trying to get away from him.

'What the hell is going on?' she whispered back.

'I cannot tell you much,' he said, 'but I believe that you are in danger. That somebody will try to hurt you.'

She looked for any sign that he was kidding, but he wasn't smiling. For the first time she felt a stab of fear.

'Who, Sylvain? Who wants to hurt me?'

He shook his head. 'I can tell you nothing. I shouldn't even tell you this. But, I am worried for you. Please believe me, this is real.'

'Is it Nathaniel?'

As soon as she said the words, Allie's hand shot up and covered her mouth.

A spark of interest lit up his face.

'How do you know about Nathaniel?'

Carter will murder me.

'I . . . I just . . . must have heard a rumour or something . . .'

He searched her eyes as if looking for clues.

'Who threatens you,' he said smoothly, 'matters less than what could happen if we do not keep you safe. I think you should stay with friends as much as possible—do not spend time alone. Especially not outside.'

It still seemed strange to Allie that Sylvain was the one telling her about this. She tilted her head to one side dubiously.

'Does Isabelle know?'

'Yes, but she does not want to scare you and thinks she can protect you. Everyone thinks they can keep you safe. I am not so sure. Please believe me. This is real.'

The warmth of his body still pressed against hers was disturbing. His familiar scent reminded her of how she'd once felt about him—of kissing him.

Suddenly she needed to be far away from him.

She exhaled. 'OK. Fine. I'll stay with friends, and I won't go outside much. Don't freak out.'

She expected him to walk away at that point, but he stayed where he was, his eyes holding hers.

'What? Is there more?' she asked. 'Please say there's not more.'

'No. I am still trying to figure out how you know about Nathaniel.'

'And I'm still trying to figure out who's trying to hurt me,' she said tartly. 'So I guess we're even.'

She could see something in his eyes that seemed to mirror her own conflicted emotions, and that worried her too. Manoeuvring her way out of his arms, she picked up her coffee and began walking back down the hallway. He stayed right by her side.

When they reached the library door hc said quietly: 'Just remember. Be careful.'

'On it,' she replied, her voice grim.

*   *   *

Allie couldn't decide whether or not to tell Carter about her conversation with Sylvain. She was fairly certain he wouldn't be happy that she'd spoken with him at all. Definitely not happy that the conversation took place the way it did. But not telling him felt wrong. Not like cheating, necessarily. More like lying. A little.

But when she returned to the library he was gathering his books to leave for Night School so the decision was made for her—she had time only for a quick goodbye, and she didn't see him again that night. The next day, because he had time off to sleep, he wasn't in morning classes. So she never had a chance to tell him.

At least, that's how she explained it to herself. And to Rachel, who, to her surprise, took the news very seriously.

'Sylvain's very high up in Night School, Allie. He may be a complete tosser but if anybody's going to know this sort of thing? It's him.' Rachel's brow furrowed as she thought about it. 'Have you spoken to Isabelle?'

They were sitting where Allie and Sylvain had talked the night before, each holding a steaming mug of tea and an untouched biscuit. Even though there was nobody around, they spoke in whispers.

'Should I?' Allie asked. 'It's been bothering me. He didn't say I shouldn't. But it all seemed kind of . . . I don't know. Off the record. Like she didn't want me to know.'

'But if you're actually in danger, why on earth wouldn't she want you to know?' Rachel looked worried.

'I don't know—the whole thing sounds totally weird. But the look on his face . . . it seemed to me he was really worried.' Allie leaned back with a sigh. 'Something's wrong.'

'Let me think about it,' Rachel said. 'I'll come up with something.'

But Allie thought she looked worried too.

*   *   *

With Sylvain's warning hanging over her, Allie slept poorly on Monday. By Tuesday night, after another day of intense classes and an evening spent finishing her essay in the library, she was exhausted when she climbed the stairs to her room at midnight.

Her teeth had only the most fleeting visit from a toothbrush, and she was half asleep by the time she pulled on her pyjamas.

Leaving the window open to the warm night breeze, she muttered, 'Night-night, room,' and fell into a sleep so sound she couldn't recall a single dream.

When she awoke about two hours later, at first she didn't know what had disturbed her. Her eyes fluttered open. Still deep in the hazy space between asleep and awake, she saw a figure bent over her bed, watching her. At first she thought she was dreaming.

Then she heard him breathe.

'Carter?' she murmured, stirring.

She sensed rather than saw the sudden movement as the figure jumped lithely onto the desk and then slipped out the window with the ease of an acrobat.

That isn't Carter.

That realisation yanked her from her torpor and she sat bolt upright in bed, staring at the open window for a split second before leaping up to turn on the overhead light.

The room was empty. But somebody had been

386

there, she was certain of it. The books and papers on her desk had been disturbed. A pen that had rested on a notebook when she went to sleep now lay on the floor.

She hadn't been dreaming.

Forcing herself to keep breathing steadily, she climbed up onto the desk and looked out the window, but all she saw was countryside, bathed in the faint glow of a sliver of moon.

Shivering despite the warm night, Allie closed the window and latched it tightly—testing the strength of the lock before climbing back into bed and wrapping her arms around her knees. She sat awake for a very long time.

CHAPTER TWENTY-EIGHT

'Maybe you were dreaming,' Carter suggested, but she could see that his muscles had tensed.

'I wasn't,' Allie insisted. 'Things were moved. Besides, I saw him.'

They were sitting with Rachel at the summerhouse. Classes had ended for the day a few minutes before. The sky was grey and ominous, but it hadn't yet begun to rain.

'You see people in your dreams,' he pointed out. 'Everybody does. How can you be sure you weren't asleep and the wind didn't blow things around?'

'Did you pinch yourself, Allie?' Rachel asked. 'Or, do something to make sure you were awake? Sometimes dreams seem very real.'

'I *saw* him.' Allie was increasingly frustrated. 'Why don't you believe me? I sat up in bed as he went out the window. It wasn't a dream. He was in my room.' She shuddered. 'He was in my room.'

'Hey, it's OK.' Rachel put her arm around her. 'You're OK. We believe you. We just want you to be sure. Tell us exactly what you saw. What did he look like?'

Screwing up her face, Allie tried to remember everything. 'He was shorter than Carter, and more slight. He wore all black, and he was fair. I'm pretty sure his hair was almost blonde.'

For a while they went half-heartedly through a list of all the students who could conceivably match that description, but dismissed them all.

'Nobody in Night School looks like that,' Carter said finally. 'And only Night School can get up on the roof right now.'

'Night School and whoever was in my room last night,' Allie said. 'Carter, there's something else I have to tell you . . .'

Until that moment she hadn't told him about her conversation with Sylvain, so now she filled him in. As he listened his jaw tightened. When she finished he jumped to his feet without a word and strode out of the summerhouse to the edge of the woods where he stood with his back to them.

'Uh-oh,' Allie said, making an abortive move as if to get up and walk to him and then changing her mind and sitting back down again.

'Give him a minute. He'll be fine,' Rachel said. 'And then I'll really piss him off with my news.'

'News?' Allie raised an eyebrow curiously.

'Let's wait,' Rachel replied, watching Carter. 'I kind of only want to tell this once.'

Allie saw that he was walking back towards them now. The rush of colour that had flooded his face as he listened to her story had receded and he seemed calmer.

'I believe him,' he said. 'He's an arse, but if anybody would know, he would. He should have told me. Not you.' He looked angry. 'But he has this thing for you so he decided to do it this way. Fine. Now we know.'

Allie looked over at Rachel, who winced before leaning towards Carter. 'You're not going to like what I have to say.'

'What?' he growled. 'Are you telling me this day gets better?'

'I told my father what's going on.'

'Oh good. It *does* get better!' Carter ran his hands through his hair. 'I had no idea that was possible. You know, between the two of you everybody's going to know everything about us before the term ends on Friday. Should we just take out a billboard and put all our secrets on it? Maybe we could set up a website—AllOurSecrets dot com.'

'There are no computers here,' Allie reminded him.

'I am fully aware of the lack of internet technology at Cimmeria,' he snapped. 'But thanks for reminding me.'

She ducked behind Rachel.

'I am truly sorry,' Rachel said. 'I realise you don't know that you can trust my father, but believe me, you can. And I'm scared for Allie. So I borrowed Isabelle's phone and I told him everything. He knows who Nathaniel is.'

The last sentence seemed to hang in the air.

Allie was the first to gather her wits. 'Who is he?' she asked eagerly.

'Here's the thing,' Rachel said, shooting Carter a worried look. 'He won't tell me.'

'Of course not,' he said sarcastically. 'But he's completely trustworthy.'

'He really is.' Rachel was fighting to stay calm. 'He said he couldn't tell me that. But he did tell me some things about him. He said Nathaniel is for real. That he and Isabelle used to be very close— those are the precise words he used—but they had some sort of falling out and now he is determined to take over Cimmeria and Night School—to sort of be the new her. If that happened, my dad said, it would be a disaster. He loathes Nathaniel. Says he's ruthless. Possibly insane. And that he'll stop at nothing to have what he wants.'

'Oh good,' Allie said.

'It gets worse,' Rachel continued. 'Some members of the board are on his side. There's something Isabelle's doing that they don't like. It has something to do with the larger organisation. Anyway, some people would like to see Isabelle gone, and they think they could use Nathaniel to do it. Just let him get rid of her, and then they think they'll get rid of him. But Dad says it won't work and that it could ruin everything.

'He's going to talk to Isabelle about it on Friday when he comes to get me. But he said something else.'

She looked at Allie, her brow furrowed. 'He said for you to watch your back.'

Images of the night before flashed in Allie's mind and she shuddered. Then she stood up, her eyes resolute. 'Let's go and talk to Isabelle.'

'What . . .' Rachel said. 'Now?'

'Now.'

'She's right.' Carter stood and walked to Allie's side. 'I'm out of ideas. And somebody was in Allie's room last night. It's time.'

'Well,' Rachel stood up and joined them, 'maybe she won't expel all of us.'

* * *

'And you're certain you weren't dreaming?' Isabelle's eyes were piercing but Allie didn't falter under her gaze.

'Positive,' Allie said, her voice more confident than she felt.

After they'd approached her with their story, Isabelle had invited Matthew and Sylvain to join them, and they were all now crowded into her office. Allie and Carter perched on the top of the cabinets they'd rifled through two weeks before. Rachel sat cross-legged on the floor beneath them. Sylvain, Isabelle and Matthew all sat in the headmistress' leather chairs.

When Sylvain and Matthew had joined them, Isabelle introduced Matthew as a 'security expert', then asked Allie, Rachel and Carter to tell their story again.

Now as they processed the information, the room was quiet.

'It will be one of Nathaniel's people,' Sylvain said, breaking the silence.

Isabelle looked at him incredulously but he didn't back down.

'They know already, don't you Allie?' he said, looking at her steadily.

Flushing, Allie nodded.

'How do you know about Nathaniel?' Isabelle

said, her voice taut with anger.

Allie glanced quickly at Carter, then looked back at Isabelle. Her jaw worked as she thought about what to say. 'Does it really matter?'

Isabelle held her gaze for a long moment and Allie couldn't read her expression.

'No. I suppose it doesn't.' She took in Carter and Rachel. 'Do you all know?'

They nodded mutely.

'Fine then. Matthew?' She turned to her advisor.

'Who else could it be?' Matthew asked.

'Right. There are two days left in the term,' Isabelle said to the room as a whole. 'Already Night School is stretched to capacity trying to ensure the grounds are safe. But there are not enough of us—somebody made it through and we noticed nothing. I don't know what you think you know about Nathaniel, but I can tell you he is very dangerous and vindictive. He was behind some of what happened the night of the summer ball. So we need to change our strategy. I will speak to the others but in the meantime, Sylvain and Carter, your role from now on will be to stay close to Allie at all times. Night and day. At least one of you will accompany her constantly. Never leave her side. Work in shifts. Agreed?'

Carter glowered at Sylvain, but he nodded.

Sylvain looked beatifically innocent. 'Agreed.'

'Allie,' Isabelle turned towards her. 'I want you to continue your life as normal. Go to class. Sleep in your own room. But do not go anywhere without Carter or Sylvain.'

Although she was unable to imagine how this was going to work (*What about the bathroom?*) Allie nodded, mutely.

'Rachel, I know you're doing this already, but stay with Allie as much as possible, too. She will need your support.'

'Of course,' Rachel said.

Isabelle continued, 'I will speak with your father to make sure he's fine with this, but I'm sure he will be.'

'Now.' Isabelle's eyes swept the students. 'Please leave us. We have work to do.'

*   *   *

In the hallway outside her office, tension was thick in the air. Carter gripped Allie's hand possessively.

'Would you like me to take the first shift?' Sylvain's voice was pure silk.

A tendon worked in Carter's jaw.

'I want you to go f . . . ' he started, but Allie grabbed his arm.

'Carter no. Calm down.' She looked at the two of them. 'You can both stay with me until one of you has to go somewhere, OK? Then the other will take over. No fighting. With each other, anyway.'

Neither of them responded.

'I'll be in the library with Rachel for the rest of the day. We can all study together,' Allie continued. 'It will be fine. It's just two days.'

'That is fine with me,' Sylvain purred.

Carter still hadn't spoken and now Allie looked up into his face, stroking his tense cheek with her fingertips.

'Come on,' she whispered.

'Fine,' he said through clenched teeth. 'We'll both take care of you.'

Allie breathed out. 'Good.'

'Anyway . . . There's a chemistry book calling my name,' Rachel said.

Allie shot her a grateful look. 'And I've still got to finish that bloody history paper. I just need to run up to my room to get my notes.'

'I'll go with you,' Carter and Sylvain chorused.

They glared at each other.

'Oh God,' Allie muttered wearily. 'This is just *perfect*.'

*　　　*　　　*

For the rest of the evening, aside from a brief break for dinner, the four of them worked in the library where the no-talking rule meant no fights, something for which Allie was grateful. But whenever she took a coffee break, Sylvain and Carter both stood up to accompany her. Carter would glower at Sylvain, who always innocently shrugged. 'But I am thirsty.'

'Bloody cheek,' Carter would mutter, reaching for Allie's hand.

Allie turned to Rachel as he pulled her away, mouthing: 'Help. Me.'

Rachel grimaced sympathetically.

Later, when Rachel suggested a loo break, Allie followed her eagerly. Sylvain and Carter waited outside the door.

'So, basically, this is my worst nightmare. My current and former would-be boyfriend at my side constantly . . . together.' Allie splashed cold water on her face.

'Carter's handling this really badly,' Rachel sighed as Allie dried her face. 'I wish for his own sake he'd have a big steaming cup of calm the hell down.'

'He has to. No way can I take this for two whole days,' Allie said, applying a sweep of pale pink lip gloss. 'I'll lose it.'

She stared at herself in the mirror. Her hair had grown while she'd been here, and the henna had faded away. Now it hung in glossy dark waves to her shoulder blades. Her wide-set grey eyes were framed by long lashes, feathery black against her pale skin. She wore only minimal makeup; she didn't need more. The crisp white blouse and pleated short skirt of her uniform emphasised her curves and made the most of her athletic legs. It struck her that she didn't look anything like the tomboy she'd always been. For the first time she thought she could see something of what Carter and Sylvain saw when they looked at her.

I've changed, she thought, and saw a pleased expression in the mirror. *I'm kind of . . . pretty.*

'Ready?' Rachel asked, tossing her paper towel in the bin.

Allie tucked her lip gloss into her pocket.

'Ready.'

*   *   *

'It's got to stop, Carter,' Allie said. 'It's just two days. I really want you to do this.'

'But I can never forget the way he treated you . . .' he said, his shoulders tense.

'I know. But he's apologised and I've forgiven him, so now you have to,' she said. 'He's helping me. Isabelle wants us to work together, so please stop being so macho. It's not like you.'

It was after midnight and they were sitting on

the bed in Allie's room. The window was closed and locked, and a bar had been affixed across the shutter to secure it more snugly. Isabelle was insisting that one of them should spend the night outside Allie's room, but they were both insisting on staying. Sylvain was outside the door now.

'I'm sorry,' Carter said. 'I know I'm being jealous.'

'Ya think?' Allie laughed.

He smiled back shame-faced. 'A little, maybe.'

'You're the one I want, Carter West.' She climbed up onto his lap so that her legs straddled him and her face was inches from his. 'You have nothing to be jealous about.'

His hands slid down her back as she wrapped her arms around his neck. 'Only you,' she whispered, leaning forward to kiss him.

They kissed until all thoughts of Sylvain left their minds and they were entirely focused on each other. Carter's hands slid down to her hips and pulled her tightly against him and she did not resist. When his hands pulled her blouse out of the waistband of her skirt and ran up and down her bare back her skin tingled. When she nipped at his ear with her teeth she could feel his heart race.

When she pulled back from him, they were both breathless; Carter's face was flushed.

'I'll be the grown-up this time,' Allie said.

'Do you have to?' he whispered. Her skirt had hiked up, and he stroked her bare thighs.

'Unfortunately.' She climbed to her feet and, leaning forward, lightly brushed her lips against his, pulling back before he could grab her. 'Somebody's got to and I get the feeling it's not going to be you.'

'Not this time,' he said.

Running her hands through her hair to smooth it, she said. 'So, I'm glad we had this little talk . . .'

He laughed.

'Will you try and not be so jealous?'

'I'll try,' he said. Standing up, he reached for her but she was at the door in two seconds and flung it open.

'Good night then.' She looked around outside until she saw Sylvain sitting with his back to the wall watching her door, expressionless. 'Good night Sylvain.'

'Good night, *ma belle* Allie.' She thought she heard regret in his voice.

Carter walked past her out the door, leaning over to kiss her lightly. 'If you hear or see anything at all, just shout, OK?'

'I promise.'

As soon as he was gone she changed into clean white pyjamas and climbed into bed. After she turned out the light, she re-ran the evening in her mind, remembering the way his lips felt. How much he'd wanted her.

Not once did she think about Nathaniel, or danger, or needing bodyguards. Instead, suffused in the warm glow of happiness, she floated into sleep.

*　　　*　　　*

Later, she would wonder what woke her. Maybe it was footsteps in the corridor. Or voices outside the door. Either way, when her door burst open and the light switched on, she was already sitting up in bed. It was three o'clock.

'Get up, Allie,' Carter's face was grim.

'Nathaniel's coming.'

CHAPTER TWENTY-NINE

Allie worked to stay calm. Still groggy from sleep, she tried several times to put on her slippers but couldn't seem to make her feet slide into them.

'Leave them. There's no time.' Carter reached for her hand and pulled her into the corridor where Sylvain stood alert, waiting for them.

'This way,' Sylvain said, leading them away from the staircase.

'Where are we going?' Allie whispered.

'Out of here,' Carter said.

They ran to the end of the hallway, where Jules waited for them by a un-numbered door Allie had always assumed was a broom closet. Without a word she pushed it open to reveal a narrow, winding stone staircase, dimly lit by exposed bare bulbs.

They ran down at breakneck speed, Sylvain in the lead, Allie and Carter in the middle and Jules bringing up the rear. Nobody spoke. When they reached the bottom, Sylvain opened a door leading into a room Allie had never seen before—a crypt-like space that seemed to be hewn from rock, with thick limestone pillars covered in elaborate carvings, lighted by flickering gaslight. The stone floor felt dusty and cold beneath Allie's feet.

I don't believe it. There is *a dungeon.*

'Where are we?' she whispered.

'Cellar,' Jules said.

She, Sylvain and Carter had formed a ring of

sorts with Allie at the centre. They each had their backs to her, peering into the shadows.

'Should we get her out of here?' Jules asked.

'Isabelle said get her out if it's safe,' Carter said. 'But how do we know if it's safe?'

'Stay here.' Sylvain's voice came from behind Allie.

Soundlessly, he disappeared into the shadows.

The other three stayed where they were in silence. After about five minutes, Sylvain reappeared and gestured for them to follow.

In the same formation they'd adopted on the stairs, they ran to a door hidden in the shadows. He motioned for them to wait as he slipped through the door, then he returned again and nodded at Carter.

They followed him up a flight of stairs and through a door so small they had to duck to get through it. Once outside, they stood in a line with their backs against the school wall. Carter's arm stretched out across Allie protectively, holding her still.

The night was cool and damp—clouds covered the moon. Allie could see nothing at first, but gradually her eyes adjusted.

It reminded her of the night that she and Carter had followed Isabelle to her meeting with Nathaniel. Uneasy, she looked off to the treeline, black on the horizon.

Is somebody there now, watching us the way we watched them?

Carter tugged her hand: they were on the move. They ran around the west wing to the back of the school building, past the terrace lawn and towards the walled garden. Stones cut into Allie's feet but she ignored the pain. Just before they would have reached the garden gate, Sylvain turned off the path and disappeared. One at a time they followed him.

The grotto he led them to was so well hidden behind trees and thick foliage that Allie had never noticed it before.

She couldn't fully make out its features in the heavy darkness, but she could feel that it was made of stone and wood, and she could just make out a statue of a nude, graceful woman dancing in the middle.

Communicating only through hand gestures, Carter, Sylvain and Jules again formed a protective shield in front of Allie, looking back towards the school. Allie tried to be as still as the statue behind her.

For a long time nothing happened. Allie had counted one hundred and thirty-seven breaths when she saw Jules gesture at a tiny point of light in the distance. Allie narrowed her eyes to try and focus on it.

Within seconds there was another. And another.

Then there were half a dozen of them moving so smoothly that they seemed to float. And they were getting closer.

Allie stood between Jules and Carter trying to get a better look.

'What are they?' she breathed.

It was Sylvain who replied. 'Nathaniel.'

Allie's breath caught in her throat. 'What are we going to do?'

'Wait,' Jules said.

It took five minutes for the points of light to become lighted torches. And they were close enough that Allie could see the shadowy shapes holding them when she heard Isabelle's voice ring out.

'Nathaniel! Stop this. It's not too late.'

'I know it's not too late.' That familiar disdainful voice chilled Allie's blood. 'That is why we're here.'

'Leave this school alone,' Isabelle said. 'No matter what you do, you will never have Cimmeria.'

'You sound so certain,' he said. 'But then you were always arrogant.'

'Lucinda doesn't want this, Nathaniel.' Her voice held a warning. 'You go against her wishes at your peril.'

'If that's true then where is she?' he scoffed. 'I don't see her rushing here to protect you.'

As they argued, something in the air caught Allie's attention. A change in temperature? Or was it . . . smell?

What is that?

Her hand shot out and she grabbed Carter's arm urgently. 'Smoke. I smell smoke.'

Sniffing the air, Sylvain turned to Carter and for the first time she saw alarm on his face.

'There!' Jules pointed to the boys' dormitory wing. Smoke poured from a second-floor window and flames danced behind the glass.

'Oh my God,' Allie whispered.

'Jules, stay with Allie,' Sylvain said. 'Carter, come with me.'

Before following him, Carter grabbed Allie by the shoulders.

'Stay here.' It was dark, but she could see fear in his eyes.

Wordlessly she nodded, reaching up to grip his hand in hers so tightly it hurt.

And then he was gone.

Now alone, Allie and Jules stood side-by-side watching the school.

Isabelle's voice had lost none of its confidence. 'Is that your plan, Nathaniel? To destroy what you cannot take by lying? By cheating? By demanding? I always knew you were petulant, but this act will destroy you. Not Cimmeria.'

He laughed. 'Your arrogance shouldn't surprise me, Isabelle. But, please do not insult me. I'm smarter than that.'

A light on the top floor of the west wing caught Allie's eye. Touching Jules' shoulder she pointed. It flickered in a window.

'The girls' dorm,' Jules whispered, staring at it.

'What should we do?' Allie asked.

'Sylvain and Carter will take care of it,' Jules whispered.

But time stretched on and nothing happened. The flames in the girls' wing seemed to take confidence and grew quickly. The smell of smoke was strong now.

'Jules, we have to do something,' Allie said urgently.

'I promised Sylvain . . .' Jules said, but Allie could hear the worry in her voice.

Allie made up her mind. 'We'll stick together. Let's go.'

She didn't wait for Jules to make up her mind—she shot out of the grotto towards the treeline, but Jules caught up with her quickly and grabbed the sleeve of her pyjamas, directing her around the side of the school to an entrance away from Isabelle and Nathaniel.

They ran through the door together into a light

haze of smoke. They were in a room with shelf after shelf of books.

We're in the back of the library.

They were near where she'd met Carter several weeks ago—Ancient Latin. She'd never known there was a door there.

'This way,' Jules whispered.

And then she disappeared.

Bewildered, Allie spun in a circle looking for her, but she was alone.

'Jules?' She hissed into the darkness. 'Where are you?'

There was no answer.

'Jules?' Allie could hear the panic in her voice. Taking a shaky breath, she tried to decide what to do.

Something was wrong. She was sure Jules wouldn't have left her . . . or would she?

Her heart beat frantically. *Did she lead me into a trap?*

She coughed. The smoke was getting thicker.

Suddenly she knew what to do.

She dashed out into the main library, past the study carrels and the tables where she'd sat with Rachel and Jo so many times, then out the library door. There was a fire alarm switch right next to it and she yanked it down.

Nothing happened.

She stared at it, baffled. Then a memory came back to her—something Gabe had said before the summer splash: *'None of the alarms in this building are real. There are no alarms.'*

Without stopping to think she ran up the main stairs towards the girls' dorm. As she reached the landing and turned towards the next staircase, she saw a figure at the end of the hall. He held a flaming torch in his hand.

She froze. He hadn't seen her yet. If she stayed very still he would never notice her and then she could get upstairs to the girls' dorm.

But then he would set more fires. The school would burn down. Nathaniel would win. She felt torn. What was more important? Warning the girls or stopping him?

It was an impossible situation. There was nobody there to tell her what to do.

This always happens to me. An unexpected surge of rage shook her and she took several steps towards him.

'Hey! You!' She shouted at the top of her lungs, and she saw him stop and turn.

For a moment that was as short as for ever neither of them moved as they stared at each other. The flame was close enough to his face that she could make out his features.

'Christopher?' she whispered.

She saw recognition in his eyes, and something else. And then he ran.

'Christopher!' She was screaming now. 'Christopher! Don't leave me!'

Through the tears that ran down her face, she saw that he was gone.

The world spun, and she leaned against the wall for support while she took a steadying breath. But the smoke was too thick now and she coughed so fiercely she thought she might faint.

OK, she thought, gasping for air. *Calm down, Allie.*

She could hear Carter's words in her head, telling her to focus on her breathing. She took slow steady breaths, filtering the air through the fabric of her sleeve. When the world stopped spinning, she looked around. The smoke was getting thicker.

She didn't have much time.

Pulling her pyjama top up over her mouth she bent down low and raced up the remaining stairs (*seventeen steps*) to the girls' dorm. She threw open the first door she saw. Smoke hadn't made it in here yet and she could breathe. The girl lying in bed sat up.

It was Katie.

'Fire!' Allie shouted taking a welcome breath of clean air. 'Katie, get up and help me. We have to get everyone out.'

'What?' Katie's voice was groggy and confused, but she soon focused on Allie. 'What the . . . ?'

'The school's on fire, Katie. Please!'

Smelling the smoke, Katie jumped out of bed.

As Allie ran out the door she shouted over her shoulder, 'Every door! Knock on every door! Tell them to follow me.'

Katie took one side of the hallway and Allie the other and they raced down the hall, throwing open doors and, if necessary, shaking girls in their beds to wake them.

Allie dashed to Rachel's room, but she was already up, disturbed by the voices.

'Help me,' Allie said, breathlessly.

'Right behind you,' Rachel said.

By the time Allie reached Jo's door, most of the girls were up. Jo's room was full of smoke, and Allie could see her blonde head still on the pillow. She dropped to the floor and crawled across the room.

'Jo,' she gasped, her voice a hoarse croak. 'Wake

up.'

But she didn't move. Even when Allie shook her violently she didn't react.

Reaching back, Allie slapped her face hard.

Her eyes fluttered.

'Ow,' she whispered faintly and Allie felt a hysterical urge to laugh.

'Get up, Jo. You have to get up.'

With her arm under Jo's shoulder, Allie shoved her upright, but she was too heavy for her to lift alone. When Rachel walked in a few seconds later she quickly assessed the situation and put her arm around Jo's other shoulder. Together they got her on her feet.

'Lisa,' Jo whispered.

Allie shot a panicked look at Rachel.

'I've seen her,' Rachel said. 'She's in the hall.'

As they half-carried Jo from the room, Allie looked around worriedly.

'Is this everyone?'

'I did a count.' The voice was Katie's. 'The only person missing is Jules.'

Allie felt like she'd been punched.

'She was with me downstairs,' she said, breathlessly. 'I lost her.'

'Let's get out of here first,' Rachel said gently. 'Then we can look for her.'

Allie could see the sense in her words. 'This way.'

Jo's feet were moving now, and Rachel could support her alone, so Allie led them out along the route Sylvain had taken earlier that night. That stairwell was still free of smoke.

As they emerged into the cellar, Allie turned to Katie. 'Do another headcount.'

Without hesitating Katie quickly tallied their numbers. 'We're all here.'

Allie gestured for everyone to follow her and led them up the short staircase to the door, praying it would open.

It did.

They poured out into the darkness, coughing and inhaling the fresh air deep into their lungs. Allie walked far enough away from them all that nobody could see. Then she vomited onto the grass.

When she returned to the group, Jo was standing on her own, although she still looked woozy.

Allie straightened and tried to look like she had it all together.

'Jo, can you get everybody into the walled garden?' she asked huskily. 'I think you'll be safe there.'

Jo nodded, and walked weakly down the path. All the others followed her except Rachel and Katie.

'Where are you going?' Rachel sounded suspicious.

'I have to find Jules,' Allie said. 'She could be hurt.'

'Then I'm coming with you,' Rachel said.

'Rach, no.' Allie could hear the worry in her own voice. 'You could get hurt.'

'So could you,' Katie pointed out. 'And I'm coming with you, too. Jules is my best friend. We're not going to let you do this alone.'

'Oh God,' Allie groaned. 'You guys, this is bad.'

'Lead the way, Allie.' Rachel's voice was firm. 'Where did you see her last?'

Allie stared at them doubtfully, but time was passing. She knew she'd never talk them out of it anyway.

'In the library. There's a secret door.'

'I know where it is,' Rachel said.

'You do?'

'Of course I do,' she said. 'I know everything about that library.'

Sticking to the shadows they ran to the door and shoved it open. Smoke poured out in a thick grey wave.

Allie felt her heart sink. This was impossible.

'Stay low,' Rachel hissed, and they dropped to their hands and knees, covering their faces with clothing.

'Where were you when you saw her last?' Katie asked Allie.

Allie didn't want to tell her that in the thick smoke it all looked unfamiliar. That she wasn't sure at all. Holding her breath, she climbed to her feet and looked around, then dropped down again.

Ancient Latin dead ahead.

'Fifteen feet ahead. I think.'

They crawled forward. But when they reached the spot Jules was nowhere to be seen.

Rachel coughed. 'I don't see her.'

'Let's split up.' Katie's voice was muffled by her shirt. 'Go no more than ten feet in three different directions then meet back here.'

'Carefully . . .' Allie added.

Staying as low as she could, Allie crawled away from the others, counting her progress in her head. But she went more than ten feet in the end— when she didn't find Jules she went twenty. Then twenty-five.

But Jules wasn't there.

The smoke was thicker here and it was difficult

to see much of anything. Her eyes burned and the tears blurred her vision even further.

Too far. I've gone too far.

She turned to return to the others but was instantly disoriented—which way had she come? In the dark and smoke it all looked the same. Had she passed that tall bookshelf before? The one with book titles in Cyrillic? Had she ever seen it before at all?

She coughed viciously. When she tried to catch her breath, even through her shirt the smoke was so thick it was like being under water. There was no air. There was no oxygen. Her breath came in short, futile gasps.

When she tried to move faster, the edges of her vision began turning black.

She wasn't going to make it.

Far away she heard a voice cry, 'I've got her! She's here.'

Another voice called her name. She tried to crawl towards the sound but she couldn't move.

'Here,' she croaked, but she knew the sound was too weak to travel.

She'd never felt more tired. *If I could just rest for a second I'd gather my strength. A short nap and I'll be able to help more. I'm just so tired.*

Her head felt so heavy. She let it drop to the floor.

As unconsciousness wrapped around her like a warm blanket, she sighed with relief.

Suddenly she was flying, supported by something strong and loving. She leaned into it. Safe. Protected. Floating.

Warm air filled her lungs, and went away. Filled her lungs, and went away. Over and over.

And then a beautiful voice. 'Please don't leave us. Don't go.'

Warm lips on hers. Warm air in her body.

Pain racked her and she coughed so violently her body shook convulsively. When the convulsion stopped though, fresh air caressed her and she breathed in gratefully.

Her eyes fluttered open. She was lying in Sylvain's lap, his arms tight around her. She reached up and touched his face wonderingly.

'Why are you crying?' she whispered.

He didn't answer. Instead he rocked her like a baby, his face in her hair. Listening to her breathe.

CHAPTER THIRTY

'This time, Isabelle did call the fire brigade, then?' Allie asked in a hoarse whisper.

'For, like, the first time ever.' Rachel smiled at her. 'After you and Jules scared the life out of everyone.'

It was morning and they were sitting in a bedroom in the teachers' wing. Allie was propped up on pillows, clutching the cup of tea with lemon and honey that Rachel had brought to soothe her sore throat. Rachel was perched on the foot of the bed, filling her in on 'everything that happened after you died'.

'They put an oxygen mask on you, although they had to pry you away from Sylvain to do it.' Rachel arched one eyebrow. 'He wouldn't let you go.'

'Was it Sylvain who found me then?'

'Yes.'

'How . . . ?'

'He and Carter had cleared the guys' dorm. Then they saw the other fire. Carter went to get the teachers out. Sylvain was going to clear the girls' dorm, but when he realised it was empty he found us outside,' Rachel explained. 'Katie and I had just brought Jules out and saw that you weren't there . . .'

She stopped mid-sentence and Allie realised that she was crying. Reaching across the bed she squeezed her hand.

'I'm OK,' she whispered. Rachel nodded and wiped tears from her eyes.

After a second, she continued, but now her voice shook. 'When we told him you were missing nobody could stop him. He ran into the library like he couldn't burn.'

She took a deep breath.

'I didn't see you when he brought you out, I was giving Jules CPR. But Jo told me he gave you CPR for a long time before you came to. After that he wouldn't let you go. Guess he was afraid you'd stop breathing.'

'Guess he was,' Allie echoed.

'Anyway, as soon as Isabelle called the fire brigade, Nathaniel and his cronies melted away— and I wish I meant that literally.' Rachel leaned back against the wall. 'You and Jules and three members of staff all needed oxygen. Jules and this one guy, Peter? Do you know him?'

Allie shook her head.

'He's one of the younger students. Well, they're both in hospital for smoke inhalation. They wanted to take you, too, but nobody would let them. Isabelle, Carter and Sylvain just weren't having

411

it. So they put you in here and Carter sat here all night to make sure you kept breathing. Which you did,' she finished brightly.

'Yay me,' Allie croaked weakly.

'Indeed. Yay you.'

'How bad is the damage?' Allie asked.

'I'm not sure. I know three or four rooms are totalled. They won't let anyone into the dorms, and the whole building reeks of smoke.' She wrinkled her nose. 'The fire in the library was started at the librarian's desk and spread to the stacks nearby. They don't know how many books are gone.'

She looked genuinely sad and Allie had to hide a smile.

'They think the dorm rooms where the fires were set were all unoccupied, and a fire was set in an attic and on the landing near the stairs,' Allie had a flash memory of Christopher with a flaming torch, 'but they're still assessing. Isabelle's running around like a mad woman.

'Contractors are coming in this afternoon to assess the damage, and everybody's being sent home. We're all writing essays to replace our last few exams. I think we should insist on doing ours on fire safety.'

Allie's chuckle sounded like sandpaper on rough wood. 'I could change my history essay to the Great Fire of London.'

'Yeah, right? You've already done the research.'

Someone knocked on the door. Allie tried to say 'Come in,' but it came out as a whisper.

'*Entrez-vous*,' Rachel called.

Jo opened the door and ducked in nervously, closing it behind her. 'Hi Allie. Are you OK?'

Allie smiled weakly. 'I'm going to live—again—I

412

think,' she said. 'Rachel was just telling me everything that happened last night.'

'It was crazy,' Jo said. 'Really scary.'

'But here we all are,' Rachel said. 'And I got to do CPR on a real person for the first time ever. So it wasn't all bad.'

'Totally worth it,' Allie agreed.

'That's what I thought.'

Looking uncomfortable, Jo turned to Rachel. 'I hate to ask but, would you mind if I had a few minutes alone with . . .'

Rachel jumped off the bed. 'Of course. Allie, I'll go and get you some food. What do you want?'

Allie's throat hurt. 'Something cold,' she said. 'Nothing sharp.'

An affectionate smile lit up Rachel's face. 'Right. No sharp food. Leave it to me, babe.'

When the door closed behind her, Jo sat gingerly on the edge of the bed.

'I just wanted to tell you I'm sorry.'

Allie started to tell her it wasn't necessary but Jo shook her head. Her face was red and Allie could see that she'd been crying.

'You saved my life last night—and you risked your own to do it. I believe you did the same thing on the roof a few weeks ago. Katie told me she lied to me because she was angry at you.'

Allie gaped. 'She did *what*?'

Jo nodded. 'You saved her life, too, you know. She might be a bitch but she's not an ungrateful bitch.'

A hoarse laugh burst out of Allie before she could stop it, and soon they were both giggling, although that set off a fit of coughing from Allie.

'I'll tell her you said so,' she managed to sputter.

413

When they calmed, Jo looked at her seriously. 'I know I have a problem, Allie. I just have these . . . what the shrink called "episodes" where I'm not rational. And I really shouldn't ever drink. I'm sorry you got caught up in it. I wish so much that it had never happened. If I could take it back I'd do it in a second. But I want you to know I'm working on it.'

'It's OK,' Allie said, although it wasn't.

As if she'd heard her thoughts, Jo said, 'It's not OK, actually. I know that.'

'Good.' Allie's voice was gentle.

But Jo wasn't finished. 'The thing is,' she said, 'each time it happens something sets it off. It used to be my parents. They'd do something stupid or forget about me and off I'd go. But this time it was . . . what happened to Ruth.'

She looked up at Allie. 'It's just . . . knowing something awful and not telling anyone . . . I think it makes you crazy.'

Allie felt a tingle of fear, like icy fingers against her skin. She couldn't tear her eyes away from Jo's.

'I think it does. What did you know that nobody else knew?'

Jo's round, cornflower-blue eyes held hers. 'I know who killed Ruth. And I couldn't handle it. Just knowing. I couldn't . . . be the only one.'

Two breaths in, one breath out . . .

Allie stared at her steadily as her heart pounded in her ears.

'Who killed Ruth, Jo?' she whispered.

'Gabe did it.' Jo's voice was dull with grief. 'Gabe killed Ruth.'

*   *   *

414

When Rachel returned a few minutes later with yoghurt, ice cream and strawberries ('See? Nothing sharp . . .') Allie was holding Jo in her arms as she sobbed.

Over Jo's head, Allie whispered to Rachel: 'Get Isabelle.' Without a word, Rachel dropped the food on the desk and ran.

'It's going to be OK,' Allie whispered, over and over, although she wasn't sure it would be. She felt sick, and took deep, settling breaths to try and steady her own nerves as questions rushed through her mind too fast for answers to catch up.

Gabe did it? Gabe killed Ruth? Why?

She remembered hiding from Gabe on the path that night she was out with Carter. Something in his voice—some element of menace—had kicked a self-protective instinct into action and led her to hide. She'd been as scared of him at that moment as she'd ever been of Nathaniel.

But murder?

That seemed inconceivable. Why would he do something like that? Ruth was his friend. What could she have done to make him want to hurt her? Much less to kill her.

'Jo, Isabelle's coming here in a few minutes and you have to tell her the truth,' Allie rasped. 'Will you do that?'

Her face puffy and red, Jo nodded. 'That's why I told you. I think everybody needs to know. He's dangerous.'

When Rachel and Isabelle ran in a few minutes later, Jo was still crying. The headmistress wore the same dark leggings and tunic she'd worn the night of the parley, and smelled faintly of smoke.

'Allie?' she asked, taking in Jo's tears and Allie's pale face. 'Is everything OK?'

'Jo has something she needs to tell you,' Allie whispered.

Jo told Isabelle what she'd told Allie. As she talked, Isabelle sank slowly to her knees beside the bed, never taking her eyes off Jo's face.

'But why, Jo?' she asked finally. 'Did he tell you why?'

'He said Ruth talked. And that she knew too much about what was really going on. She wanted to tell people. I think she wanted to tell you,' Jo said. 'But then he wouldn't tell me what that meant—like what was really going on.'

Allie could see the shock on Isabelle's face, but the headmistress kept her voice preternaturally calm.

'Rachel,' she said, 'would you go and get Matthew and August, please?' She reached out for Jo's hand, wet with tears and clutching a damp, crumpled tissue. 'Did he tell you how he did it?'

'A little. Enough to scare me,' Jo said. 'It was during the ball. Everyone was happy and dancing. He only left me alone for a few minutes but when he came back I saw blood on his hand. I thought he'd hurt himself. He said he'd had an accident—a cut—nothing serious. But he didn't tell me then . . . about Ruth. He told me a few weeks ago. He didn't want me hanging out with Allie any more. He told me what happened to Ruth could happen to Allie too. Or any of her friends.'

Remembering Ruth's body—her face so pale it was almost unrecognisable; her pretty pink dress dark with blood—Allie swallowed hard. Gabe had been threatening her. That could have been her

416

face. Her pretty dress.

She counted her heartbeats. . . . *twelve, thirteen, fourteen* . . .

'What else did he tell you?' Isabelle asked.

'He didn't want me to tell Allie anything about Night School, or anything about what he was doing.' Jo's voice sounded tired. 'He said Allie was to blame for all the bad things that were happening and that you and Zelazny were weak. He said Nathaniel was right and you should just let him have her . . .?'

Isabelle and Allie exchanged a startled look.

'How did Gabe know Nathaniel?' Isabelle asked gently.

'I don't know,' Jo said. 'But they just . . . know each other. Like Gabe meets him sometimes. To talk.'

Allie gasped. She saw colour drain from Isabelle's face.

'They're . . . friends?' Isabelle's voice shook, just a little. Jo wouldn't have heard it, but Allie did.

'Kind of.' Jo thought about it. 'I think Gabe admires him.'

At that moment Zelazny and Matthew walked in and Isabelle rose to her feet and stepped outside to talk with them. She returned to the room alone and sat on the bed next to Jo and Allie.

'Why didn't you tell us sooner, darling?' she asked quietly.

Tears streamed down Jo's face. 'I didn't know what to do,' she sobbed. 'I love . . . loved Gabe. I couldn't . . . I didn't know what to do. I'm sorry. I'm so sorry.'

'It's OK,' Isabelle whispered. But Allie could tell she was lying.

After Isabelle led Jo away to her own room, Rachel returned long enough to make Allie eat some melted ice cream and warm yoghurt. She stayed until Allie fell asleep.

When she woke up, Carter was sitting on the foot of the bed watching her, his dark eyes unreadable.

'Hey,' she rasped.

'How're you doing?' His voice was gentle.

'Never better.' But waking up set off a round of coughing and he handed her a glass of water with a straw.

After she sipped it she felt better and scooted up in the bed until she was sitting up.

'Did you hear about Gabe?' she whispered.

He nodded, his muscles tense. 'I should have seen it, Allie. Why didn't I see that it was him?'

'Nobody could see it,' she said. 'Don't blame yourself or we'll all have to blame ourselves. Have they found him?'

'No—they're all looking. Nobody knows where he is. He might have done a runner.'

She digested this information for a minute.

Then she said: 'Rachel told me that you saved lots of people last night. That's amazing.'

'And you saved people, too.' But he didn't say it was amazing and she could see the tension in his face.

'What's the matter?' she said.

He shook his head and didn't speak for a moment, when he did, his voice quivered.

'Why didn't you stay in the hiding place, Allie?

418

You would have been OK if you'd listened to me.'

'I'm sorry, Carter. But I was scared for the girls,' she said. 'I had to help. I couldn't just let them die.'

'We would have got them out,' he said.

'We didn't know that,' she said. 'The fire spread fast.'

'Whose idea was it to go in? Yours or Jules'?'

Allie thought longingly about lying. 'Mine,' she said. 'Jules wanted to wait a while longer.'

'And you both nearly died,' he said angrily.

'But we saved people, Carter.' Her hoarse voice was indignant. 'We did help.'

'I would sacrifice every single one of them for you.'

She stared at him, aghast. 'Don't say that,' she whispered. 'That's horrible.'

'I know it's horrible.' His fingers flicked a tear off his cheek and he avoided her eyes. 'It's also true.'

She had no idea what to say, and she studied him worriedly.

'I'm OK, you know.'

'I know.'

'So, let's not freak out OK? Let's just be glad that we're both all right.' She reached for his hand and held it against her cheek. 'I'm so glad that you're OK.'

Saying nothing, he wrapped her in his arms.

'Carter and Allie save the world,' she whispered.

*   *   *

That afternoon, Rachel brought Allie a skirt and blouse that smelled like a bonfire.

'They let me in the dorm for all of three seconds.

419

I raided your wardrobe for these,' she said. 'Sorry about the stench.'

'No worries,' Allie said. 'I'm just psyched to finally get out of these chargrilled pyjamas.'

'They said we could go up to get our stuff tomorrow,' Rachel said. 'With supervision, of course.'

'Of course.' Allie gave a wry smile. 'Health and safety.'

'Everybody's going home today and tomorrow— my dad's coming tomorrow morning,' Rachel said. 'The offer still stands if you want to come stay with us.'

'Thanks, Rach,' Allie said. 'I still might take you up on it.'

After a shower in the teachers' bathroom to scrub the soot out of her hair, Allie began to feel human again. Rachel had forgotten shoes though, so when she padded down the stairs later she was still barefoot. But she walked with purpose straight to Isabelle's office and knocked.

The door opened before her knuckles left the wood and without a word Isabelle wrapped her in a bear hug. Then she held her at arm's length and studied her face.

'Are you OK?'

'I think so,' Allie whispered.

The headmistress held the door open for her. 'Come in, sit.'

'How's Jo?' Allie asked.

'Not good,' Isabelle said, sitting beside her as the kettle rumbled in the background. 'She's very upset, understandably.'

Allie hesitated—not sure if she could even bring herself to ask the next question.

'Gabe?' she whispered finally.

Isabelle shook her head. 'He's gone. When Zelazny and Matthew went to find him he'd disappeared. We think he might have gone last night during the fire.'

Somehow Allie wasn't surprised. She took a steadying breath.

'So . . . what happens now?'

'We will look for him.' Isabelle busied herself making tea. 'We'll let his parents know. We will try to make sure he's safe. We will take care of Jo. And then we will find a way to deal with Nathaniel.'

'I want to help,' Allie said.

'You will,' Isabelle said. 'I promise you that.'

'No, Isabelle.' Allie's voice was firm. 'I mean I want to *help*. I want to be involved in everything from now on.'

The headmistress looked at her blankly and Allie tried not to let the frustration and tension she felt into her voice. If she ever needed to act grown-up, now was the time.

'I'm in the middle of all of this. In some ways, Gabe was right and this is about me. Nathaniel has Christopher and now he wants me, too. That's true, isn't it? All this term I've been rescued and saved and helped, and everybody's all about protecting me, which is wonderful, and I am grateful. But I want to protect myself. Right now, I can't ever save myself. I don't know how.' She steadied her nerves. 'But there's one place where I could get the skill to do that.'

Isabelle spoke slowly. 'You want to join Night School.'

'Doesn't it make sense?' Allie wrapped her arms around herself. 'I need to be stronger and faster.

I need to know how to fight. And I need to know what's happening so that I can do the right things. I'm never just going to do what you say if you say "Allie don't go outside". But if you include me in stuff . . . That's different.'

A heavy silence fell. She could see that Isabelle was thinking. After a second the headmistress handed her a cup of strange-smelling herbal tea with lemon.

'For your throat. Drink it.' She sat down beside her. 'OK, then. I agree. I'll talk to the others.'

A thrill of excitement rushed through Allie. As if she'd seen that, Isabelle hurried to quash it. 'It's not my decision alone, Allie. Others will have to agree. But I will back you up.'

Even though she heard Isabelle's caution, Allie didn't believe it. She knew Isabelle could do anything she wanted.

She was in.

Changing the subject, Isabelle said, 'You sound terrible, by the way. Did the doctor look at your throat?'

A doctor had visited Allie an hour ago to examine her. He'd pronounced her throat 'Not as bad as it could have been', and given her a bottle of pills and something to gargle.

She nodded. 'He said I'll live. But I'll never sing with the opera.'

'Puccini will get along without you,' Isabelle said. 'It could have been much worse.'

'That's what I thought. How's Jules?'

Isabelle nodded. 'She's doing very well. She has a concussion—she tripped and hit her head. It knocked her unconscious. But she was spared the worst of the smoke and heat, so her lungs weren't permanently damaged. She'll be back here tonight.'

Guiltily, Allie remembered how she'd doubted Jules up to the last minute in the library.

'I'm so glad she's OK,' she said. 'She was very brave.'

'She said the same thing about you.'

Allie asked the next question with trepidation.

'Have you seen Sylvain?' Her throat tightened. 'I . . . wanted to thank him.'

'He's avoiding you,' Isabelle said bluntly.

Allie's head shot up. 'Why?'

The headmistress' eyes were kind. 'You know, don't you?'

The heat of the tea radiated through the porcelain of the teacup, burning Allie's fingers. 'Know what?'

'He has feelings for you.'

At that moment Allie realised that she did know. She remembered his tears falling on her face. Emotions she didn't even recognise flowed through her.

'But I'm with Carter,' she said weakly.

'I know.' Isabelle held her hands up. 'So there we are.'

Allie watched the slice of lemon floating aimlessly in her cup. 'There we are.'

The headmistress curled up in the deep leather chair next to her—the circles under her eyes betrayed her exhaustion.

'I don't think you'll see Sylvain again this term. He needs time to think. And to heal.'

'Would you tell him . . .' Allie thought about what to say. 'Just . . . thank him for me?'

'I will.'

Allie set her cup down. 'And I've decided I'm

going to go home, rather than to Rachel's. I need to talk with my parents.'

Isabelle looked worried.

'I think it's the right thing to do, and I'm glad you're doing it,' she said cautiously. 'But now that we know Christopher is with Nathaniel and Nathaniel is interested in you . . . Well, things are different. The situation is more dangerous. I'll explain this to your mother. But, Allie, at home you will be in more danger. I will do what I can to protect you, but don't take any chances.'

Allie thought about Ruth. 'I'll be careful,' she promised. 'I'll lie low.'

'The autumn term starts in three weeks,' Isabelle said. 'But I can't let you stay home that long. I'll give you a few days at home, but after that I really think you should go to Rachel's. Her father is completely capable of protecting you and he will be expecting you. I'll send a car for you.'

There was something awful about being told that home—once the safest place she had ever known— wasn't safe any more. But Allie didn't argue. She'd seen what Nathaniel was willing to do.

'OK,' she said again.

Isabelle took a piece of paper off her desk and wrote something on it. 'If you get concerned or frightened at any point—if anything feels threatening or just wrong . . .' she folded the piece of paper then handed it to Allie, 'call me, and I'll send somebody for you. Don't take any chances. Will you do that for me?'

The paper had Isabelle's name embossed on the top, and Allie saw that she'd written a phone number on it.

Allie nodded. 'I promise.'

424

They stood and Isabelle gave her another hug. Allie walked to the door. As she turned the handle, Isabelle stopped her.

'One more thing,' she said. 'Ask your mother to tell you about Lucinda.' Allie's eyes widened but she said nothing.

Isabelle finished: 'Tell her I said it's time.'

CHAPTER THIRTY-ONE

'Come on, bag. Zip!'

Allie had stuffed the last few things into her bag and now it bulged at the sides and refused to close. Even when she used all of her strength she couldn't get it to zip up.

The girls had all been given fifteen minutes in their rooms to pack. It turned out most bedrooms were fine. But the teachers were worried the fire and water might have made the ceilings and floors weak.

'Oh, bugger it.'

Panting from the exertion, she flipped it open and looked for something to jettison. Her scuffed dark red, knee-high Doc Marten boots lay right on top. She pulled them out and tried again.

It closed easily.

She picked up the boots lovingly. *No way am I leaving these behind.*

Holding them in front of her she studied the scuffs on the toes, the way the leather had moulded to fit her ankles. She'd been in love with these boots since the day she saw them in the window of the charity shop down the road from her school.

When she found out they were the right size, she knew they were destined to be hers. For two months she'd gone to that shop every day to make sure they were still there. Eventually she convinced the workers to put them aside for her until her birthday. The thick soles, the sturdy leather, the sheer aggressive power of them made her feel strong again. They were like her armour.

I know I've changed while I've been here, she thought. *But I haven't changed so much that I don't think these are bitchin' boots.*

Kicking off her school-issued sensible shoes she pulled on the Docs, lacing them up with happy familiarity. Paired with her school uniform, they looked . . . *perfect*.

Then she looked around one last time, running her hand along the top of her desk. She'd hated this place so much when she first arrived. Now she couldn't wait to come back.

She hoisted the bag to her shoulder and hurried through the door crashing full-force into Carter, who stood on the other side.

'Hey Speed,' he laughed, steadying her with a hand on each shoulder. 'Where's the fire?'

'Ha ha, you're hilarious,' she said, rolling her eyes.

He smoothed her hair. 'Are your parents here already?'

'They'll be here any minute.' She made a face. 'I'm only hurrying because my dad hates waiting.'

His eyes clouded briefly, and she remembered that his parents would never come to pick him up again.

'Where will you live during term break?' she asked with a worried frown. 'They won't let you stay in the guys' dorm.'

'I'm moving into the teachers' wing while they're fixing the smoke damage,' he said. 'It'll be fine.'

'I hope you won't be too lonely.'

'I'll be OK,' he assured her. 'This is home for me, remember? And I won't be alone. Jo and Sylvain are staying and Jules is only going home for a few days. Most of Night School will be back after a week or so.'

Hearing Sylvain's name, Allie felt an unwanted tug on her heart. She hadn't seen him since the fire.

'Good,' she said. 'But I'll worry about you anyway.'

'And I'll worry about you. Write to me,' he said. 'And I'll nick Isabelle's phone and call you.'

'You still have my number?'

He held up his hand—she'd written her number just below his knuckles an hour ago.

'I'll have it tattooed while you're gone,' he joked.

A sombre silence fell, and Allie rested her bag on her foot and gently bounced it with her toe.

'You're going to be careful, right?' he said, tugging lightly at the hem of her shirt, pulling her a step closer to him. 'You'll stay safe?'

Even though he kept his voice light, she could hear the concern behind his words.

'Don't worry. I'll be good as gold. I'm only home a week then I'm off to Rachel's country pile, which is apparently as secure as Buckingham Palace.'

'Good,' he said, pulling her into a tight hug. 'As long as you're careful. We need you around here, you know.'

'Yes you do. This whole place would fall apart without me,' she said with an ironic smile.

Burying his face in her hair, he breathed in

deeply.

'Time! Everybody out!'

Zelazny's voice rang out in the hallway outside the door. Allie lifted her face for a quick kiss, pulling away almost immediately. It was too late for long goodbyes.

She picked up her bag and threw it over her shoulder.

'I'm going to go down by myself, OK?' Her eyes searched his face, but she knew he would understand. If he really kissed her properly or asked her to stay—if she just kept looking into those eyes—she'd never make it out the door.

Moving briskly she walked to the door and opened it.

He called after her: 'Nice boots, Sheridan.'

She didn't look back.

'Stay cool, Carter West.'

She was halfway down the hall when she heard his reply.

'Always.'

ACKNOWLEDGEMENTS

This book started on a dare. I never thought I could write a novel but my husband thought I could. One day he dared me to try. *Dared me.* Told me I'd be a coward if I didn't try. I never back down from a reasonable dare and he knew that.

Thank you my darling, for daring me.

The dare started it but everything else that happened was serendipity and kindness and generosity. And while you can only thank the gods for serendipity, kindness and generosity deserve to be recognised.

Without the enthusiasm and energy of Madeleine Buston and everyone at the amazing Darley Anderson Agency (especially Clare Wallace and Mary Darby), there's no way this book would have made it onto shelves. Your phone call *changed my life*, Maddy. There aren't enough words in the world to thank you for that.

To the fabulous Samantha Smith, editor extraordinaire at Atom Books, a million thanks. Not only is she a brilliant editor but she's funny too. Working with her is a dream come true. Frankly, the whole crew at Atom/Little, Brown is incredible: Gina Luck, Kate Agar, and Darren Turpin—you all helped to make *Night School* happen. Thank you all so much! I owe you *so many* cupcakes . . .

This book was shaped and honed with the help of friends who read it while I was writing it, and told me the truth about it. Their honesty and brilliance made it so much better. Hélène Rudyk, Kate Bell and Sally Davies—you are all *goddesses*.

To the staff at the Starbucks on Memorial Drive at Dairy Ashford in Houston, Texas, thank you for letting me sit and write in your icy air-conditioning for hours on end—sometimes until you were stacking the chairs around me and sweeping the floor under my feet—without ever asking me to buy more coffee or get out of your way. Basically, thank you for ignoring me. *Night School* was fuelled by your iced mochas.

While this book was being written my mother passed away, so she never got to see that everything worked out. That this wasn't just another of my crazy dreams. They say sometimes people watch over you after they die so . . . Look Mom! I did it.